"LaVine Rathkey spins a heartwarming tale full of adventure, emotion, and drama. *Chalk dust and Choices*, though set in the Pacific Northwest, is drawn from a universal source that resonates with the reader's heart, and is a pleasure to read. No wonder LaVine Rathkey is one of my favorite authors."

Jane LaMunyon
Teacher and author of *Escape on the Wind*

"LaVine Rathkey's skillful writing transforms devoted teacher, Kathleen O'Brien and her friends into our real-life next-door neighbors, whose lives lead them toward crucial decisions. Readers label *Chalk Dust and Choices* a can't put it down book."

Betty M. Hockett
Writer, teacher, speaker

To Birdie,
Thanks for all
your help
Blessings!
La Vine

Chalk Dust and Choices

Chalk Dust and Choices

LaVine Rathkey

Tate Publishing & *Enterprises*

This title is also available as a Tate Out Loud product. Visit www.tatepublishing.com for more information.

Published by Tate Publishing & Enterprises, LLC
127 E. Trade Center Terrace | Mustang, Oklahoma 73064 USA
1.888.361.9473 | www.tatepublishing.com

Tate Publishing is committed to excellence in the publishing industry. The company reflects the philosophy established by the founders, based on Psalm 68:11,
"The Lord gave the word and great was the company of those who published it."

Cover and Interior design by Jacob Crissup

Published in the United States of America

ISBN: 978-1-60462-886-9
1. Fiction: General: Romance
2. Fiction: Religious: Romance/Contemp
08.03.19

Acknowledgements

First of all, thanks to the Lord for the talent He gave me. I strive to perfect it and honor my Savior.

Two awesome teachers, Betty H. and Jane L., never failed to provide helpful lessons, critiques, and encouragement. You have my gratitude. Thanks, also, to my friends in Creative Writing class who've listened to this story again and again, laughed, asked for more chapters, and always you were supportive.

To my editor, April, for helping me polish this manuscript, and to all the staff at Tate Publishing, from first contact, to the last, your kindness, and help haven't gone unnoticed. Thank you.

My thanks, too, belong to family and friends; you've listened, bailed me out, and supported me all along this journey. Last, but surely not least, Eldred, I thank you for your longsuffering, patience, and most of all, belief in this writer. I couldn't have done it without you.

Chapter 1

Kathleen O'Brien braced her feet and held the classroom door open with her backside. She breathed deeply, drawing oxygen into her lungs as the wind whipped hair that flashed like fire when touched by the sun. If she were handed one more thing to hold, she'd have to grip it in her teeth.

"Patti, don't forget your mittens. You'll need them if it snows." First-graders struggled with coats, caps, and mittens while the teacher held paper sacks, workbooks, a half-eaten cupcake, and one gooey candy cane waiting to be stuck back in a mouth.

"Um, thanks, Miss O'Brien. Merry Christmas."

"Bye, Miss O'Brien. Merry Christmas."

"Merry Christmas," the teacher parroted for the zillionth time.

Kathleen's heart swelled with pride as she watched "her kids" reclaim their sacks laden with gifts and prepare to leave. The children waved as they boarded the school bus. A few forgot until seated and then, hands smearing moisture on windows to clear a spot, waved frantically. Patti Williams, next to last in line to board the bus, turned to wave once more to her teacher.

My arm is going to fall off if I wave one more time. Kathleen sighed, waved once again, and watched helpless, as the little sprite dropped her sack spilling the contents on the ground. Her blonde curls made a halo round her head as she bent to retrieve her belongings.

The air smelled fresh, crisp and clean as a new day in paradise. Indeed Kathleen thought of Pleasant Grove as a bit of heaven on earth. This picturesque country school tucked close to the foothills, eight miles from the thriving timber town of Fir Valley, Oregon, seemed next to perfect. In her mind, it equaled exclusive schools where the wealthy sent their children.

Cows cropped lush green grass in the field next to the playground. Half a dozen horses grazed and frisked nearby. Evergreen trees, mixed with maple, dotted the hills beyond. Here and there, a house could be seen snuggled down on the hillside. The hardwoods had lost their leaves long before now, but in the fall, they were a riot of color. On clear days, Mount Hood stood out in bold relief, its snowy peak looming in the background.

She shivered and pulled her sweater closer around her. Before she could return to the classroom, a late model, blue Honda raced past the school bus and slammed to a halt. *That driver is going much too fast for school grounds. I've never seen that car before. I'll have to find out who it is and have Mr. Steele speak to them.* She swallowed her irritation as another disturbing thought occurred to her. *I hope it isn't someone wanting a last-minute conference. Our principal may be lenient, but Dick would never condone being rude to a parent even if he did say we could leave early.*

A tall, blond-haired man with shoulders like a football player leaped from the car. Kathleen watched in amazement as Patti turned, saw the man, dropped her sack once again, and sped to his waiting arms. The stranger ran fingers through his hair, pushed it back. He stooped, caught Patti and lifted her high in an embrace. Small arms hugged the man's neck—the wide grin on her face as he placed her in the car left no doubt of her delight to see him.

The stranger slammed car doors, gunned the engine, and tore from the parking lot seconds ahead of the school bus. Kathleen heaved a sigh, marched out, and retrieved Patti's sack and the spilled contents. A cheap ring and matching necklace, a package of gum, two candy canes, and Santa Claus stickers she had gotten from the teacher at their party that afternoon, lay on the ground. *One more thing to go in the box of miscellaneous caps, mittens and sundry items no one ever seems to claim.*

The classroom smelled of chalk dust, warm bodies, peppermint, and Kool-Aid. She picked up trash, straightened desks, and put away books. Her mind was already flying through the clouds when her friend and coworker, Rosie Kestler, popped in and plopped down in one of the larger first grade desks.

Rosie groaned. "Now I know why I never teach anything lower than fifth grade. How do you ever fit behind one of these desks?" She squirmed. "Never mind. I admit I'm Christmas green with envy of your slim trim little figure that I've never had and never will. To say nothing of that coppery hair and those green eyes that have the men falling all over themselves.

"Speaking of men, when are you going to marry *Mr.* Connors, have lots of babies and get fat, frumpy and flustered like me." Rosie snickered. "Who am I kidding? You'll never look like me no matter how many kids you produce."

"You sound just like my mother. Who, by the way, would think you're beautiful, as do I, and she certainly would applaud you and your four children. She can't wait for *me* to marry and have a dozen kids."

In truth, Rosie wasn't pretty, her nose too big, mousy hair that generally looked as if it needed combing, and at least thirty pounds overweight. But she had an unflappable personality and a smile that made you want to hug her. Kathleen counted herself blessed to have her for a friend.

"Do I detect a sour note here? When we're about to be set free?—*Vacation,* remember?" She lifted an eyebrow. "Edward (she pronounced it Ed-waard) no doubt, is planning to whisk you off to some romantic rendezvous. Just in case he doesn't, I'm inviting you to join me and my tribe for Christmas day. Though I'm sure I don't know why anyone would sacrifice peace and quiet for the bedlam at my house."

"I'd *love* to come. I adore your kids. They're angels compared to my brother's six. How Mary retains her sanity... and Michael just seems to tune it out, I'll never know. But in all fairness, I must say their children are happy and well adjusted."

"Let's see if I remember. Michael is your brother in Ohio, right?"

"Yeah, and I've promised Mom and Dad I'll fly back there for the holidays." Kathleen sighed. "My parents are coming up from Florida. It's more than a year since we've all been together. I haven't the heart to say no."

Rosie struggled to pry herself from behind the small desk and did a hilarious imitation of a very old woman. In a quavering voice she mimicked, "I can't sit here dear. *Help me*, or I'll be permanently bent." Kathleen grinned at her friend's theatrics and waited while she continued. "I don't get it; I thought you had a good relationship with your parents."

"I do. At least I did. Dad is tops. Mom means well, but she thinks being twenty-six and single is the unpardonable sin, the old maid school teacher and all that malarkey." She groaned. "My mother married at eighteen. She doesn't understand waiting." Kathleen shoved a book back on the shelf. "I haven't worked this hard for a career just to chuck it all, the way my sister-in-law has, to raise a family. I love teaching.

"You'd think six grandkids would be enough, but Mom wants more. She's bad enough on the phone long distance, but when she gets a crack at me in person for two weeks she'll show no mercy."

She laughed but it lacked mirth. "She'll grill me about Edward. She'll want to know his pedigree, where he was born, how much money he makes, and most important, are we setting a date for marriage? She suggested I might want to invite him to come back with me. Ha! After two weeks of my mother scrutinizing his every move, and weighing his every word, he'd be ready to bail."

Rosie started to reply when the door burst open and the school secretary, Hazel Brooks, stuck her head in the room. "Kathleen, Mrs. Williams is on the phone. She says Patti didn't get off the bus and she wants to know if she's being kept at school."

"No, of course she isn't being kept. A man came and picked her up, just before the bus left, someone Patti obviously knew. I would have reported it, but Patti ran to him; she would not have if he were a stranger. Do you want me to come and talk to Mrs. Williams?"

"No, I'll tell her," said Hazel.

Moments later she was back—followed closely by their principal. A tall man, in his early fifties, dark hair starting to gray around the temples, he exercised regularly trying to stave off the inevitable growth around his middle. A man who commanded respect, usually with a twinkle in eyes framed by wire rimmed glasses. Alarm rushed through her at the grim look she now saw on his face. *Something is terribly wrong.*

"Kathleen—we've got a problem. I need to see you right now—in my office."

Fear clutched like a vise around the throat. Her thoughts kicked into overdrive. *The man in the schoolyard…Who was he? Can Patti be in danger?* She shot a quick look at Rosie—a mute cry for help—as obediently she followed the secretary and principal to the office

"I'll pray," her friend mouthed as she quietly slipped out to return to her own room.

Mr. Steele closed the door and turned to his first grade teacher. "Okay, tell me, did you get a look at the man that took Patti Williams? Can you describe him?" The principal's voice sounded harsh and too loud.

She gripped the back of a chair. Her hands were sweaty, and she felt lightheaded. "He's tall, six foot or more, broad shoulders. He had on a black leather jacket. Jeans, I think. And his hair, blonde, almost the color of Patti's, hung below his collar. I think he combs it straight back. Mr. Steele, what is this all about?"

"Mrs. Williams called and said Patti did not get off the bus. When Mrs. Brooks told her what you said, Patti was picked up by a man in a blue car; she became hysterical. She is on her way here and threatens to sue the school for letting an unauthorized person take her child."

"Dick," Kathleen appealed. "This man is no stranger to Patti. She *ran* to him and threw her arms around his neck when he picked her up. She would not go to a stranger. We've talked about safety in our class, and it included not approaching strangers for any reason. We've play-acted similar situations, and Patti knows the dangers."

The principal softened his tone. "Okay. I wanted to make sure of what you saw. When Mrs. Williams gets here we may be able to get this all sorted out. Did anyone else see the car and what happened?"

"I'm sure Mr. Benchly, the bus driver, saw him…and John Walker. He saw. He was right behind Patti. I don't know who else might have seen but those two for sure." She took a deep breath and tried to slow her racing heart. "I know we have a policy stating anyone who picks up a student must report to the office unless previous notification is given. Whoever this was didn't know or didn't care. He came and left so quickly, I couldn't possibly have stopped him.

"Well, I'm glad you saw what happened. Otherwise we'd have nothing to go on."

The sound of a car door slammed and feet running up the stairs forestalled further discussion. Mr. Steele quickly opened the office door and a distraught Mrs. Williams rushed in.

"My baby, why did you let someone take—"

Kathleen interrupted. "Mrs. Williams, I'm Kathleen O'Brien. Patti's teacher." She spoke softly from her heart. "I'm sorry Patti hasn't come home. I know you're upset—"

"You *bet* I'm upset. How *could* you?"

"But, I *assure* you your daughter didn't leave here with a stranger. Are you sure you don't know who might have picked her up? Maybe as a surprise...a bit late getting home?"

"Please. Be seated," said Hazel, as she pushed a chair forward.

To everyone's astonishment, Mrs. Williams seemed to wilt before their eyes as she collapsed into the proffered chair. A tiny woman with long dark hair, dressed in a pink jogging suit, she didn't look to be more than a teenager.

"It has to be Patti's father," she blurted. "We've gone through an ugly divorce—battle over custody." She leaped up, as though she found the seat too hot, and began to pace, back and forth, back and forth. "I won the right to keep my little girl, and my ex-husband has only visitation privileges. He can have her two weekends a month. And the judge awarded him three weeks in the summer." The distraught woman continued to pace, wring her hands, and stop repeatedly to look out the window. Did she expect Patti to magically reappear?

"Al wanted her part time over Christmas. But it isn't his regular time—I thought it best to not change the routine." Mrs. Williams stopped pacing to perch on the edge of the chair, her eyes brimming. "I thought it less disruptive if he saw her after—". Mr. Steele interrupted. "But surely she's safe with her father, and he'll return her to you before long. Perhaps he just wants a little time with her to give some Christmas presents in person."

"*No!* You don't understand," she bleated. "He's *kidnapped* her. He'll take her off to England. He has an uncle there. His uncle married to a British girl. If he has his way — I'll never see my baby again." She grabbed for the phone across the desk. Mr. Steel reached it first, and Hazel handed him a card with emergency numbers from her desk drawer. It took only minutes for the principal to call the sheriff's department and the state police. But it seemed an eternity as the teacher watched the young mother shred a tissue, her eyes imploring a calm principal as she silently mouthed, "Hurry—hurry—please, please—*hurry*!"

Kathleen had no intention of becoming embroiled in a custody battle between Patti's parents. But she couldn't help thinking Mr. Williams a jerk as she watched the frantic mother. How could parents who professed to love their child play tug-of-war with their daughter's life? *What were they thinking*?

Neither parent came for scheduled conferences to discuss Patti's grades and how she did in school. Anger seeped in to replace the butterflies in her stomach. Her Irish temper slowly inched toward the red mark. *If Mrs. Williams had only let me know what was happening maybe I could have helped, been more on guard.* She bit her lip and clenched her fists behind her, letting the long nails bite into her palms.

"I've notified the authorities, Mrs. Williams. I'm sure they'll do their best to get Patti back to you." Dick touched her shoulder. "Is there someone we can call? Someone to be with you?"

She shook her head. "I need to get home. Cancel appointments. Maybe Al will call me with some *ridiculous* demand. *Oh*," she howled. "I hope the police can stop him!"

"Wait! You forgot your purse." Kathleen scurried to hand it to her as she blasted out the door and started down the steps.

"Thanks. I'm sorry I accused you," she threw over her shoulder as she ran for her car.

Chapter 2

The three looked at each other and breathed a collective sigh of relief. What did one say after a scene like that? Kathleen feared if she didn't escape soon she too, would burst into tears or spout something purely unprofessional. Hazel quickly bunched papers, closed and locked desk drawers.

"Well, that's that," Dick said. "I think it's out of our hands, though I don't take this lightly. I'll make a couple more calls. See what I can do." He took off his glasses and rubbed the bridge of his nose. "You're free to go. I hope you won't let this unduly upset you. Enjoy the holidays, and I'll see you here next year. Hopefully with Patti back in your classroom, Kathleen." The principal managed a weak smile, and an even weaker, "Merry Christmas."

Kathleen hurried past Rosie's darkened room. *Everyone has gone. No chance to pour out my frustration on my friend. No time either.* She grabbed her purse from the desk drawer, shut off the lights, locked the door, and sprinted for her car.

Settled into the seat of her old white Chevy, she started the engine, switched on the lights, and buckled her seatbelt.

It started to rain as she pulled out of the school parking area onto the highway. *I'm really late. Edward is not going to be happy.* Luckily, she had less than a mile to drive to Mrs. Fisher's country home where she had an apartment. She hated days when headlights seemed ineffective, the road a black ribbon absorbing light. *I'm glad Edward is driving me to the airport.*

She noted his light green BMW parked in the circular driveway as she pulled into her spot in the double-car garage. It took only moments to run upstairs to her domain, slip out of her skirt and into a pair of warm charcoal-gray wool slacks, tuck in her champagne colored silk blouse, kick off her shoes, replace them with fur-lined boots, snatch her green wool coat from the closet, grab her one suitcase, and carry-on. Breathless, she descended the stairs.

Not fun having to rush but a sixty-mile drive to Portland airport laid ahead of them. They could make it easily, but no time remained for the intimate dinner Edward planned. She suspected he might have other plans as well. A week ago, while they Christmas shopped and looked in stores at jewelry, he'd drawn her attention to rings and asked her opinion of different sets. Aware of his many fine qualities (it didn't hurt that he was gorgeous) she liked and admired him. Secretly, she admitted she might be falling in love. The seniors at church thought Edward walked on water since he provided transportation for those who could no longer drive, and the music department had a new sound system thanks to him. Bill Kestler, the choir director, marched around smiling these days.

She felt the attraction growing. But was it real love? Infatuation? Or worse, habit? How did one tell? She had steered away from the jewelry department unwilling to admit, even to herself, she wasn't ready to become engaged.

The idea she might be immature, a thought her mother unobtrusively planted, she quickly rejected. Kathleen further discounted the suggestion she was rebelling against her mother's pushiness. She should know her own mind, and her mind was set on teaching school—something Edward said *his* wife wouldn't need to do.

"Hi! Sorry I'm late," she puffed, as she threw a beseeching look in the direction of the man drumming his fingers on the mantle.

Edward, dressed in white shirt, blue striped silk tie, wearing gray flannel trousers, and shiny black loafers, leaned against the fireplace, every inch the executive—except for that one strand of dark wavy hair that refused to obey and kept falling over his forehead. It was there now, and she thought it made him look boyish, despite the scowl on his face.

A fire blazed on the hearth and the room smelled of fresh evergreens. Martha, seated in her faded rose-colored wing chair beside the fireplace, turned her white head and peered up at Kathleen over the top of gold-rimmed spectacles.

She rose stiffly, and gestured with crooked fingers toward the front window. "Mr. Connors has been such a help. While he waited for you, he brought in the tree and got down the ornaments for me."

"Shall we go?" He directed as he took charge of the luggage she'd dumped on the floor.

Age thirty-two, district bank manager of local branches in the area of Fir Valley, he worked at looking older and dignified. Kathleen smiled at him as he reached for his dark blue sport coat on the arm of a chair and slipped it on. His eyes were serious behind horn-rimmed glasses.

"Yes, we must," she answered. "It's starting to rain and driving may take longer."

Martha, dressed as usual in a flowered calf-length, shirtwaist dress, sleeves rolled to the elbow, white apron tied around where her waist was presumed to be, bent her ample, barely five foot frame over the coffee table. "Here. You must take some of my fruit cake."

She wrapped four generous slices in a napkin and handed them to Kathleen. "I wish you didn't have to leave so quickly, but I suppose planes won't wait."

"Thanks for the refreshments, Mrs. Fisher. It's been a pleasure visiting with you," Edward said while propelling Kathleen out the door.

"Drive carefully! I do wish you a Merry Christmas!" Martha waved and called from the open doorway.

The tension began to leave her body as she relaxed against the soft leather seat of the nearly new BMW. Edward selected a CD, and The Mormon Tabernacle Choir filled the car with "The Halleluiah Chorus."

"I'm sorry we're getting such a late start, but you won't believe what happened at school." She turned the volume down a bit and filled him in on the traumatic events, leaving out few details, unaware her voice had risen.

He threw her a look, and turned off the stereo. "The Halleluiah Chorus" was over.

"We may *never* see Patti again," she wailed.

"So you say, but isn't that a bit melodramatic? Divorce happens every day." He pushed the hair back off his brow. "Fathers duck their responsibilities. Refuse to pay child support. Sometimes they take their own kid. It happens. Let the authorities handle it."

She barely noticed when they entered the freeway. "But it doesn't happen in *my* school—to one of *my* students."

"Well, I don't see that it's your problem. You did nothing wrong. Kathleen, you get too emotional over those kids. You're a teacher. Your job begins and ends in the classroom."

"*What?*" she barked. "Edward! I care about my students, and that doesn't end when I leave the classroom."

The windshield wipers made a steady whish-swipe across the glass as they sped along the freeway. Rain came harder now and mixed with a few snowflakes. Neon lights blinked on and off. They passed Rudolph the red-nosed reindeer and Santa's sleigh atop peaked roofs. Green and red garlands swayed in the breeze between lampposts. She saw none of it. Her eyes brimmed with tears as she turned away and pretended to look out the window.

He braked to a gentle stop in the parking garage and glanced at her. She continued to look away. He opened the door, retrieved his black raincoat from the backseat and slipped it on before reaching for her coat and going around the car to open the door for her.

"I'm sorry I hurt your feelings."

She shrugged into her coat, refusing to look at him as he held it for her. He turned her to face him, tracing a tear on her cheek with his thumb.

"I understand you have a big heart; it's part of who you are, and part of what makes you so special. I just hope there's room in that big heart for me, or have I totally blown it?" He retrieved her luggage from the trunk and handled it as easily as a bank teller counts money.

"Sorry, I guess I don't see it as such a bad thing that Mr. Williams wants his daughter. Sure, I concede, he shouldn't have taken her the way he did," he sighed. "But maybe he isn't being heard. Kathleen, my old man walked out and never looked back. He never wrote, and he never called."

"I thought your father died." She gasped. "You told me he's dead."

"Yeah, he is. I didn't lie to you." He put an arm around her shoulder as he guided her to the sky bridge. "What I didn't tell you is, he died four years ago. My dad walked out on my mother and me, when I was three years old. I never knew him."

He tried to grin, but it looked more like a grimace and died before it could reach his eyes. "Sorry, this is a lousy way to start the holidays." He gave her a little squeeze. "Not at all what I visualized, what I wanted. I'd like to be totally selfish, ask you to chuck your plans and spend the time with me. But

I know you need to see your family. So..." He looked down at her. "Am I forgiven or still in the dog house?"

She moved closer and directed a tremulous smile upward. The unruly lock of hair fell across his forehead, and she visualized the little boy whose father didn't have time for him. A lump formed in her throat. *Father, forgive me,* she silently prayed. *I'm blessed with a wonderful family, a mother and father who love each other and me. And I haven't always appreciated what I've been given.*

They entered the terminal amidst a crush of humanity. Impatient to get to the ticket counters, trailing luggage behind them like some added appendage, anxious to get through security and to the boarding gates beyond, people dashed everywhere. Kathleen's eyes darted around looking for uniformed policemen. *Is anyone looking for Patti and Mr. Williams? Could they already have apprehended him?* She hadn't seen any squad cars around the building.

"Do you think the authorities are here? Do you think they are looking for Mr. Williams? I don't see any uniforms other than airport security. Would they stop him?"

He squelched a groan, a frown worrying its way between his eyes. "I'm sure I don't know. Maybe there are undercover agents here. We do know airport security is tight since 9/11. Speaking of which, we'd better get your suitcase checked through, and pick up your boarding pass."

"Oh. Right."

"Did you see the tall decorated tree over there?"

"Um, what? Oh, yes. Pretty, isn't it," she murmured.

"Is it a noble fir or a Norwegian spruce, do you think?" he pressed.

She half-turned and followed his gaze, blinking in surprise at the tree professionally decorated with pink miniature teddy bears, and old-fashioned porcelain dolls dressed in pink with white pantalets. But it wasn't the tree that made her gasp, it was the little girl in a red jacket exactly like Patti's. "*Edward*! Over there—that little girl." The child turned, Kathleen tightened her grip on his arm, then sagged like a helium-filled party balloon after the third day.

Chapter 3

Al Williams fought the strong urge to speed. He set the cruise control at a safe limit and let his eyes do double duty between the rearview mirror and the road ahead. He didn't need the police to stop him for speeding.

"Daddy, I didn't know you were going to pick me up. Mommy said you wouldn't come till after Christmas. Does this mean you can spend Christmas with us? Will you take me to see Santa Claus like you did last year?"

Patti's happy chatter thrummed in his ears like a familiar song, but he couldn't have told a judge the words if they put him on the witness stand and made him swear to tell the truth. His one thought ran like a chant, *get to the airport and on that plane. Get to the airport and on that plane.*

"That dumb ol' Jimmy says there isn't really a Santa Claus. It's just some ol' fat guy dressed up. And it's just for babies anyway…I told him to shut up. That you said it's okay to believe in Santa Claus…so will you? Take me?"

"Umm-hmmm," Al mumbled.

How long before Amber figures out I'm the one grabbed Patti? How long before she sets the police on me? Probably not long, he thought. *My ex-wife may be a lot of things, but stupid isn't one of them.*

He hoped he had at least a half hour head start, but it could be less. He hoped too, they expected him to go to PDX, the largest and most logical Oregon airport. And the closest to the school where he'd snatched Patti. A half-smile formed around his mouth as he thought of authorities looking for him in Portland while he and Patti flew out of Eugene.

"Daddy?—Dad-*dee!*"

"Yeah, Patti? What is it?" Al tried to keep the irritation out of his voice and remember what it was his daughter last said. But he simply didn't know; he hadn't been paying attention.

"I forgot my present and stuff from school. Can we go back and get it? Please? I want to show it to you."

"Not now, sweetheart. You can get it later."

Several minutes passed before Al realized it was too quiet in the back seat.

"Patti?" Tears ran down the cheeks of his daughter's crumpled face when he glanced back to check on her. Except for a few sniffles, she emitted no sound. The silence cut him to the quick. Off in the distance the Golden Arches of a McDonalds reminded Al of happier occasions when there had been plenty of time for laughter, food, and play. His knuckles turned white as he gripped the wheel, his jaw clenched, and his eyes grew cold. He swore under his breath. He didn't like having to lie to his daughter.

I didn't start this convoluted custody battle crapshoot and the end justifies the means. What the Sam Hill does Amber think? That she, as Patti's mother, is the only one with rights? That I'll just roll over and play dead? Pay support and let some judge tell me when I can see my kid? Never!

• • •

Nearly two hours remained until scheduled departure time, Edward steered Kathleen to a small coffee shop. He found a place for two in the corner, pulled out a chair and seated her.

Poinsettias—red, white, various shades of pink, burgundy, and a kind of green she said she didn't like—decorated the tables. Glad the more familiar red adorned their table, he watched her turn the pot in her hands; she looked like a kid, who's read too many fairy tales and thinks if she rubs the right bottle, a genie will pop out and grant her wish. Bing Crosby's *White Christmas* played softly from strategically placed speakers around the room, creating a nostalgic mood for those tuned in.

"What would you like, Kath—"

"I'm not very hungry," she interrupted. "Maybe just coffee."

The evening hadn't gone at all the way he'd planned. No nice dinner, no intimate time alone with his girlfriend. The incident at the school made her late to begin with, and even now he didn't have her attention. He felt frustrated, like he'd just invested a hefty amount of money in a growing company only to have the stock market plunge.

He ordered coffee and two pieces of what he knew to be her favorite—Pecan pie. He reached across the table, closed his hand over her fingers and stopped her fidgeting. "It's going to be okay, Kathleen. They'll find her."

She threw him a startled look, blushed, and dropped her gaze. The cup clattered slightly against the saucer as she reached for her coffee; she picked up her fork and broke off miniature pieces of pie the waitress had placed on the table before her.

He pulled a small box, wrapped in shiny green paper and tied with silver ribbon, from his pocket and set it on the table. *Maybe this'll draw her attention back to me.* "Merry Christmas," he whispered. "I hope you like it."

She froze mid-bite and stared at the ring-sized box. "What…what is it?"

"Go on. Open it. It won't bite you."

Her fingers trembled as she pulled the ribbon and undid the paper, careful not to tear it. "Oh—Edward." Her eyes, wide with surprise, flew to his. "Thank you. It's perfect." She expelled a ragged breath, and like a teenager on a first date, emitted a nervous little giggle. "I love Giorgio's sandalwood. It's my favorite perfume." She twisted a lock of hair around her index finger, and sat up straighter.

A blush suffused her face. "I'm sorry. I forgot. Your gift is on my bed, back at Mrs. Fisher's." Reaching across the table, she squeezed his hand, then picked up her fork, and finished her pie.

"This pie is delicious. Aren't you going to eat yours?"

He chuckled, the first happy sound all evening. "Kathleen, that's not too subtle." He pushed his pie toward her. "Go on, eat it," he smirked. "I'll get something later."

She reddened and ate the pie.

Kathleen stacked the plates and pushed them to the edge of the table, as the waitress, clad in a short red dress and Santa hat, poured more coffee. With the plates removed, Giorgio's perfume winked up at them from the center of the table. She reached for the bottle, twisted the cap, sniffed, and dabbed a little on each wrist. Grinning, she waved an arm under his nose.

He leered back at her and made a motion as if to bite the wrist she so adroitly exposed. She withdrew her arm, opened her purse, and tucked the perfume inside. A pleased look changed to one of puzzlement, and then to enlightenment, as long fingers probed the contents of her bag.

She withdrew the napkin-wrapped fruitcake and placed it on the table. "Umm…this probably won't mix well with the perfume." She tried for a wide-eyed innocent look, as she pushed it carefully toward him. "Do you think it might make it through the checkpoint?"

He squelched an all-out laugh and turned it into a discreet cough. "I don't think I'd chance it. Though, I suppose it's pretty good, as fruitcakes go." He winked at her. "Dump it. I suffered my share back at Mrs. Fisher's."

She checked her watch. "What time do you have, Edward?"

He bit back the sarcastic reply that his tongue could easily have uttered. *Ten minutes later than when you asked before.* He knew they could probably squeeze in another twenty minutes together, but there didn't seem to be much point in doing so.

"I guess it's time for you to go."

They joined the line of harried people waiting to clear United Airline's checkpoint. Not used to having an audience when they kissed, and highly self-conscious, they stopped and faced each other. A glance around told them people weren't especially interested in them, and could care less what they did. They embraced, and Edward kissed her decisively, if quickly, before letting her go.

He shoved his hands in his pockets and watched as she cleared the checkpoint then rushed down the concourse without so much as a backward glance.

Back in the car he removed his tie, folded it carefully, unlocked the glove compartment, and placed it inside. His fingers, as though operating independent of him, grazed the ring-box resting uneasily in its temporary location. Tonight it would go back in the bank vault. He took it out and carefully opened the lid, turning the diamond until it caught the light and flashed. *Enough icy fire to melt one redhead if I can get it on her finger—If I can get her out of that classroom—If the two of us can escape this one-horse town. If…*

A whole lot of ifs.

Am I deceiving myself, or is it just the timing that's off? How could something I deemed to be so right, straightforward, and easy a month ago, become such a mental quagmire? This is becoming more complicated than approving a bank loan for a widow. His thoughts on Kathleen, he felt like a kid trying to fit a round peg in a square hole. He wanted her but was getting a sinking feeling she wasn't going to fit well in the compartmentalized desk drawers of his neatly arranged life. *I like a woman with spirit, but I* want *a wife that will climb the ladder with me and live the style of life I can provide.* It wasn't just the school thing, though that was a large part of it. He wanted to have his own kids, not take on twenty-six he didn't even know. It was her whole obsession with the rural, country-style living she had adopted. *She's enamored with chickens, cows, and horses, for Pete's sake.* Edward had no intention of remaining in some back-water, shabby little town, with mostly rednecks, any longer than absolutely necessary.

He first met Kathleen at church. She sang in the choir, sang solos like an angel. Right then and there he'd decided to join the choir. It had been a good move, not only did it put him closer to her, but the choir director turned out to be amazingly knowledgeable on a variety of subjects, as well as gifted in music, a friend he could converse with.

The choir itself, a motley crew made up of young and old, male and female, lacked professionalism, but there weren't too many to draw from in a small congregation. What they lacked in talent, they made up for in enthusiasm and a desire to worship God with their music. He figured it didn't hurt his image around town, to be one of them.

Some of his business associates had explicit suggestions of what to do with a girlfriend who looked like Kathleen. He'd smiled and kept his own counsel, though he wasn't entirely adverse to some of the ideas. This wasn't, after all, the dark ages. People were liberated in today's society. If they wanted to live together, they did.

The trouble is, Kathleen swallows all that Bible stuff about purity and waiting, and she favors going places with a group rather than spending much time alone with me. She's downright prudish. He respected her for it, but wasn't convinced God cared that much what people did or did not do in their private lives. Surely a God of the universe had more important things to take care of than monitoring someone's sex life.

Back on the freeway, he set the cruise control and plugged in a medley of Christmas songs. It stopped raining and a few stars could be seen twinkling against a dark sky. Traffic was lighter; he relaxed and sang along with the "Little Drummer Boy." "Come they told me…"

He prided himself on his acceptance of a wide variety of music. Gospel, Country-Western, some of which Kathleen liked, though his taste ran more to the classics.

He combed fingers through his hair, pushing back that stubborn strand, and sighed. *Kathleen is a jewel worth waiting for, but a man can't be expected to wait forever.*

Chapter 4

Kathleen pulled her boots back on after having the heels checked for explosives and clomped her way down the corridor without a backward glance. She entered the waiting area with all the enthusiasm of a patient entering a dentist's office. Not that she minded flying, she thrilled at the takeoff and thrust of the mighty jet engines. She loved soaring above the clouds. No, it was the body-numbing sitting that put her mind in comatose.

Before that could happen, she checked the area for one misplaced little blonde girl. Not easy in a crowded room of people sitting, standing, changing positions, and milling around like cattle waiting to be let in the barn. Children were present, some carbon-copies in miniature of the parents who kept them close but again, no Patti.

The first leg of her journey, from Portland to Seattle, seemed a nightmare lasting an eternity. From the time she wedged herself in beside a grandmother, who should have bought two tickets, and discovered the woman was first cousin to an auctioneer, the verbal assault had been ceaseless.

"I'm going to Seattle to spend Christmas with my daughter and son-in-law and those precious grandchildren Billy's three and smart as a whip. You wouldn't believe the things he can do—why—he can *read.* Mary's five and cute as a button she likes to help cook..."

Doesn't this woman ever take a breath?

"Does a good job, too. Joe is seven and the spittin' image of my Bertha bless his little heart he wants to be an airline pilot now wouldn't that be something I'd get to fly free maybe."

The lady gulped air faster than a swimmer in a race and never broke stride.

"Selma is six months and just a darling I love her to death, looks like her daddy though..."

At another time, she might have found the woman amusing, but the day's emotional roller coaster had depleted her sense of humor. Kathleen's temples throbbed by the time she disembarked at SeaTac airport. "*Thank God, she gets off in Seattle. My ears are red from overload, and if my brain were a computer, it would have crashed.*

"Well, bye, Dear. I hope you have a nice time. Merry Christmas."

• • •

With a cheeseburger, small salad, glass of milk, and two Excedrin to fortify her, Kathleen felt she might again join the human race. She pulled her cell phone from her bag and dialed Edward's number. Maybe, just maybe, he had heard some news about Patti. *I wish I'd asked him to get Mrs. Williams' number.* So I could *call her.* She counted each ring, one, two, three *(pick it up, Edward)* ten times. No answer. Kathleen dialed the number for his cell phone. *Shoot, he has it turned off. Where is he anyway?*

She paid the check, shoved the change in her billfold and watched people, pacing, looking, and pacing some more. The clock on the wall said one thing and her wristwatch backed it up.

Tomorrow I will be with my brother Michael, Mary, and their brood in Ohio. It'll be good to talk to Mary. Her sister-in-law had an uncanny way of peeling off the varnish and getting to the heart of a matter. When Mary sorted things out it could be plain as writing on a chalkboard. *She won't just tell me what she thinks I want to hear, she'll call it as she sees it. I wonder what she'll think of Edward.*

Kathleen hadn't asked Michael about the snow, but it would be unusual if they didn't have at least five or six inches. In Ohio everyone expected a white Christmas. She looked forward to romping in the powdery fall-out with her nieces and nephews, building snowmen and snow forts. Those kids knew how to challenge her. They'd have her laughing till her sides ached.

• • •

Kathleen entered the plane like a hen looking for a nest and tried unsuccessfully to stow her carry-on in the overhead. Her face matched her hair when she whapped the person sitting on the aisle with her shoulder bag. Ready to apologize, she looked down into eyes as blue as Crater Lake on a summer day.

"Carrot Top? Is that you?"

"Danny?—Daniel Lee Davis?"

A grin lit his face around teeth straight out of a toothpaste ad. "Yeah, it's me. Who else do you go around hitting?"

"Danny!" she exploded. "The last time I hit you, we were in *fifth* grade. And as I remember, you hit me back."

"Probably," he conceded. "Now I just rescue damsels in distress." Still grinning, that cat-got-the-cream satisfied smirk, he got up and stowed her carry-on with all the ease a flight attendant might have, which only made her turn a deeper red.

During high school days, Daniel Lee Davis could make me madder than anyone, she recalled. *But he could be pretty nice, too. Like the time I had a bad cold and missed the prom, he brought me six long-stemmed red roses the next day. Then he sat with me through a comedy on television while I sniffed, blew my nose, and inhaled chicken soup. And he wasn't even my date.*

About to take her seat beside the window, she noticed the open Bible he'd placed there before getting up to help her. It didn't fit with the Danny she remembered. A question in her eyes, she handed the book over to him.

"Curious?"

The mischief in his eyes, she did know. "Well…Yes. Don't tell me you are a preacher or something?"

"Preacher? No. Something? Yes." I went to Promise Keepers last summer." He lifted the pocket-sized Bible, then closed and laid it aside. "Some of us sort of agreed to be accountable to each other. Helps keep us on track."

Interest stirred, she wanted to know more, but Danny neatly switched the topic to her.

"So…tell me about you. What are you up to these days?" He lifted her left hand, then released it. "Hmm—I don't see a ring on that finger. I figured you'd be married with six kids by now."

"No, not married. I'm teaching in the nicest little country school you can possibly imagine. Public school just outside Fir Valley, Oregon, but it could as easily be a private instruction for the rich and famous."

"Ah, still bossing kids around, huh."

"*Danny*."

"Just teasing. You always did have a way with the small fry, Kathleen. I'm not surprised you're teaching." He squeezed her hand and his eyes had that devil may care look she well remembered. It was as if eight years just fell away, they might have been back in school together, but she didn't remember his touch or his eyes making her feel giddy, the way they seemed to be doing now. *I'm just tired,* she thought. *And my emotions are about as stable as a six-year-olds on the first day of school.*

• • •

For years their parents owned homes in the same block; Danny had been a frequent visitor in the O'Brien house. He'd dogged her brother Michael, whom he hero-worshipped, especially while in grade school. High school ended, and their parents, facing the empty nest syndrome, sold out and moved away. The kids went off to college and lost touch. Kathleen hadn't seen Danny since their high school days, when they slaved and stewed together over the school paper. He was the photographer. She had charge of layout. He delighted in catching her in unflattering poses and snapping her picture. Some of which found their way into print, despite her efforts to keep them out.

• • •

"I don't see a ring on *your* finger, Mr. Danny "Flashbulb" Davis. What's keeping you from the clutches of matrimony?"

"Ah! I've been waitin' for you, my darlin'."

"Will you be serious?" She punched him lightly on the arm. "What's the real reason? In high school you were pretty serious about Susan Landon."

"Puppy love leads to a hound's life," he chortled. "No—I'm never home—it wouldn't be fair to a wife. Besides, Susan wised up and married a dentist."

"Explain."

"Explain why Susan married a dentist?"

"No, you idiot." She had to laugh. "Why are you never home?"

"I trot around the globe hiding behind a camera."

"You're a photographer?"

"You don't have to sound so surprised." He feigned insult. "I wasn't *that* bad."

"Actually, Danny, I always thought you were pretty good."

She grinned. "Unscrupulous, but good. So, who are you working for?"

"I'm on the staff of a Seattle paper...and I freelance."

A flight attendant interrupted. "Would you like something to drink?"

"Kathleen?" Danny turned to her.

"Sure, orange juice would be nice."

"Make that two," he ordered.

They sipped quietly on their drinks, each thinking of the multitude of questions still to ask. Eight years of catching up takes time. She gazed at him. He was taller than high school days; she guessed five-feet-ten or eleven inches—better looking too. Maybe not handsome in the classic way but cute—definitely a hunk. Perhaps he was on the go, but she bet he frequented a gym.

His muscular Levi-clad legs stretched the denim tight, and ended with feet encased in cowboy boots. He wore a warm wooly pullover the same shade of blue as his eyes. If he spent the winter in the pale Northwest, he didn't look it; his blonde hair, short and curly, looked like sun-bleached straw, and he had a tan to make celebrities envious.

"So, where do you live? When you're not globe-trotting, I mean?"

"Well, I hang my hat in Chicago some of the time. Seattle when I'm on the West Coast. Sometimes I get out to see Mom and Dad. I just came from there."

"Oh, how are your folks?" She remembered Mr. Davis sold his hardware store in Portland and moved right after she and Danny graduated. "Are they still on the ranch in central Oregon?"

"Yeah, and loving it. You couldn't rope my dad and drag him from there. Mom either. Would you believe, she has her own horse, a gentle little black mare named Coaly, and goes riding almost daily? Your folks?"

"Florida. Michael's in Ohio." She wriggled in her seat and sat up a little straighter. "That's where I'm going now. The folks are flying up."

"Well then, tell them old Daniel said hello." He smiled, then totally surprised her by reaching over and taking her hand again. "Kathleen?" His eyes were completely serious, making shivers go up her back. "I may be jumping in here where angels fear to tread. I know I haven't seen you in a long time. But you looked as if the world rested on your shoulders when you boarded." He hesitated, searching her face, then plowed on. "You smile, but your eyes look like a storm about to break. Is everything okay?"

Dumbfounded at his perception and that he cared enough to ask, she simply stared into two dark blue pools one could drown in. Without realizing she'd been holding her breath, she let it out in a rush, like a blown-up balloon someone forgot to tie.

It felt good to unburden herself to someone who honestly seemed to care. Danny never interrupted her disclosure of Patti and the abduction one time, but he often nodded encouragement and his eyes shown with compassion while gently squeezing her hand and patiently waiting for her to continue when a lump in her throat threatened her voice.

When he was sure she was finished, he said in a voice kinder than she thought possible, "Kathleen, I'm sorry. No wonder you were upset," He smiled, hesitating. "With your permission, I'd like to pray." He released her hand and reached for the small Bible pocketed earlier.

> "Do not be anxious about anything, but in everything, by prayer and petition, with thanksgiving, present your requests to God. And the peace of God which transcends all understanding, will guard your hearts and minds in Christ Jesus."
>
> Phil.4: 6-7 NIV

With her hand again gently tucked in his, he prayed softly for her ears alone. She heard her name, Patti, wisdom, peace, something that sounded like guidance, and leaving it in God's hands. She yawned. Feeling more peaceful than she had in a long time, one weary schoolteacher succumbed to sleep after they prayed. Gravity played a part, and Kathleen's coppery curls just naturally came to rest against Danny's shoulder.

• • •

The intercom crackled to life. "Ladies and gentleman, we will be landing at O'Hare airport in about twenty minutes. It's a cool seventeen degrees in Chicago, and it's snowing. I hope you brought your overcoats. Happy holidays, and thank you for flying United."

Seats came to upright positions, trays were stowed, and seatbelts snapped like a well-rehearsed litany.

"Hey, O'Brien. You snore. Did you know that?"

"Hmmm...what? I do not" Kathleen murmured, while attemting to rub sleep from her eyes.

He grinned at her. "Sure you do, but I won't tell." He put his arm around her shoulders and gave her a squeeze. "It's been great seeing you again, Kathleen. I hope we can keep in touch." He handed her a card with his Seattle address, phone number, and e-mail. "I'll be praying. Things will work out with Patti. You'll see."

Quickly, she dug in her purse, retrieved a pen, and scribbled her e-mail address, cell phone, and home phone number on the back of another card he handed her. With an overwhelming lump in her throat, she reached up and hugged his neck as though she'd been offered a life preserver on a sinking ship.

A face, briefly red as Santa Claus's suit, she didn't look at him as he retrieved her carry-on, and helped her into her coat. She watched him slide into his leather jacket. Then when his hands were busy with his own paraphernalia, she gave way to memories, a tinge of nerves, and school-girl silliness. Kathleen giggled and did what she'd wanted to do since she sat down beside him. Her hand lifted and two fingers touched those tight springy curls.

She leered at him. "Just as I expected. You wear a wig."

He chuckled. "Watch it, Carrot Top! Those are my golden locks you're talking about."

They exited the plane together. She stole looks at him, unwilling to admit their meeting made more of an impact than warranted. The likelihood of seeing him again any time soon appeared slim and left her with a feeling of loss she didn't understand.

She watched through tear-dimmed eyes until he stopped, turned, and waved.

Chapter 5

Thankful for forty-five minutes in which to stretch her legs before the connecting flight to Youngstown, Kathleen sought a quiet corner. After tunnels, moving walkways, and people, people, people, it was nice to find a niche where bodies were less intrusive. Dark outside, it was difficult to see much, but she maneuvered to a window and looked out anyway. Floodlights revealed it was still snowing—snowing hard.

The swirling flakes mesmerized the weary teacher, until an elderly woman paused beside her. "It doesn't look good out there, does it?" Before the lady could say more, a young man grasped her elbow, and gently pulled her away. "Come on Mother, let's get some breakfast."

A seed of doubt planted, Kathleen bit her lip and went to check the monitor for incoming and outgoing flight schedules. Two cancellations and five delays.

Fifteen minutes later, everything changed.

"Ladies and gentlemen, we are sorry to announce all

flights to and from O'Hare International Airport are being cancelled due to a severe snowstorm. We apologize for the inconvenience, but safety must come first. We'll be back in the air as soon as possible."

Smiles on faces of holiday-travelers vanished quicker than cookies on Christmas Eve. Her heart plummeted, she didn't relish time spent waiting in an airport. *Things could be worse,* she told herself. *I'd rather be here than out there in that storm.* Nothing to do but wait...perhaps morning...only a few hours away, would bring change.

• • •

Daylight struggled against a dark snow-laden sky. Another look out a window revealed snow being blown before gale-force winds, an alarming sight. It was like looking at a white wall about ten inches from your nose.

I need to call Michael. Kathleen headed for one of the many pay phones in the terminal. *It will be cheaper,* she reasoned, *than paying a roaming charge and I may need my cell phone later. Michael is an early riser, I hope he's up.*

Three rings and her brother's alert voice came over the line. "Hello."

"Michael," she croaked around the lump in her throat. "It's me. Guess where I am?"

"Snowed in at O'Hare airport."

"You know? How could you know?"

"Baby Sister, it's all over the early-morning news. They're saying it's the worst blizzard to hit in ten years, and it's supposed to be heading this way.

"Oh, no…Michael?"

"Sorry, kid. I'm disappointed too, but you may be better off there. Mary's in bed with the flu. I think Bobby is coming down with it also. He didn't want any dinner last night, and he loves hamburgers.

"I phoned the folks," he rushed on. "They're not coming, afraid of catching the flu. And this whole storm thing has the planes up in the air."

"Michael, she giggled. "Big Brother, don't you mean, planes grounded?"

"Yeah, whatever." He chuckled, but it sounded forced. Kathleen could hear a ruckus in the background.

"Sis…I'm really sorry—Bobby's crying. I'd better go. Call later?"

"Yes, sure. Bye. Love ya."

"Love you, too. Bye."

• • •

She and Michael had had their share of squabbles while growing up, but, she thought, they were closer than most. Five years older, he was protective of his little sister. She was almost eight the Christmas their parents gave them bicycles. Michael received a new updated ten-speed, and she got her very first shiny new bike—complete with a big red bow tied on the handlebars.

Her brother had to be eager to try out his own new wheels, but he had spent hours helping her, running alongside the small bike, shouting directions and keeping her from falling when she wobbled. By evening, she'd learned to ride.

• • •

Feeling deflated, and seeing like emotions reflected in more faces than she could possibly count, Kathleen determined to make the best of a bad situation and not feel sorry for herself. She imagined she could hear Danny saying. *God's in control.* It brought a smile and a sense of peace.

A professional brass ensemble, there to entertain passengers as they funneled through the terminals, performed bravely for the stalled and disgruntled humanity. Shops, boutiques, and restaurants put forth their best holiday finery, decorations guaranteed to enhance the Christmas spirit under normal conditions. A good place to grab a last-minute gift and hop on the plane, today seemed a grim reminder they weren't going anywhere—at least not as soon as they wanted.

Uneasy travelers, killing time, crowded the stores and quaint little boutiques. Shopkeepers beamed hopefully and were generally met with hollow-eyed stares. Kathleen mingled with the lookers, smiled bravely and hoped her grin didn't look as plastic as those on the faces she saw. She giggled quietly to herself when "White Christmas" played over the loudspeakers for the third time in as many hours. *Be careful what you wish for,* she thought. *You just might get it.*

The day wore on, and still it snowed. People wandered around, some preferred to sit and read; still others had a card game going. The lucky ones managed to catch a nap. Children ran around in close vicinity of their parents, whined and fussed while their distraught mothers and fathers searched for ways to distract them.

She pulled a paperback from her purse and tried to read. When she repeated the same paragraph for the third time and had no idea what she was reading, she decided it was time to lay it aside. She continued to watch people, her mind free to windmill from one topic to another. Always, it returned to one missing little girl.

Surveying the children and hoping one might turn out to be Patti, was becoming a habit. *I have about as much chance of seeing her as I have of finding a diamond in a snow bank,* she admitted. *By now, she's probably out of the country.* She looked anyway. Prayed and hoped.

Darkness settled in. People ambled away to eat in restaurants, visit bars, kill more time, eventually ending up back in the concourses, wishing they were anywhere but O'Hare airport. Officials did what they could to prepare for a long uncomfortable night. Cots were brought out and blankets dispensed. Children were tucked in and most slept.

Bodies stretched out on anything resembling a couch. Others made use of the floor, backpacks and luggage serving as pillows. Midnight came and went. Still it snowed. Kathleen, seated in an end chair by a table, eased off her boots, tucked her feet beneath her, stowed her purse securely under her arm, and shut her eyes. With hundreds of people around her, she had never felt more alone—or more vulnerable.

I'd like it if Edward were here with me now, make me feel safe. But he wouldn't like sitting around, she acknowledged. *He'd probably start another bank branch. Or maybe organize crews to clear away the snow.* The thought made her smile. *I'll call him tomorrow.* Tired out of her mind, she finally slept.

Day two repeated day one. Tempers grew shorter, people forgot to smile, children cried more, babies screamed, and the bars were packed. She took a whole hour over a cup of coffee and a doughnut. Still more tired than she could remember, she found an unoccupied space, stretched out on the floor with her head propped on her baggage, and took a long Sunday nap. Later, feeling a little better, she killed more time taking two and a half hours to finish her evening meal of steak, baked potato, salad, dinner roll, coffee, and sherbet for dessert. The lettuce was none too fresh, the croutons stale, and the tomatoes tasteless, but she ate it anyway.

Back in the waiting area, she offered to hold a fussy toddler while a weary mother, who sat down beside her, stretched her cramped limbs.

"Oh, thank you. It's hard traveling alone with a little one." Her eyes glistened with unshed tears. "My husband is in Iraq. I know I should have stayed home, but I so wanted to spend the holidays with his parents in Pennsylvania." Eyes downcast, she shrugged. "I never dreamed we'd be stuck in a snow storm."

Kathleen flashed her a sympathetic smile. "None of us did." She put the tiny boy over her shoulder and gently patted him on the back while quietly talking to his mother. In no time, the baby was asleep.

Bedtime came. She and the young mother sat on a couch, the little guy asleep between them. Tonight they each rated a blanket. Wrapping it around her, snuggling into its fuzzy warmth, and trying to imagine herself home in her own bed, one redheaded schoolteacher slept.

• • •

Day three. Monday. And still it snowed. *Am I going to be here Christmas day?* Weary beyond belief, her brain stuck on hold with boredom, Kathleen ventured farther a field. She made it all the way to outside. Gasping at the cold, astonished at so much snow snowplows had tried to clear, she quickly turned and retraced her steps.

An airport official called in passing, "It's supposed to quit snowing today."

Oh, I hope. I'm so tired of this. She entered a restroom she'd never been in before. *I'm never going to complain about Oregon's rain again,* she vowed. Bent over the bowl washing her face, she didn't notice the small schoolgirl exiting the stall behind her.

The youngster stopped beside her, a teddy bear clutched under one arm. "Miss O'Brien. What are *you* doing here?"

"*Patti?!—" Oh, dear God.* It's really *her*!

Kathleen smiled, her mind raced, trying to quickly assess the situation, and decide what she could do without raising undue alarm. The child seemed pale and her eyes looked as if she'd been crying.

"Patti, I'm so happy to see you. Here…I'll hold your bear while you wash your hands." *How long can I detain Patti before Mr. Williams sends someone or comes storming in here himself?*

"Where are you going, Patti?"

"My daddy didn't telled me." She held up the teddy bear. "He buyed me this bear." Big blue eyes looked up at her teacher. "Miss O'Brien? My mommy's gonna be mad at me. I was 'spose to go home. But Daddy taked me on the airplane."

"Oh—Patti." Kathleen hugged her. "Your mommy isn't mad at you. But she is worried." The teacher took her by the hand and led her to a lounge. "I know—lets see if we can call her. Patti—do you know your telephone number?"

"I think so."

Kathleen whipped out her cell phone and punched in each digit as one of her brightest students proudly recited the phone number to her teacher.

One. Two. Three rings. *Please answer.* Four. Five…*It must be about four in the morning back home.* Six…"Lo?"

"Hello. Mrs. Williams? This is Kathleen O'Brien. I'm sorry to wake you. But I have very good news. Patti is *here.* At O'Hare airport.

"My *baby*! You *saw* her?"

"Mrs. Williams, she's right here with me. At the moment we are in a restroom. I'll put her on the phone to talk to you."

"Mommy? I'm in Chawgo." Patti gripped the phone. "Mommy you sound funny—are you mad at me? Daddy buyed me a teddy bear." Patti, seated on the lounge, began to squirm as tears formed in already red-rimmed eyes. "Mommy? Why are you crying?" The little girl pushed the phone toward her teacher. "My mommy wants to talk to you."

"I'm here."

"Miss O'Brien—can you keep Patti away from that *bastard*?" she screeched. "Get her back to me?"

Kathleen flinched, bit her lip and moved the phone a

fraction away from her ear. "Mrs. Williams—I promise to do the best I can..."

"Get the police," the woman, near hysteria, interrupted.

"Mrs. Williams, I *will* do the best I can from this end. Right now planes are grounded because of a blizzard. I'm not sure..."

"*Call the police.*"

She half turned away, lowered her voice, and enunciated each word carefully into the phone. "*You* need to call the authorities from *there.* Alert them. *Now.*"

Troubled eyes watched the teacher. Kathleen smiled reassuringly and forced herself to stay calm.

"Mrs. Williams, I'll do my best—and I'll call again—when I can —I have to hang up now. Goodbye."

"Patti, is your daddy waiting for you outside the restroom?"

"Uh-huh." Blonde head bobbled up and down, her tousled curls bouncing.

"Well, I'd very much like to meet your father." *God in heaven, help me. Give me wisdom.* Kathleen silently shouted a quick prayer upward while handing the bear to Patti. "Let's not keep him waiting any longer." Phone safely shut off and stashed in her purse; she took the child's hand and smiled encouragingly into trusting upturned eyes. Together, they exited the restroom.

Patti led the way straight to the large sandy-haired man who stood within ten feet of the restroom door. "Daddy, this is my teacher."

"Mr. Williams. Hello—I'm Miss O'Brien." She manufactured a bright smile and held out her hand as if she were welcoming him to her classroom for a scheduled conference.

Fear, fast as lightning, flashed in his eyes, and he darted a glance around him. But he stood his ground and hesitantly reached to shake hands.

I'm an unwelcome surprise he didn't count on. He can't be sure how much I know. If only she could keep him off balance until she determined what to do or the authorities took control. *Please God, don't let Patti tell her father we called Amber Williams.*

Chapter 6

"I was thinking of getting some breakfast." Mentally, she kept her fingers crossed and prayed unseen powers were at work. "I wonder if you and your daughter would join me?"

"Can we Daddy? Please?" She looked up at him with trusting eyes.

Al took a step backward. Sweat popped out on his forehead. His face darkened. Eyes narrowed. Wary.

"My treat." *Will he run?* She hardly dared breathe as she forced a smile. "Where would *you* like to go, Patti?"

"McDonalds. Can we Daddy? Please?"

She counted on the child to sway her father, but Patti seemed to lack real enthusiasm. It niggled her mind, but she couldn't guess the reason. *Maybe she's just tired.* She wondered too, why Mr. Williams hadn't dressed his daughter in warmer clothes. He himself seemed comfortable enough in sweater and a leather coat, but Patti still wore the red jacket from school, not nearly warm enough for Chicago weather.

Kathleen gabbled on, hoping to throw him off guard and

lower his defenses, as if she could hold him with mere words. "This blizzard. It's nice to see someone from home—someone with whom to spend a little time while we're waiting for the weather to clear."

He glowered and seemed on the verge of refusal when Patti tugged on his arm, her eyes imploring. "Daddy? Can we?"

"Well, maybe a cup of joe," he grudgingly conceded.

The man couldn't be described as handsome, but he certainly commanded a second look. For one thing, he was larger than he appeared when she saw him in the school parking lot. *A man it might be dangerous to cross,* she thought. He had the rugged look of a football player, or maybe a boxer, and sometime or other his nose had been broken. His hands were enormous.

True to his word, Mr. Williams only nursed a cup of coffee. Kathleen ordered hot chocolate, toast, and an egg for herself and Patti. He consented to French fries for his daughter, when she begged.

Seated across the table from them, Kathleen watched Patti play with her food, and noted her flushed cheeks. "So, Mr. Williams, what do you do when you aren't on vacation?" *What is he thinking? Does he suspect I know he shouldn't have taken his daughter?*

"Huh? Oh...I drive truck. Log truck." He sipped his coffee, eyes mostly downcast. "I have my own truck." He frowned and admonished his daughter, "Patti, quit fooling around and drink your chocolate."

To Al's consternation, in response to his rebuke, Patti began to cry. "What the… *Now* what's wrong?"

"Mr. Williams, I believe your daughter is ill. Maybe she needs—"

"*Miss* O'Brien—this *isn't* your classroom." He abandoned any pretense of niceties. "Patricia is just tired. She'll be fine—once we get out of this bleepin' airport. *I'll* take care of her." He shot a venomous look at Kathleen and started to get up from the booth they were sitting in. "I think *I* know what's *best* for my daughter."

"Mr. Williams!" Kathleen flared. "Was it *best* for Patti when you took her unannounced from the school grounds? Or is it just *best* for your selfish interest?" Before he could escape, Kathleen's arm shot out and a hand gripped his arm. "Man, *look* at your daughter! It's my guess she's running a fever. She needs attention. *Now.*"

Eyes locked and blazing, a flicker of doubt stole over him as Patti began to cough and shiver with a chill while they sat there glaring at each other. "Patti?" He wavered and looked down at her. "Are you really sick?"

"Daddy—my head hurts. I want to go home," she wailed.

He looked more like a frightened child himself than a man in control. Angry words died on his lips as he turned stricken eyes on the teacher. "Ma'am—if you're gonna stick tighter than pitch to a log, maybe you can tell me what to do. How in the name of God, do you take care of a sick child when you're stuck in a terminal?"

"Well, Mr. Williams—you might start by praying. We may need all the help from God we can get."

He scooped his daughter up as easily as though she were a three-year-old. She clung to him, letting tears dribble down his neck, wetting his shirt. Kathleen followed close in his wake, close enough to hear him mutter, "And when did God ever help me?" Trotting to keep up, she reached a hand and felt Patti's forehead. The child burned with fever.

The concourse was littered with baggage strewn everywhere. She followed as he stepped over, around, and kick-shoved his way through the obstacles. Curious looks turned to glares, bounced off him and slapped her. She kept her eyes on his back and tried not to notice when people scowled. He stopped before a vacant chair, eased Patti down, and turned anxious eyes on the teacher.

"I'll stay with her while you get some help," she said. "Tell an official you have a sick little girl here. Tell them she may very well be contagious..." She had another *tell them* on her tongue, but Al wasted no time striding away to find someone to come to their aid.

She took off her coat and wrapped it around Patti. Then sat in the chair and pulled the child onto her lap. The heat transferred to her fingertips, as she gently smoothed damp hair back, set off alarm bells in her brain.

"I want my mommy," Patti whimpered.

"I know, honey, maybe we can do something about that." She hugged her. "But your daddy is here, and he loves you very much. You're going to be okay." *Please, God. Let it be so.*

"Teacher?" Another cough wracked her little body. "Teacher, will you stay with me, too?"

Tears threatened, filling her throat. Before she could answer, a determined Mr. Williams returned with an airport official in tow.

Kathleen watched the scowl on the woman's face quickly change to a look of concern and then compassion, as Patti peered up at her with fever-bright eyes and tried to suppress another wracking cough.

"Bring her to my office," she said.

• • •

Patti lay on the couch, hiccupping, coughing, and crying. Sandy Jones, her name tag read, reached in a cupboard, took out a warm blanket and covered her.

"Can you get us a doctor?" Al barked, big hands clenched at his side.

She shot him a look and turned her attention to Kathleen. "Maybe I can—I just saw Dr. Macy. She's a friend of mine. If I can catch her," she finished in a rush, "I'll send her in."

Al paced the floor of the small office like an animal on a short chain, jerked to a halt by the misery on the face of his daughter. His eyes, muddy pools of pain in a face gone white, looked to the schoolteacher for some ray of hope.

She could argue, he brought it on himself, and no doubt he would pay for it. He paid now, for he loved his child, and had to shoulder large responsibility for her illness. Blame, however, or finger-pointing, wasn't going to help now.

She sat on the edge of the couch, holding Patti's hand and

brushing the hair from her face. *Please, God, let her be well,* she silently pleaded and tried in vain to muster a smile, when she wanted only to cry. There was no room left in her heart for anger—only sympathy.

The door opened and a tall, no-nonsense woman strode in. "I'm Dr. Macy," she announced while shaking hands. "What seems to be the problem?"

Kathleen rose quickly and looked at Al, waiting for him to say something. Before he could get words out, the doctor took her place beside the little girl and didn't wait for his answer.

"What's your name?"

"Patti."

"How old are you, Patti?"

"Six."

"Okay, Patti. Tell me where it hurts—here?" She felt the glands in her neck. "Here?" The doctor felt her tummy. "Your head hurts?—Uh-huh."

"Are her immunizations up to date?" She fired the question at the woman she thought was Patti's mother.

Al shrugged when Kathleen glanced his way. She wasn't sure if that meant he didn't know if Patti had her shots, or if he left it up to her discretion to explain the awkward situation.

Time enough for that later, she decided. *We could be here all day if I try to explain why the schoolteacher's here and Patti's mother isn't.* "Yes Doctor, Patti's health record is up to date. She's had all necessary immunizations for first grade."

The doctor tucked the blanket back around the girl and faced Kathleen, "I'm limited here without my medical bag, but there is no doubt she is running a fever, I suspect fairly high. My educated guess is, she has the flu, but I can't be sure unless I run some tests. I want to get her in hospital."

"You can do that?" he spluttered. "The snow—we—you can get her there?"

"Oh yes. We'll get her there," the doctor affirmed while retrieving a cell phone from the pocket of her trousers. "Not as soon as I'd like." She punched numbers. "But we have some good men with snowplows. We'll…Sandy? Joyce Macy. Can you make sure there's a cab at the front entrance, and get Joe on the snowplow, I need to get this little girl in hospital—And Sandy, can you get me some chipped ice? The more the better."

Dr. Macy motioned them to chairs while she draped a hip over a corner of the desk. Plain-looking, her well-cut salt and pepper hair fit like a cap around a face devoid of makeup. Warm brown eyes intent behind rimless glasses looked directly at Kathleen. "You've been stuck here three…"

The door flew open and Sandy Jones entered with a large paper cup filled with chipped ice. "The cab and Joe with the snowplow are waiting, Doctor."

"Thanks, Sandy…now then …your names?...

"I'm Kathleen and this is Al—"

"Kathleen, I want you to feed these ice chips to Patti—as quickly as she will take them—she's dehydrated. Al, wrap that blanket around your daughter as closely as you can.

Dr. Macy's long legs led the way through the airport. *No doubt, I look ridiculous,* Kathleen thought as she trotted and hopped along beside Al, trying desperately to keep up and poke ice chips in a ready little mouth. She felt like Momma Robin minus the wings.

Chapter 7

A ride in a taxi, behind a snowplow, will never make it in brochures designed to entice visitors to the Windy City nor was it in Kathleen's top-ten favorite things to do. But it got them to the hospital, and for that she was grateful.

Dr. Macy phoned ahead and staff were waiting and ready when they arrived. Little doubt remained of her status and authority in Children's Hospital; it was, "Yes, Dr. Macy—right away, Dr. Macy—it's being done, Dr. Macy."

Relieved it was out of her hands, Kathleen wilted into a seat in the designated waiting room while Patti's father went to fill out admittance papers. Waiting in an airport, traded for waiting in a hospital, and one concern for a deeper worry. *How sick is Patti? Will she be all right?* The questions went round and round in the teacher's brain, like forgotten luggage on a carousel.

Back from filling out papers, Al sank in a chair beside her, buried his head in his hands, and moaned as if in physical pain. He glanced up when she lightly touched his arm. "Shouldn't you call Patti's mother?"

His head snapped up and he stared at her as if she'd suggested he strip and go naked. She waited, and watched as comprehension dawned, and he deflated before her eyes. "I don't have a choice do I?"

"I could make the call, but I think the news should come from you." She hesitated. "You can use my cell phone if you like." Tired as she was, she dredged up a weak smile.

"No. That's okay—I'll go call—get it over with—don't worry—I'm not going to run, if that's what you think. My *daughter's* in there." His voice broke.

Something more than worry showed in his face when he returned from calling, was it resignation, or anger? She watched, with barely concealed curiosity, as he took a billfold from his pocket and removed a fistful of bills. His hand shook as he turned to face her.

"How did your ex-wife take it?"

"About like you'd expect, I suppose," he sighed. "She's scared, worried, and madder than a trapped bear robbed of her cub. She'll have the hounds on me soon as she can figure out which number to call first. She was still screamin' obscenities at me when I hung up." He tried to grin and failed. "She's coming here soon as she can get a flight out of Portland. She wanted to know where you are—guess you musta talked to her before."

Kathleen nodded.

"Well, Ma'am, I know you think I'm seven kinds of devil, and there ain't no need of me trying to convince you otherwise." He hesitated. "I want you to take this money. Help Amber get Patti home if she needs it. She's such an airhead—and I have no idea how much money she has—"

"I will on one condition," she interrupted, trying to make it easier for him. "Al, stop calling me Ma'am; call me Kathleen, or Miss O'Brien if you must. I know I'm older than you, but you're making me feel antiquated."

He pressed the bills in her hand. "I know I don't have the right to ask." He swallowed. "But will you stay here—if they come—you know?"

Kathleen thought he wanted to say more, but a white-coated Dr. Macy appeared, and walked over to talk to them. Apprehensive, they both stood to face her.

"Your daughter has double pneumonia, and a mild case of influenza. For now, she'll be in ICU."

"Can we see her?" they said almost in unison.

"You can see Patti in a few minutes. June at the front desk will show you where to go." The doctor looked at Kathleen. "She's frightened, of course, and asking for her mommy... and her daddy, too." Dr. Macy smiled. "Our nurses are well-trained and excellent with children; she's had medication and will sleep soon." She clapped Al on the shoulder. "We'll get your daughter fixed up." The pediatrician turned on her heel and left.

Kathleen rushed to catch her in the hallway. "Dr. Macy—*please*—I need to talk privately with you for a minute. It's important." She motioned Al to go ahead and see Patti without her.

Dr. Macy frowned, waiting. Kathleen lowered her voice

and spoke quickly, "I'm not Patti's mother. I'm her schoolteacher, Kathleen O'Brien." In an economy of words she explained the situation to the doctor.

"I see—and you say Patti's mother is on her way here from Oregon?"

"Yes. Mr. Williams called her."

"Well, Kathleen O'Brien, I'd say Patti Williams is lucky to have you for a teacher, and a friend. I'll have to report this, you know."

"Yes, I thought so—thanks for your time, doctor—I'd like to go see Patti now, if I may."

"Good girl…I'll talk to you later," the doctor called over her shoulder as she turned and hurried away.

Kathleen sought directions and was courteously directed to the right unit.

She slipped in beside Al and stared down at the little girl lying so still. She looked small and fragile in the hospital bed, hooked to an IV, soon to be enclosed in an oxygen tent, and eyelids fluttering. The nurses bathed her flushed face, and brushed her hair until it waved softly, shining like a halo on the pillow. Teddy bears danced across Patti's hospital gown. *We forgot her teddy bear, it's back in that office at the airport,* Kathleen remembered too late.

"I have to go now, Patti cake," Al whispered, frowning at the oxygen tent. "You're almost asleep." He bent over the bed and two little arms reached up to encircle his neck.

"I love you, Daddy."

"I love you too, Princess," he choked, hugging her gently. "Sleep tight, don't let the bedbugs bite."

• • •

Monday morning, not yet noon, was that possible? It felt like weeks since she'd slept in a real bed, and even longer since she'd had a shower or a soak in a tub of hot water. Coffee, the beverage you reached for because you didn't know what else to do when consigned to the purgatory of waiting rooms, tasted bitter.

Kathleen set the plastic cup on the end table beside her, and thumbed through a magazine, not really seeing the pages. She glanced, surreptitiously, at Al as he paced, looked out the window and worked on the strong coffee in his cup.

Suggestions they go to the cafeteria for something to eat, met with defeat. "Sorry, but I don't think I could force food down with a long-handled fork; you go ahead if you want." He dropped onto the chair beside her. "This waiting is hell, isn't it?" Al, elbows propped on his knees, held his head in his hands, and stared at the carpet.

Kathleen watched as two men hesitated in the doorway and scanned the room. Eyes pinned on their suspect, they marched over and stopped in front of him.

"Mr. Williams?"

"Yes?" Al's head came up as though jerked by a puppeteer.

"FBI." Badges flashed. "You're under arrest for custodial interference."

• • •

Curious looks, directed at her, eclipsed the worry-masks worn by people in the waiting area. She couldn't blame them for wondering what it was all about when they led Al away in handcuffs. Being stared at, the object of their speculation was another matter. She grabbed up her things and fled to the restroom, before questions in their eyes reached a bold tongue, and someone gave voice, asking for explanations she wasn't ready to give.

Closeted in the lavatory, Kathleen let the tears spill over. Prepared to dislike Mr. Williams, the hours spent with him and Patti, altered her feelings. Taking his daughter in the manner he did, was wrong, but she no longer saw Al as an evil person.

Dear God, I know You are in control, but why did Patti have to get sick? Why couldn't the authorities have stopped Al in Portland? Why? Why? And why am I in the middle of all this?

Kathleen pulled out her cellular phone. She needed to talk to Edward. *He probably thinks I'm in Ohio with my brother and family. I'll bet he's tried to call me and wonders why my phone's turned off.* She let his private number at the bank ring several times. When he didn't pick it up, she tried his cell phone. It was shut off. *Where could he be?*

Frustrated, she dialed his home number, not really expecting him to be there. She left a message on the answering machine. "Edward, it's me. I'm in Chicago. I've too much to tell you, for the machine. Call me."

She stood before the mirror, applying lipstick, when her cell phone rang. "*It's Edward, calling me back,*" she thought, and yanked the phone from her coat pocket.

"Hello, Ed...?"

"Kathleen?—Finally! I've been trying everyday to call you. Are you still at O'Hare?"

"Danny?" She gulped around the lump in her throat. "Danny! You aren't going to believe what's happened."

In less than twenty minutes, Danny came striding through the door to Children's Hospital. Before she could think about what she was doing, she rushed to meet him, tears coursing down her cheeks. He gave her a fierce hug. None too quick to let go, he gently released her. "Hey, Carrot Top. You're getting me all wet." His eyes warm and mischievous, he pulled a clean, white handkerchief from his pocket and handed it to her. "Here, mop your face, and don't forget to blow your nose."

It was so like him to say something ridiculous; she snickered, and did exactly what he'd suggested. Making sure he knew she wiped her nose, she wadded the hankie up and handed it back to him.

"Keep it." He made a face at her.

Kathleen laughed, a genuine, tension-releasing giggle.

He took her hand as they moved from the lobby. "Kathleen, if I'd known no planes were going to be flying for three days, I'd never have left you alone in that airport."

"But you couldn't know. And didn't *you* tell me, God's in control?" She turned needy eyes to him. "Could you tell me again? Please."

He took her carry-on and slung it over his shoulder. "You *know* He *is*." He smiled, and gave her a one-armed gentle hug. "In fact, I'd say God's very much in control."

"But what am I going to tell Patti, when she asks me why her daddy isn't coming in to see her?"

"Tell her the truth, Kathleen. God will give you the right words. Chances are she's a lot more perceptive, than even you, realize."

They reached the ICU waiting room, and she knew it couldn't be put off any longer. With a promise he'd pray, Kathleen left Danny and went in to see her little charge.

Relief flooded her being when she looked down and discovered Patti asleep. *Maybe I can slip out and come back later.*

The child stirred and opened her eyes.

"Hi, Miss O'Brien.

"Hello, Sleepyhead. How do you feel?"

Dee said I could have ice cream when I waked up." Patti looked at her nurse. "She said my mommy or my daddy could feed it to me. Teacher, is my mommy coming?

Kathleen glanced at the nurse. *Does she think I'm Patti's mother?*

"Yes, dear. Your mommy is coming soon as she can get a plane from Portland. She should be here sometime tonight." She smiled. "Will I do in the meantime? I'd love to feed you some ice cream."

Big eyes looked up at Miss O'Brien. "Okay...Teacher? Where's my daddy?"

"Patti—Honey. Your daddy had to go away for awhile." Kathleen took a deep breath. "Remember when you thought your mommy didn't know where you were?...Well, you were right. She didn't know." She hesitated, watching the little girl's eyes.

"Sweetie, your daddy loves you very much, but he forgot to ask permission before he took you from the school grounds. And just like at school, when you forget to ask for a special privilege, there are consequences. Patti, do you understand what I'm saying?"

"I think so." She nodded. "Sometimes we can't play at recess if we forget. Like when Jimmy didn't ask if he could take the ball out. He lost it. And you made him stay in. A *long* time."

Patti's chin quivered. "Teacher? Will my daddy have to stay in a long time?"

"Oh, honey. I don't know." Kathleen struggled to smile and hold back the tears. "I'll tell you what. When he does see you, he'll want you to be all well. So...how about that ice cream?"

She shook her head. "Teacher, I don't want it now." Tears spilled over.

Before Kathleen could think what to do, the nurse laid a gentle hand on her shoulder. "It's okay," she whispered. "I'll talk to her. She just needs a little time to digest the news." The nurse, called Dee, gave her a kind smile. "Miss O'Brien, get some rest yourself. By the time Patti sleeps more, and her mother gets here, she'll be fine."

Chapter 8

Her thoughts with Patti and wondering if she'd be well by Christmas, Kathleen breathed deeply of the fresh air, and gasped at the intensity of cold, when her lungs burned. Deep snow blanketed the city, a harmony in white, to soften and redefine harsh realities of a great metropolis. The weather forecast uncertain, a blue-cold sky hovered above the snow, looking like a freshly painted picture on an artist's easel, a scene from a Christmas card.

"Right nippy, don't cha think?" Danny took her hand, and pulled her along, to the waiting taxi. "Cold enough to freeze the ears on a statue. Send a brass monkey indoors for his overcoat. Make the ducks wear ice skates."

"Danny, you're goofy," she giggled.

"Huh...What? What'd I say?" He grinned impishly.

"It's a winter-spectacular out here, but you're right. It's *cold.* Is it always this frigid here?"

"Well, this is Chicago—The Windy City and all that. We

don't often get so much snow at one time, but it can get a lot colder. This'll make you appreciate good ol' wet Oregon."

Surprise registered on her face when the cab stopped in the street, and let them out in front of a large apartment building. She watched as Danny, looking smug, negotiated a tall mound of less-than-pristine snow, then pulled her up and over.

They entered a luxurious, columned foyer, with plush carpeting on the floor, and took the elevator to the sixth floor. Down the hallway, third door on the right, his key fit in the lock. He opened the door and gently ushered her inside.

"This is your apartment? It looks cozy, and it's *warm.*"

"Yeah, this is my bachelor pad. I thought after three days in an airport, you might like to take a shower."

"Danny Davis, I think I love you."

"Ah, you're just sayin' that cause you want my hot water."

"True." She gave him an alluring grin.

"Through there." He pointed to an open doorway. "Just dump your stuff on the bed. The bathroom is to the left, down that little hallway. The towels are fairly clean, the cockroaches are friendly, the soap's cheap, and there's a ratty old bathrobe on the back of the door, if you need one."

Kathleen laughed and not a musical little tinkle, either, an all-out hoot, the kind that released tension. Danny looked quite pleased with himself as he chuckled and set to work in the little kitchen. One redhead, giggling as she went, lost no time in scurrying down the hall to find the shower.

• • •

Danny removed a warm loaf of bread from the bread-machine and gave another quick stir to the chowder. He rummaged in a drawer for napkins and placemats, things he didn't ordinarily bother with when dining alone. A red pillar-candle placed in the center of the table, by the lady who came to clean periodically, his only concession to Christmas.

Two cellular phones, his and Kathleen's, rested on the counter, plugged in to outlets, batteries recharging.

The clean smell of freshly washed hair, still damp from the shower, reached his nose. He thought he detected a more subtle fragrance of perfume, a strictly feminine scent. Before it had more time to rattle his brain, he turned and grinned at her.

Still clad in charcoal-gray slacks (the bulk of her clothing no doubt circling a carousel in Youngstown), she had managed a change of underclothes from her carry-on, a fresh tee shirt and a downy green pullover. Jade earrings twinkled in her ears. Her feet were snuggled into wooly white socks.

"Hey, Carrot Top. You clean up pretty good. I can see the freckles on your pert little nose."

"Why, thank you. I do feel like a new woman." She beamed at him and made a mock curtsy. "All due to you, and your shower, I just may make it through another day."

"Well, I hope you're hungry. I've been slaving away here over a hot stove." He gave her his mischievous 'Danny-look.' "Just for little ol' you."

"Something smells wonderful. What is it? Can I help?"

"Sure ya can. Grab those two bowls and dish up the chowder while I slice some of this bread."

Seated at the small round, glass-topped table, he took her hand, bowed his head, and offered a short blessing, not forgetting to ask God to watch over Kathleen and restore Patti to good health.

"This isn't clam chowder out of a can, Danny. This is *good.* Hot, too." She took another cautious spoonful. "Did you make this?"

He beamed and handed her a thick slice of fresh bread slathered with real butter. "It's my own recipe. Have I managed to impress you?"

"I've never eaten clam chowder so *good.* Where did you learn to cook like this?"

"Ah." He managed to look pleased and slightly embarrassed at the same time. "I shouldn't divulge my culinary secrets here, but eating in restaurants every day, can be a great motivator—not to mention expensive. With a little help and advice from some good food-jockeys along the way, I made a few mushy mistakes, some downright disasters, and finally learned how to feed myself.

"I haven't mastered pastry yet. Probably won't. But we do have pumpkin pie, thanks to Mrs. Sanchez." Danny rose, winked at her, and poured fresh steaming coffee into their cups, coffee that smelled heavenly and had to be Irish Crème. "Mrs. Sanchez cleans for me, and she likes to bring something that, 'she just happens to have left over.' She's an incredibly nice lady, but she thinks I'm skinny."

"Well, skinny isn't going to apply to me if I keep eating

like this." She twinkled up at him, making her hazel-green eyes round and innocent looking. "May I have another helping of your chowder? This is really good."

It was his turn to laugh. Clearly pleased, he dished her up another bowl of clam chowder.

"Danny, this has been so nice, but I need to get back to the hospital. I don't know what time Mrs. Williams will get here." She sighed. "I don't want Patti to think she's been abandoned. She felt pretty awful about her daddy, when I left her."

"No time for pie?"

Kathleen blushed. "I ate too much of your clam chowder."

• • •

Danny didn't try to detain her. He simply called a taxi and climbed in beside her. "You don't have to come with me," she protested. "You must have better things to do than play nursemaid and sit around in a hospital waiting room."

The sun hurled yellow beams through a narrow break in a cloud-darkened sky. It shone like a gem displayed against blue velvet. The brightness fell across her face, and when she squinted, he reached out and pulled her against him.

"Kathleen, I'm flying out early tomorrow morning, and I'd like nothing better than spending some time with you before I leave. We have more catching up to do. You haven't yet told me about all the broken hearts you've left along the way." His tone was light and teasing, an echo from high school days (But they both knew they were no longer those kids).

The cab pulled up close to the front entrance of the hospital. She quickly slipped the driver a bill—before Danny could do so—as they climbed from the taxi. Cold forced them to hurry indoors.

"I'm beginning to understand why Chicago is called The Windy City," she said. Her cheeks were red with cold and her hair wind-tossed around her shoulders.

It seemed natural to hold hands as they walked gleaming corridors, buffed to a high-gloss, which mirrored their reflection. They passed a gift shop displaying more cuddly stuffed animals than most department stores. Decorated trees reminded them Santa Claus was coming soon. A room with child-sized furniture and toys invited children to enter and play.

Three kids, two boys and a tiny girl, not sick enough to be in bed and not well enough to go home, sat at a red table quietly stacking blocks. Anxious parents hovered, watched, and waited.

Back in the ICU lounge, Kathleen glanced surreptitiously around the room. A few people looked up when they entered, but no one paid them much attention. They were immersed in their own problems. With a gentle sigh of relief, she headed for a corner chair and as much privacy as one ever has in a waiting room.

"I'll go see her and be back soon. Visitors aren't allowed to stay long when a patient is in ICU."

• • •

Danny looked up from his magazine. "That was fast."

"Patti's asleep. The nurse says she is doing much better. Her breathing is less labored. She thinks they'll be moving her out of ICU soon."

"Well, that's good news."

"Sure is. You know what?" She giggled. "Now, I wish I had a piece of that pumpkin pie."

He chuckled. "I like that about you Carrot Top. You're not one of these finicky women that are eternally on a diet. Wanta go back to my place and polish off the pie?"

"It's tempting, but I should keep an eye out for Mrs. Williams." Kathleen sighed. "I haven't a clue when she will get here, and I need to check on Patti again before long. I don't want her to think I've left her. You know, I'll bet we can find a cafeteria if we try, and maybe even get some exercise climbing a few stairs." She challenged him. "What do you think? Sitting around makes me tired. At home, I run almost every day. I've missed it."

"You're on. Let's go."

They climbed stairs fast, all the way to the top floor, but it wasn't a race. He walked beside her, only dropping back to let people pass. Exercise accomplished, the two friends explored the hospital until they found the cafeteria.

Kathleen's phone on standby remained strangely quiet. When it did ring, as she was about to take another mouthful of pumpkin pie, she jumped. Danny, who had already finished his dessert, walked away to give her some privacy.

"Hi Sis. How's Patti doing by now? And how are you holding up?"

"Much better to both. I think Patti will be out of ICU soon. How're things there?"

"Yucky. Throw-up everywhere. Believe me, you *don't* want to come here."

"I thought as much. Hey, Big Brother, guess who's here at the hospital with me? *Danny*. Daniel Lee Davis. Remember him? He's a photographer, can you believe it?"

"Yeah Sis, I can and a pretty good one, too. He's had some pictures in *National Geographic*."

"What? He has? How come I didn't know that?"

"Maybe you spend too much time with the Dick and Jane crowd," Michael teased. "Anyway, tell old Danny boy, Mike says hello."

She swallowed. "Michael...has anyone tried to call me there?"

"Oh, yeah, I nearly forgot. Kerry said Edward somebody-or-other called and asked for you. She told him you weren't here. He hung up before I could talk to him."

Phone call ended, Kathleen walked up beside Danny. "Brother Michael says tell you, hello."

"Ah, good old Mike. Do you know, I had the worst case of hero worship on him when we were kids? I don't know how he put up with me. I was like a second shadow, dogging him everywhere. Are you spending Christmas with Mike and his family?"

"No. I won't be going. Michael says they have the plague at their house. Everyone but him is sick with the flu." She shrugged. "If Mrs. Williams doesn't need, or want my help with Patti, I'll fly back to Oregon when she gets here. Danny, you said you're leaving early in the morning, but you haven't told me where you'll be Christmas day."

Eyes unusually solemn, he reached across the table for her hand. "Kathleen…I'll be in Iraq." He stroked her hand with his thumb, eyes locked on hers. "Will you pray for me?"

"But isn't that terribly dangerous? Do you have to go there?"

His grin returned, but his eyes no longer teased. "They seldom shoot photographers, unless, of course, they take a really bad picture." He squeezed her hand a little tighter. "I don't plan to get myself killed."

Chapter 9

At a loss to know what to say, feeling as if her emotions had hit overload, she choked back tears, determined to be cheerful for Danny's sake. If her smile faltered, it nevertheless shown warm in her eyes.

"Kathleen, since you don't know how long you'll be in Chicago, I'd like to give you a key to my apartment. You can go there and crash when you get tired." A hand held up stopped her protests. "If you're in my bed, you'll remember to pray for me." He smiled and winked, making her laugh.

"Oh, Danny, I don't know."

"I promise I'll change the sheets before I leave. Hot water. Showers any time you want. You can even finish the pie. And, hey Carrot Top, don't forget, I'll be long gone. No one to harass you. No one to tease you. Nothing but peace and quiet."

"Danny, you're incorrigible. One minute you have me laughing, and the next minute I want to cry."

"So, just take the key." He placed the metal in her palm

and closed her fingers gently over it. "It's a spare. When you're finished with it, leave it on the table. Or if you forget, mail it to me."

"I don't know what to say. This is so generous of you. Thanks."

He released her hand. "And now, I really should go. Walk out with me?"

• • •

She touched his shoulder and reached up to kiss him on the cheek before the cab stopped. Danny grabbed her in a fierce hug, and without either quite knowing how it happened, his lips found hers. The kiss left them breathless. She clung a little too long, and felt him tremble.

"I'll call you when I get back," he whispered in her ear, before the taxi could whisk him away.

Kathleen could argue the reaction was a result of being under stress, the excitement of seeing an old friend. Two souls caught up in the magic that seemed to float in the air during the holiday season. But how was she to convince the person who looked back at her in the mirror? Could she deny the chemistry between herself and Danny? Did she want to?

What about Edward Connors? Exactly what did she feel for him? *Oh, it's too hard to sort out, and I'm much too tired. I'll deal with it all later,* she promised herself.

Ready for this supercharged day to end, emotions in turmoil, she watched the hands on her wristwatch inch toward midnight. Most parents, tired from a long stressful day, were already asleep on cots set up earlier by the staff. If Mrs. Williams didn't arrive soon, one tired schoolteacher would be asleep as well. Questions, Patti's mother might have, could wait for answers until morning.

As if on cue, Amber appeared in the doorway of the ICU lounge. Breathing rapidly through her mouth, eyes darting around the room, she looked on the verge of panic. Kathleen knew in the dimmed lights, she didn't see her. Crossing the room as quickly and silently as she could, she laid a gentle hand on her arm and whispered. "I'm glad you made it. Let's go in the restroom, where we can talk and not wake the sleepers."

"Oh, thank God, Miss O'Brien. Am I glad *you're* here. Patti? How is she? Do you think they'll let me see her? This late?"

She looked even worse in the harsh light of the restroom. From her appearance, one might believe she'd flown the entire distance from Portland, Oregon, to Chicago on a broom behind a witch. Dark rings circled red-rimmed eyes, her nose shone red as Rudolph's, and her hair wasn't just windblown, it was a tangled mess.

"Please, call me Kathleen. I'm sure they'll let you see Patti now, if they understand how far you've come, and that you just got here."

"First, I have to know. Did they get that son of a—*bean eater?* Or did he run? I could *kill* Al for what he did to Patti and me."

Surprised at the vehemence, she gave her a sharp look. "He's been arrested. The FBI took him away in handcuffs."

"Well, thank God for small favors!"

More disturbing than appearance, was the strong smell of tobacco on Amber's clothes, and liquor on her breath. *Is she reacting to stress, or is there a more serious problem involved here?* Managing a weak smile, she steered her to the ICU nurses' station. Dr. Macy's instructions admitted the mother immediately. For Patti's sake, Kathleen fervently hoped the liquor and cigarettes were temporary.

• • •

In the hospital, people awoke early; barely six in the morning and already cots were folded and stored away. Showers were available to visitors with children in ICU. Kathleen went with Patti's mother to bathe and prepare to face the day.

"I've never been in a hospital this big," Amber exclaimed. "The last time I was in hospital was when I had Patti. I was barely seventeen when she was born. I was scared to death. I didn't like hospitals then, and I don't like them now."

She took a deep breath and chattered on. "If there's any way to get Patti home when she's released, other than *flying*, I'm taking it. I'm terrified of planes. Is there anyplace here I can go for a cigarette? I don't suppose they want us to smoke in the bathrooms?" She frowned, and withdrew a pack from her pocket. "I know. I shouldn't smoke. I'd almost quit, but this has made me so nervous."

By mid-morning Patti was out of ICU and in a two-bed ward. Dr. Macy bustled in, glanced at Kathleen, checked Patti, tousled her curls, and eyed Mrs. Williams. "I'm Dr. Macy…you're Patti's mother?"

Quickly, Amber ran a cold, sweaty palm down her pant-leg, then shook the doctor's hand. "Yes, I got here rather late last night. I can see my daughter's better. Can I take her home soon?"

"Hmmm. Patti's better. Yes. But she's not ready to go home yet. We'll give it a couple of days and see how she's doing then." Dr. Macy winked at Kathleen and spoke directly to Mrs. Williams. "Mothers are free to spend the night in their child's room. We'll set up a cot for you, but don't try to spend the entire day with her. You'll just wear yourself out—and Patti needs to sleep."

The busy doctor turned on her heel and strode from the room, saying as she exited, "We'll talk again later. I make rounds between seven and eight in the morning."

"Patti, it's good to see you feeling better." Kathleen beamed at her. "Looks like you might be going home soon. At any rate, I'll see you back in school after the holidays if I don't see you before."

"Noooo—I don't *want* you to go." Tears brimmed in her eyes. "*Please*, Mommy. Make her stay. My teacher keeped me from being scared. My daddy—" She coughed and a tear rolled down her cheek. "I want *both* you to stay with me."

"Oh, Patti, honey, I don't know. We've imposed enough on Miss O'Brien. I'm sure she has her own family to be with over the holidays."

"Well, actually, my plans have been cancelled. I *could* stay if you'd really like me to."

"Oh my goodness! You'd really do that?" Amber reddened. "I think God just answered my prayers though I don't remember praying." She tittered. "I *hate* the thought of being here on my own. With Patti in hospital, I could really use your help if you're sure it isn't asking too much."

"I don't mind at all," Kathleen responded. "It will give us an opportunity to get acquainted. I like to get to know the parents of my students." She sighed. "I may have to insist on getting some breakfast though. My stomach is starting to protest rather noisily." She grinned at Patti, who definitely had heard the rumblings, and was rewarded with a giggle and two arms reaching up to give her a hug.

Reassured her mommy *and* her teacher were there to care for her, Patti collected more hugs, closed her eyes and promptly fell asleep. Amber followed Kathleen to the hospital cafeteria.

They loaded trays with coffee and orange juice, filled plates with scrambled eggs and bacon, buttered toast and jelly.

After easing into a chair, she waited while Amber sat opposite her. She watched in surprise as she lifted her fork and crammed a large bite of egg into her mouth, all the while continuing to talk. Kathleen gave an imperceptible shrug, reached for her napkin, and silently thanked God for blessings.

Around a mouthful of food, Amber said, "It's so *cold* here. I'm tempted to buy myself a fur coat. You know? I wonder how much they cost. Do you have one? But you don't really need one in Oregon do you? Still..."

. "It *is* cold here, isn't it? Speaking of which, have you thought about warmer clothes for Patti? The jacket she was wearing seems a little light."

"Patti? Oh. Wouldn't she look cute in a little fur coat? Maybe I could find *her* one." She forked in more food. "I can just *see* her in a little white fur coat. It could be her special Christmas present." She giggled. "And wouldn't Al just have a hemorrhage if he knew *his* child support bought us fur coats?"

Not sure how to respond to such diatribe, she remained silent, sipped her coffee, and contemplated the day ahead.

"Miss O'Bri...I mean Kathleen. Do you have a boyfriend?" She giggled around a bite of toast, not waiting for an answer. "I do. I met this guy. Patti hasn't met him yet. Spike. He plays guitar in this band."

She reached for her orange juice and finished it. "They have a gig in Portland the twenty-seventh of December. I'll go hear him if we get back to Oregon in time. Oh—I hope my kid'll be okay, and I get home in time. Of course I won't leave her if she's still sick."

Barely halfway through her meal, Kathleen lay down her fork, rubbed her temples, and observed Amber. Head bent, she cleaned her plate and fished a pack of Camels from her pocket. She stuck a cigarette in her mouth, seemed to remember where she was, and hastily withdrew it.

"Ummm...I guess I need to go outside. I don't mean to be rude or nothin'. Excuse me? Please? Could we just meet back in Patti's room?"

"Sure." Relieved to be alone, she wondered if she could stand an entire day listening to such prattle.

• • •

Except for varied time spent with Patti, they shopped until they dropped; mostly in the big Sears department store. Amber, shocked by prices, ogled the fur coats, but didn't attempt to buy one. Glad she couldn't read her mind, and know about the large amount of money Mr. Williams had entrusted to her, with instructions to help his ex-wife if she needed it, Kathleen tactfully steered the young mother to areas of more sensible clothing where she bought a red wool car coat for herself and a fleecy pink snowsuit for Patti.

Since the bulk of her clothes had gone to Youngstown, Kathleen purchased more underwear, a white cotton blouse, and a pink cardigan, a Christmas present to herself.

• • •

She heaved a sigh of relief and quietly let herself into Danny's apartment. Her head ached. She felt like an escapee from an all-night slumber party of giggling adolescent girls. Amber chattered enough for ten teenagers.

She stepped into the shower and let hot water soothe away the day's frustrations. Thankful she'd included her old flannel nightgown in her carry-on, she dropped it over her head and climbed between the sheets.

Motivated by guilt, thoughts more on Danny than her almost-fiancée, Kathleen tried again, unsuccessfully, to call Edward. *Why doesn't he answer? Where could he be?* Tired and confused, she let anger override worry and replace guilt.

As a concession, she left her cell phone on standby and placed it on the table beside the bed. A tear slid down her cheek as she turned out the lamp. She punched the pillow once, before resting her head, and eventually fell asleep whispering a prayer for Danny's protection.

• • •

Startled by the sharp ring of her cell phone, it took a moment to awaken, to remember where she was, and to identify what woke her. She fumbled for the lamp, found the switch and turned on a light. A quick glance at the bedside clock, told her it was after midnight.

She managed a sleepy, "Hello?"

"Kathleen?...It's me...I hope I didn't wake you. I forget about the time difference."

"Edward!—Where have you *been*?" Now wide awake, she carefully enunciated each word, in her schoolteacher voice. "I've tried again and again to call you."

"What do you mean? Where have *I* been*? You,* obviously, aren't where you said you'd be. I tried to call you at your brother's. Michael, is it?"

"*Edward*—I was stuck in O'Hare airport for *three days* because of a snowstorm. Or don't you listen to the news?"

"Oh, I listen to the news all right. I *tried* to call you. Your cell phone was turned off. I finally just gave up."

"I don't think I like your tone of voice."

"You don't like *my* tone of voice*?* Are you by any chance listening to yourself?—And if I may be so bold as to ask, *where* are you? You can't be still snowed in at the airport."

She could hardly miss the sarcasm, dripping from his voice. "You mean where am I right now? This very minute?" Frost coated her speech.

"Yeah—Right now?—Where are you?"

"I'm in Danny Davis' bed."

Loud silence reigned on the other end. A nervous giggle escaped her. *Why did I say that?* Before she could get the words out to explain, Edward hung up on her.

Chapter 10

Warm and snug beneath the blankets on Danny's bed, auburn hair fanned across the white pillowcase, she might as well have been sleeping on a hard floor. She tossed and turned like a hyperactive child short on medication. When she finally did doze off, disturbing dreams not even Steven King could think up, moved through her mind. Patti, lost in a snowstorm. When she tried to search for her, her feet felt as if they were encased in cement. She couldn't move. And all the while, Amber, seemingly unaware of her daughter's plight, kept chattering and giggling.

The lesser nightmare turned out to be reality. Edward had hung up on her.

Kathleen opened one eye and squinted at the digital clock on the bedside table. Not quite six thirty on Christmas Eve morning. She groaned, slipped out of bed and tiptoed to the window to look outside. Streetlights glowed in the darkness; across the way Christmas tree lights glimmered on and off, bright red, green, pink, blue, and white bulbs proclaiming a happy holiday message.

Tomorrow, all over the world bright-eyed children would awaken early and urge their parents out of bed to see what Santa Claus left them. "Bah humbug!" She muttered to herself, as a tear slid down her cheek. *I know, I know. I should be ashamed of myself. Danny's in Iraq facing danger. Others are giving their lives on this day of peace on earth, and here I am, safe and sound and feeling sorry for myself.*

She crept back to bed and pulled the covers up to her chin. The mental talking to she gave herself didn't help much. *This ranks as the worst "Joyous-Holiday-Season" in all my twenty-six years. I'm not with family.* With little effort, she could work herself into what her mother called a real Irish snit. *Stuck in Chicago with a chatterbox who can give me a headache in ten minutes. Edward and I had a fight. We've never had a real fight before. Why did he have to hang up on me? I would've explained—in a minute.*

Kathleen squirmed in the bed, her conscience pricking her. *Well, I did kinda provoke him. Maybe I should try calling him back. Explain why I'm here in Chicago. He doesn't know about Patti.*

She sat up in bed, folded her arms across her chest and glared at the cell phone, as if it alone were responsible for the ache around her heart. *Or maybe I should just turn the stupid phone off, crawl in my mental cave and wait for the holidays to be over. If only I could sleep until Patti is ready to get on a plane and fly back to Oregon.* She sighed. *Now that's pretty juvenile thinking.*

She turned on the bedside lamp and reached for the Bible. His Bible. Left so conveniently on the table, within reach of her pillow. *Did he think she would eventually pick it up? Had he left it there for her? Oh, what's wrong with me?* Tears threatened. *Why am I reading something in to this? It's simply a habit. Danny's never too far from a Bible.*

She held the book in her hands and let the pages fall open where they would. A note or card lay wedged between the pages where the Bible fell open. Closer inspection revealed a name on the front. Kathleen. Spelled out carefully, in red block letters. With eyes misted over, she opened it and peered at the message.

> Merry Christmas, Carrot Top. Sorry I can't be there with you. Remember, *all* God's promises are yours. Danny.

She swiped a sleeve across her eyes, gave up when more tears threatened and padded barefoot to the bathroom for toilet paper to blow her nose. She gave a final honk, threw the tissue in the commode and flushed it. Back in bed, she hugged Danny's pillow to her and read the words again and once more after that. *Merry Christmas, Carrot Top. Sorry I can't be there with you. Remember, all God's promises are yours. Danny.*

She held the card against her cheek before she laid it aside. Was there something more he wanted her to read? She scanned the pages where she found the card. Her eyes fell on a verse in the eighth chapter of Romans that he'd highlighted with a yellow marker pen. "And we know that in all things

God works for the good of those who love him, who have been called according to his purpose" (Romans 8:28, NIV).

A gentle reminder that God's in control. How she wished Danny was here to say the words to her. She brushed away another tear, turned out the light, snuggled into his pillow and promptly fell asleep.

• • •

Startled, not sure what had awakened her, Kathleen bolted upright in bed and glanced at the clock. Eight in the morning and someone insisted on ringing the doorbell. *Should I answer it, or ignore it? It has to be for Danny. Someone who doesn't know he's gone. No one knows I'm here. What if it's a girlfriend? She wouldn't expect me to be here. I'd better ignore it.*

The doorbell chimed for the third time. Whoever it was didn't seem willing to give up and go away. She scrambled out of bed, and reached for Danny's old bathrobe on the hook behind the bathroom door. She slipped her arms in the too-long sleeves and inhaled the fragrance of his aftershave. With a lump in her throat the size of Rhode Island, she cautiously made her way to the front door.

The ringing grew insistent. She stood on tiptoe and peered out the peephole. A short woman, with snapping brown eyes the color of melted chocolate, dark hair cropped short, and enveloped in a long black coat, stood there. Two grocery bags clutched in her arms, her finger persistently pressing the doorbell.

Kathleen slipped the bolt aside, unlocked the door and pulled it open.

"Well! I think you not let me in." The woman pushed past her and headed for the kitchen with her sacks. "I have key. I maybe let myself in, but I not want scare you. Maybe I scare anyway. You sleep?"

Slowly the light began to dawn. "Mrs. Sanchez?"

"That right, honey. I make you breakfast." She looked Kathleen up and down. "My, you a pretty one. Too skinny though, just like Danny. Some babies fix that."

Kathleen felt herself turning red and thought it best not to comment on that remark. "Please, Mrs. Sanchez, you don't need to fix me breakfast. You must have family to care for on this holiday."

"Oh, phoo. They not need me." She waved an arm. "All married now. I go to my daughter tomorrow. Help cook. Danny say you care for sick little girl." She tied an apron around her ample waist and began to pull things from sacks. "He say you maybe alone. He say look out for you."

In no time, Kathleen was sipping the best hot chocolate she had ever tasted. A plate of French toast topped with blueberry compote, placed before her, couldn't be denied.

"Eat, eat," she urged. "I make you more."

"It's truly delicious and so nice of you to do this. But I must tell you, if I eat any more, I'm going to burst."

"Ah, but it's Christmas Eve. No? You have one more cuppa chocolate and these baby oranges. So sweet." She pushed a green glass bowl of tiny tangerines toward her. "Try."

Mrs. Sanchez leaned against the counter, peeled a tangerine and stuck half in her mouth. "Danny is good man. Kind. You marry? Yes?"

Kathleen nearly choked on her swallow of chocolate and felt her face growing hot again. Before she could catch her breath and think of a proper answer to that remark, her cell phone, tucked in the pocket of Danny's robe, jingled incessantly.

Please God, don't let it be Edward calling me back now. Not in front of Mrs. Sanchez. With a quaver in her voice she answered. "Hello?"

"Kathleen? It's Amber. They're releasing Patti this morning. Can you come right away?"

Mrs. Sanchez followed her to the bedroom, scolding and admonishing. "You not make bed. I take care. You go. Little girl need you. Yes?"

"Thank you, Mrs. Sanchez." She smiled at her. "Danny is right. You are a treasure."

The older lady, already stripping the bed, beamed as Kathleen gently closed the bathroom door. She showered and dressed quickly in slacks and sweater.

When she re-entered the bedroom, the bed was made and the room looked tidy. Her carry-on, coat, and purse were placed carefully on the bed. With a minimum of motion she packed her dirty underwear and scanned the room for anything she might have missed. Thankful Mrs. Sanchez had left the room, she dug in her purse for pen and paper to write a note to Danny.

Pen poised, she chewed her lip. *What should I write? Should I tell him how much I enjoyed seeing him?* It felt as if they were destined to be more than friends, but how could that be? Reality reasoned her chances of seeing him again, anytime soon, were little better than winning the lottery, especially since she never bought a ticket. Didn't he tell her he traveled a lot? That he didn't have time for a serious relationship?

She would go home to Oregon and Edward. She'd say she was sorry. Edward would apologize. He'd take her somewhere nice. They'd kiss and makeup. *Everything's going to be fine. Mother is right, I'm just skidding my wheels and passing up a golden opportunity. Edward is a brilliant man, and he wants me. Or at least he did. "A bird in the hand" and all that.*

With that thought in mind, she wrote the date, and quickly scrawled a few lines.

> Danny, I pray for your safety. Please be careful. Thank you for "the Bible lesson" and for letting me stay here. Your housekeeper is a gem. Kathleen.

She stuck it between the pages in the Bible, where she had found his note. There was nothing left, but to thank the housekeeper and go. Amber and Patti were waiting for her.

Mrs. Sanchez laid aside her dishtowel and came to tell her goodbye. Her dark-chocolate eyes danced with merriment, as if she knew a secret not yet revealed. "You go now? I give you hug? Yes?"

Kathleen dropped her things and opened her arms to the little woman. So short a time to know each other, but already she seemed like an old friend.

"I see you again? Yes? You ask me to wedding? No?"

"Wedding?" she puzzled. "Mrs. Sanchez, I don't think you understand. Danny and I are just good friends."

"Friends?" Mrs. Sanchez shook her head. "No, no. I think you marry up with Danny. Danny, he take good care you." She shook a finger at her. "I tell Danny, you nice lady. He should marry."

Mrs. Sanchez thrust a package in her hands before she opened the door. "I bake cookie for you." The housekeeper continued to wave and call, "Happy Christmas! Happy Christmas!" Until the elevator door closed, and Kathleen could no longer see her.

• • •

Alone in the backseat of the cab, she didn't know whether to laugh or cry. *Mrs. Sanchez is a wonder. She's wrong about Danny and me, of course. But it's impossible to feel sorry for yourself around such a bubbly little woman.* A few hours ago she couldn't wait to leave Chicago. Now she thought it might have been fun to spend Christmas with her, and her family.

The cab pulled up in front of Children's Hospital. Kathleen paid the fare, tipped the driver, wished him a Merry Christmas, and for what she hoped was the last time, rushed through the door.

She walked into the room and found Dr. Macy talking with Amber. Kathleen suffered a moment of uncertainty when she saw Patti's empty bed. The doctor had her back turned and didn't see her come in, but a white-faced Amber glanced up and alerted her of another's presence.

The doctor turned, and seeing her, smiled. "Patti is next

door in the playroom. She's ready to go home." Dr. Macy stood, but didn't seem in any hurry to leave. "Kathleen, you're flying back to Oregon with Patti and Mrs. Williams?"

"Yes. Yes, I am."

"Good. Exellent. I've spoken to my friend, Sandy Jones. She'll help you board the plane with a minimum of difficulty. I want Patti home in as short a time as possible."

She turned back to Amber, but continued to address Kathleen. "Mrs. Williams tells me she is afraid of flying. I'm giving her enough Valium, so she should sleep most of the way."

The doctor looked full in her face, and in a stern voice said, "Don't mix alcohol with these pills. No cocktails. And don't drive yourself home when you get to Oregon."

For once, Amber seemed unable, or unwilling to talk. She nodded and listened, pale-faced, as Dr. Macy gave her prescriptions and instructions for Patti's care.

Chapter 11

A pretty nurse appeared with a small-sized wheelchair. "Shall we go next door and collect our passenger?

The trio hesitated in the doorway of the playroom and watched for a moment. The scene brought smiles. The girls obviously were having fun in the small kitchen specially equipped for children.

"Patti, you get to go home now," the nurse spoke. "Ready for your ride?"

Amber quickly zipped Patti into her warm pink snowsuit, while dark eyes watched.

"Don't be sad, Misha, you'll go home soon, too." The two little girls, one chocolate, one vanilla, hugged.

Patti grinned, as if she had a ticket to an amusement park, as she climbed into the wheelchair. The nurse smiled at mother and teacher, nodded her head, and began the long trek down the hallway. "No matter how much fun they're having, they're always ready to go home," she said.

• • •

The taxi sped along boulevards still lined with snow. Wide-eyed, Patti watched from her seat in the middle. Amber remained quiet, almost sullen. The landscape flew past, as Kathleen watched and said nothing. It began to snow again. Patti looked from one to the other and voiced her fear. "Will we be snowed in at the airport again? How will Santa Claus find me?"

They looked at each other over Patti's head. Amber appeared about to panic and remained mute.

Striving to keep uncertainty out of her voice, Kathleen smiled at her first-grader. "I don't think so, honey. I think you'll wake up in your own little bed tomorrow morning, but Santa Claus will find you, no matter where you are."

The terminal pulsated with people, a little less crowded than during the three-day snowstorm but still plenty of last-minute-travelers intent on reaching their destination before Christmas day. All seemed to be flowing in an orderly manner. Kathleen soon spotted Sandy Jones. Thanks to Dr. Macy, the airport official watched for them.

With Ms. Jones clearing the way, Amber purchased the necessary tickets with a minimum of hassle. Kathleen's three tickets, to Youngstown, Ohio, back to Chicago, and on to Oregon, were quickly exchanged for one ticket and boarding pass. A flight on United, straight through from O'Hare to Portland, Oregon. With the difference in time, they would be in Portland almost before they left Chicago. Never missing an opportunity to teach, she explained the difference in time zones to Patti.

"That's funny, Miss O'Brien," she giggled.

With tickets and boarding passes in hand, enough time remained to buy and eat hotdogs. The best hotdogs, a nurse at the hospital told Kathleen, you could find anywhere. The nurse claimed they were even better than the ones at Coney Island. When questioned, Ms. Jones laughed and said, "Yes, and if you happened to watch *Jeopardy*, you know we sell more hotdogs here than they do at Coney Island. They're good. I have to have one at least once a week."

Kathleen purchased a hotdog for each of them. *I can't believe I was marooned here three days and didn't know to try these.* As she handed one to Ms. Jones, she beckoned her aside, and with back turned to Patti and Mrs. Williams, whispered one more request. The airport official nodded and hurried away.

Patti devoured the last of her hotdog, mustard smeared on her face, as Sandy returned clutching something under an arm. "Patti. Look what I have."

A grin spread across her cheeks and eyes widened like puddles of snowmelt when the sun shines. "My bear! Look Mommy." She tugged on her mother's arm. "My bear that Daddy buyed me. I thought it was lost. Forever." She reached up with eager arms and hugged the bear to her.

It might have been a smiling contest until Amber diverted their attention with a cough and dark scowl.

"A teddy-bear. Hmpf! Your father is just *full* of surprises, isn't he? Yes— Well,... You'd better wipe the mustard off your face." The corners of her mouth turned up in a simulated smile as she handed her daughter a paper napkin. "Or your bear is going to look like he ate hotdogs too."

Kathleen didn't know she'd been holding her breath until air escaped like a safety valve on a pressure cooker. She no longer knew what to expect from Patti's mother. *Talk about hot and cold.* The woman had gone from chatterbox to nun-like quietness, and back to limited dialogue, in less than twenty-four hours.

Ms. Jones walked them through security; they were first in line to board the plane without knowing quite how it all happened.

Ready for takeoff, the jet screamed down the runway and lifted. Patti, buckled in the middle, hugged her bear. Amber scrunched her eyes shut in a face the color of chalk. White knuckles gripped the chair-arms and she breathed through slightly parted lips.

Passengers began to relax when altitude was reached and the fasten-seatbelts sign blinked off. More than one sigh reached Kathleen's ears as belts unsnapped and chairs tipped back. A flight attendant came by with the offer of food and drinks. Kathleen declined. Patti wanted nothing, and Amber sat with eyes closed, hands still gripping the chair arms.

A man across the isle pulled a cellular phone from his pocket and placed it on standby. Kathleen turned on her own. Not that she expected any calls, it was habit. Happy to be headed back to Oregon, she shoved the phone deep in her coat pocket and gave herself permission to relax. In no time, she slept.

It took a minute or two, and Patti's hand jiggling her arm,

before Kathleen realized the annoying jingle was her own cell phone. She fumbled and extracted the instrument.

"Hello?"

"Kathleen? It's me. I'm sorry I hung up on you. When are you coming home? We need to talk."

• • •

Thankful Edward had agreed, while they talked on the phone, to drive her home in his comfortable car, she hoped he wouldn't be too astonished when she showed up with two more passengers. It wouldn't be the intimate time alone, she knew he wanted. And he might be a bit stiff, but he could be counted on to play the gentleman.

A quick look at Patti, revealed a little girl on the verge of sleep. The child's eyelids fluttered as she hugged her bear and whispered secrets too private for adult ears.

It brought a smile that quickly faded as she glanced across. Amber looked as if she expected to have a tooth pulled without benefit of Novocain. The medication Dr. Macy gave her didn't seem to be helping. *Maybe she didn't take the pills soon enough.*

Too tired to worry over it for long, Kathleen leaned her head back, closed her eyes and fell asleep. A little later, Amber brushed past her unnoticed and headed for the lavatory. On her return trip, she stumbled, and caught herself, while trying to regain her seat. The shoulder bag she carried clunked and rattled as it hit the floor. The weary redhead moaned softly but didn't awaken until the plane was flying down the Columbia River.

The intercom crackled to life. "Ladies and gentlemen. This is your captain. We will be arriving at Portland International Airport in about twenty minutes. It is a cool thirty-nine degrees in the City of Roses, and it is raining. Thank you for flying United. We hope you'll join us again. Happy holidays."

Instantly awake, Kathleen placed her chair in the upright position, and fastened her seatbelt. Patti looked over at her mother for help. When she didn't rouse, the little girl struggled on her own to fasten the seatbelt. A little assistance from her teacher and the belt snapped in place. Patti's fleeting smile was quickly replaced with a worried frown.

"Mommy?" She pulled on her mother's arm. "Mommy. Wake up! You haveta fasten your seatbelt. The plane's gonna land." She shook her again. "Mommy! Wake up."

Kathleen stared at her. *What's going on? Is she that drugged?* All the poking, shaking, and the woman hadn't batted an eyelash. Alarmed, she reached across Patti, grasped Amber by the arm, and shook her. *Hard.*

"Amber! *Wake up*!" She ground between her teeth, before she added a pinch to the flesh she gripped. "*Now!*"

Her head rolled slowly to the side, and her eyes slid open. She stared at the teacher as if she were seeing her underwater. Confused, she looked down at the child beside her. Slowly, comprehension dawned.

"Fasten your seatbelt!" Kathleen repeated, trying to keep the edge out of her voice. "We're landing."

The woman moved like a programmed robot whose response-time is out of sync, but she did manage to get her chair upright and secure her belt. As the plane began the descent to the runway, Amber blanched as if she'd awakened and found herself at the top of the most fearsome roller coaster ever designed. Her eyes widened in terror before she clamped them shut, and strangled the arms of her chair. She made a sound, low in her throat, like a wounded animal.

It was a tossup, who felt the most relieved to be off that plane and back on terra firma. Kathleen heaved a sigh of relief and thought if she never got on another flight with Mrs. Williams it would be soon enough.

Patti squeezed her bear, looked solemnly into the bear's eyes, and announced in a small voice, "Well, Pooh-bear—we made it."

Slowly, a tinge of color returned to Amber's face. Her eyes didn't appear as glassy, and she looked as if she might be on the verge of speech.

The thought barely had time to circulate her brain, when Kathleen's cell phone, back on standby, chimed.

"Hello?"

"Kathleen? I'm so frustrated; I don't know what to do. There's no *way* I can get there to pick you up. Not any time soon, anyway. There's been a bad accident on the freeway, both north-bound lanes are closed and traffic is backed up for miles."

He groaned. "I can't even cross the median, turn around, go back, and find an alternate route." She thought she heard him pound the steering wheel. "Can you possibly find another way home? Rent a car. I'll pay for it. Better still, stay in a hotel. I'll come get you as soon as I get out of this snarl. We can have a late dinner."

"Edward, I'm sorry you're being held up, but don't worry. I'll get a way home. I found Patti in Chicago. She and her mother are with me. Patti's been in hospital. Pneumonia. She's okay—but she needs to get home as quickly as possible. I'll rent a car."

"You have *who?—Patti?*—The little girl whose father took her from the school grounds? Kathleen, *you* didn't tell me that." He took an audible deep breath and let it out slowly. "I'm glad, of course, the child's been found. But I fail to see why you're so involved. Why can't they find their own way home? Why are you always in the middle of everything? Why, if I may be so blunt, are you babysitting a grown woman? Kathleen—I feel like I'm always last on your list of priorities."

She struggled to keep her voice even. "I'm sorry—Edward—I'll explain it all later. I have to go now. Bye."

Her eyes two round question marks, Patti clutched her bear, and looked up at her teacher. For once, Miss O'Brien wasn't paying her any attention. The child turned to her mother and again tugged on her arm. "Mommy?"

"Huh? Whas wrong?"

"I'm sorry. We just lost our transportation home. Edward can't pick us up. There's been an accident on the freeway. He's stuck in traffic. I'll rent us a car."

"Mish O'Brien—Kathleen—No." Amber grabbed her by the arm. Whether to stop the teacher or steady herself wasn't clear, but the result was the same. She had her attention.

I'll call…Spike. He livesh here—She fumbled in her bag for her cell phone. "Can be here—ten minutes and take us home."

"Spike?"

"My boyfriend."

Apprehensive, and doubtful, she barely had time to be nervous. Spike pulled up outside the main entrance, where the taxis waited, in just under ten minutes. He leaped from his '98 black Chevy, with the one dented front fender; ran around to the passenger side, and embraced Amber in a fierce hug, before stepping away and eyeing Kathleen.

"Spike…Miss O'Brien…Patti's teacher."

"Glad ta meetcha."

He shook her hand with a grip that made her think of a slippery fish.

"This is, Patti. Patti—you can call my friend—Uncle Spike."

"Hiya kid." The man flicked his eyes over the little girl. "So your mom says, like, ya been sick, huh? That's tough."

Patti studied the toes of her shoes and remained mute.

Glad to be rid of the bag that made her identify with a turtle carrying it's shell, Kathleen let Spike take it from her. For all she knew, her large suitcase, checked all the way through, was still going round and round on the carousel in Youngstown. Ms. Jones, the ever-helpful airport official, had assured her the luggage would be returned to Fir Valley. Relieved she didn't have to deal with it now, she could only stare at the interior of the car's trunk.

Two cases of Coors, a bottle in a brown paper bag, obviously some kind of liquor, and grocery sacks that contained God only knew what occupied the interior. Little room remained. Kathleen frowned and shot a look, sharp enough to cut steel, at Spike. *Should I withdraw my bag?*

The young man read her look, but wasn't about to have his holiday spirit spoiled by any over-zealous schoolteacher. He smirked a devilish grin at her. "Hey, teach? Wanta party?"

"Spike. Behave!" She giggled. "Kathleen's okay. He's teasin'…Spike don't drink and drive. Do ya sugar?"

"Nope. I'm jober as a sudge." He held up his hands, palms out, before giving Amber another playful squeeze and slapping her on the bottom. "Not like my little chicken here, huh?" He looked at Kathleen. "You comin'?"

She didn't like him on general principal, but she could detect no liquor on his breath, and standing here glaring at him wasn't going to get them home. Whatever he intended, at not yet three o'clock, the party hadn't started. She quashed the retort on the tip of her tongue and climbed into the backseat beside Patti.

Chapter 12

Spike, a slight-built young man, looked as if he might not be out of his teens. He wore baggy blue jeans, a green flannel shirt that hung to his hips, or where his hips were presumed to be, and the requisite baseball cap turned backwards, the "uniform" seen on nearly every street corner and especially around the high school. Dress guaranteed to raise the ire of parents and the scorn of educators—kids in rebellion, wanting to be different but requiring the approval of their peers.

Kathleen sat behind the driver and tried to decipher the writing on his cap. Something about a band? *He's a guitar player in a band? Is that what Amber said? What else does he do?* She wondered. *Does he have a job?* His hair, a nondescript brownish color, only partially hidden by the cap, hung well past his collar and curled up at the ends. She was relieved to note, his tresses had the shine only clean hair affords.

With the rain and dark fast approaching, visibility

became poor. One of those times when the asphalt appeared to swallow any illumination cast by the headlights. Car lights seemed about as effective as a penlight in a tunnel. Kathleen admitted, if only to herself, she was glad she didn't have to drive.

Spike might, to her way of thinking, be an unsavory young man, but he drove carefully, staying well within the speed limits, and only changed lanes when it was appropriate to do so. She relaxed. Before they entered the freeway, Patti fell asleep.

They'd gone only a few miles, when flashing lights up ahead and a siren wailing behind alerted them of the accident responsible for Edward's delay. Traffic slowed to a near crawl and funneled into the right lane of the southbound freeway. A police car, lights flashing, siren screaming, whizzed past them in the far left lane.

"Hey, babe?" He gave Amber a not-so-gentle nudge. "Move over—there's cops swarmin' all over the place. I think we're gettin' close to that accident."

She pried herself loose from Spike's hip and scooted to her own side of the seat as another firetruck raced past. Any attempts to relax were shattered. A loud blast from an emergency vehicle woke Patti. She sat up and rubbed her eyes with two balled fists.

Nerves on alert, Kathleen strained to see through the gloom. Officers with flashlights motioned cars to keep moving. The line of traffic crept forward, stopping and starting. Even knowing there was a bad accident, she wasn't prepared for what she saw.

A tanker truck and trailer lay on its side across all lanes of the northbound interstate, like some giant's twisted toy. Whatever the tank contained, proved flammable and had ignited. Firemen were still hosing everything down. A blackened car rested on its top in the median.

What looked to be a red Toyota, front end now smashed, windows broken, had careened across the center-strip and stopped, right side up, just short of the southbound lanes. Kathleen couldn't tell if people might still be inside. Three or four cars were nosed toward the ditch on the far side of the northbound interstate, but it was impossible to tell if they were involved in the accident or merely trying to get out of the way.

Packages, once wrapped in brightly colored Christmas paper, were strewn over the grass—presents, now unrecognizable in their tattered and sodden shape.

Ambulances and other emergency vehicles were on the scene. More were arriving. Workers strived to keep curious onlookers at bay and assist the scared and injured.

"Man, oh man!" Spike ejaculated. "I'll bet somebody died in that mess."

"Well, I hope you're wrong!" Amber came to life. "What an *awful* Christmas for somebody."

Kathleen shuddered. She wanted to call Edward on her cell phone. Tell him what she'd seen, the reason for his holdup. But she didn't want to rehearse it for Patti's listening ears. It was hard to know how much she could see from her shortened advantage. *Will she have nightmares?* The teacher thought her student entirely too quiet. She could only hope she had missed most of the distressing scene.

Maybe Edward is right. Maybe I need to step back. How does one draw the line between caring and professionalism? How could Patti's mother be so concerned for her daughter's health on the one hand, and so oblivious to her needs on the other? *Maybe if I see parents at conference time, that's enough.* She thought she knew Patti's folks a little too well now.

Amber seems to have forgotten she has a daughter in the backseat. Why doesn't she offer a word of reassurance to her? Inwardly, Kathleen fumed as she moved closer and reached out an arm to draw the child close to her side.

"Miss O'Brien?"

"Yes, Patti?"

"Will we get in a assi...dents?"

She caught her breath. "No, honey. Bad accidents are rare. You'll be home all safe and warm in your own little bed soon. And Patti, tonight, Santa Claus comes." She smiled into upturned eyes.

"Miss O'Brien, can I hug you?"

The teacher bent her head and the child's arms encircled her neck. "I love you," she whispered. Kathleen smiled, and hugged her back, though she had to wipe the moisture from her eyes.

• • •

"Hey, teach? Enda the line here." Spike reached down, pulled a lever to pop the trunk, and turned his attention to necking with Amber. If the two in the front seat heard her "Thanks for the ride," they uttered no response. Only Patti whispered, "Goodbye, Miss O'Brien."

"Bye, sweetheart. Crawl in bed as soon as you get home, honey, and stay warm." The teacher spoke softly, and stroked the little girl's cheek. "Merry Christmas, Patti. I'll see you again when school starts." *Will those two lamebrains in the front seat take care of her? And what can I do if they don't? Please, God. Watch over her.*

She was *home*. Half of her vacation time gone, and she felt like an emotional wreck. Still she could count her blessings. She planned to spend a good part of the remaining time sleeping.

I don't know when I've been so tired, she lamented as she retrieved her bag from Spike's car, ducked her head and trotted through the rain to Mrs. Fisher's backdoor. *Sorry, Spike. I think I forgot to close your trunk.*

She was tempted to bolt for her rooms, but Martha would expect an explanation of her unplanned return.

She dropped her bag and purse in the hallway at the foot of the stairs, squared her shoulders, and entered the living room.

"Kathleen! What are you doing back here? And on Christmas Eve?" Martha laid aside the afghan she was crocheting and leaned forward in her chair, her brow puckering in surprise. "I thought you were one of the grandchildren coming in the backdoor. Well, come on in dear. Sit here by the fire and tell me what's happened."

"Oh Martha, it would be easier to tell you what *hasn't* happened." She unbuttoned her coat, but left it on as she perched on the edge of the chair. "I'll give you the abbreviated version and fill you in later if I may. First, a snowstorm in Chicago halted all air traffic for three days. Then my brother's family came down with the flu." She hesitated, not sure how to proceed.

Martha's discerning eyes peered at her over the top of her glasses. "What? What is it dear, that you don't want to tell me?"

"Do you know about Patti Williams?"

"About her father taking her from the school grounds and running with her? Yes, I know. It doesn't take long for a thing like that to get around this neighborhood." She sighed. "Alvin Williams isn't a bad boy. I've known him since he was knee-high-to-a-duck. He used to cut my grass. Hard worker. But he's a hothead who tends to act first and think later. Formidable on the football team—I'm sorry, Kathleen. Forgive me for rambling on. It's an old lady thing. What were you going to tell me?"

"Mr. Williams has been arrested and Patti is back with her mother."

"Ah—I see. Well—what he did was wrong. He was bound to be caught. And I expect it is better now than later. Though I'm not sure, Patti is better off with her mother. That girl has some growing up to do." She picked up the afghan crocheted in shades of green and blue, pushed the glasses back on her nose, and wound the yarn around arthritic fingers still nimble enough to make the crochet hook fly.

"Kathleen, you look dead on your feet. Get some rest. We can talk later. Join us here tomorrow for Christmas dinner, you and your young man, if you don't have other plans. I'm roasting a turkey."

"And your turkey's always so good. I appreciate the invitation, but you just made me remember; I need to call Edward. There was a wreck on the interstate, and he's stuck in a very long line of traffic. He's not a happy camper right now. I think I'll let him tell *me* what we're going to do."

The landlady smiled. "Well, we eat about two, if you change your mind, you'll be very welcome."

She suspected there were more questions she'd like to ask. However, she knew how to wait and pick her time. Always kind, she simply brewed the best pot of tea ever, smiled and encouraged her renter to share the happenings of her day when she came home, weary from a day of teaching.

Martha wasn't the only one with questions. Kathleen wondered what her landlady, a teacher herself, who had lived here all her life, could tell her about Al and Amber. What had Martha meant, when she said Patti might not be better off with her mother?

Chapter 13

Kathleen dumped her bag in the bottom of the cedar-lined closet. Dirty laundry could wait. She hung her winter coat on a padded hanger, kicked off her fur-lined boots, and eyed the bed. *Her bed.* There in the middle of the spread lay Snowball, Mrs. Fisher's Persian cat. In her haste to greet Edward and get to the airport, she'd neglected to close her door tightly. All this cat needed was an inch or less to gain entrance.

The cat stretched, winked an eye, and twitched his tail. "Sorry, old boy." She picked him up and stroked his fur. "Christmas Eve and all that, but this is *my* bed and I'm ready to crash."

Purrrrrrrrrrrrrr.

"Oh, sure. You rascal. Purr. You know I'm an old softy, don't you?" Kathleen rubbed her cheek against his silky head and deposited him back on the foot of her bed. There was one more object to remove. The leather attaché case she forgot to give Edward. She moved the package, wrapped in shiny silver paper and tied with a blue curled ribbon, to her desk.

"Well, Snowball, he'll get it tomorrow." She smiled and tickled the cat under his chin. "We just won't tell him it has your paw prints all over it, will we?"

Kathleen stretched out on the bed and reached for her phone on the bedside table. Edward answered on the first ring.

"Hello?"

"Hi. It's me. I'm home—finally." She took a deep breath. "That accident looked terrible. Really bad! It took us a long time to get through there."

"Yeah, I've been listening to the radio. They say there are two fatalities and numerous injuries. I don't know when *I'll* make it back home."

"I'm sorry you're being held up. If I had spotted your car, and we could have stopped, I would have come and waited with you. I didn't have to rent a car after all. Mrs. Williams' boyfriend drove us home."

"Thanks, Love, for saying you'd wait with me, but I wouldn't wish this torture on anyone. I'm just glad you're home safe." He groaned. "Believe it or not, we've started to move. I'm creeping along here at about ten miles an hour. It's stop and go. If I make it back within a couple hours, do you want me to come and get you? I don't know if anything decent will be open in Fir Valley, but we could maybe come back to my place. Have some hot chocolate. Talk."

"Oh Edward, I don't know. I don't want to disappoint you,

but I'm afraid I wouldn't be very good company. I'm so tired; I can barely hold my eyes open."

"Well, okay then. I guess I'm not exactly the Energizer Bunny myself. And I don't feel much like Santa Claus either." He sighed. "This has been some day. One lousy Christmas Eve. Wouldn't you say? Shall I pick you up, say about ten tomorrow then?"

Snowball rubbed his head against her, as she cradled the receiver and absently petted him with her free hand. "Could you make it a bit later, please? Say eleven, and you just might have a date that can stay awake."

"Okay. Eleven it is."

She hung up the phone, pushed the cat aside and rushed off to brush her teeth. Snowball jumped from the bed and followed her to the bathroom, tail thrust in the air like a symphony director's baton. Kathleen washed her face in warm water and patted it dry with a fluffy towel. The cat, one eye on her, jumped to the commode and began grooming himself. His rough pink tongue made wet lines down his expansive chest, like small sled runners in snow.

He looked surprised when she chuckled softly and tucked him under one arm. "Okay, Fuzzbutt. Out you go. It's nighty-night time." She put the cat on the floor and gently shoved him through the door before closing it firmly behind him.

She undressed quickly and slipped into a clean pair of flannel pajamas, relieved to crawl between the sheets and turn out the light. Could it really have been only this morning she left Danny's bed? His apartment? Talked to motherly

Mrs. Sanchez? Was it only three days ago she'd been with Danny? It seemed like an eternity since she left Chicago.

"Please, God, keep Danny safe in Iraq." She closed her eyes and was instantly asleep.

• • •

Kathleen woke a few minutes after nine. Christmas day! Already smells of roasting turkey were drifting up the stairs, causing her stomach to growl. She had awakened in plenty of time to shower, shampoo her hair, do her nails, dress and be ready for her date. *What should I wear?*

Not having a clue what Edward planned and knowing he had a bent for the elegant, the safest bet seemed to be away from the casual. He might freak if she wore blue jeans, attire she found perfectly comfortable on holidays with her family.

She chose a long black acrylic skirt with a slit up the left side. It had been spendy for a teacher's salary, but bought on sale, she considered it a bargain. Paired with an eggshell, long-sleeved satin blouse, her black leather, calf-length boots, a gold bracelet, diamond earrings winking in her ears, she felt ready for anything Edward might suggest. They had things to discuss, and looking her best gave her confidence.

The redhead applied foundation with a deft touch, and quickly brushed on a light dusting of face powder. The merest hint of shadow brought out the green of her eyes. Mascara enhanced already thick lashes. Tweezers eliminated a stray hair or two, and quick strokes with an eyebrow pencil defined arched brows. A little of Giorgio's sandalwood, her Christmas present from Edward, dabbed behind her ears and on each wrist provided the finishing touch. She might be dressed to conquer, but it did nothing for her empty stomach rumbling like a clogged drain that had just been unstuck, a decidedly unladylike sound.

Martha looked up from where she was stirring something on the stove. "Oh my! Don't you look nice." She smiled. "I sometimes wish my brood would dress-up for the holidays, but they'll come in here looking like field-hands and eat like an ol' time threshing crew. Guess they're most comfortable in their jeans. Girls too. Jeans. Different in my day. I suppose I don't really mind, so long as they come for dinner."

Three pumpkin pies, along with one pecan, and two mincemeat, lined the counter, as well as freshly made cinnamon rolls. "Pour yourself some coffee. It's fresh." She waved a hand in the general direction of the pastry. "And have one of those sticky buns."

"Martha, how do you do it? All this baking and preparing a big dinner?" Kathleen poured herself a cup of coffee and pinched off a cinnamon roll. They smelled heavenly and she took a big bite just as her stomach gave another plaintive growl her landlady couldn't help but hear. "Oh my, I guess I forgot to eat last evening and my tummy is letting me know about it." She smiled a bit self-consciously.

"Well, dear, you were pretty tired last night. I'm not surprised you forgot to eat. Take another of those buns; it won't spoil your breakfast, or whatever your young man has planned." She turned to survey her. "Maybe you should eat a big breakfast now, before you go. Do you have time?"

"I really don't." She laughed and winked as she snatched

another pastry. "We won't tell anyone I'm about to devour two of your delicious cinnamon rolls."

Martha chuckled and continued stirring.

"Thanks, and Merry Christmas," Kathleen called before filling her mouth with a big bite as she climbed the stairs back to her rooms. Edward would pick her up in less than a half hour. Quickly, she devoured the second bun and gulped her coffee. Thankful her stomach had quit rumbling; she brushed her teeth again and applied fresh lipstick.

With twenty minutes to spare, she switched on her computer and checked her e-mail. She had twenty-nine messages. Most were spam she could delete later. Two messages from her mom and dad. Her nieces and nephews sent her some jokes. Michael wrote and Mary added a few sentiments. None of which she took time to read now. But the one that stopped her, was a few lines from Danny:

> Hi, Carrot Top,
>
> Alone in my hotel room, I just finished reading the story of Jesus' birth, found in Luke. Not too much like Christmas here, but dinner with the troops was nice. So was time spent with you. How's Patti? Wishing you a happy holiday.
> Danny
>
> P.S. "Pray about everything. And the peace of God which transcends all understanding, will guard your hearts and your minds in Christ Jesus" (Phil. 4:7, NIV)
>
> "Glory to God in the highest, and on earth peace to men on whom his favor rests" (Luke 2:14, NIV)

Pray about everything? Is that in the Bible? I'll look it up later.

Kathleen slipped on her three-quarter-length black leather coat, tucked Edward's present under her arm, grabbed her purse, and went to wait for him.

On her way out, she left her bedroom door cracked a fraction of an inch. With all the company swarming the house today, Snowball might be looking for a quiet place to escape. She smiled to herself. It could be their little secret.

Chapter 14

Edward smiled to himself as he pulled the BMW into Mrs. Fisher's driveway. *It's going to be a good Christmas after all. Finally, things are going my way. Kathleen and I can get married. She can quit teaching; I can now afford to give her anything she wants. That teacher's salary she makes is nothing.*

Dressed in charcoal wool-flannel slacks, black loafers, and a blue pullover lambs-wool sweater, atop a white button-down shirt, he looked like a candidate for best-dressed man of the year. His glasses were left behind today in favor of contacts, and his leather jacket lay flung across the backseat. He shoved his hands in his pockets, whistled a wordless little tune, and strode briskly to the back entrance.

His date opened the door before he could ring the bell. She stood before him, lovelier than the angel on top of the Christmas tree. It took his breath away. What a beautiful woman Kathleen was, and soon she would be his. He put his arms around her and, without saying a word, kissed her possessively and a bit roughly, right there on the porch. It still galled him that she'd slept in another man's bed. He wanted her in his bed, and *only* in his bed.

"Well...and Merry Christmas to you, too." She quipped as soon as she could catch her breath.

"That's only the beginning of what I have in store for you." He smirked as he put an arm around her and ushered her to his car.

The weather had turned colder during the night, Kathleen shivered as she buckled herself in. Oregon juncos, looking for all the world like plump, black-bonneted matrons, were busy hopping around, searching for food on the lawn. Kathleen smiled as she watched the little feathered creatures some referred to as snowbirds.

Edward drove slowly, his eyes doing double duty watching the road and feasting on the woman beside him. "Kathleen, I should take you somewhere special for Christmas brunch. But as you know, nothing is open in this flea-bitten, one-horse town of Fir Valley. We'd have to drive to Portland, and I just don't think I can face the freeway again today." He gave her a winning smile.

"Do you mind too much if we just go to my apartment for awhile? I can scramble a few eggs. Brew coffee...I'm not a good cook, but I promise I won't let you starve." He reached over and squeezed her hand. "We're invited to Bill and Rosie's for dinner later. Rosie asked me earlier, probably out of pity for a lonely old bachelor. I called this morning and told her you're back. She squealed in my ear and nearly broke my eardrum, so I take it she's delighted to have you come, too."

Kathleen laughed. "No—no—and yes. No, there is nothing open on Christmas day in Fir Valley. No, I don't mind going to your apartment. I don't think I can face Portland again just yet, either. And yes, I would love to go with you to Rosie and Bill's for dinner. Rosie did invite me earlier before she knew I was going to my brother's in Ohio. I'm glad we're going there."

• • •

Seated in front of his gas-lit fireplace, she looked exquisite. He could go far with a woman of her beauty and integrity beside him. Perhaps he would eventually get into politics. The idea intrigued him.

Did she seem a bit distant today, or was it his imagination? *Perhaps she's still tired from her trip.* He wouldn't allow her to help in the kitchen, though she offered. If he was careful, and kept it simple, he could make a decent breakfast for the two of them. It wouldn't be long until he could hire all the help they might need. *His wife* would never be a household drudge.

Kathleen smiled and laid aside the *Money Magazine* she had been idly thumbing through. Edward set a tray on the table in front of her, plates laden with little link sausages, scrambled eggs, and toasted bagels spread with cream cheese. Fresh-squeezed orange juice in fluted glasses, and coffee that smelled heavenly steamed in matching white mugs. Thoughtfully, he'd provided over-sized paper napkins with a Christmas motif.

Bette Midler's medley of Christmas songs from her album

White Christmas played softly in the background on the Dolby surround-sound. "Edward, this looks scrumptious, and here, in front of the fire, is much cozier than dining in the swankiest restaurant. I'm impressed." Kathleen smiled into his eyes.

He sat beside her, and before picking up his plate, he reached over and kissed her on the mouth with lips as tender as a butterfly's caress. He handed her a champagne glass of orange juice and then picked up his own and proposed a toast. "To us, Kathleen, and to the future."

Breakfast finished, he whisked the dirty dishes back to the kitchen, brought the pot and poured them more coffee to sip in front of the fire. He winked. "The maid will clean up the dishes."

"Edward, let me help you with clean up. I'm pretty good in the kitchen. Really, I am."

"Ah, no, my love. I don't want those pretty little hands in dishwater. I want you here beside me, on the couch. Besides, I have some great news to share with you, but first maybe a little question or two." He set his coffee cup down and reached for her hand.

"Kathleen, who is this Danny person, whose bed you were in? And how did you meet him?"

A giggle escaped. "Why, I think you're jealous."

"You bet your socks, honey. When it comes to *my* girl in another man's bed, I could just maybe commit murder."

She quickly sobered. "But you have nothing to be alarmed about. Danny is simply an old friend. I've known him since fifth grade. He's like a brother. He used to tag Michael around.

Hero worship, I suppose. All through school, he was in and out of our house."

"Yeah, uh huh...So how did you hook up with him in Chicago? Have you kept in touch? Just in case? Did you have a little rendezvous planned? Or something?"

"*Edward!* —Don't be ridiculous! This isn't like you."

"Yeah—Well—You still haven't told me what you were doing in his bed. I'm going to assume he wasn't in the bed with you. Or was he?"

"*How dare you*!" She jumped up, coffee sloshing over the sides of her cup before she plopped it back on the tray.

"Okay—Sorry." He held up his hands. "Maybe that's a little over the top. But, *Kathleen,* you're a beautiful woman, you can't blame me for being jealous."

Barely controlling her temper, fists balled at her sides, she clipped her sentences and spit the words at him as if they were ice cubes. "Danny *left.* For *Iraq.* We met on the plane. To Chicago. There was a *snowstorm.* Danny *worried.* He reached me by cellular phone. Offered me the use of his apartment. Long as Patti remained in hospital. *End* of story."

"Okay—okay. So how come *I* couldn't get you on your cellular?"

"*You* are asking *me?* Why you couldn't get me on *my* phone? Edward, I tried repeatedly to call you when Patti was in hospital. I called every number you have. Including your private number at the bank. I talked to your secretary. You were simply *unavailable.*"

"Touché. Shall we call a truce? I could cut you some

fruitcake." He deadpanned and watched her eyes turn from stormy to mischievous.

"Go ahead. Serve me fruitcake, but cut yourself a big piece first. I'll match you bite for bite." They challenged each other and burst out laughing at the same time.

"Ah, Kathleen, my love. Life with you will never be boring. Which brings me to my surprise and the reason you couldn't get me by phone." He reached out and took her hand. "I have the most exciting news. I've been in California, Sweetheart. Sacramento to be exact. I didn't want to say anything until I knew for sure. But Grandfather called two days ago, and I have the position of finance manager down there. It's a step up, and not the last I plan to take. Finally, we can get out of this backwoods, red-neck settlement with the one stoplight in the center of town."

"What are you saying?"

"I'm saying, I'm transferring. To Sacramento. Leaving Hicksville behind. Honey, I want you to come with me. Marry me. We can live with Grandfather until I can find us a suitable house. His place is so huge he'd never know we were there, and he employs live-in help."

Kathleen remained silent a fraction too long. "I don't know what to say. I suppose I could blush and say 'this is all so sudden,' but I guess that went out with the horse and buggy. The truth is, you *have* caught me by surprise. When, exactly, are you being transferred?"

"I leave here the end of January, and take over the new management the middle of February. Kathleen, please say you'll come with me. If there isn't enough time to plan the wedding you want, big church, whatever, we can do it later. You can have anything you want. Just come with me now."

She gasped. "The end of *January?* Edward! I couldn't possibly go with you then. *Hello?* I'm a *teacher.* I have a class to teach. I'm under contract till the end of the school year."

"But, of *course* you can come with me. Tell them you quit. You'll never have to work again. Don't you understand? You don't *need* that or any other job. I can support us, and soon I'll be able to give you anything you want." He moved away a little and looked into her face. "You'll find other interests once we're married."

"No—I don't think *you* understand." She threw up her hands. "I can't...okay...*won't,* just walk away from my job in the middle of the year. It goes against everything I've been taught. Everything I believe in."

"Oh yeah!—I suppose I knew you'd balk at that. But, Love, I don't know if I can wait 'till June. Will you at least come to Sacramento during spring break? Maybe we could get married then? You *will* marry me, won't you, Kathleen?"

"Edward?—do you pray about everything?"

"Huh? What kind of answer is that? What are you talking about?"

"I'm just asking a simple question. I think it's in the Bible. Do you *pray* about everything? You know...decisions?"

He expelled a ragged breath. "I believe in God. Okay? I even go along with *most* of what pastor Jim spouts from the pulpit. But *pray* about *everything*? You don't take that literally, do you?" He ran a hand through his hair. "Sounds a little off the deep end to me. I believe God gave us a brain and expects us to think for ourselves. I might pray about an illness, cancer, something like that. But no...I don't bother God with things I can handle myself."

"You haven't asked God, then, if I'm the one you should marry?"

"Kathleen?—Why do I feel like a simple proposal has ended up mired in the mud? I *love* you! I can take *care of you!* Isn't that *enough?"*

"I'm sorry. I don't mean to upset you. Really, I don't. I'm happy for you that you're being transferred. I know it's what you want, and you honor me by wanting me to be your wife. I do care for you, but marriage is a big step. I need time to think about it, and yes, pray about it."

He slapped his knees, stifled a groan, and ran fingers through his hair; he knew better than to push Kathleen. His hope of presenting her with an engagement ring on Christmas day faded. The thought that she somehow changed, since her stay in Chicago, continued to torment his mind. Could it be the upset with Patti? Or did seeing this Danny person have something to do with it?

Needing answers and knowing none were forthcoming, he thought it best to change the subject. "Hey, beautiful, is that intriguing package you're courting over there by your side, by any chance for me? Or do I just get a lump of coal in my stocking this year?" His grin was decidedly boyish. "I've been a good boy, you know. I'm kind to old ladies, dogs, babies, and I rarely tease cats."

"Oh...I nearly forgot." She giggled and handed the

brightly wrapped package to the man sitting beside her. "Of course, it's for you...Merry Christmas!"

He shook the package.

"Go on. Open it. I hope you like it." She rose to stand in front of the fireplace and watch his face.

"An attaché case—With my initials, EFC, on it." He held it up and turned it for inspection. "This is very nice. And exactly what I need. Thank you, Love."

"You're welcome." She smiled and then asked the question that had been on her mind since the announcement of his intention to go to Sacramento at the end of January. "Edward, about your grandfather? Didn't you want to spend Christmas with him while you were in California? Why did you come back? *I* wasn't supposed to be here."

"Ah, Kathleen, you have to understand Grandfather." He grimaced. "He did his duty by me. Pulled a few strings. Got me the promotion. We did spend a couple days together. But Grandfather hasn't been much for family life since Grandmother died ten years ago. By now, the old gent is off on a holiday cruise with his latest 'lady friend.'"

"And your mother? Didn't she want to spend Christmas with you?"

"Huh? Well...yes. I suppose she did. If I could fly to Paris."

"Oh, dear. I'm sorry."

"*Well*, don't be. I'd rather be here with you. Kathleen, we'll have our own family. We won't need anyone else."

She bit her lip, carefully refolded the paper napkin and laid it on the tray.

Chapter 15

Edward parked in the circular driveway close to the front entrance. He took her hand, and together they strolled up the front walk.

"Oh, look! Isn't their home beautiful?"

Bill and Rosie Kestler lived three miles out of town in a spacious two-story house custom-built for them the year before. A deck graced three sides of their home, and a daylight basement provided a terrific view of their manicured backyard and five wooded acres beyond.

"I suppose its okay, if you like the farmhouse look."

Kathleen glanced at his face and saw he was serious. She began to suspect they wouldn't agree on their taste in architecture, as well as in other areas. Unwilling to commit herself further, she didn't divulge her propensity for old farmhouses.

Deer, squirrels, and raccoons shared the acreage with the Kestlers. The children worked to make pets of them; they took tempting morsels and left them in hidden places for the animals to find. Rosie hadn't the heart to scold her youngest, five-year-old Nathan, when he tried sneaking his broccoli out for the deer to eat. The little boy tried hard to copy his sisters, but he had yet to learn what deer liked.

Cedar boughs were entwined around the porch banisters. Thousands of tiny white lights intermingled with the branches and twinkled a welcome. White velvet bows, placed strategically, gave a touch of elegance to the greenery.

"Did you ever see anything more gorgeous?" Kathleen tugged gently on his arm. "Look at all Rosie's done."

Miniature white lights framed tall windows, designed to look small paned, and blinked on and off. Fake snow clung to lower window corners and gave greenery a frosted look. Seven large white poinsettias were grouped in a tier beside the front door. A fresh wreath made from mixed evergreens, wired with small pinecones in groups of three and tied with a huge white velvet bow, adorned the front door.

Kathleen couldn't wait to see what her friend and coworker had done to decorate her house. Rosie, appointed their decorator at school, could be counted on to come up with clever ideas no matter what the season, but Christmas was Rosie's favorite time of year.

She breathed in the heady scent of pine and juniper as they waited for someone to answer the doorbell. Edward sneezed three times in rapid succession and held a clean white handkerchief to his nose. Rosie opened the door.

"Welcome. Come in, come in. Merry Christmas!" She stepped back and opened the door wide. "Well! Don't you two look like dolls from Santa's sleigh, all gussied up, pretty, pretty, pretty." She laughed.

Edward squelched another sneeze as he handed their hostess a large box of chocolates.

"Kathleen, I'm so glad you could come, though I'm sorry things didn't work out with your family." She took their coats and hung them in the hall closet. "The men are all downstairs, playing ping-pong, I think. Just go on down, you know the way."

"Rosie, I love your decorations. I never would have thought of using white the way you have. And those poinsettias are gorgeous. Where ever did you find them?"

"They are pretty, aren't they? Bill's friend in the nursery business got them for us." She drew her aside. "We'll go to the kitchen in a moment. It's a beehive out there, but first, come see the trees.

"Edward said you found Patti. That she's back home. But he didn't seem to know any of the particulars, and I'm dying to hear all about it."

"It's quite an involved story. I think you'll be surprised, when I have a chance to tell you all about it. I want Dick to know too. Our principal needs to be informed." She sighed. "Rosie, I just don't think Patti's dad is such a bad guy. He had every opportunity to run, and he didn't."

"I called Dick as soon as I heard. He'll probably call you—maybe even tomorrow. He's as curious as I am."

A tall, perfectly decorated, white-flocked noble fir, displaying blue and silver ornaments, revolved slowly on a turntable in the living room. Electric candles on the tips of the branches winked a silvery glow.

The Douglas fir in the family room became the children's to decorate, and Rosie gave them a free hand. Something less than perfect evolved, and Kathleen loved it. Every handmade item the children created over the years hung somewhere on the branches. Strings of popcorn, cranberries, and paper chains circled the tree in haphazard fashion. A star made out of cardboard and aluminum foil, shone from the tip of the tree; an ornament their oldest, fifteen-year-old Rachel, made while in first grade.

Delicious smells of roasting turkey, hot-spiced cranberry juice, and baked goodies wafted throughout the house. The fragrance of burning candles mixed with the fresh scent of evergreens reminded Kathleen of Christmases past. Always, in her growing-up-years, there had been a live evergreen tree. She wouldn't tell her parents, but Christmas in Florida, with the artificial tree, didn't compare.

Rosie's mother stood in front of the stove and stirred gravy. "Well, hello, Kathleen. How nice that you can join us. And how pretty you are. That's a lovely blouse."

"Why, thank you, Anita. You look lovely yourself."

The gracious lady, attired in a sparkly blue pant suit, dark hair pulled into an upsweep and pinned with silvery combs, laughed, a musical little trill. "How can you tell, dear, beneath this voluminous apron?"

Kathleen giggled. Indeed all three ladies wore huge, white bib aprons; the kind she hadn't seen since she was a little girl, and her grandmother made all her aprons.

A slender woman turned from the counter where she was making a fresh green salad and smiled. “Hi, I’m Joanne, Rosie’s sister-in-law.”

Joanne wore a simple, short black dress that hugged her body; gold hoop earrings the only adornment. Her shoulder-length hair, bleached almost white, flowed straight as a jet-stream. Her black high heels showed off a good pair of legs, but it was her cornflower-blue eyes that Kathleen noticed first.

Rosie stopped mid-scurry, a bowl in hand. “Oh, I’m sorry. I forgot you two hadn’t met.”

Kathleen, however, felt as if she already knew Joanne, and Bill’s brother Tom, from Rosie’s many diatribes. She knew Tom at thirty-eight was four years younger than Bill and six months younger than Rosie. Joanne was thirty-five, but often lied and said she was thirty. Tom, an attorney in Portland, Oregon made good money, but Joanne, a stay-at-home mom, could dish it out with a teaspoon faster than Tom could bring it in with a shovel. Or so Rosie claimed.

“Can I help with something?” Kathleen volunteered.

“Sure.” Anita, spoke up. “Reach in that drawer down there and get one of these aprons. I made five for Rosie, so there should be another one or two. You can stir this gravy. I’ll try and carve the turkey.”

“I could call Bill,” Rosie said. "Mom, however, can carve the turkey better, and with a lot less mess.”

“I say lets keep the men out of the kitchen.” Joanne winked and gave an impish little grin. “Until maybe *after* dinner, they can clean up, don’t cha think?”

• • •

Fifteen people were seated around the table, including Bill and Rosie's four children and Tom and Joanne's three. Rosie wasn't one to banish her children to the kitchen. She taught manners by example. Kathleen approved and silently applauded her friend. She was surprised to see a fleeting frown on Edward's face when she glanced his way.

Bill asked everyone to join hands as he returned thanks. Relieved to see she wasn't overdressed, Kathleen breathed her own thanks. Rosie looked especially nice in a red blouse and dressy black trousers. Even the children wore their finery, younger girls in frilly dresses, and little Nathan, the only boy, adorable in white shirt and bow tie. Rachel and Becky, fifteen and twelve, looked quite grownup, in long sheath dresses.

The men were a bit more casual in their attire, slacks and sweaters ruled. Mr. Smith, clad in dark slacks and a wool plaid shirt, could have doubled for Santa Claus. He only needed the white beard and white hair. Quite bald, a merry twinkle in his brown eyes put one immediately at ease. The Kestler clan had gone all-out to make this a festive occasion.

Conversation, in quiet tones, ebbed and flowed with the passing of dishes around the table. Plates were filled and forks were put in motion when Bill's voice boomed from the end of the table. "Kathleen—I'm glad you made it back in time to spend Christmas with us. But I have to tell you—I'm a bit disappointed in you."

Heads swiveled and forks paused as all eyes turned to Bill, and then focused on the object of his attention. "I thought you'd keep our boy here nailed down a while longer." The choir director and hardware-store owner smirked at Kathleen. "Quite a promotion he's gotten himself—but I don't like seeing him leave our fair town. I'm guessing you'll be bailing out next. Am I right?"

Kathleen smiled and remained quiet. She could feel her face growing hot and past experience told her it was turning crimson—the curse of redheads.

"Well, Bill, it's true, you do have a nice hardware store here, but I never thought Fir Valley had *that* much to offer." Joanne chided her brother-in-law. "Who wouldn't jump at a chance to leave this dinky town? Where will you be going Mr. Connors?"

"Edward—Call me Edward. I'm transferring to Sacramento. Leaving the end of January."

"Sacramento!" Joanne squealed. "I *love* Sacramento. I'd move there in a minute." Her blue eyes sparkled and she beamed as if he'd announced he was moving into a million dollar house on the Street of Dreams and she could be his neighbor. "We have friends there, don't we, Tom? He's an attorney. She's a nurse. I'll have to give you their address and phone number. I *know* you would like them."

Tom, seated on Kathleen's left, cut a bite of turkey, and aimed a smile in her direction. "My wife is from L.A. She thinks people up here in Oregon are still playing cowboys and Indians. A shootout our idea of Saturday night entertainment."

Joanne stuck her tongue out at Tom. "Ignore him—Kathleen, I know you would like Sacramento. California has so much more to offer when it comes to the arts and entertainment. And their restaurants—well, I haven't found anything in Portland to compare."

Edward sat up straighter. "Sacramento is only a start. I don't intend to *stay* there." His voice sounded a bit frosty. "I think the real cultural advantages are in the east. Maybe New York City."

Tom, gave a barely perceptible snicker and grinned across the table at his wife. Of the Kestler boys, Bill had inherited the tall good looks, an average-sized nose, dark curly hair, and brown eyes. Tom was tall enough, but his nose was startling. It was the first thing you noticed. If it were Halloween, and not Christmas, one would think he wore a false nose and glasses. His myopic eyes were neither brown nor green.

Kathleen pushed food around on her plate. Her smile felt plastic and her head began to ache.

"Bill, please send the turkey around again, and the potatoes and gravy, too," Rosie said.

When everyone declared they couldn't hold another bite, the three older girls, Rachel, Becky, and Ruth, helped Rosie clear the table and serve three kinds of pie for dessert, lemon meringue, peanut butter, and pumpkin. Mrs. Smith brought her specialty, a four-layer chocolate-cherry cake. If this wasn't enough, Rosie had candy dishes filled with fudge, divinity, and nuts. A Santa Claus tray held four kinds of cookies.

Kathleen sipped her coffee and prayed she could do justice to a small portion of lemon meringue pie. Edward, beside her, polished off a piece of peanut butter pie, and an ample serving of Mrs. Smith's cake, and still had room for three pieces of fudge.

Rosie looked at her husband and smiled sweetly. "Bill, the ladies and I are going to retire to the basement. You may have the honor of clearing the table and loading the dishwasher."

"Well, guys. You heard the boss. Shall we?"

"And don't try to con the girls. They've helped all morning. They're free to change their clothes and go play."

The Kestler's party room was designed for fun and comfort. Cozy chairs and couches invited one to sit and relax. A Douglas fir stood in the corner, decorated with red cardinals, white doves, bluebirds, and miniature bird's nests.

Anita sank on the sofa beside Kathleen. "My dear, you're quite pale. Are you feeling all right?"

Before she could answer, Joanne, still smarting from Edward's remark about Sacramento, gave her a pointed look. "Pardon me, but your Mr. Connors seems a bit snooty. Do *you* think New York City has *that* much more to offer, than say California?"

Rosie looked shocked and started to protest, but stopped when Kathleen erupted into laughter. "You know what, Joanne? I couldn't agree more. He did sound snooty. I wouldn't know about the east, since I'm an Oregonian. Born and reared here. I rather *like* small towns, and the little elementary school, where Rosie and I teach, suits me just fine."

Joanne stared at her, but had no more to say.

I've done it now. Kathleen thought, her head beginning to pound. Ashamed of her outburst, she sent an apologetic look to her friend and caught Rosie's wink. There'd be time for talk later.

Chapter 16

It looked as if the kids might get their wish. The temperature dropped, and a few scattered snowflakes floated through the air, in no rush to reach the ground. The local weather forecast projected one to two inches of snow down to the valley floor by morning.

"Rosie, I think your father and I better head home," Anita said. "It looks like the storm could be arriving a little sooner than predicted, and those west hills, as you know, can get pretty slick."

"Mom, you and Dad could stay overnight."

"I know, dear. But you know your father. He'll want to get home."

The women trooped upstairs to find and consult with the men. Tom wasn't worried about driving in a little snow, and he, Joanne, and their brood opted to stay. A football game was underway on TV. Mr. Smith, true to Anita's prediction, wanted to leave for home. Kathleen felt relieved when Edward suggested they go, too.

"Merry Christmas. Thank you for a lovely dinner." Voices of departing guests mingled. "Good Bye. Look! It's snowing... Merry Christmas." Arms waved and happy calls echoed.

Edward guided the BMW onto the two-lane highway. "I don't mind telling you, Kathleen, I'm glad to get out of there. Haven't the Kestlers ever heard of an artificial tree? Three live trees in the house, for Pete's sake—and greenery everywhere. My sinuses feel like they've been sandpapered." He wiped his nose. "It's a relief to be back in the car and away from all that—that *forest.*"

"I'm sorry. I suppose Rosie didn't think of anyone having allergies. The trees were beautiful, though, don't you think?

"The one in the living room wasn't bad, but what was with that tree in the family room? It looked like a discard from a refugee camp. And I can't say I'm particularly wild about birds and bird nests. Unless they're out in the woods, where I can avoid them"

"The one in the family room? That's the children's tree. Rosie lets her kids decorate their own tree."

"Yeah? Well, it looks like they could have used a little supervision," he groused. "And while we're on the subject of kids, did they have to eat at the main table? Nathan chewed part-time with his mouth open. And what's-her-name, Susie? slopped gravy on herself. Couldn't they have eaten in the kitchen?"

She didn't answer, and the silence stretched between them with only the hum of tires on wet pavement, and a few intermittent snowflakes hitting the window, for distraction.

"You don't agree, do you? I might have known you

wouldn't. Kathleen, you've really got a thing when it comes to kids, you know that?"

"You haven't had a very good day have you?" She spoke in carefully measured tones. "Is there anything about this Christmas you've enjoyed?"

He threw her a sharp look. "I like time spent with *you.*" His voice conciliatory as he reached over and took her hand. "Kathleen, let's go back to my place. It's only seven o'clock. Make hot chocolate. Watch a movie. I have several classics, any one of which I wouldn't mind seeing again—with you."

"I don't think so, Edward." She withdrew her hand. "Maybe I'm still tired from the ordeal of the last few days, but I have a headache, and I'd really just like to go home."

"You could take some aspirin. Lie down on my bed for awhile. Come on, Kathleen. It's early. Spend the rest of Christmas with *me*."

"I'm sorry. I really am tired, and it's starting to snow harder. The roads could get treacherous. Please—Just take me home now."

"Okay!—If that's the way you want it—I will." He accelerated and the car picked up speed. "A *blizzard* didn't keep you from cavorting around Chicago with your old boyfriend. Did it? Or from sleeping in his bed. But now you won't even spend the *evening* with me. And your excuse is—the roads might get a little *snow* on them?"

Not wanting to start World War III, she bit her lip, massaged her temples, and struggled to hold her temper until he'd parked in the driveway. With one hand on the door handle, the redhead turned to her escort. "Edward, you have many fine qualities." *Though right now, I can't think what they are.* The thought flashed unbidden through her mind like a neon sign. "I predict you will go far. But—I know now I'm *not* the woman to go with you. I wish you well—but I don't think we should keep seeing each other—I'm sorry."

Before he could react and stop her, Kathleen stepped from the car and sprinted for Mrs. Fisher's back entrance. Startled, he fought the need to go after her. Drag her out (maybe by the hair) and make her see reason. He swore, slapped the steering wheel, and spewed expletives he'd forgotten he knew. He wanted to break something. Instead, he could only back from the driveway and ease onto the highway.

He was tempted to drive fast. But snow fell in earnest now. He wasn't such an idiot, no matter how angry, that he wanted to wreck his car. But if Kathleen thought he'd lay down and play *dead*.

• • •

Trembling, Kathleen eased off her boots and crept down the hall and up the stairs in stocking feet. A peek in the living room had revealed Martha alone, dozing before the fire, chin resting on her chest, afghan forgotten in her lap. Snowball slept curled up in his basket.

Thankful to be alone, she closed her door and eased to the window to touch her hot forehead against the frosty glass. Fat snowflakes danced and swirled in illumination from the yard light. It was hard to recall a time of being excited about a white Christmas. She'd seen too much snow recently. Bears had the right idea. Hibernate.

A tear escaped down her cheek. She felt disconcerted, like she'd failed an important test. At the same time it felt as if she'd been relieved of a burden carried too long.

She should phone her mom and dad, but her mother was sure to catch the nuances in her voice and guess that something was amiss. Kathleen loved her mother, but she didn't feel like playing twenty-questions on this Christmas day that had been less than perfect. Maggie O'Brien could be relentless when uncovering mysteries in the life of her daughter—especially if she suspected someone of mistreating her. She peeled away layers, faster than winter-wet clothing from a four-year-old.

Instead, she sent an e-mail. She told them about Rosie's wonderful dinner. *I ate too much.* About the children's happy faces. *Little Nathan's so adorable.* How the fragrant smell of evergreens reminded her of their own tree when she was a little girl. *Remember, Mom, Dad? We always had a fir tree. You let Michael and me help pick it out.* A nice, safe Christmas letter, guaranteed to make them smile.

If only Mom doesn't think it strange, I don't mention Edward. Or if she did, she wouldn't ask until Kathleen could think of some soul-satisfying explanation—one that didn't call for her one-and-only daughter becoming an old maid.

She crept about the room, undressing and quietly arranging her clothes in the closet. Mrs. Fisher never intruded on her private domain, but if she suspected her home early, she might well call up the stairs. Something about Christmas, people naturally assumed you didn't want to be alone.

Glad she'd saved her mother's gift until now, she shook

out the flannel nightgown and slipped the cozy comfort over her head. The yellow butterflies, flitting across a pale blue background, made her smile. Silently she blessed Maggie for mailing the package in time for Christmas. *With all the changes in plans, I'm surprised she remembered.* Kathleen's own packages for her family were going to be very late.

One more peek out the window told her it was snowing hard.

Her cell phone off, she reached over and took the receiver from the cradle of the land phone and laid it on the bedside table. If bears could sleep through a storm undisturbed, one weary confused human should have the right to do the same.

Edward looked angry enough to chew ice cubes and spit fire, Kathleen thought as she knelt beside her bed. *I can't talk to him now. Maybe this snowstorm will give us time to cool off and think clearly.* If she spent a little longer than usual on her knees, the bed felt no less welcoming. She nestled beneath the covers and soon fell asleep.

• • •

Kathleen rolled over, slid one eye open and squinted at the clock. Nine? *Could that be right?* She yawned, stretched, opened both eyes and peered at the clock again. *I can't believe I've slept for twelve hours. Not since I had the flu, have I stayed in bed this long.* Maybe she should play Rip Van Winkle more often. She felt wonderful.

She hurried over to the window, pulled aside the drape, and stared at the ground below. Martha's boot prints tracked from the house to the birdfeeder hanging in the apple tree.

Chickadees, nuthatches, and Oregon juncos vied for the sunflower seed. Robins fluffed their feathers, managed to look thoroughly miserable, and systematically stripped the holly tree of berries.

At least six inches of snow transformed the world beyond the window into a potential winter playground. *I hope Patti won't try to play in the snow. She should stay indoors and warm.*

Apparently, the cattle didn't think much of the white stuff. They stood in little knots around the barn, heads lowered, noses puffing out small clouds of steam into the frosty air. The sun made a weak effort to shine, but it lacked heat.

Warm from her shower, and thinking she might like to hike through the woods, Kathleen dug her old gray sweat pants from the bottom drawer and pulled them on over even older blue leotards. A baggy cable knit sweater, of indeterminate colors, new ten years ago, fit loosely over a cotton tee shirt and long-sleeved yellow turtleneck.

Two pair of socks, the last heavy woolen, encased her feet before she stuffed them down into fleece-lined zippered boots that hugged her calves. She gathered her hair into a ponytail high on the back of her head, and secured it with a red rubber band. Her face, scrubbed clean and devoid of makeup, glowed pink.

Officially, Kathleen rented the upstairs apartment from Mrs. Fisher. One bedroom had been converted into a tiny kitchenette/living-dining area. A former sewing room, off the bedroom, with a large window facing the road, now served as her office. Her own bathroom, with both tub and shower, offered privacy and comfort.

Within two weeks of her moving in, Martha had treated her more like a member of the family than a renter. She invited her for meals and insisted she feel free to use the larger kitchen. They slipped into an easy camaraderie of cooking, eating, and visiting. Kathleen contributed to the groceries and usually did the evening cleanup. She found Martha now, sitting in the sunny breakfast nook, nursing a cup of coffee.

"Ah, Kathleen, good morning. You look all bright-eyed and bushy-tailed on this snowy day."

"Thank you. I think I may have finally caught up on my sleep."

"Well, the coffee's hot. You can make yourself a proper breakfast, or you can do what I did and breakfast on leftovers."

Martha twinkled up at her as she reached for a cinnamon roll and pinched off a piece to dunk in her cup before popping it in her mouth. "I'm lazy this morning. I've been sitting here an hour just looking at the snow, watching the birds, and studying the tracks. A deer has walked right up the driveway, jumped the fence, there by the garage, and trotted off across the field"

She sipped her coffee and pushed the cinnamon rolls toward Kathleen. "I'd guess it's that old doe, the one I've seen under the apple tree, probably went through here just after daylight. My Earl would've known. He read tracks like a pro."

Kathleen poured herself coffee and cut a piece of pumpkin pie. She sat at the table where she could see the driveway and the road beyond. "Sure is quiet, isn't it?"

"Yes, it is that. Not much traffic this morning. Guess the snow has kept a few people from rushing to the after Christmas sales."

"Oh, Martha, Look! Coming up your driveway."

"Quail. Aren't they pretty? How many are there? Six, a dozen?...More? Hard to count them, they move so fast. But there must be at least fifteen. Martha got up from the table and stood by the window for a better look. "I'm glad I put feed out for them this morning."

Kathleen joined her by the glass to watch the birds, but their attention was diverted when a Jeep slowed on the road, and then turned into the driveway.

"Oh my, who can that be? I don't recognize that car," Martha stated. "Do you?"

"No, but I think I may know who it is. I'll go to the door."

Arms folded across her chest, shoulder leaning against the entryway, she watched as he climbed from the jeep. Hands shoved in his pockets, head down, he strode up the walkway.

"Hello, Edward."

His head snapped up. "Kathleen! I've tried *repeatedly* to call you. What did you do, turn off your phone?"

"Yeah—I did."

He glared at her. "Well, that's kinda juvenile, isn't it?"

Chapter 17

"Kathleen, you can't just *dump* me, and not tell me what this is all about. You at least owe me an explanation. Come to town with me? We can go for pizza."

"Yeah. I think maybe you're right. I suppose I do owe you an explanation. But I must warn you—I don't think it's going to change anything."

He surveyed her less than stylish outfit and offered, "I'll wait in the jeep and keep the heater running if you want to change."

"No—I'm dressed for the day. I don't have any plans to change clothes. I'll just be a sec while I grab a coat."

They made small talk, punctuated by heavy silence, on the drive to Fir Valley. Neither willing to launch the discussion destined to terminate their relationship.

"This is a nice Jeep. Goes good in the snow. Where did you get it?"

"I borrowed it from the new teller, Jeannie, the girl I hired a month ago. She's the only one who didn't have a problem getting to work this morning." Edward scowled. "The city just started plowing the streets when I left. You'd think they'd never seen snow around here before. They seem ill prepared."

• • •

Fortified with a couple slices of pepperoni pizza and mugs of hot cider in front of them, he spoke first. "Kathleen, what is this all about? Is it something I did—said—yesterday? Were you offended when I said I didn't like looking at kids eating with their mouths open?" He shrugged. "Or did something happen while you were in Chicago? I don't know—Kathleen—you seem different—more distant. Are you sure you don't have a thing for that guy you met?"

She struggled to hold the lid on a temper threatening to boil over. "Edward—this is the third time you've thrown Danny in my face. I don't like it, and I'm not going to justify my actions again. If you didn't believe me the first time—you won't believe me the third or fourth time."

"Okay—*Okay*." He held up his hands. "I'm sorry. But I can't help being jealous. Especially when you say you don't want to see me anymore. What am I *supposed* to think? So, are you going to tell me what it is that I've done—that's so *wrong*?"

"I don't know that you've done anything *wrong*. I think you are just being you. In the end, that's all any of us can do. Be ourselves. If we try to be what we're not, we're going to be miserable." She took a deep breath and let it out slowly.

"You're highly intelligent Edward. You have good taste,

and, you're a gentleman. But we are two entirely *different* people. We have different likes, dislikes, and goals. Do you even *know* who I am—and what *I* want?"

He pushed his pizza aside, and stared at her while his face turned red. "What—exactly—is *that* supposed to mean? Do I *know* you? We've been going together almost a year."

"Think about it, Edward. What do you want in a wife? Don't you want someone who will stay home, entertain, join organizations, do charity work? You don't like the idea of having *your* wife work. Do you?"

"But, Kathleen. You won't *need* to work. I'll be able to give you anything you want."

"My point exactly. You haven't been listening. I *want* to teach school. I love children. I love my job. It's what I struggled through five years of college to do. I don't want to throw that away."

He grimaced, took his arms from the table and ran his hands through his hair. "I guess I didn't realize it was *that* important to you. If you really want to teach that bad—I suppose it would be okay for awhile."

"No—it wouldn't be *okay for awhile.* If I married you, I'd know every day I worked—you really didn't want me doing that. You haven't even wanted to know about Patti. Not really."

She looked away, took a deep breath, and met his eyes again. "My involvement with her has been an irritant to you from the beginning—and I really care about that little girl. I'm sorry—Edward—it just won't work. I do wish you well. But I'm not going to marry you and make both of us miserable."

Edward scraped his chair back and rose from the table. The pizza lay between them, cold as a hockey puck, grease congealed. "Well—If you'd rather play nursemaid to a horde of kids—than be my wife—there's nothing more for us to talk about. I'll take you home. Just remember—Kathleen—what I offered you, when you get tired of riding herd on a bunch of ungrateful little brats."

• • •

Kathleen bit her lip and studied her boots as she scrunched across the roadway and into the forest beyond. An egg-sized lump threatened damage to her trachea. *I didn't know a breakup could feel like this.* She gave the snow a kick. In the shelter of the woods, with trees her only witnesses, she released tears and let them flow unchecked down her cheeks. *How could I ever have thought he was the one? I don't think he even likes children, and I'm beginning to wonder about his relationship with God.*

She trudged along, hands jammed in pockets while her chin fraternized with her chest. Gradually the awesome surroundings soothed her bruised heart. Head up, she began paying attention to the beauty around her.

The moss-covered ground remained almost free of snow under the thick canopy of old-growth fir trees. Tall stately giants like these were generally found in parks, but this timber stood on private property. Martha's brother and sister-in-law were the owners, and lived at the edge of the woods in a modest house across the county road from Martha. Both in their late seventies, the Martins had no plans to log off the prime timber, though they were approached by many speculators wanting to buy. Neighborhood children were welcome to play here; in summer, the grove often rang with their laughter.

Trails crisscrossed the forest and a narrow road snaked its way to the river beyond. It was here Kathleen tread, ever so softly. A hush lay over the land today, a feeling of awe, as if she dwelt in a cathedral designed by the masters. The added weight of snow on the branches silenced even their whispers. She stopped in the deepest part of the woods, brushed snow off a mossy log and sat down to listen and worship her Lord at the altar of nature.

A Steller's jay landed on a limb across from where she sat and sent a cascade of snow crashing. Seemingly pleased with his feat, the jay let out a loud squawk, shattering the reverence of quiet and making Kathleen laugh before he flew away.

The somberness of her mood lightened, she got up and journeyed on. Smaller birds hopped in the roadway ahead of her, their weight hardly making a mark in the snow. She rounded a curve, stopped, drew in her breath, and tried to remain perfectly still. There in the path, looking at her, sat a fox. *I wonder if he has a den nearby.*

Thrilled to see this creature of the wild, Kathleen smiled, let her breath out slowly and watched as the fox left his place in the snow, turned and trotted away down the trail. His tail, a magnificent black-tipped brush he brandished behind him, while tiny feet made dainty tracks in the snow.

Maybe she could bring her first-graders here in the spring. The fir grove would make a wonderful nature walk, and it was close enough to the school to provide a good hike for the children. They wouldn't need the school bus. *I'll have to talk to Principal Steele and see what he thinks.* Seeing a fox was unlikely, noisy children being what they are, but they could look for birds and bird nests, wild flowers in bloom, and if she timed it right, they might see the nearly extinct lady slippers.

Kathleen traipsed through the woods and came to the wire gate leading to the river and ultimately the swimming hole where the kids gathered in the summertime to swim and play. No cattle or goats grazed in the fields today and the gate lay sprawled on the ground. She skirted the edge of the hayfield and trod the path beside the water, admiring snow-covered rocks and pristine beaches at the river's edge. Tall evergreen trees, drooping branches draped with nature's fluffy whipped frosting, made a perfect backdrop for steely gray water reflecting today's darkened sky. *What a picture. Wish I'd thought to bring my camera.*

The forgotten camera made her think of Danny. She knew *he* could capture the scene and turn it into something to rival a *Currier and Ives* print. Maybe she could ask his advice on taking pictures of some of the giant old-growth trees. Or better yet, perhaps he might take the pictures himself, if she explained how exceptional they are. Kathleen sighed. *But I'm dreaming. Danny has more important things to do.*

She retraced her tracks through the forest with a decidedly lighter heart. This time she didn't linger, but kicked the pace into fast-forward. Her thoughts raced ahead to the classroom. She'd tell her students about the fox she'd seen. Their eyes would dance with excitement; they loved stories about animals. And first-graders liked to share what they learned at school with their parents. *Has Patti ever seen a fox,* she wondered. Kathleen wasn't sure what kind of fox she'd met on the trail. Was it a gray or a red fox? It's difficult for a novice to distinguish between the two, as their dark winter coats are much the same. If she described it accurately, her landlady might know.

• • •

Something smelled wonderful as soon as she entered the house. A race up the stairs to rid herself of coat, cap, and mittens, and Kathleen sought out the cook. She found Martha in the kitchen adding rice to a large pot.

"Your nose is red. I'll bet you're cold. I looked at the thermometer a bit ago and the temperature is just above freezing. Did you have a nice walk?"

"I did, but I'm glad to be back inside; my fingers and toes were starting to complain. Is that turkey soup that smells so good?"

"Yes," Martha acknowledged. "I thought I'd better make use of all these leftovers. If it snows more, and they're saying we could get another six or eight inches tonight, soup ought to go down pretty good, don't cha think?"

"Oh, I *love* soup, and turkey-rice is one of my favorites. Is there something I can help with?"

"No, I'm about through here in the kitchen. You could add another log to the hearth, though, if you wouldn't mind. I think we'd better keep the fire going just in case we lose our electricity."

"I'll be happy to take care of that. When I finish, I want to tell you about the neat animal I saw."

Martha stopped her stirring. "That sounds exciting, but first, *I* need to tell *you* about the phone call I got while you were gone. Alvin Williams called me. He really wanted to talk to you, but wasn't sure where you were or how to get hold of you. He's worried about Patti. He said he tried to call Amber, but some man answered and hung up on him. I told him what I could."

"Do you know where he called from? Did he give you a number?"

"No. I think he may have been calling from a pay phone. I told him you would be back, shortly. He thanked me, but didn't say if he would call again."

"I wonder if he'll call back? Maybe he's only allowed so many calls."

Martha stirred the soup one more time and laid the wooden spoon aside. "I don't know—that idea troubles me."

Thoughts of Patti were never far from Kathleen's mind, and anticipating a call from Al caused her to replay all the known facts and move on to fears real and imagined. How might she reassure him when her own doubts lay deep? *Will Patti want to play in the snow? And if so, will her mother let her? Doctor Macy warned that Patti needs to be kept warm and dry until all danger of reoccurrence is past. Will Amber remember?* It seemed about as likely as a teacher spending an entire winter day with first-graders and not hearing one cough, sniffle, or sneeze—Possible, but not probable.

"Well, I guess all we can do is wait—and hope." Martha lowered the heat to simmer and slapped a lid on the pot. "I know Alvin's done wrong. However, I can't help feelin' a bit sorry for him, and even sorrier for little Patti. She's gonna miss her daddy—but stewin' about it won't help. I'll fix us a cup of tea."

Chapter 18

They sat by the hearth, drank an entire pot of tea and willed the phone to ring. For awhile they attempted to make small-talk, but finally gave it up and sat gazing into the fire—each lost in her own thoughts. Martha rose to check on the soup. Kathleen thought it a good time to excuse herself and go upstairs. That's when the phone rang.

"It's for you," Martha called from the kitchen.

"Hello."

"It's me...Al Williams."

"Al—I'm glad to hear from you. Where are you?"

"Well, I ain't bustin' rocks on the chain gang. If that's what you're thinkin'."

"Um, something like that, I suppose."

"Kathleen—I guess I'm one lucky dude—But I ain't feelin' very lucky right now. I've screwed things up royally for Patti and me." He coughed. "I'll be lucky if I getta see my daughter before she's eighteen. And my weekends are gonna be pretty busy for awhile."

"You got off with hours of *community service?*"

"Yeah—Ain't that a kick in the head? Amber has full custody of Patti now. I don't dare show my face unless she says I can, and I sure as shootin' can't come anywheres close to the school—unless I wanta do time."

"I'm sorry, Al—How can I help?" Kathleen twisted the phone cord around her fingers.

"Well, I was hopin' you could tell me about Patti. How she is?" He cleared his throat. "I tried callin' Amber. Some jerk—answered—and hung up on me. I'll tell you one thing. If I catch that son-of-a-knock-kneed-goat out somewhere—he won't be hangin' up on anyone for awhile. I'll break both his arms."

"*Al*—If you do that—you *will* go to prison. You don't want your daughter to have to say her father's in prison—do you?"

"Yeah—I suppose you're right. But if I can taunt him into hittin' me first—I can bust his nose."

She made sure he heard her exasperated sigh. "*Al*—Stay out of *trouble*."

"Yeah—teacher—I suppose I can try." He sounded like one of her first-graders. "About that other little matter you were handlin' for me. You still got it? Or did you bank it?"

"I have it."

"Okay. That's cool. Can you meet me in Fir Valley? I ain't gotta car—I havta do somethin' about that—I can't come out there, so can you make it in here? They got the roads plowed and sanded. At least they have in here."

She had told no one about the money. It seemed wiser

if people didn't know she carried cash given to her by Mr. Williams—most especially his ex-wife Amber. Kathleen had considered asking Edward to set up an account at the bank and handle the transaction for her, but decided at the last minute to say nothing.

"I'm pretty sure I can make it to Fir Valley if I can get onto the highway. They plowed the road here about an hour ago, but backing my car out of the garage could be a problem. I wasn't expecting snow or ice this soon, and I've neglected putting snow tires on my car. There's about six inches of snow in the driveway. Where should I meet you? Assuming my car leaves the garage."

"I'll be waitin' in the drugstore. It's warm, and there's chairs over by the pharmacy. They plowed the parkin' lot at that grocery store across the street. You could park over there." Al sneezed. "They got the curb here blocked with snow. Don't worry if it takes ya awhile to drive in here. I'll wait—I got nowhere to go."

Kathleen found Martha seated in her rocker beside the blazing hearth, her hands busily crocheting an afghan. "I need to go to town for awhile if I can get out with my car. And I think I can if I maybe shovel a bit of snow first, and get a run at it. Is there anything I should pick up while I'm there?"

"Oh, no Dear. You shouldn't have to shovel snow," the landlady protested. "Frank called about noon and said he'd be right over with his tractor and plow my driveway. I can't imagine what's keeping him. Maybe I better give him a call and see if I can hurry him along."

Well, some things work out. The timing couldn't be better. Mr. Fisher chugged up the driveway with his tractor and began blading away the snow before she had time to button her coat.

"That should do ya," Frank called as he bladed snow from the driveway and pushed it into a dirty pile beside the road.

"Thanks a million. I can make it for sure now." Kathleen backed her old Chevy slowly down the driveway and eased the car out onto the highway.

• • •

She found Al sitting in a chair by the pharmacy, as he said. What she didn't expect was the smile he flashed her. He looked a bit haggard, like a truck driver too long on the road. She sensed, as she took the chair beside him—this was a man refusing to be beaten. She wouldn't want him for an adversary. It was more than the physical, though she doubted there were many men he couldn't beat in a fair fight. No, it was something deeper than that.

Kathleen opened her purse and handed him a plain white envelope with all the bills sealed inside. "It's all there, but you maybe should count it."

"Nah. I trust you. Besides, it'd just be my word against yours. And who'd believe *me*?"

Few people were in the store. Cashiers stood around visiting. A gentleman waited for a prescription to be filled. And one or two brave souls wandered the aisles looking for after-Christmas bargains.

"What will you do now, Al? Will you be living in Fir Valley?"

"Nah. I don't think I wanna hang around here. Kinda depends on what I end up doin'. I wouldn't mind gettin' me a little trailer, settin' up in the woods somewhere." He ran a hand through his hair. "If I'm real lucky, I might get my old job back. Drivin' truck for Orwell. He's the guy bought my rig." He flashed her another grin, but it was pure plastic. This time, Kathleen caught the look of sadness in his eyes.

"Anyway, I thank you for your help." Al stood and shoved the envelope with the money down an inside pocket. "Come on, I'll walk you to your car. Who knows, maybe someday, if I ever get ten minutes to call my own, you'd have a cupa coffee with me?"

She smiled, but didn't comment.

"Maybe you could let me know how Patti's doing? Send a copy of her report card? That's if Amber don't raise a fuss." He looked at the floor.

Preoccupied, Kathleen glanced up just in time to see the couple trip the automatic glass doors and enter the drugstore. Too late, she put out a hand to warn him. By the time he looked up and saw his ex-wife, they were within inches of each other.

Startled, it took a few seconds for Amber to comprehend who she saw. "*You!*" she hissed. Faster than a rattler strikes, she drew her arm back. With the determination of a home run hitter; she smacked Al Williams across the face.

The sharp crack of an open hand striking flesh resounded throughout the quiet drugstore—more riveting than a holdup.

Kathleen took two steps back before her feet behaved as if she'd stepped in a fresh spill of quickset glue. She gasped, horrified, as Al's ears turned red as tomatoes and his face looked hot enough to fry eggs.

Clerks stopped their gossip mid-sentence to stare open-mouthed at the disturbance taking place in the front of the store. The pharmacist stepped from behind the high counter and peered around the corner trying to see what the ruckus was about. One customer, a lady wide as a loveseat, waddled and puffed her way up the isle to stand and stare unabashed.

Everyone stood frozen, waiting to see what happened next. Kathleen sucked in her breath and prayed Al wouldn't explode and physically retaliate. The heat of anger beginning to cool, Amber turned pale and stepped back as her ex-husband pointed a finger directly under her nose.

"Congratulations! *Amber*!" Al snarled. "You assaulted me. Think I should press *charges*?" He lowered his voice, clipped his words, and spat them at her, like ice pellets from a winter storm. "Feel better? Or would you like to try for *scratchin'* an *bitin'*, too? *Go ahead.* Make a scene—you're *good* at it. We could *both* end up in the slammer," he threatened. *You* might just end up *losin'* Patti for good, and this time it wouldn't be *me* takin' her. Then neither of us'll know what happens to her."

"Hey, jerk. You can't talk to her like that," Spike spluttered.

"Listen—*Sonny Boy*—this is none of your business. And if it were—you're not man enough to stop me." Al thrust his chin out and glowered at him, daring Spike to make something of it. "And if you're the hound that hung up on me when I called earlier today—I warn you—*don't* try it again. I'll look you up and shove the phone down your throat.

"Amber, you wanted *your* daughter back so bad, but you just couldn't wait to start chasin' around again—could you? What rock did you find this little weasel under? And where'd ya dump Patti *this* time?"

"Now just a cotton-pickin' minute," Spike blustered.

"Oh, *shut up*! Both of you!" Amber snapped. "For your information—*Al*—I didn't *dump* Patti. I'm here to pick up a prescription for her, and as for where she is, you won't get *your* hands on her again. I'll see to that. So don't bother asking."

She shot Kathleen an accusatory look before lifting her chin and striding back to the pharmacy. Spike shrugged his shoulders, brushed past Al and followed in her wake like a dinghy behind a speedboat.

Kathleen wasn't sure if Spike was brave or just stupid. It took guts to confront an angry man who could easily break him in two. Of one thing the teacher felt confident, the news of the near-fight in the drugstore would spread all over town faster than an outbreak of influenza through a school.

I can just imagine what they're going to say. People will wonder what Patti's teacher was doing there. Was she with Mr. Williams? It certainly looked as if she were. With as much dignity as she could muster, eyes straight ahead, she strode to the doors and like Moses parting the Red Sea, bid them open and let her escape.

Safely back in her car, she locked the doors and gripped the steering wheel with white-knuckled fingers. A tear slid down her cheek, and she fought the giddy impulse to laugh as she dropped her head on her hands. The whole episode in the drugstore took less time than it takes to pick up a phoned-in prescription. She felt wrung out, as if *she* were the one needing medication. She didn't like having attention focused on her, even if she was an innocent bystander.

The thought of Patti brought fresh tears to her eyes. Children were hurt in the most amicable of divorces, and these two seemed intent on tearing each other apart. Not for the first time Kathleen wondered if they ever considered what they were doing to their daughter, or if she was just a pawn in their spiteful war.

She brushed the tears from her face, fastened her seatbelt, and started the engine. Slowly she began pulling out of the parking lot. She glanced at the automobile parked nearby, and braked for a closer look. *That's Spike's car.* And there sat Patti in the backseat, a fuzzy yellow blanket wrapped closely around her. Only her eyes and nose were visible, and her eyes were shut. One relieved teacher breathed a huge sigh of relief, and smiled as she drove away.

Chapter 19

A dark and threatening sky loomed overhead. Instead of going home, she turned left and drove to Les Schwab Tire Center. It was time to get snow tires.

The waiting room bulged with customers. Kathleen took a seat in the corner and quickly hid her face behind a magazine. Seated two chairs down on her left, sat the large lady she recognized from the drugstore. The woman held an animated conversation with the person sitting next to her, a fairly accurate blow-by-blow description of the fracas in the drugstore being recounted.

"I don't know who those people were," she wheezed. "But I thought there'd be a knock-down-drag-out right there. I'm here to tell you, the sparks were a flyin'. The only thing I can't figure—is what the schoolteacher was doin' there, looked like she was with that man got slapped. I'm pretty sure it was Miss O'Brien. She's my little grandson's teacher, you know." The woman gulped air as her enormous chest rose and fell. "I only seen her that once—but that red hair an all—I'm sure it was her. And I hear tell she's engaged to that banker fella, too. How do ya figure?"

Oh, mercy. This is even worse than I imagined it might be. Kathleen cringed knowing the story would soon reach Edward's ears, and though she owed him no explanation, she wanted her reputation untarnished when he left town. Her Irish temper did a slow boil. She dropped the magazine to her lap and leaned toward the lady doing the talking.

"Ma'am?" She waited until the woman's attention focused and she saw comprehension dawn in her eyes. "I know for a fact the schoolteacher isn't engaged to the banker, and she wasn't with that man in the drugstore. If by *with*, you mean dating."

Already beginning to regret her outbreak, she smiled, hoping it wasn't too late to relieve the woman's red-faced embarrassment. It never worked for good when one spoke in anger. "I'm sorry. As you've guessed by now, I'm Miss O'Brien. Did I hear you say your grandson is one of my students?"

"Oh, yes." She gushed, relieved to have the subject diverted. "Johnny—I'm Mrs. Walker, Johnny's grandma. Miss O'Brien, my Johnny just *loves* you—talks about you all the time."

"I'm glad to meet you, Mrs. Walker. It's a joy to have John in my class. He's a very bright little boy."

She beamed and laid her hand gently on the arm of the woman sitting between them. "Miss O'Brien, this is my neighbor, Nancy Truaxe."

"Nice to meet you. Forgive my rudeness for talking over you. I'm afraid this hasn't been my best day."

"Only if you'll forgive us for gossiping about you."

"Miss O'Brien, that little girl that was taken from the school. Have they found her?

• • •

She knew it was only a matter of time until the ladies, and the rest of the town, learned the identity of the people causing the ruckus in the drugstore. They wouldn't, however, hear it from her. She longed to shield Patti from the gossip. If only there were a prescription to heal the hurtful things people say. Regretfully, all she could offer were her teaching skills and her love. Would it be enough to help one little girl through the turmoil her parents generated?

• • •

It started snowing again the moment she left Fir Valley; at first, only tiny insignificant flakes floated willy-nilly toward earth. Before she could drive the eight miles home, huge flakes tumbled from dark clouds intent on dumping their load. The closest thing to a whiteout she'd ever experienced. Thankful to be home, she parked her car in the garage and trudged through snow to the backdoor.

Martha's granddaughter, Charlene, the ever present cell stuck to her ear, let the storm door bang. They nearly collided as Kathleen struggled up the back steps.

"Oh. Hi, Miss O'Brien. I just brought in a ton of wood for Grandma. You guys won't haveta worry about being cold. Boy! Lookadit snow. I gotta get home and help Dad feed cattle—Bye."

The lights flickered once, brightened, and then went out while she helped herself to a cup of hot tea in the kitchen. Cup balanced, she made her way carefully through the darkened house and found Martha already lighting kerosene lamps previously placed in strategic spots in the living room. A fire blazed cheerfully on the hearth and a large carrier of wood stood at the ready.

"Kathleen. Thank God, you're home. I was about to call out the cavalry to go look for you. I think we're really in for it. I didn't expect the power to go off this soon."

"I'm glad to be home, it's wicked out there! I stopped and had snow tires put on the car; just in time I'd say." Kathleen pulled her chair a little closer to the fire, savored her tea and took the plunge. "Martha, I might as well tell you, as I'm sure it will be all over town before it quits snowing—"

She listened, nodding her head, to indicate she was paying close attention. "Well, I'm not too surprised by the fracas in the drugstore. Theirs was a stormy marriage from the beginning. I'm just sorry for little Patti. Her mother will tire soon enough of taking sole responsibility for her, especially when the fun of locking horns and punishing Al grows old."

Martha rose, traipsed to the kitchen and brought back the teapot. She replenished their cups with liquid kept hot by the tea cozy, settled back in her chair, sipped slowly, and began a narrative to enlighten the young teacher.

"Clara, Alvin's grandmother, has practically raised Patti from the time she was born. They lived with Clara and Henry up until about a year ago. Clara mothered them all; Amber was pretty much free to play momma or not as the fancy struck her. Clara loves that little great-granddaughter, but she scarcely sees her now—and she can't baby-sit even if Amber would allow it."

Like *Caspar the Friendly Ghost,* Snowball appeared from the shadows. He stationed himself before the fire and wrapped his substantial tail around his feet like an old man's lap robe. But not before going to each lady in turn and rubbing his silky head against their legs by way of greeting. Martha reached to pet him before continuing her narrative.

"No, I'm afraid Clara has her hands full. Henry doesn't even try to get out of bed now; his arthritis is so bad."

"Al's *grandparents*? Does he not have parents, then?"

"No, and that's a sad story. Both killed in a light plane crash when Alvin was about a year old. I think, if I remember correctly, Alvin's father, had just gotten his pilot's license; they were celebrating an anniversary." Flames blazed high in the fireplace as Martha continued. "Clara and Henry were keeping the baby until they got back. They crashed somewhere in the mountains—took weeks to find their bodies."

Beyond the reach of the fire the room began to cool. Kathleen helped fill bowls with soup, still hot from the long simmer on the kitchen range. They ate turkey-rice soup, and fresh-baked bread slathered with butter, in the living room in front of the fire.

Does Mrs. Williams have anyone to help her with her husband?"

"I know what you're thinking," Martha said. "Why isn't Alvin there helping his grandmother? Well, you have to know Clara; if Alvin stayed there she would boss him around, mother him, and insist on doing for him, too. It would just mean more work for her."

Old fashioned kerosene lamps cast a cheery orange glow around their chairs, an island of light closing them in. Martha continued, "I go once a week and sit with Henry so Clara can go grocery shopping or whatever she needs to do. I might vacuum or do a load of laundry while I'm there. Clara objected at first, but we've been friends a long time. I generally get my way. Friends from church help out, too. She has a pretty good support system."

Kathleen stepped to the window and peered out when she heard a truck lumbering by on the roadway. The headlights revealed snow coming down faster than ever. She opened the door and stepped out onto the porch. Nothing she knew of smelled quite like snow, air scrubbed cleaner than a breeze off the ocean. *I wonder if I'll ever see snow without thinking of Chicago, Patti, and Danny.* The four had become almost synonymous in her thinking. Danny? Where was he tonight?

Lost in her thoughts, a moment or two passed before she realized Martha stood beside her. An almost reverential awe fell over them as they witnessed falling snow blanketing the earth, a silence that called for like response.

"It's beautiful isn't it? Kind of takes your breath away. But I suppose we'd better go in before we catch pneumonia." Neither woman had bothered to put on a coat before venturing out, and Martha shivered.

With cheeks beginning to take on the hue of burnished apples and a nose akin to Rudolph, they sought the warmth of the fire. Curiosity stirred by what she had learned, Kathleen prompted her companion to continue the narrative.

"What about Amber? Does she have family?"

"She has a mother. I'm afraid Velma isn't much help. The polite term for what she is, is alcoholic; but most people simply refer to her as the town drunk. Or worse—Velma wanders from bar to bar and will leave with anyone who cares to buy her a few drinks and maybe a meal."

"And her father? Does she have a father?"

"If she does, I don't think she has any idea where he is. Some say he left them when Amber was very young. Others say Velma didn't know who the father was." Martha sighed, pushed the glasses up on her nose, peered at the young woman across from her, and reached for the afghan she crocheted, before continuing the account.

"To her credit Velma worked hard, cleaned houses for people, slung hash, baby sat, took odd jobs, and raised Amber pretty much on her own. Though by the time she became a teenager, it was a question of who took care of whom.

"Velma never liked Alvin, and Alvin detested her. She visited some, after the baby came, wanting to see Patti. Clara always tried to be nice to her. If Alvin was there, he'd get up and storm out of the house.

The fire crackled, popped, and sent a shower of sparks upward. Kathleen added another log to the flames. There was something about an open fire and the soft glow of lamplight that invited intimacy. And with the power off, there wasn't much to do but talk. Her computer dark, there would be no e-mail. She really didn't mind; Google couldn't give her the information to help Patti but listening to Mrs. Fisher might.

"What does Amber do? I've never heard her say. I assume she works."

"She's a beautician and quite good, I'm told. She always did Clara's hair...before the breakup. Henry sent her through beauty school.

"Charlene's done some babysitting for Patti, and she said Amber asked her to stay overnight New Year's Eve. Wants her to come early, about five. Sounds like a big night is planned, but this snow just may change things."

"Patti must be doing all right then, or surely her mother wouldn't leave her."

If neither lady believed Amber could be trusted to put her daughter's needs first, they preferred a fairy tale ending to voicing those fears.

"I shall try to keep the fire going all night; if I let it go out, the house is going to be colder than the freezer in a meat market." Martha yawned and stretched. "I'll set my old alarm and get up every few hours and add more wood. There's extra blankets in the upstairs closet, and you'll surely want them. It's bound to be frigid up there."

"I have a better idea. Why don't I make a bed for myself, here on the couch? I'll tend the fire, and you won't need to get up. That way, we'll both stay warmer and sleep better."

Martha protested, but only mildly. "Well then, I'll wish you good night. Try not to worry over-much about Patti. Things have a way of coming right."

Chapter 20

Kathleen parked her Chevy alongside Rosie's Ford station wagon and shut off the engine. Snowplows had cleared the parking area and pushed snow into sodden dirty heaps around the perimeter. Other teachers would no doubt be coming to prepare classrooms on this Saturday before school started again, but so far it seemed they were the only two brave enough, or crazy enough, to leave their beds and come so early. Unsullied snow carpeted the playground, but it looked tired and deflated, like meringue on a pie after three days in the refrigerator.

She took her box of materials from the car and trudged through the slush to Rosie's classroom. Lights were on and her co-worker sat at her desk making out lesson plans. She looked up and smiled when Kathleen entered.

"I'm glad you're here. I've wanted to call you ever since that fiasco at Christmas, but it seems I haven't had a moment to call my own. Tom left Joanne and their kids with us until yesterday and it's been a circus, let me tell you. Only not the kind you'd pay to see. One more day—and I might have strangled Joanne."

Rosie snorted and motioned to a chair. "I'm really sorry about that stupid remark she made in relation to Edward being arrogant. Sometimes I think Joanne has sawdust for brains, and if anyone is arrogant, she is. As well as lazy, thoughtless, and rude, since I'm being charitable," she grumbled. "I'm lucky to escape to my classroom, or I might be in jail for murder."

She laughed, set her box down, and slid into a seat near the teacher's desk. "Well, I'm glad you haven't murdered your sister-in-law. I know she gets under your skin, but you have to admit there's validity to what she said. Edward *was* arrogant."

"Well, if he was, and mind you, I'm not saying it's so, she had no right to confront *you* the way she did."

"It's okay, my friend, you can be honest. You're not going to hurt my feelings. Edward and I have agreed to disagree. I'm not sure why it's taken me so long to admit the truth. We could never make it as husband and wife. We're just too different."

"Oh dear!" Rosie scanned her face. "Then it's not just the Christmas debacle? You've split up?"

"He isn't taking it very well, but we're no longer an item."

"He's angry?"

"You might say that."

"Well, that puts a different light on things." Rosie leaned back in her chair and surveyed her co-worker. "You know,

Bill couldn't figure it out, he saw Edward in the restaurant with the new teller. Bill said 'if she'd been ice cream, Edward would have eaten her with a spoon.' People were staring and snickering."

"Oh? That doesn't sound like him, but it's none of my business; he can do whatever he wants. I just hope the girl doesn't get hurt."

"Honey, he's doing it to make you jealous. He's counting on it making the rounds and getting back to you."

"Rosie, he's wasting his time. I don't *care* what he does." The corners of her mouth turned up in a smirk. "What I do care about, is my students. I'd better get to my room and make some preparations. I thought about doing a thing with snowflakes, but I'm so tired of looking at snow, I've about changed my mind."

"I know whatcha mean. I'm tired of snow, and I haven't dealt with being snowbound in Chicago, as you have. All I've done this past week is dry wet clothes and wipe up tracks while Joanne sat on her duff and watched television. The kids must have made twenty trips a day out to play in the snow," Rosie huffed. "I think even they are tired of it.

"I know you're eager to get to your room; I won't keep you now, but I'm anxious to hear all about your adventures—and Patti. Come to my room for lunch, and you can tell me all the juicy details then." She looked up and winked. "I brought enough sandwiches to share in case you didn't bring any."

"I did bring a sandwich, but I'm not averse to seeing what goodies you have." She snickered. "I'll fill you in at noon, and I might even divulge some privileged information if you brought some of your chocolate chip cookies."

Back in her classroom, the young teacher deposited everything on her desk and took special notice of the room. The janitor had waxed and buffed the floor until it gleamed like new vinyl in a showroom.

Desks arranged in groups of four throughout the room encouraged children to share and learn. At the beginning of the school year, she set up a book corner with two white-painted bookcases pulled together to form an L. Delightful books, with pictures and illustrations designed to capture the attention of even the most challenged learner, lined the shelves. Bright red, blue, and yellow baskets placed along the wall, held more books. Two small-sized beanbags—one yellow, one blue—rounded out the reading corner.

I just need to change a couple bulletin boards, she thought. Put up some new backgrounds and go with a winter theme—maybe even a few snowflakes. I don't know, I'll have to think about it.

Kathleen sang as she worked and time passed quickly. She stepped back and surveyed the room with satisfaction. Words written with a green magic marker on yellow strips of paper and pinned to form an arch against a blue background said:

Read Winter Books—Write Winter Poems

Fun-to-write poems, poems to challenge and teach. A refresher for students to spell and identify their colors. Four-line poems: first line a color, second line a noun, third line a verb, and then write a sentence using the color, noun, and verb. When completed, their sentences would be read and displayed on the bulletin board.

Mr. Steele pushed the door open and strode into her classroom. "Mornin', Kathleen. I just talked to Rosie; you guys certainly got here early today. Are you ready for all those little bodies to troop in here Monday? Ready for the next big push?" Hands on hips, he surveyed the room. "Looks like you've been busy. New bulletin boards up, aren't they? Interesting."

"Yes, I've made a few changes for our winter season."

"Well, we'll get down to business Monday morning. It's my experience, learning really gets going after the Christmas holidays. Before January, there's too many days off. Too many distractions. Too much time taken just establishing order and routines when school starts in September."

The principal eased into the large white rocking chair. "I like the idea of a rocking chair in this room, but it would never do for me to have one. I'd sit in it and go to sleep."

Kathleen laughed. "That's my story-time chair. I sit in it to read to the children, and my helpers use it as an exemplary behavior privilege. It's working quite well. Two at a time can read and rock if they don't get too boisterous."

"Uh-huh." Dick nodded and smiled. "Well, we need incentives. I wish we had more than two computers for this room. I think we will next year. I'm trying to convince the school board to budget for them. They're a good teaching tool and shouldn't have to be limited. I know you're using time on the ones we have as a privilege, but I hope you'll work it so everyone gets some experience on them."

"Oh, I do. New helpers are appointed each day, and they earn time on the computers by passing out materials for me, straightening books on the shelves, things like that."

"Swell...And what about that little Williams girl? How'd that turn out? Will she be back in school Monday?"

"I think so. I hope so. Patti's back home with her mother. Mrs. Williams has full custody now. The judge gave Mr. Williams about a zillion hours of community service; I thought he'd be in prison, but he's not. Of course he's lost all rights and contact with Patti; he doesn't *dare* come close to our school."

Kathleen exhaled. "I wanted to ask you, Dick, about the advisability of sending reports of Patti's progress to Mr. Williams. I know he'd like to hear how his daughter is doing, and Mrs. Williams hasn't forbidden it, but then I haven't asked her either. There's an awful lot of animosity there, and I think if I do ask her permission, she'll say no."

"I see—okay...I'll check. Don't do anything until I find out what the law is on this. I'll give the judge a call. We wouldn't want to get into litigation over something so asinine. I'll never understand why parents have to fight over their kids." He heaved a sigh. "Some people should never have children."

The principal turned to go. "Kathleen, do you like teaching first grade better than, what was it you taught before, fifth?"

"Oh, yes. I love teaching first grade. I think I've found my niche."

"Well, you'll do okay. You're dedicated, and I'm glad to have you on our team. I hope your vacation wasn't too stressful, that you were able to get some rest. From what I hear, you did an incredible job of rescuing the Williams girl."

"Thanks, Dick. But I must tell you, Patti's father turned out not to be the ogre we thought he was. He behaved quite admirably when she became ill."

• • •

It started to rain as Kathleen left the building and hurried to her car. Clouds obscured the mountains, and the afternoon gathered gray and dismal, weather typical for the Willamette valley in January.

The short drive to Mrs. Fisher's passed unnoticed, her mind back in the classroom on plans she'd formulated for winter season and the remainder of the school year. She felt excited, and a little apprehensive at the same time.

Life on a personal level remained on hold. Maybe she should take a deep breath and just tell her parents everything in one big burst. Get it over with. Her family didn't know about the breakup with Edward; she had yet to learn what their reaction might be. *If I tell my parents about running into Danny, will they read more into it than it merits? Mom has this intuitive way of reading between the lines. But what is there to read?*

She'd devote her time and energies to teaching and to helping one special little girl cope with changes in her life. Of one thing she was certain, Patti needed her.

Chapter 21

A tall blond lady smiled as she propelled two children ahead of her. She spoke softly, "I've brought you double trouble. I'm not saying they're badly behaved children, just precocious and energetic."

Startled from her Monday morning routine, Kathleen looked up to see a young woman and two little boys.

"Oh, hello. I'm afraid I didn't hear you come in." She rose from her desk. "I'm Miss O'Brien."

"And I'm Mrs. Daniels." She held out her hand. "These are my sons, Robert and Jerome, better known as Bobby and Jerry—or, *The Twins*!"

The boys mumbled a polite hello and eased away to inspect the classroom. Their mother fiddled with the strap on her purse and didn't quite meet the teacher's eyes. "They're not bad boys," she repeated. "But, I guess they are a bit mischievous. The teacher at their other school got a little upset when they switched shirts and fooled her. She couldn't tell them apart, and of course the children giggled when they corrected her. I'm afraid she didn't think it funny."

Kathleen wrote her name on the board for the benefit of her new students. Robert and Jerome Daniels took their assigned seats and stared bright-eyed at their new teacher. Identical twins, as much alike as corn kernels in a can.

And how am I ever to tell them apart? I wonder if they'd consider tattoos? Maybe on the end of each pert little nose? Aloud she said, "Welcome boys. The bus will be here soon and you will meet your new classmates."

"I'm Bobby, he's Jerry." One blonde curly-haired twin announced, brown eyes sparkling.

"Yes, I know," she responded with more confidence than she felt.

The boys were dressed alike, except Bobby wore a sea-green sweatshirt, Jerry royal blue. Identical mischievous twinkles sparked from their eyes. This teacher didn't doubt they could fool her. But maybe she could make lessons, free time, and privileges enticing enough, they soon wouldn't bother.

The Daniels bought the run-down old Adams place, a fact she learned from the twins' mother. The grapevine, usually the fastest source of information, hadn't yet circulated the news around the neighborhood. *Or at least it hasn't reached Martha,* Kathleen surmised. *She's usually first to know what's going on in the community.*

The previous inhabitants, an older couple with four children, rented the house and were forced to move to another district when the place sold. One child, Sally Ann, had been in Kathleen's class. She would miss the little girl, though the child was borderline retarded.

The school bus rumbled onto the grounds and disgorged it's occupants. Children streamed to their respective rooms eager to greet their teachers and share holiday experiences.

"Hi, Miss O'Brien. Guess what I got for Christmas."

"Miss O'Brien, can we play in the snow?"

"Yeah. I wanna build a snow fort. Can we?"

"Miss O'Brien, guess what we did over the holiday? My daddy drove all the way to Utah. Grandma said he's crazy, but she gave him a big hug anyway."

"Hey. Who're you?" Freddy gaped at the twins.

Kathleen did her best to respond to each child. The chatter continued until the bell rang and the children took their seats.

Twenty-five open faces turned curious eyes on their teacher and waited for the day's instruction and enlightenment. Patti wasn't among them.

"Class, we have two new students, Bobby and Jerry Daniels. I hope you'll show them around at recess and lunchtime and answer any questions they might have."

"I'm Bobby, he's Jerry."

Well! Does Bobby always takes the lead? Kathleen wondered. *Maybe it's a way to tell them apart. They haven't had time to switch shirts, but if they do, will I know?*

"Class, lets stand and recite the Pledge of Allegiance," the teacher said. "Then we'll take a few minutes for 'Show and Tell.' Please tell our new students your name before you begin."

"I'm Freddy. I got a new sled for Christmas and my dad and I played in the snow," one of the children said after they had finished the pledge.

"I'm Lisa, we drove to Utah. Grandma gave me a new dress."

"Thank you, children, for sharing. I'm glad everyone had a nice vacation. Today we're going to write winter poems. I'll put an example on the board."

WINTER POEM
color—white
noun—snow
verb—run, play
sentence—I like to run and play in the white snow.

"Jerry, Bobby would you like to be my helpers today? You may come forward and take papers to hand out. Give one paper to each student."

Bobby bounced from his seat and strode forward, but Jerry remained in his chair. "I'll give Jerry his," his brother crowed.

"No. Jerry will come and get his own." The teacher smiled at Jerry and the child left his seat and came forward like a chick for a bug.

Kathleen circulated around the room, observing and helping individuals get started with their winter poems. It was impossible to keep her eyes from returning to the vacant chair beside John's. Why hadn't Patti come to school? Was she sick again?

A little hand shot up. "Yes, John, do you have a question?"

"Miss O'Brien, where's Patti? I heard she got kidsnatched 'er something. Is she comin' back to school?"

"Class, Patti was in hospital with pneumonia over Christmas vacation, but she's better now and I'm sure she will be back in school soon."

Activity in the classroom settled down to a happy hum; time passed quickly and children were dismissed for morning recess. While Kathleen thought about grabbing a cup of coffee in the teacher's lounge, a knock sounded on her classroom door, and she hurried to answer.

Spike and Patti, face flushed, stood there. Kathleen wondered if she might be feverish again or if the little girl had been crying. For an instant, Patti lifted tear-filled eyes to her teacher; before her chin dropped, and she stared at her shoes.

"Uh...I guess Patti's kinda late, huh...teach?" Spike spluttered. "Patti says she needs an excuse or somethin' for bein' late. So, I suppose I'm here to giveya one. We like sorta overslept."

"Yes, well we're glad Patti is here now. Thank you for bringing her, Mr. Spike." The teacher smiled at her little student. "Patti you may hang up your things and play on the computer for the remainder of recess."

Kathleen stepped outside and closed the door behind her. "I know you only as Spike, or I would address you by your surname. *You*, however, *do* know my name, and it isn't, *Teach*.

I would appreciate it if you would call me *Miss O'Brien*, especially in front of my students."

"Uh—yeah, sure, okay…tea…*Miss* O'Brien. That's cool. I can probably like do that."

"And Mr. Spike, would you please inform Mrs. Williams tardiness goes on Patti's record and it can lower her grade. I hope you will make an effort to see she's here on time." She swallowed her annoyance as she watched him retreat. If her threat wasn't totally true, she could only hope it produced the desired effect.

She pulled a chair close and sat beside Patti while she played a math game on computer. With elbows on knees and chin propped in her hands, Kathleen waited patiently for the child to make eye contact. "Patti, are you feeling okay?"

"I'm sorry I'm late, Miss O'Brien." Round liquid orbs threatened to spill more tears. "Mommy didn't wake me."

"It's all right, honey. I know you couldn't help it." Kathleen pulled Patti into her arms and hugged her. She felt warm, but not feverish. "Would you like to wash your face before the bell rings and your classmates troop in?" The teacher winked, gave her a reassuring smile and a gentle nudge.

"We have two new boys in our class. Bobby and Jerry. They're twins, and pretty cute—I think you'll like them."

"Ugh," Patti made a face. "Girls are nicer. I like girls better." She giggled.

The teacher laughed but kept her thoughts to herself. *My darling girl, you will change your mind soon enough, but for now I'm glad to see you smiling again.*

• • •

"You look tired, dear. How did your day go? Any surprises? Please don't tell me Patti wasn't there."

"Now that I have time to think about it; I am tired, Martha" Kathleen affirmed. "I've lost one pupil, a girl, and gained two new students, twin boys cute enough to be in sitcoms and never have to learn a line..."

"Hold that thought...I'm bringing you a cup of hot tea, then I want to hear all about your day." She called from the kitchen, "The twins—are they from that family that moved into the old Adams place?...Clara told me today, someone bought the house and has moved in there."

Kathleen accepted the tea and squelched a need to giggle. "Thank you, this is really good. Orange spice is it?"

"Um, yes." She perched on the edge of her chair and balanced the teacup on her knee. "Go on, dear. I won't interrupt again. Tell me about these twin boys. Are they identical twins? Look alike do they?"

"Martha, they're as alike as berries on a bush, and I think they may be smarter than I am. Their mother told me they're mischievous; they like to swap shirts and confuse the teacher. I think they did that today, and after lunch they changed desks, though I can't be sure."

The silver-haired matron set her cup aside, tipped her head back and chuckled. "Well, dear, they sound perfectly delightful. Maybe you will need to stamp them with indelible ink or something to tell them apart." She laughed again then nodded her head. "You know, it's been my experience there's always some little difference even with identical twins. You'll find it dear, then you can turn the tables on them—And Patti?"

"Oh, Martha," Kathleen sighed. "I'm not sure what to think. I believe Patti's recovered from pneumonia, but she got to school two hours late. The children were out for morning recess."

"Her mother brought her two *hours* late?"

"I wish her mother had brought her, but a man I know only as Spike came with her."

"Well, for land sakes! Where in the world was Amber? I sure don't like the sound of this."

Kathleen frowned and finished her tea. "I know, but what can anyone do?"

"Oh, I'm not sure, but I think Clara may be able to intercede. She won't like hearing her granddaughter was late for school. And for *sure* she won't like hearing about Spike somebody-or-other. If nothing else, she'll call and wake Patti in time to get dressed and get on the school bus, I should think."

"Martha, what if Amber takes Patti and moves away?"

"Well, dear, I suppose it's possible, but I don't think she will. She has a pretty good clientele built up at her shop in town. She has friends here. Whether she admits it or not, she knows she can count on Clara and Henry if she needs help.

Kathleen sighed and rose to go upstairs. "I suppose we won't solve the world's problems tonight, but before I drop the subject entirely, who cares for Patti after school? Do you know? Surely her mother wouldn't leave her home alone."

"I think a neighbor might be keeping an eye on her. Tiffany lives next door, and I know for awhile she watched Patti in exchange for having her hair done. I'm not sure; she may have gone back to work at the grocery store."

"I'm probably worrying too much about Patti and things that are none of my business, but I'm not sure how to overcome that."

"Well dear, you've been through a lot with that little girl. I don't suppose in college they cover how to deal with such situations. No doubt the two of you have bonded, but Kathleen, need I remind you, you're her teacher. You're not her parent or guardian. I wouldn't like to see your heart broken over what may not be helped. Unless there is real neglect or abuse, we should stay out of it."

Chapter 22

Friday evening, the weekend stretched ahead with no plans. Oh, she could wash her hair, do some laundry, write a few letters, and send e-mail jokes to her nieces and nephews. For the first time in more months than she cared to think about, her schedule didn't revolve around Edward.

Kathleen took inventory of her tiny kitchen—three teabags, half a jar of peanut butter, four rice cakes, one apple, one banana, and about a half dozen withered grapes. *I could raid Martha's refrigerator, or maybe even eat with her, but I really don't want her to know I've nothing to do.* They had long since agreed to not share meals on weekends as she seldom found time.

She preferred hibernating the entire weekend, rather than chance an encounter with Connors while alone in Fir Valley. *But I have to eat, and that means a trip to the store. Or driving to another town and eating in an obscure restaurant.* That thought had about as much appeal as swallowing raw oysters in the dark.

Paranoid or not, I wish I had caller ID. I have a feeling he will call. I don't want to talk to him. I don't want to hear his voice on my answering machine, either. Outdoors, a cold drizzle continued to fall, by 4:30 it was totally dark, and Kathleen convinced herself she didn't need to go out. At least not this evening.

As she lay on her bed, a nap claimed her until the phone startled her awake. *Is that Edward calling me?* On the fourth ring, she gathered her courage and answered.

"Hel-lo."

"Kathleen?"

"*Danny.* Is it really you? Where are you? Are you all right?"

"Yeah, it's me."

"Where *are* you?"

"Well, I'm in Portland."

She bolted upright on the edge of the bed and began twining a lock of hair around her right index finger.

"Portland? You're in Portland?" *Good grief Charlie Brown! I sound like a parrot. Why can't I say something intelligent?*

"Yeah, I flew down from Seattle. I've got a little time coming. I thought if you could maybe spare a couple hours from your busy schedule, we could have coffee or something..."

"You'd come to Fir Valley?"

"Sure, I'll swing by that way if I can see you for a little while. I've rented a car—if there isn't too much snow, I'll drive over the mountains, go see the folks. How about it, Carrot Top—do you have a little time for ol' Dan?"

She tugged hard on her hair, tried to slow her racing

pulse, and prayed he didn't notice when her voice sounded a little breathless. "Danny, I'd love to see you."

"Great. I was hoping you'd say that. When? You probably have a hot date tonight. Tomorrow morning, sometime?"

"Actually, I'm free as a bird. I don't have any plans for the weekend. Whatever time is convenient for you…I could meet you somewhere in Fir Valley."

A slight hesitation, an expelled breath and then, "Wait a minute—are you telling me you're free this weekend? The entire weekend? You don't have a date tonight? Saturday? Sunday?"

"Shameful, isn't it? I have no pride."

"I can't believe my luck. That's if you'll spend the weekend with me? We could go to the coast…to the mountains…is it too late to come out now and take you to dinner? Have you eaten?"

"I haven't eaten, but it'll take you two hours, at least, to get out here, you crazy man." A giggle erupted. "Do you really want to wait that long to eat?"

"I will, if you will. Come on, Kathleen. Let me come get you. We have some catching up to do. How's Patti?"

"She's fine. I'll tell you all about her later. Do you know how to get out here?"

"I know how to get to Fir Valley, but you'll have to tell me how to find your place from there."

Quickly, she gave him directions. "If that isn't clear, call me again when you get to Fir Valley, and I could just meet you in town somewhere."

"Oh, no, I come get my women."

"So hang up already," she snickered. "Get in your car and drive, but not too fast. I'll wait for you."

Kathleen showered, shampooed her hair, twice, changed clothes three times, and finally decided to wear the navy slacks and soft blue sweater. In exactly one hour and fifty-three minutes from the time he hung up the phone, Danny pulled in to Martha's driveway.

Instructions were to come to the back door, and she stepped out before he could knock. A peek in the living room, on her way down the hall, revealed Martha asleep in her favorite chair. She probably wondered why she hadn't seen Edward in a few days, but Kathleen hadn't felt like filling her in on the breakup, and so far she hadn't asked.

Danny gave her a quick hug, ushered her to his car, and opened the door for her. "Ready to roll?"

"You bet…I like your car…this is a Honda?"

"Yep. Short and snappy. Runs like a scared rabbit. So where we going? I'm not familiar with this area, you'll have to direct me."

"Oh, well, I'm afraid there's not a lot to choose from in Fir Valley. No really good restaurants here or nearby. I guess I should have told you that before you drove all the way out here. Huh?"

"What? They don't make hamburgers out here?"

She laughed and felt tension drain from her body. "Well, yeah, they do make hamburgers. Jimbo's makes pretty good ones as a matter of fact. We have a Mexican restaurant, a Chinese place, a pizza parlor, and if you want steak, probably The Stagecoach is the place."

"What would be your preference, Kathleen?"

"You know, Dan, I could go for just about anything, but when you said hamburger I started salivating."

"You got a deal. It's crazy, but when I was in Iraq, I kept wishing I had a hamburger. The kind they only seem to make in the good ol' U.S. of A. One about three inches thick with onions, mushrooms, tomato, mustard, ketchup—the works. Where do I find this Jimbo's place?"

• • •

Danny placed their order for hamburgers, milkshakes, and french-fries, then leaned back in the booth and grinned at her, his blue eyes friendly as a lake in July. "Seems like we did this once before, when we were about fourteen. You were pretty then, and you're even prettier now. How is it you're unattached this weekend?" He leaned forward, elbows on the table. "When you were in Chicago, I got the impression a man was waiting for you back here."

She reddened. "Yes—well—we broke up. Our lives weren't going in the same direction. We don't want the same things out of life."

Kathleen studied her hands for a few seconds before meeting his gaze across the table. "I thought about you a lot while you were in Iraq. Were you in much danger there?"

If his eyes were summer blue before, they now turned gray as a rain-filled Oregon sky. "I didn't feel in particular danger." He grimaced. "We were with the troops most of the time, and they do their best to protect us. But it's hard to know who and where the enemy is. A vehicle two lengths ahead of us took a hit. A colleague of mine lost his life, along with two soldiers...but it's incredible, Kathleen, everyone does their job no matter what. I took pictures of the explosion. Pictures of the medics. And pictures of the air vac."

"Will you show me your pictures sometime? I'd love to see your work. Perhaps you could show me your cameras, your equipment, a time when it's convenient?"

"Sure. I'll show you more pictures than you'll probably want to see. Not all my pictures make the papers or magazines. Some of my favorites are never published."

She sipped her milkshake, hesitated, then bleated the question uppermost on her mind. "Danny, will you be going back to Iraq?"

"Yeah, probably. But not too soon. There'll be other assignments, and right now I have some R and R time coming."

She groaned, but smiled to take away any reproach that might be perceived. "Why can't you just take pictures of cows, eroding sand dunes, or something? Something *safe*?"

He chuckled, "Be gory, Carrot Top, you sound just like me mither. Actu..."

Kathleen snickered. "I'm sorry...please, you were saying..."

"Actually, I have taken pictures of cows. You may recall a story about a dairy herd in Tillamook county being struck by lightning. Well, the same thing happened to a farmer's stock in Washington state. His prize bull fried on the hoof. I took their pictures. Made front page in Olympia. Unfortunately, there isn't a whole lot of interest in cows."

She smiled and dawdled over her hamburger while Danny

polished off his second one and told her about some of the children in Iraq. “I have to warn you, darlin’, my heart belongs to another. She has the prettiest big brown eyes I’ve seen anywhere, and she knows how to use them. I’d ask her to marry me, but she’s only four years old.” He kept the tone light, but there were nuances and inflections in his voice saying more than words alone conveyed. *What?* she wondered, *is the story he isn’t telling.*

“They’re cute kids. And they’re curious, like kids everywhere, as soon as they get over their initial shyness they want to know about the strange Americans. Of course a little candy doesn’t hurt. I took some great pictures.”

Focused on each other, they were oblivious to people around them. The gang of teenagers in the restaurant went unnoticed until they were ready to leave and a girl spoke to her.

“Hi, Miss O’Brien.” Her voice said hello, but her eyes questioned, whose the hunk you’re with?

“Oh. Hello, Charlene.”

If she hesitated a moment too long, she could only hope it went unnoticed. “Charlene, this is an old friend of mine, Danny Davis. Dan, Charlene Fisher, my landlady’s granddaughter.” *How long before Charlene lets her grandmother know she saw the teacher with a man they haven’t seen before? How long before the whole neighborhood hears?*

“It’s too late for a movie, and way too early to call it a night,” Danny quipped. “How about you show me your school?”

"My school? You want to see my school? Tonight? I don't think you can see much in the dark."

"That's okay. You can show me again when it's daylight. Maybe I can take a picture of your school."

"You'd do that? You'd take a picture of my school?"

"Sure. Why not?"

"Wow, that would be fantastic."

A smile spread over his face as he drove slowly on to the schoolyard. "You're right, of course, I can't see everything, still the front of the building is rather like I pictured it." He let a minute or two pass before shutting off the motor and the lights. They sat in silence another minute or two before he eased her to him and gently planted a brief kiss on her lips.

"So. Are you going to show me your room? You must have a key, don't you?"

"Umn—what?" she stammered. "A key?" She stared at him. "You want to see my room?"

"Of course. I'd like to see where you work. It's all right, isn't it? If I see your room?"

Her hand trembled slightly as she unlocked the door to her classroom, switched on the lights, and shut off the alarm. When she turned to see his face he wore a big grin and the light dancing in his eyes reminded her of devilment the twin boys in her class pulled.

"Well, Miss O'Brien, teacher, ma'am," he drawled. "I'd like to be a kid in your classroom. Can I sit up front and be teacher's pet? Huh, can I? Pretty please?"

"Danny, you're a nut." She giggled.

"Yeah, I know, but you like me anyway." He strolled

around the room, noticing bookshelves, picking up books, reading titles before replacing them. Bulletin boards caught his eye and he stopped before them and read each word. Aloud.

He sat behind her desk, winked at her, then moved quickly on to the white rocking chair. "Kathleen, this has to be your own special touch. You sit here and read to the kids. Am I right?"

"Yes. How did you know? I also let children read and rock as an earned privilege."

If he weren't so big, she could easily imagine him as one of her mischievous little boys claiming the rocker and setting it in motion. The chair slowed, and his eyes became serious. "What's your biggest teaching concern right now?"

She stared at him. "I worry I'm neglecting certain children and not giving them the attention they deserve. I don't mean to, but shy children work quietly and wait while others waggle their hands and it's 'Miss O'Brien, Miss O'Brien'. It's hard to ignore persistent kids. I have twenty-seven little bodies needing direction and I worry, too, I won't bring the slow learners along quickly enough."

A nod encouraged her to continue.

"Then, of course, there's Patti. My landlady reminds me I'm her teacher not her mother, but I want so badly just to comfort her. I'm not sure what all is going on in her home, but twice this week she burst into tears when she didn't get a hundred on her paper. I'd like to give Patti extra help. There just isn't time. I have two new students, twin boys. Identical twin look-a-like little boys. Danny, they're cuter than the wings on a hummingbird and can move just about as fast. Smart, too, but rascals. They like to switch clothes and fool the teacher. I confess, I don't always know when they're doing it."

He chuckled. "Ah, me darlin', I always knew you'd be a great teacher. Only good teachers worry over their kids. Even back in grade school you had a way with the small fry. Your students may not know it, but they're lucky."

Kathleen's face matched her hair. "Sorry to run on so, I'm afraid it isn't often someone asks me about my teaching."

"Well—I plan to ask you again. So there. And now maybe I should get you home. Will you spend the day with me tomorrow?"

"I'd love to spend the day with you, but aren't your folks expecting you?"

"Yeah, but I'll call 'em. They won't mind if I take a detour. Especially when they know I'm spending time with you. They've always liked you, you know. Besides, I'll have all next week with them."

Danny drove her home and walked her to the back door. "See you tomorrow," he whispered. He waited until she was safely inside, but he didn't kiss her goodnight. If she were fourteen again and living at home, she might well slam a few doors and stomp upstairs. However, at twenty-six, one is mature. Therefore, one creeps up the stairs to the apartment on the second floor, opens and closes doors quietly.

Once inside her bedroom she switched on a light and scowled at her reflection in the mirror. "Why didn't he kiss me goodnight," she muttered. "He kissed me in the car. What? I've got bad breath or something?"

Chapter 23

"A little rain won't quench our outing to the beach. I may have been in Iraq, but I'm still a native Oregonian," Danny chortled. Wipers on the black Honda swooshed back and forth in slow cadence like a metronome for a beginning piano student. Headlights smiled bravely into the gloom.

"Right." She postulated. "We Oregonians like rain, don't we? Liquid sunshine and all that."

He lifted an eyebrow and noted she was about to burst into laughter behind that serious demeanor.

"Students at our top universities are Ducks or Beavers, water animals, and everyone knows we have webs between our toes." She continued. "No true child of Oregon carries an umbrella." A giggle escaped after a glance in the backseat. "Well, maybe, if it's really pouring."

"Think you can hold out for breakfast 'till we get to the coast, or do ya wanta stop somewhere nearby?"

She returned his smile. "I can wait. It's fun eating and watching the ocean, but I might like coffee to sustain me until we get there. How about you? If you'll stop at the Coffee Hut up ahead I'll treat us to a coffee-hazelnut-mocha. They're to die for."

"You got it."

He guided the car to the window of the little building, stopped and placed their order. "Hmmm. This smells rich enough to eat with a spoon. Thanks, Carrot Top."

"You're welcome, Boone."

He tipped his head back and roared. "Oh, no, I thought you'd forgotten about that nickname."

Her emerald eyes were electrified. "With you calling me Carrot Top? No way."

Comfortable in his Levis, blue woolen plaid shirt, and cowboy boots, Danny watched the road and stole glances at the woman beside him. She looked good in jeans and a green monogrammed sweatshirt, but then he thought she could probably wear a shapeless burka and still appear sexy. They dated a few times while in high school, never anything serious, more often just part of a group of kids having fun. He doubted she ever suspected the crush he had on her since fifth grade, seeing it was her brother Michael he hero-worshipped. In their senior year it all changed. Susan Landon entered the picture, his brain stuck in burst mode, and all his focus was on Susan. He was in love. It all seemed so long ago. Now, at twenty-six, Danny supposed he was mature, but the attraction to the redhead beside him made him feel about sixteen again.

They rode in comfortable quiet, sipping their coffee, listening to Linda Ronstadt on a CD. "So, how long's it been since you went to the coast?"

"Umm, not since last summer. A couple teacher friends and I stayed in Seaside one long weekend. Seems kinda ridiculous when I think about it, to wait so long between times. I do love the beach, and I'm not really that far away." She finished her coffee and stashed the cup. "How long's it been since you were on the Oregon coast?"

He sighed. "You know, I can't remember the last time—at least five or six years, before the folks moved across the mountains. I don't get many assignments for local pictures, which somehow seems wrong. I dreamed about seeing the Pacific Ocean again while I was in Iraq. I determined then to come back and take more pictures of the Oregon coast. The scenery along this particular coastline is spectacular. No place like it anywhere else on earth."

The road entered the H.B. Van Duzer forest corridor and they grew quiet again, struck by the magnificence of the stately Douglas fir trees lining each side of the highway. Snow clung in tenacious patches among the green-leafed rhododendron, like strips of white in an heirloom quilt.

Danny laid his hand lightly on the back of her neck. She turned to look at him and his breath caught. "What would…" But when she caressed his cheek with the backs of her fingers, he forgot, for the moment, what he started to say. "You think about eating at the mouth of the shortest river in the world?"

"Dee River? That would be super. We could see the ocean at the same time couldn't we?"

"Yeah, from the restaurant I'm thinking of, you can eat and watch the waves roll in, maybe even spot a ship out at sea." *But who's got time to watch the ocean? I'm busy watching you.*

• • •

An hour later they were seated in the restaurant; the waitress arrived with carefully balanced plates. She set their orders of ham, scrambled eggs, hash browns, and toast before them. A caddy of jellies and jams followed. She fished a bottle of catsup from her apron-pocket and plunked it on the table. Fresh-squeezed orange juice and steaming cups of coffee rounded out the menu. "Can I get you anything else?" she asked.

Danny's eyes questioned Kathleen before answering, "No, thank you, I think this is all we need."

"Enjoy your breakfast."

Left to themselves, he reached for her hand, bowed his head and in a voice only she could hear, offered thanks to God for the food and other blessings.

"The ocean never fails to fascinate me," Kathleen remarked. "Even on a gray day like today, I think it's beautiful. I don't think I'd want to be out there on it though, those waves look really rough."

"Have you ever been out on the ocean deep sea fishing?"

"No, never. You?"

He gazed at her. "Yeah, a few times. Maybe that's something we'll have to do. We could go out from Depot Bay, the world's smallest harbor. That's fun. Or maybe take a charter from Newport."

Her eyes grew large as sand dollars and her face turned the color of sea-foam.

Danny chuckled. "Oh, not today, fair lady. We'll pick a time when the sky's blue and the sea calm as a lake. But you really should go out at least once. They have whale-watching excursions, too. That might be fun."

"I've heard about that. However, I'm not sure I want to get that close to a whale. A friend of mine told me they smell really bad when they blow."

"Yeah, that's true. They don't smell any too good. I don't suppose they ever heard of Listerine. Small wonder Jonah was ready to do what God said after riding around in one of those animals for three days. Do ya think?"

They talked, laughed, and joked their way through breakfast. Getting reacquainted couldn't be better.

"Which way would you like to go? Up the coast or down the coast?"

"I don't know. Either way is bound to be nice. There's plusses and minuses both ways, isn't there?"

He pulled a quarter from his pocket. "I don't really care which way we go, either.

Wanta flip for it? Heads we go north? Tails we drive south?"

"Sounds fair."

He flipped the coin in the air, caught it and slapped it on the back of his hand.

"Looks like we go south."

Happy to drive, look at the scenery, and survey the lady beside him, it was nice to discover she didn't need to talk all the time. He had dated women that seemed to think it their duty to fill any and all pauses with chatter—even when there were spectacular things to see. It drove him nuts.

"Kathleen, if you'd like to stop any time and look at something, sing out. We're not in a race here. We can poke around some of these little shops on the coast if you'd like."

"You wouldn't mind? I thought men hated that sort of thing."

He smirked, gave it up and exploded into laughter. "As long as you promise not to drag me through a women's clothing store, I can probably stand it. I may regret admitting this, but I rather like shops with kitchen stuff. Since I'm my own chief cook and bottle washer, finding that one magic gadget appeals to me."

• • •

When they exited the kitchen store, ceramic pitcher for her, omelet pan for him, an eerie feel to the atmosphere made the hair on the back of his neck stand at attention. A definite smell of ozone mixed with the salty smell of ocean. The sky looked as if a giant finger had poked a hole in the clouds to let sunshine tumble through. The parking area around his car glowed like high noon on a summer day. Danny said the first thing that popped into his mind. "Wow! If you don't like the weather, stick around, it'll change in a few minutes."

Kathleen scowled. "Danny, I don't like the look of that

black cloud over there. Maybe we'd better make a dash for the car."

He reached for her hand when a clap of thunder *boomed* loud enough to blast the birds from the trees. Gravity lost it's hold on Kathleen; she jumped and shot like a rocket headed for the car. A split second behind her and with automatic key in hand to unlock the doors, he launched himself next to her in the car. The urge to laugh died in his throat when he noticed her pallid face.

"Come 'ere, honey." His arms encircled her. "If lightning gets you, we'll check out together."

"I'm embarrassed. I guess I've never gotten over my childhood fear of thunderstorms."

"Well, that was a particularly close strike. And the thunder was loud enough to wake the dead. If you noticed, I might have outrun you getting to the car if I hadn't stopped to fish the key from my pocket."

A familiar flash lit up the sky followed by more thunder. Clouds ruptured and a deluge tortured the roof and sluiced the windows.

Arms still around her, he nuzzled her cheek. "How about a walk on the beach?"

The question teased a small upturn of her lips. "You know, I was hoping we might do that; but I think I'm going to vote for exploring more shops until it quits raining."

"I'll second that thought. Maybe we'll see how many places we can check off the list. We're not that far from Depoe Bay. Coming to the coast and not stopping at Depot Bay would be tantamount to driving to a large shopping mall and sitting in the parking lot. Do you agree?"

• • •

Danny parked the car between Highway 101 and the ocean. They watched in dry comfort as waves crashed against the abutment and sent plumes of salty spray skyward high as Old Faithful. The rain slowed to a halfhearted effort of bird pecks against the windshield.

He reached in the backseat and retrieved her pink London Fog raincoat. He shrugged into his own windbreaker and opened the door for her. A mad dash, hand in hand, across the highway barely dampened their feathers.

They prowled shops the length of Depot Bay's main street and back again and didn't buy a thing.

"Hold on. I think we need some saltwater taffy." He propelled her in to Ainslee's candy store.

"So many flavors and pretty colors to choose from, all of them enticing." Kathleen lamented while helping fill a sack. "How does one pick with so many choices?"

The couple watched a worker pound and shape a block of taffy. The store made their own candy right there, and it was fascinating to see the process. To tempt one further an assortment of fudge and chocolates beckoned. A dangerous place when one is already hungry.

Danny snickered. "You just get one now, 'cause I plan to feed you dinner."

She grabbed the sack out of his hand and shoved it in her pocket.

"Hey, no fair."

"So, who gets only one piece now?"

Laughing, he grabbed her around the waist, spun her around, and kissed her on the cheek "That's gonna cost you lady."

She made a face at him.

Hand in hand they entered the Spouting Horn and ordered fresh salmon for their dinner. They lingered over coffee and dessert unwilling to see the day end. Rejecting yet another offer of coffee the couple grew embarrassed. Danny paid the bill and together they sauntered out the door.

He took the long way home, still the ride ended too soon. They sat in Mrs. Fisher's driveway, tired, happy, and reluctant to say good night. An entire day on the coast hadn't been long enough.

"Danny, I've had such a good time. I can't remember when I've laughed so much."

"Yeah, me too."

He walked her to the door. "Until tomorrow then?"

"Yes—Tomorrow."

She turned to go in, but he stopped her, drew her gently into his arms and kissed her like the world might end before midnight.

Back in the car rationality set in. *I shouldn't have done that. But I'm only human, and she has no idea how beautiful she is. She's so innocent and sweet. Is it wicked of me to want one perfect, stress-free day with her?* "Give me the strength, Lord," he whispered. "Tomorrow I'll break it off. I have no right to drag Kathleen into my chaotic life."

Chapter 23

"Hi, handsome."

"Hello, yourself, Beautiful Lady. Ready to go?"

She nodded. "I like your Sunday-go-to-meetin' clothes, Danny. Nice."

He grinned, a beam to make the winter sun envious. "Why thank you, ma'am. I clean up pretty good, you think?"

From a window on the porch, Kathleen had watched him exit his car and stride to the back entrance. He wore gray trousers, shiny black loafers, and a blue v-necked sweater over a white button-down shirt. A black leather coat fitted loosely over his shoulders reminded her of his high school letterman's jacket.

The sun hadn't been up long, but it looked like it might be a nice cloud-free day as they headed to Fir Valley.

"Sure you don't mind missing services at your own church?"

"I not only don't mind, I'm happy as a spring lamb in a field of clover to be going elsewhere. It's a small church I attend, where everyone knows everyone else. In many ways that's nice. It's like a big caring family." She twisted in the seat and crossed her legs. "However, there are drawbacks, like right now. I don't want to face curious stares because I'm not with Edward. I'm not ready to offer explanations. It'll be easier once he leaves town. Even then, I'm not sure I want to go back. Maybe I'll find another church home."

Blue eyes assessed her. When he spoke, the subject headed another direction. "This is a pretty area, Kathleen. It definitely has some things going for it, clean air, sparkling streams, unpolluted river, not too heavily populated."

"A low crime rate, too."

"And I'd guess not the drug problem some of the larger schools have. It's certainly off the beaten path, and I'm wondering what drew you here. How'd you, a city girl, happen to end up teaching at a little country school out in the sticks?"

"It is pretty amazing isn't it? A college chum brought me here one weekend. She had a niece going to school at Pleasant Grove, where I'm now teaching. My friend's sister and niece couldn't say enough positive things about the area and the school in particular. I fell in love with the locale, and when an opening came up, well, like they say 'the rest is history'...Oh, Danny. Look! Out there in the field—Swans. They're here again. Aren't they beautiful?"

Danny pulled to the side of the road and quickly retrieved a camera from luggage in the backseat. In no time, he was out the car and taking pictures of the white birds against a green-field background. The photographer's trained eye spotted movement at the edge of the pasture—a coyote. Faster than a robin can pull a worm, the professional had his wildlife pictures.

All business, he didn't seem to notice when she quietly stood beside him watching. *What is he waiting for?* Then she knew. The majestic white birds lifted as one, like some great fantasy ship against the blue sky. An unbelievable picture.

"Kathleen. Stay right there. Now turn your head just a little my way. That's it. Perfect. Thanks, love—Wow! No wonder you like it out here. All this wildlife. A photographer's dream come true."

"Isn't it awesome? What a treat seeing the coyote. I sometimes hear them at night, but it isn't often I see one." She laughed. "Don't get me wrong, Daniel, I have nothing against the city. The convenience of good restaurants, the accessibility of concerts and quality entertainment is something I miss. It's a long drive from here to the Arlene Schnitzer Concert Hall in Portland, but I've fallen in love with the country. To me it's worth the tradeoff."

Sunday morning traffic on the eight-mile drive to Fir Valley, the little town everyone depended on for weekly needs, ran light. One pickup rattled by when they stopped to photograph nature. Danny drove faster now, making up for time lost.

When he stopped at the Coffee Hut in Fir Valley and ordered a repeat of yesterday's mocha, she laughed.

"Thought you might need a little fortification before we drive on to Portland."

"Thank you…I do love these things."

"You're welcome. So, did you have time for breakfast?"

"Well, sorta. You?"

"Yeah, continental at the motel."

"I had tea and a rice cake smeared with peanut butter."

Danny hooted. "Carrot Top, you need me. I'll feed you good when we get out of church."

Content to sip her hot coffee and watch the scenery slide by, Kathleen didn't notice the somber look that stole over her companion's face. Nor did she notice how many times his troubled eyes darted her way. If he was a little quieter than usual; she attributed it to traffic and driving on the freeway.

The large church they attended as youngsters looked pretty much the same from the outside. "I'm impressed, you drove straight here with out once turning the wrong way. I'm sure I couldn't have found the church so easily. How long has it been since you were here?"

The question sparked a grin as he guided the Honda into the large parking lot and found a space between a late-model Toyota and a Buick. "Not since high school. You?"

"No, I haven't been back. I wonder if we'll know anyone."

"Let's go find out." He squeezed her hand; together they strolled up the long sidewalk and entered the massive double doors. A greeter welcomed them at the entrance to the sanctuary and handed each a bulletin. They took a seat down the right aisle toward the back.

Kathleen opened her bulletin and scanned the program. She didn't see a name she recognized, the staff, strangers all. The youth pastor they'd been so fond of no longer attended here.

The organist began to play and Kathleen poked Danny in the ribs. "That's Hattie Stockmeyer. I would never have believed she'd still be playing organ. She must be eighty at least."

"You're right, that's Hattie. I thought that style sounded familiar. No one plays quite the same as she does. She played organ, and sometimes piano, when I first started coming here with my folks."

The choir entered from both sides of the platform and took their places on risers. It was time for the service to begin. The buzz in the sanctuary, sounding for all the world like hens in a chicken house—or so Kathleen's mother always declared—quieted and the congregation gave themselves up to worship.

They sang hymns and choruses of adoration and praise to the Lord. Thankful to be in church, Kathleen tried to focus on the words before her. Painfully aware of the man beside her, his rich baritone sent shivers up her spine. Or maybe his shoulder grazing hers did odd things to her heart. How could she be so responsive to this man when she had so recently broken up with another?

The pastor, a man in his early fifties, stepped to the lectern. He sported a full head of blonde hair, and a generous paunch. The result of too many socials, Kathleen thought.

With an effort she strove to bring her thoughts into submission and concentrate on the sermon entitled, "How Is Faith Worked Out In Our Lives?" The pastor read from Matthew 18:20 in the NIV, "For where two or three come together in my name, there am I with them." A pause while the preacher scanned the congregation. "Folks, we need each other. Live in dependence upon your Lord *together*." There was that word again. Together. Leaping out at her.

The service ended. People stood for the benediction. Glad she didn't have to take a test on the contents of the sermon, Kathleen dropped her head and breathed her own prayer for guidance. *Please, Lord. Don't let me care too much for this man if it's not your will.*

Danny's palm was warm on her back as they made their way down the aisle. Individuals on each side stopped to shake hands, and invite them to come back again. They were strangers. Kathleen thought she recognized a few people in the choir, but no familiar faces appeared until Danny whispered in her ear. "Don't look now, but I think that's our old Sunday school teacher headed this way."

"Daniel Davis. It is you, isn't it? I thought you looked familiar. How nice to see you!" The silver-haired lady gripped his hand. "And this lovely lady with you...wait a minute... I know you...don't I?...Kathryn? She reached to shake Kathleen's hand. "No, that's not right. *Kathleen*—Kathleen O'Brien."

"That's right, Mrs. Gregory. I'm surprised you remember me. It's been a long time. How are you?"

"Well, I'm fine, dear. A little older. A little fatter. A bit more forgetful." She stepped back and peered up at them through her bifocals. "But the good Lord keeps right on blessin' me. But tell me about you two. It's so great to see you—and together—are you married? Or what is it, the young people say today? An item? Are you living here in Portland again?"

The lady might be older, and yes, heavier, but the same twinkle lit up her brown eyes, and she hadn't lost her ability to talk fast.

Danny chuckled and jumped in when Mrs. Gregory paused for a breath. "No, we're just visiting today. Part of a little trip down memory lane..."

"Wonderful, come home with me, and we'll have dinner together. You can tell me all about what you're doing now. Oh, this is just so wonderful seeing you two again."

"That's very kind of you, Mrs. Gregory, but I have a long drive ahead of me. And I need to get Kathleen back home. Thanks, anyway. Maybe another time."

• • •

She watched him shove a piece of steak around on his plate. The electric blue eyes he lifted to hers looked as if they needed recharging. Apprehension knotted her tummy.

"Kathleen, I hope you know this weekend has meant more to me than just a trip down memory lane." He cleared his throat. "It's been great. No—better than great—it's been a dream come true. But if I had an ounce of brains, I would have had coffee with you and rushed on over the mountain."

"*What?*"

He lifted a hand to forestall her. "When we met on the plane, and I found you again after the snowstorm—at the hospital in Chicago—it seemed like the answer to prayer. A respite for me before the fire of Iraq, and if I helped you through stress with Patti." He gulped coffee then continued, "Well, that was just an extra blessing."

"Danny, for me, you were the answer to an unspoken prayer, too. I didn't know how much I needed you, until you were there."

He continued, not quite meeting her eyes. "When I got back from Iraq and crashed at my apartment in Chicago, I could smell your shampoo in the bathroom. Your perfume on my bathrobe—It was like you were still there—I wanted to call you right then."

He sipped water and set the glass down. "I told myself it was just to make sure you were okay. I'd ask about Patti. But it was two in the morning. Not a good time to call."

Beverly, their waitress for the afternoon, refilled their cups. "May I bring you dessert? We have some really nice cherry cobbler. The chef makes it himself."

"Kathleen?"

"Um, no, thanks."

He vetoed dessert and the waitress hurried to another table.

"What I'm trying to say—and making a complete mess of it—this can't be a casual relationship for me. I'm in over my head here. You're everything I've ever dreamed of in a woman. What I'd want in a wife. You're intelligent, compassionate, you love children. But—"

He turned his water glass round and round and studied the wet rings on the table. "Kathleen, *but* is a small three letter word—but— the implications are *enormous*. I need for you to understand that."

"Are you talking about your job? You don't want any entanglements because of your work?"

"I suppose I might learn to do something else. The thing is, I love what I do. I like being a photographer, and I like trotting all over the globe." He raised distraught eyes to hers. "I just can't ask you to be part of such a chaotic lifestyle. I care way too much for you, to drag you into my way of life. I don't think we should see each other again."

Chapter 25

"So you're saying what? You're *dumping* me because I won't like your *job?*"

"Kathleen, you don't understand. When you most needed me, I could very likely be in some African bush jungle taking pictures of pygmies or pythons. I could tell you I'd give it up, but it wouldn't be three months until I'd be resentful."

"So, do *I* get a voice in this at all?" Her eyes met his across the table and her question nailed him. "Or do you just make the decisions and that's that?"

Her back stiffened straight as pencil lead and her voice grew serious as a teacher about to reprimand a child. "First, I would never ask you to give up a job you love. I like what I do—and I just broke up with a man who wanted me to give up teaching. It's so unfair. Second—others have survived a 'chaotic'—as you call it—lifestyle. What makes you think you're so different?...and third—third..." she spluttered. "Well...I don't know what third is?"

She reached across the table and gently touched his hand.

"Danny, what about Walter Cronkite and his wife, Betsy? They had a great relationship that lasted for years, and certainly Mr. Cronkite was all over the world, and probably not home when, quote, *needed*."

Danny was speechless. He hadn't counted on one little redhead's iron determination or depth of feeling.

She dug in her purse, withdrew a carefully folded note and handed it to him. He opened it and read: Merry Christmas, Kathleen. Sorry I can't be there with you. Remember, all God's promises are yours, Danny.

"You had Romans 8:28 highlighted in your Bible." Tears threatened her eyes. "I assume you believe it." She looked down, unable to meet his gaze. In a barely audible whisper she said, "Danny, I'm in over my head, too."

"Oh, blazes, Kathleen. I doubt you know what you're lettin' yourself in for, but I can't withstand my own feelings and yours, too." He gave her a boyish grin, as glowing as a kid turned loose with a new camera and no restrictions on picture taking.

The waitress breezed by and poured more coffee. Danny stopped her. "Miss, we might need some of that cherry cobbler after all. Warm it up and slap some ice cream on it. Please."

"Good for you. You won't be sorry. Everyone raves about Max's cobbler." She served them and watched out the corner of her eye. When she returned the coffee pot to the burner, she nudged the behind-the-counter waitress, and whispered, "See that couple over there? Something has changed from when they first came in here. They look as if they've swallowed lighted candles. They glow."

Sally shrugged. "They look like they're in love."

"Yeah, but he looked miserable when they first came in."

"Well, people can act pretty sappy when they're in love."

"I hope they like the cobbler, but the way they're making calf eyes at each other, I suspect I could serve them cardboard and they wouldn't know the difference." Beverly glanced their way again. "They're wrapped in that euphoric insular bubble that's been around since time immemorial, and each newly-in-love pair thinks originated with them." She shook her head and muttered. "Hope the bubble doesn't burst too soon."

Danny paid the bill and left a generous tip. Hand in hand, the couple floated out the door of the restaurant, unaware of knowing looks cast their way.

"Did something pretty fantastic just develop back there in the restaurant, or am I looking in the wrong end of the viewfinder? Please tell me the picture is clear. You're willing to take a chance on me?"

She smiled up at him, her eyes luminous and warm. "With all my heart, I want to be the object of your focus."

"Oh, glory be, saints, and angels! Darlin', I'm not sure whether to laugh, shout hallelujah, or cut my suspenders and go straight up." Before she could safely settle in the car, he grabbed her around the waist, lifted her off the ground and whirled twice with her. The kiss they shared launched their relationship to a no-turning-back level.

Buckled in the car once more, Danny started the engine and drove from the parking lot. He fumbled through a carton and selected a CD. Lyrics and music poured forth. Johnny Cash sang, "I fell into a burning ring of fire. I went down, down, down, and the flames burned higher. And it burns, burns, burns, the ring of fire. The ring of fire…I fell for you like a child."

"Penny for your thoughts, Carrot Top. Tell me what you're feelin'. "

"Oh, Boone. I don't know. Happy. Excited. Thrilled. Scared."

"Why are you scared, darlin'? Tell me."

"I don't know, Danny. Scared of feeling this happy, I guess. Scared things are moving too fast. Scared it's too good to be true, that it might not last."

He squeezed her hand. "Wanta know what I'm feeling?"

"Of course, I do."

"The same things you're feeling. Mostly, I'm scared you'll change your mind—especially when I'm gone for weeks at a time. Honey, I'd like to run away with you. Right now. This minute. Just take off and get married. Snag a minister and get hitched. Before you can change your mind. Oh wait, this is Sunday. We can't get a license today. And I think there's a three day waiting period. In Washington."

He gave her a magnanimous grin. "How about it? Wanta run away and get married? We could keep it secret. Have a church wedding with all the trimmings later, if you'd like."

She snickered. "Danny, is that a proposal?"

"What? You want the whole nine yards? Me down on a knee?" He released her hand and screwed up his face in exaggerated concentration on the road. "That's gonna be a little hard when I'm driving."

"Well, I'm not running away with you until I get a proper proposal."

He pulled to the curb, parked and shut off the engine. "I'd propose standing on my head if I thought you really would run away with me." He caressed her cheek. "You won't do that though, will you?"

Surprised he read her so well, she laid her head on his shoulder. "Danny, it's tempting. It really is. But getting married and keeping it secret, and then having a wedding later, has always seemed to me like trying to frost the cake after you've eaten all but the crumbs." She smiled into his eyes. "Besides, if I eloped with you, my mom would kill me. Then shoot you. She has her heart set on seeing her one and only daughter married in a traditional wedding."

He groaned, but his warm lips on hers told her he was okay with her decision. "We'll do it up right, sweetheart. To tell the truth, if your mom didn't succeed in killing me first, my mom would strangle me for cheating her out of a wedding. The folks are going to be thrilled when I tell them the news."

"But you still haven't asked me to marry you."

"I haven't?..."

"*Dannneee...*"

"Okay, darlin'." He held up a hand. "Stay right there."

He reached in the backseat and retrieved the car robe he'd learned to carry for emergencies. The blanket was still encased in it's protective plastic envelope. Before she could blink, he raced around the back of the car and opened her door. Quickly he unhooked the seatbelt and turned her to face him.

He threw the blanket down, just missing a puddle, and knelt on one knee. With her hand in his, he asked, "Miss Kathleen O'Brien—will you marry me?"

She pretended to consider, but only for a moment. "Yes, yes, yes. I will."

Overcome with emotion, and the absurdity of this man on his knee, proposing on a city street, cars slowing, people gawking, the young teacher giggled. She peered down at the gutter. "What are you kneeling on?"

Danny beamed, stood to his feet, made her a mock bow, then straightened and erupted into laughter.

Back in the car, he pulled her into his arms. Completely serious now, he whispered, "Sweetheart, you have no idea how happy I am—or how much I love you. I plan to spend the rest of my life showing you."

• • •

With studied nonchalance, the ring glinting from the third finger of her left hand, Kathleen sauntered into her friend's classroom. "Hi, Rosie. Ready to face another Monday morning?"

"Not really. I've had a rotten weekend," she groused while continuing to sort papers. "The phone never quit ringing and my kids were horrid. I could use another day to sleep." She heaved a sigh and looked up from her desk. "Well, you look like the cat that swallowed the canary before breakfast. You musta had a good weekend. What's up?"

She shifted her hand and the light caught her ring.

"Oh, leapin' lizards! Is that an engagement ring on your finger?" Rosie reached for her hand and inspected the diamond flanked by two small pearls. "Pretty, Kathleen. Really nice. Not too flashy. Very classy. And not at all what I might have expected from our esteemed banker."

She leaned back in her chair, placed her hands behind her head. "So…Edward finally found you, and you two obviously have made up. He was looking everywhere for you over the weekend, called me twice on Saturday thinking I might know of your whereabouts. He looked disappointed when you weren't in church Sunday. I don't think he stayed for the whole service. Guess he went searching for you and apparently worked fast once he located you."

Kathleen reddened and dropped her left hand. "Um, I am engaged, but not to Edward."

"*What?* Who, then? My word, Kathleen, you work fast. Or have you been holding out on me?" The fifth grade teacher lurched from her chair and stood behind her desk. Shoulders thrust forward, hands propped on the worn surface. The look on her face one of disbelief. A scowl generally reserved for an errant student. "Kathleen! Come on girl, give with the juicy details. And this better be good. Or you're in big trouble."

She hid her left hand in the folds of her black wool skirt and stared unseeing at the large impartial clock on the wall.

"Yeah. I suppose it did happen kinda fast. Rosie, it's not *quite* like you're thinking. I've known Danny a long time. I know him better than I ever knew Edward, and, and, well—I gotta get to my room. I'll fill you in later."

Rosie moved quickly from behind her desk and hugged her friend. "Kathleen, I'm sorry. I'm happy for you. Really! I am! It's just that you knocked me over with a thunderbolt. I'll let you go for now. The bus, with all our little darlings, will be here in about twenty minutes, but you're not leaving this school until you've told me all."

• • •

Kathleen tossed her books and students' papers onto the bed, kicked off her shoes and stuck her feet into warm fuzzy slippers. Tired, disgruntled, and peevish, after her less-than-perfect day at school, she needed to face Martha and repeat yet again, the ring on her finger didn't mean she was engaged to Edward.

So far, the only ones who seemed genuinely happy she wore Danny's ring, and not Edward's, were she and Danny. Her parents had seemed reluctant to give their blessing when she'd called them Sunday night with the news. *Did she really know Danny? What about the intervening years between high school and now? Wasn't she moving a little fast? What about Edward? Wasn't he a nice man destined to go places?* The questions made Kathleen want to scream, but she had answered calmly and politely. If only they could not worry and trust her judgment.

Her good friend and colleague, claimed to be happy for

her, but she too, couldn't quite hide the uncertainty. The same skepticism she might have for a student claiming to have done her homework when she knew none of the answers on the history test. *I suppose it's justified.* She acquiesced. *But Rosie of all people, should know I'd never marry Edward.*

Kathleen squared her shoulders, lifted her chin, and marched down the stairs and into the kitchen, where she found Martha sliding a pan of lasagna into the oven. Fresh-baked bread gave off a mouth-watering aroma from the counter.

Martha straightened, turned and peered up at her. "Oh, I didn't hear you come in, but I'm glad you're home. You look tired, dear…and before I forget, Edward came here looking for you Sunday. He practically insisted I tell him where you were—as if I should know."

She took a knife and began to slowly and methodically slice bread to set on the table. Butter, in a small blue crock, and her own strawberry freezer jam in a pretty crystal dish followed. Cute little spreader knifes, each one different, both with silly handles, elicited a smile. Brightly flowered paper napkins, in rainbow colors were already laid out and waiting on the table in the breakfast nook. Instead of tea, the landlady poured tall glasses of milk.

"Sit here at the table, Kathleen, and tell me all about your day."

Chapter 26

She took a deep breath. "I do have things to tell you—and I hope you won't think I'm some kind of Jezebel when you hear my news."

Martha stopped buttering bread and stared at her. "I have no idea what you want to tell me; but my dear, I would never consider you a Jezebel. *Never.*"

Uncertain as a first-grader presenting a crayon drawing for approval, she withdrew the hand she'd kept hidden in her lap and placed it on the table in front of her silver-haired friend. The ring gleamed and glistened and silently shouted her engagement.

"Oh, my! What a beautiful ring." After wiping her fingers with a paper napkin, she lifted Kathleen's hand for a better inspection. "Very dainty. I've always liked pearls, and with the diamond, this ring is stunning." She smiled broadly and gently released her hand. "So you're engaged. And I'll bet not to that banker fellow—am I right? Could you be engaged to that nice looking man you were with in the restaurant?"

Kathleen's jaw dropped and hung there for a few seconds until she remembered to close her mouth. "Martha, it's uncanny the way you know things. Everyone at school assumed I'd gotten engaged to Edward."

"Well, in the Salem witchcraft days, they may have tried me for a witch." She tittered at the thought. "But, dear, it's not so unusual. I simply pay close attention to what I see and what I hear. Maybe because I married my Earl after knowing him for only three weeks; I know it doesn't take long to fall in love. Our marriage lasted fifty-one years, two months and seventeen days, before the Good Lord took him home. I'm sure we blamed World War II—our excuse at the time—for marrying so quickly. We were in love and wanted to grab all the happiness we could before he shipped out. I'm not sure long courtships prove anything."

Martha smiled, blinked, and pushed the glasses back on her nose. "To tell the truth, I always thought there was something missing in your relationship with the banker. That certain spark seemed to be lacking. No doubt, he's a nice man, but you appeared to be trying too hard to please him. Of course that's just one old woman's opinion, an old woman who talks too much."

This time Kathleen remembered to keep her mouth closed, but she was speechless.

"When do I get to meet this lucky young man who's won your heart?"

"Martha, you're simply incredible. Thank you for validating my judgment. Danny will be here this Friday—I'll introduce you to him then. I think you'll like him. His name is

Daniel Lee Davis. I've known him a long time, though we just recently reconnected."

Kathleen smiled, finished her milk, then excused herself and pushed away from the table. Good manners demanded she not bolt from the room. She restrained herself by easing to the window and pretending to be interested in what lay beyond, before turning again to face her elderly companion.

"What is it, dear? What's bothering you?"

"I'm angry that Edward is looking for me and questioning people. He has no right. I need to put a stop to it."

"A phone call should take care of that. That isn't what's really troubling you—is it?"

"No—you're right. It's Patti. Spike dropped her off late again—hair uncombed, and jam smeared on her blouse. I dried her tears, brushed her hair, and washed her face…there wasn't too much I could do about the soiled blouse. But what really scares and concerns me—Patti tells me, 'Mommy got sick, and Mommy yells at me.' Martha, I know you told me not to become too involved, but I can't help worrying about this child."

• • •

Early Tuesday morning fog wrapped the Willamette valley in gray tentacles. She didn't notice the familiar BMW in the school parking lot until she stepped from her car.

"Hello, Kathleen."

"Edward! What are you doing here?"

"Is that any way to greet an old friend? I came to see you, of course."

She felt her face grow hot, but when she spoke her voice dripped ice. "What do you want?"

"I came to ask you once more to come with me to California. Forget this teaching nonsense and the boyfriend I know you've been seeing. We'd be good together, Kathleen; you know we would." He took a step closer and reached for her.

"Stop it!" She knocked his hand aside and stepped back. "I'm not going with you. Not now. Not ever. I don't want you touching me."

"*Fine*!" His eyes grew steely, his voice scathing. "I thought you might say that. Actually, I'm glad. It clears the way for me to take Jeannie—Remember Jeannie?—the good looking little bank teller I hired?"

"The girl with the Jeep."

"I thought you might remember." His face twisted in a smirk. "Pretty, isn't she? And she wants me, too. We spent a week together in California. You're not the only one that can play around, my dear."

Kathleen thought she might be sick. Could this be the man she had dated and contemplated marrying? *Was he even a Christian?*

"I'm assuming you listened to the message I left on your recorder asking you to not bother my friends for information about me. You have to know—I don't want to see you."

"Well—I wanted to see you—baby," he sneered. "And where better to catch you than here at your precious school."

He turned as if to go, then whirled around and stepped forward until he was almost in her face. "By the way, that kid you're so hung up on. The Williams' brat isn't it? Guess she'll be leaving your little school. I hear her old lady's headed for stardom. Ms. Amber Williams is quitting, leasing her beauty shop—she plans to travel with a band."

"Who told you that?"

"Oh no, my dear. I don't divulge my sources—but then maybe she'll leave the kid behind."

The look on his face told Kathleen he was enjoying springing this on her.

A car slowed and turned into the school, the headlights penetrated the gloom and momentarily illuminated them before moving on to a parking spot. It was all the distraction needed for Kathleen to clamp a lid on her emotions and not let this man rattle her.

She gripped her purse and notebook and held them like a shield in front of her.

"You'll have to forgive me if I don't stay to chat." He could hardly miss the sarcasm. "Ms. Brooks just arrived. The busses with the children are next. I have a class to teach. I need to be in my classroom. Good bye, Edward—I hope you'll find happiness in your endeavors."

The ability to turn and walk sedately to her classroom, shoulders back and chin high, when every nerve screamed for a hasty retreat seemed nothing short of a miracle. Not once did she look back, but she couldn't fail to hear the car door slam. Or miss the screech of tires as he gunned from the school grounds.

• • •

Recess came and passed faster than a teacher can down a cup of coffee. Patti still hadn't arrived by the time students took their seats. The twins, Bobby and Jerry, were disruptive during reading time and had been called down by their teacher. Now they were back in their desks smirking at each other. Kathleen's head throbbed.

The children settled down to work hard on simple arithmetic when a knock on the door caught their attention. The teacher instructed them to continue counting and adding quietly while she answered. *No doubt it's Patti, late again.* The thought barely had time to whip through her thoughts before she opened the door. Spike stood there. Alone.

"Spike? What's wrong? Where's Patti?"

The young man looked at his toes and said nothing until Kathleen's heart was in her throat and she wanted to shake him.

"*Spike?*"

Slowly his head came up and he looked her in the eye. "Patti's okay. She's home today with her mother. Miss O'Brien—I told Amber she should come and talk to you, but she's got this thing about facing you. There's a letter in the office explaining the situation. Maybe in the long run things will be better for Patti. I sure don't know nothin' about bein' a dad. I told Amber I don't. She shouldn't expect it. Besides, Patti has a dad."

"And are you trying to be a father to Patti, Mr. …?

Spike dropped his chin, then raised it again and faced her, his blue eyes troubled. "George, my name is George Cooper…and yeah, I suppose I have been. Or maybe just a friend. I know Patti's been late on Mondays; but I did feed her and get her here."

Kathleen heard a titter in the classroom behind her. As much as she wished to know more, she hadn't time to stand here and pry answers from Spike. "Thank you, Mr. Cooper, I appreciate your stopping to talk to me."

"Yeah...okay...I know you have a class to teach, so, I'll be going." Spike looked at his toes and mumbled. "You're okay, Miss O'Brien, wish I'd had a teacher like you." He spun and strode to his car, but not before she saw him turn red as a checkmark on a wrong answer.

No doubt about it, Spike raised more questions than he answered. Kathleen wasn't quite ready to declare this the morning from hell, but it could certainly enter the contest. If a raging headache scored points, and frustration counted, it could easily come in a close second, and one more upsetting incident make it a winner.

The children were too quiet and too studious when she turned her attention back to the classroom. Something suspicious going on and it remained for the teacher to discover what, and quickly. A slow walk around desks and tables revealed nothing unusual, but student's heads ducked even lower and a muffled giggle from someone reached her ears.

She hesitated beside John's desk and suggested he rework problem three. Then she stopped beside Jerry's desk and scanned his work. Jerry had solved four problems and they were correct, but a slow red began to creep up the little boy's neck while his teacher stood there.

Miss O'Brien moved to the front of the classroom and

managed a plastic smile as she spoke to her students. "Class, I see some of you are having trouble with today's assignment, so I'm going to help you by working some problems on the board. Jerry, would you come forward and show the class how to do number three and number four?"

The twin wearing the yellow shirt rose from his seat and started forward. "No, Bobby, I know *you've* done the problems correctly, but I want Jerry to work this one. Jerry, you may get your yellow shirt back from your brother, and please sit at your own desk from now on. What do you think class, has their little game of deception gone on long enough?"

Heads lifted, a few children giggled, and all eyes focused on the teacher as together the class called out a thundering, "Yes."

Kathleen smiled and complimented Jerry on a job well done. The problems he worked before the class were correct and she hoped he went to his seat feeling good about himself.

"I'll give you ten more minutes to work on your arithmetic and then we're going to do something a little different this morning. I have a headache and I need you to be really quiet until lunchtime. Instead of singing before our noon break, you may color. And I need two volunteers to come forward when you've finished working the arithmetic problems, get the pictures to color and pass them out to the class."

Busy-work to be sure, but I must have it quiet if I'm to make it through the rest of the day. Substitutes hate being called with half an hour's notice. Most won't come. Kathleen didn't blame them.

"All right, Bobby, you and Molly may pass out the papers. Give two pictures to each classmate. Children, if you're extra quiet perhaps we can have a longer story time after noon recess.

It's called bribery, or maybe saving your sanity, the teacher thought as she unlocked her desk drawer and reached for the aspirin. They don't teach it in college, but every elementary teacher learns to use it at some point.

She leaned back in her chair, closed her eyes for a moment and let her squelched emotions rise to the top like mercury in a thermometer. She wouldn't want to wish Edward any bad luck, but if he had four flat tires on his way to California, and he woke up with warts all over his face, and his little playmate dumped him, well, it would be no more than Mr. Important-Bank-Manager Edward Connors deserved.

Kathleen indulged in a few more *mind pleasantries* for Edward, then switched her thoughts to worry about the letter waiting for her in the office. She'd reached the third "what if?" scenario when a warm hand touched her arm. Her eyes flew open and she jumped as though she'd been caught napping in a teacher's meeting while the Superintendent of Schools gave a talk.

"Miss O'Brien?"

"Bobby. What is it?"

The little boy looked uncertain, brown eyes round and luminous as he held out a fist and slowly disclosed his offering. "Miss O'Brien, you can have my candy bar. My mommy gets a headache when she's hungry. My daddy buys her chocolates and then she feels all better."

Kathleen melted. She wanted to hug him. She wanted to pick him up and hold him on her lap, ruffle his curly blonde hair. Of course, she did none of those things. The smile she bestowed on the little rapscallion made him wriggle like a puppy and scuff his white sneakers.

"Bobby, that's very nice and very thoughtful of you. Thank you." *Handle this one carefully, Kathleen, or you'll have the whole class bringing you treats by the carload.* "But I really think you should eat it. Coffee is what makes my headache better, and I'll get a cup at lunchtime."

Chapter 27

Kathleen entered the school office and hesitated when she saw the secretary talking on the phone. "Close the door," she mouthed as she motioned the first grade teacher to a chair. Ms. Brooks absently tugged on a lock of hair, a shade darker than the champagne blouse she wore, while she listened to a parent's concerns.

Hazel's lunch, spread out on a napkin across her desk, bore the unmistakable scent of tuna fish, dill pickle, and potato chips. The odor of fish and pickle did nothing for Kathleen's headache.

"I'll never know why parents think lunchtime is the best time to call the school. Maybe they just like to catch me with my mouth full." The secretary rubbed her narrow, slightly elongated nose and rearranged some papers on her desk. "I'm glad you came in; I was about to come find you. I have some startling news that concerns one of your students, and there's a letter here, too, with your name on it. Now where did..."

Hazel frowned.

"What?"

"Kathleen, are you ill? Do you need me to call in a substitute? If you don't mind, my saying so—you look like you were sent for and couldn't make it. You're so pale. Do you have a migraine? Have you had a rough morning?"

"You might say that. My morning kinda got off to a bad start." She managed a tired half-smile. "But no, I don't need a substitute. I've taken some aspirin...I'll make it through the day."

"Well, I'm not sure if you'll consider this good news or bad news, but it's certainly surprising after the tirade Mrs. Williams displayed here in this office when she called me after Patti was back in school and made it perfectly clear she wanted Mr. Williams given no information about his daughter."

"*What news?*"

"Oh...sorry." Hazel waved a paper in the air. "We have an order here from the judge stating Mr. Alvin Williams, by specific request of Mrs. Williams, now has full custody of their daughter, Patti. All restrictions on contact with his daughter are cancelled, rescinded, abolished—now *why* do you suppose Mrs. Williams would do such a thing?"

Kathleen's mouth flew open, her eyes grew big, and she sprang from her chair as if she'd sat on a hot coal. "*What?—* Would you mind repeating that?."

"I know. Hard to believe isn't it. Mr. Williams has been given custody of Patti." The secretary took a bite of sandwich and managed to chew and talk at the same time. "What's wrong with the woman? Has she got a screw loose? I swear, I'll never understand parents if I live to be a hundred."

Kathleen thought Amber might very well have a screw loose or maybe she was just tired of being a mother. For whatever reason it looked as though she wouldn't be caring for Patti.

"You had a letter or something for me?"

"Oh. Yes. Maybe this will shed some light on what's going on." She opened a drawer, found what she was looking for and handed Kathleen a sealed envelope with her name printed in blue ink across the front.

"Thank you." She clutched the letter in a sweaty palm, turned and left the office, but not before she noticed the look of disappointment on the secretary's face. *Sorry, Hazel. Maybe later, but no one's going to watch for my reactions while I read this the first time. If Patti's world is collapsing, I want to be first to know.*

Locked in her room, she sat in the rocker, opened the envelope and removed a sheet of tablet paper. The message was short, but the large pencil-scrawl covered nearly a page.

> Kathleen, Spike said I should come talk to you but if I don't I hope you understand I want to spend time with my baby. By now you know Al will keep Patti, Spike said its for the best I hope thats right. This is my chance of a lifetime me, and Spike have been invited to appear on the Grand Old Opry and then travel all over with a country western star thats purty famous. Pattis gonna be so proud of her mommy, and I can buy her anything she wants when

> I get rich and famous. Maybe I'll buy you something to you been a good teacher to Patti. Patti likes you so I hope you can keep on teaching her. Well I guess thats all I got to say maybe you can come see us perform sometime. Amber

Kathleen fumed for all the good it was going to do her. Amber could have told her when she was leaving. She might have mentioned what Al planned to do. Had they even talked it over? Knowing those two, probably not. Would Al pull Patti out of her class and put her in another school? As far as she knew, Al lived somewhere up in the woods in a small trailer. Would he take Patti to live in the woods where she might have bears for playmates?

Stop it. She leaned her head back and set the rocker in motion with a strong shove of her foot on the floor. *And what business is it of yours if he does? You're Patti's teacher, not her guardian, and certainly not her mother. Maybe you should listen when people tell you not to get so involved.* "You bet, and maybe I could teach school with nothing but a piece of chalk and a blackboard," she groused under her breath. "I can't help worrying." Kathleen stuffed the sheet back in its envelope and rubbed her aching temples. "Poor Patti; I'll do all I can to help her."

She returned to the office and caught Hazel popping the last of the potato chips in her mouth. She laid the letter on the desk in front of her. It paid to stay on the good side of the woman who knew the comings and goings and inner workings of the school system.

"Read it, please, and tell me what you think?"

A look of surprise on her face, the secretary read and shook her head at the ending of each sentence, or at least where the sentence should have ended. “Well—this is interesting—but it doesn’t tell you what you want to know. What’s going to happen to the little Williams girl? Will her father take her out of our school?”

“My sentiments exactly and I haven’t a clue.”

“Do you want me to try contacting Mrs. or Mr. Williams to find out? Since the child’s absent today, it shouldn’t seem too unusual.”

“No—it’s their call. Guess I just wanted someone to commiserate with.” Kathleen rolled her eyes and snatched a cookie from the desk. “Some people should raise chickens instead of children.”

“Exactly. Or maybe rutabagas.”

• • •

Wednesday passed, an uneventful day at school. Before retiring that night, she crossed the date off on her calendar. Two more days and she’d see Danny.

The sun chose to shine Thursday, and though it was only the latter part of February, it felt like a day in May. Kathleen bent the rules and let the children play an extra ten minutes while she sat on a swing in the warm sunlight and watched them. Her thoughts alternated between Danny and Patti.

Thoughts of Danny were a warm fuzzy, but Patti’s situation troubled her. The little girl missed too much school. Kathleen would do what she could to help the child if she returned to her classroom, but the downside was not enough hours in the day for concentrated individual help. *I could request an aide, but I doubt there's enough money in the budget.* With Patti falling behind, if she didn't get extra help soon, Kathleen feared she'd become discouraged.

• • •

The warm sunshine didn't last. By the time she sat down at the table with Martha, to eat a bowl of bean soup, a cold front had moved down from Alaska. The temperature dropped twenty degrees and a drizzle ran in sluggish rivulets down the windowpane.

"Excuse me, dear, is it cold in here, or is it just my old bones?" The landlady pushed her chair back and rose from the table. "I'm going to get my sweater from the closet, and I think I'll turn up the heat a bit."

No sooner had Martha traipsed off toward the bedroom, her slippers slap slapping on the linoleum, than the phone started to ring. "Will you get that, dear?" she called.

"Hello. Fisher residence."

"This ain't Martha is it? Kathleen?"

"Yes, this is Kathleen."

"Well, this is Al, and it's you I wanta talk to. Maybe you can tell me what's goin' on. I got a thing from the judge, and unless this is some kinda elaborate sick joke, I've got custody of my daughter."

"It's no joke. The school received a document from the judge as well."

"Well, I'll be double dipped—It's true then? You're sure? I don't pick up my mail every day, just junk mail and bills.

But I got this note a few days ago from Amber, sayin' she's leavin' and I can have Patti. To come pick up her clothes. No explanation. *Nothing.* I figured she was jerkin' me around—her cracked idea of a joke. A big ha ha if she could land me back in jail. Then I got this official-looking document—so—is Patti cool with this? Is my kid okay?"

"I don't know, Al. Patti hasn't been in school this week. I think Amber wants to spend as much time with her as she can before leaving."

Kathleen winced and pulled the phone away from her ear as Al let fly with a loud expletive. In her best teacher's voice, she enunciated, "Al, I'm not deaf."

"Yeah, sorry—but that woman can make me *so* mad. What's she tryin' to prove? Does she wanta make Patti fail? I'll bet she's not helping her at home neither. And I'd be surprised if she spends more than twenty minutes a day talkin' to Patti. If I know her, she's parked in front of the TV watchin' her stupid soap operas."

"Al, what are *your* plans?"

"Well, I've barely had time to make any, and I'm kinda out on a limb here. For sure I can't bring Patti to live with me up in the woods. And my trailer is hardly big enough for both of us, but it may have to do for now. That's if I can get someone to move it."

"So, will you be placing your daughter in a different school? You don't live here. I'm sure living in this district isn't convenient to your work."

Kathleen motioned for Martha to finish her soup and not wait for her. This call could take awhile.

"No. I wanta keep her there in your school. I want you to teach her. I figure the kid'll have enough changes to cope with...I'll find a place to stay in the district. Somehow. There's always the folks. Though I hate to burden Clara; she has Granddad to take care of."

"Might you rent or lease your ex-wife's place while she's gone?"

Al snorted. "Yeah. *Sure!* When loggers fall trees with axes, and *I* haul 'em out with my brand new Mack truck. Or—if you prefer—when pigs fly and hell freezes over. She'd board the blasted house up before she'd let *me* live there."

Kathleen sighed. *What do these people hope to prove by their selfish behavior?* Aloud she intoned, "Not even to help Patti?"

Al ignored the remark as not worthy of an answer.

"I'm comin' out there soon as we hang up; I need to talk to Amber. I just hope I can keep from beltin' her one. The scatterbrained—she *mighta* given me a little more time to prepare. But I'm picking Patti up this evening—whether Amber likes it or not."

"Al, hold your temper. Think of your daughter."

"I don't suppose you'd like to go with me? You do have a calming influence, you know."

She laughed. "I don't think that's a good idea, but I'm happy to know I'll still be Patti's teacher. I'll do what I can to help you both."

"Fair enough. And one way or another—I'll have the kid in school tomorrow."

Chapter 28

The next morning John clambered down the steps of the school bus first; Patti followed close on his heels. Kathleen smiled as they entered her classroom; the children's happy chatter did much to reaffirm the teacher's belief. Her students liked school.

"Hi, Miss O'Brien," Patti chirped. "Mommy and I went shopping. She bought me these new clothes. I picked 'em out myself. Do you like 'em?"

New jeans with floral appliqués, sequins, and a corresponding scarf belt; pink turtleneck sweater, and appliquéd matching denim jacket completed her outfit.

"Good morning, children. Welcome back, Patti. We've missed you. I do like your new clothes. You look very pretty."

Patti beamed. "Miss O'Brien, I have a note from my daddy." The child reached in her pocket and handed the teacher a slip of carefully folded paper. "I'm gonna live with my daddy now, and maybe my grandma."

• • •

Morning crept by with no disruption in routine. Kathleen found a few minutes before first recess to explain and help Patti catch up on some work she had missed. "Don't try to do all the pages now. Do one or two extra a day until you're caught up. You'll be staying here with me after school today, and going to your grandmother's house on the later bus with the big kids. You'll have time to play, and then perhaps we can work on your lessons together. I'll be glad to help you then."

Thankful she didn't have playground duty this week, Kathleen watched a few minutes as her students scattered for the swings, teeter-totters, jungle gym, and merry-go-round. Shrieks and laughter filled the air. Satisfied things were going well and her students were happy to play in the cold sunshine, she headed indoors for a quick cup of coffee.

She sat behind her desk, a dreamy smile on her face as she sipped the hot beverage and romanticized about her wedding and the kind of dress she wanted to wear. *One more day, and Danny will be here.* So many plans to make. So much to discuss. *Where will we be married? We need to…*

Her musings were interrupted by a courtesy knock on the door before the on-duty teacher pushed it open. "Oh, good! You're here." The fourth grade teacher ushered in a sobbing Patti and a red-faced Bobby. "Sorry to interrupt your break time. These two got into a shoving match; I'd handle it, but I think Patti may have skinned her knee.

"Thank you, Helen. I'll take care of them."

Patti howled louder, while her nose streamed, and tears

coursed down a reddened face. Kathleen led the little girl to a chair, sat her down, and handed her a tissue from the box kept on her desk. "Wipe your nose, Patti. Hush your crying and tell me what this is all about."

"He pu...pu-sh...pus-hed me." She stammered amid hiccoughs. "I felled and-and-and tore my jeans. They're all *r-u-i-n-e-d*," she wailed.

"Let's have a look and see if you skinned your knee." Gently the teacher pulled up the leg of her torn jeans. "Well, you scraped it a little bit. But it's not too bad. We'll wash it off and put on a Band Aid. That should make it feel better."

Kathleen turned to Bobby, whom she'd been totally aware of, though he'd remained quieter than a mouse in a cheese factory, while he stood behind her. He grew exceptionally interested in his shoes, scuffed the toe of one sneaker on the floor, and then tried to hide that foot behind the other. His hands seemed ill at ease as well, not knowing whether to twist in front or behind him. When the teacher didn't say anything, he raised tear-filled eyes a fraction and peered up at her.

"Bobby? Did you push Patti and make her fall?"

Tears brimmed over and slid down his cheeks. "Yeah. But I didn't know she was gonna fall."

"Why did you push her?"

"She shoved me first."

"Uh-huh...Patti? Is this true? Did you shove Tommy first?"

"But he chased me. And he put a *bug* down my neck."

"I see. Where is the bug now?"

Both children stopped their sniveling and stared at the

teacher. Kathleen repeated the question. "Patti? Bobby? Where is the bug now? What did you do, Patti, when Bobby put the bug down your neck?"

"I shaked him off."

"And the bug didn't hurt you?"

Patti stared at the floor. In a small voice, she said, "No." Slowly the elfin face tipped up, and large blue eyes looked at the teacher. "But I don't *like* bugs on me." She shuddered. "I *hate* bugs."

"I'm sure you do. How do you think the bug may have felt, being put down someone's neck? Then being shook off? Bobby? Patti?"

The children hesitated, looked at each other, and then recited in unison. "Scared?"

Kathleen finished cleaning the scraped knee and placed a Band-Aid over the wound. "There. Patti, I think your new jeans can be repaired. Please don't cry anymore."

She smiled at her little charges. "Bobby, I'm sure you didn't mean to hurt Patti. Let's leave the bugs alone after this, and absolutely no more pushing or shoving from either of you. Okay?"

The bell rang signaling the end of recess. Rosy-cheeked children trouped into the classroom and hovered around Patti like Dwarfs around Snow White, asking what happened and was she all right. Bobby got his share of attention as well. Most of his classmates thought he was in trouble and were surprised and relieved to learn he wasn't being punished.

Students quickly settled down to routine and the happy hum of contented children working on lessons filled the classroom. The teacher needn't worry over Bobby; he'd be fine. Kathleen felt Patti's outburst on the playground had more to do with changes at home, than pranks played at school. How upset she might be over her mother leaving, she could only guess and hope at some point Patti might confide in her.

The day wore on more slowly than Kathleen thought possible. She taught school by rote and let her mind jump ahead to the weekend. *Is Danny counting the hours until evening, even as I am? Why does time pass so slowly when you're waiting to see someone you love? I feel like a child waiting for Christmas.*

Only hours remained before she'd see Danny. She didn't want to share those first moments with anyone, but she'd promised to help Al and Patti.

Kathleen swallowed her disappointment and smiled at the little blonde pixie standing beside her desk. "Patti, you will be going home with me after school today. It will be somewhat late when your father picks you up, but it sounds as if you will get to ride in his log truck. That should be fun."

"Yeah, my daddy told me. And it'll be fun goin' home with you, Miss O'Brien." Patti's grin exposed two missing teeth. "I'll get catched up in my workbooks. My daddy said he'd help me."

"That's great, and perhaps I can help you, too, while you're waiting for your father."

• • •

The smell of baking cookies permeated the air as Patti and Kathleen entered Martha's house through the back entrance.

"I'll take your coat and hang it in the guest closet. You can get it easily when your father comes to get you."

Snowball climbed from his basket, stretched one back leg at a time, yawned, and shuffled over to inspect their new visitor. The cat rubbed his furry head on Patti's legs and began to purr.

"I think Snowball likes you."

"He's pretty. Can I pick him up? I wish I had a kitty."

"Snowball's pretty heavy. But yes, I think you can pick him up if you'd like. He's gentle."

A car slowed and Kathleen rushed to the window to look. *Oh, I hope that's Danny, here early.* The vehicle passed on by; she sighed and turned back to watch Patti put her arms underneath the cat and heave the animal upward.

"Boy, Miss O'Brien, this cat's heavier thana tub a lard. Bet he's eatin' more than three square meals a day. I'm puttin' this big ole cat back on the floor."

Kathleen smothered a chuckle. *Where has this child heard that kind of talk?*

Snowball continued to purr and rub his body against all available legs. Patti dropped to her knees and stroked the silky fur. She giggled when the cat stuck out his pink tongue and began a thorough wash-job on his chest.

"Maybe we should follow Snowball's example, and wash our hands. If I know Martha, she has goodies waiting for us in the kitchen."

"Something smells really good." Patti blurted as they entered the breakfast nook.

Martha smiled. "Well, hello, you two. I thought I heard

voices. Patti, you probably don't remember me, but I feel I know you. I first saw you when you were just a baby. I'm a friend of your grandmother."

Patti, suddenly shy in the presence of a stranger, ducked her head.

"Come and sit down at the table. I've made cookies. I hope you like chocolate chip."

"They smell wonderful. If we weren't hungry before, we are now." Kathleen poured a tall glass of milk and set it on the table in front of Patti.

• • •

"I talked to your Grandmother today," Martha continued in a warm, friendly voice. "She told me she is taking your grandfather to the doctor this afternoon."

"Yeah, my grandpa's pretty bad; he's got rightus or…something."

"Arthritis?"

"Yeah. That's it. But my daddy says it ain't hurt his blather none. Miss O'Brien, what's his blather?"

Martha turned away and hid a smile. Kathleen nearly choked on a cookie, and quickly covered her mouth with a napkin before she could erupt into laughter.

"Well, Patti, I think it may be a special way of talking."

"Oh." She gulped milk and reached for another cookie. "My grandpa knows lots a funny stuff. He makes me laugh. Gramma says it's fairy tales, and nursery rhymes mixed with foolishness."

Martha smiled. "Does your grandfather tell you stories of when he was a little boy?"

"Oh, yeah. Grandpa says they were real poor. But they had lotsa animals. And Grandpa had a pet goat. I liked that ole goat. He's funny. Grandpa says that ole goat ate his underpants right off the clothesline."

Kathleen laughed and checked her watch again. *Danny should be here any minute, if he didn't get held up in traffic.* "If you two will excuse me, I'll dash upstairs and freshen up a bit."

"You go ahead, dear. We'll finish our cookies and milk; and then, Patti, maybe you'd like to feed Snowball his supper?"

• • •

The cell phone chimed as she began to wash her face. Quickly, she reached for a towel, dried her hands, and answered. "Hello?"

"Kathleen?"

"Danny. Where are you? Are you held up in traffic?"

"Um...Not exactly."

"What do you mean? Not exactly. Danny?—Where are you?—Are you okay?"

" —Kathleen—Honey? I'm sorry. But I'm in Chicago."

"*What?—Chicago?*"

"I know. I'm disappointed, too. But this came up suddenly, and it's an assignment I can't turn down."

Can't or won't? Her mind raced, but her body felt frozen in time, like one of those characters in a science-fiction movie.

"Kathleen? Sweetheart? Are you there?"

She collapsed on the edge of the bed. Her heart beat too fast—and hot tears trickled down her face. The lump in her throat threatened to choke her. She gripped the phone in an icy hand with knuckles turned white. *How can you do this to us?* Aloud she managed to croak. "I'm here."

"I know this is poor timing, and you've had no warning—but I'll be back before you know it. Once I'm through with this assignment, we'll spend days together. I should be back about the time you're ready for spring break."

More silence. *If I say anything, Danny's going to know I'm crying. He probably knows anyway.* "Okay," was all she could manage to squeeze past the swelling in her throat.

"It's *not* okay, is it? I hear it in your voice. Honey, talk to me. I know you're disappointed, but I did warn you—this is what my life is all about."

"I know. You *did* warn me, but I didn't know it could happen so soon…I didn't know—" She broke off and reached for a tissue. "You must admit this is a bit of a shock. I expected you to arrive *here* any minute."

"I know, sweetheart. I'm not exactly dancing in the streets myself. I hate to leave you like this. Honey? Please tell me you're going to be okay."

A roiling mixture of disappointment and anger churned her stomach. Her voice came out sounding raspy, but stronger. "Danny, if you tell me you're going to *Iraq* again—I just may get a gun and shoot you myself."

He sighed. "Nope, not this time—Israel—maybe I'll bring you back a picture of me at the wailing wall."

So who needs a wall? I can wail without any visual aids. Thank you very much! She took a deep breath, slowly let it out, and said, "Danny, just come back in one piece."

"You got it...Sweetheart, I've got to go—You'll be okay?"

She answered in a voice she hoped sounded positive, in spite of the fact her throat felt as if she'd swallowed a goose egg, shell and all. "I'll be okay." *What choice do I have?*

Kathleen released her stranglehold on the cell phone and turned it off. She hadn't known Danny's leaving could hurt so much. It felt like rejection. Did she really want a marriage with long and sudden separations?

Chapter 29

In a matter of minutes, with one phone call, plans for the weekend had fallen apart faster than a jet trail from a Boeing 747. Danny quite effectively relieved her of several needs—the need to apply fresh makeup, the need to change her wrinkled skirt and less-than-fresh blouse, and the need to spend time on her appearance. She splashed cold water on her face, and ignored the mirror above the bathroom basin. The two people waiting for her downstairs wouldn't care how she looked, if they even noticed.

Of course little escaped Martha's eye, and if Kathleen thought otherwise it only indicated the extent of her turmoil. She kicked her shoes across the room and found a slight satisfaction in hearing them strike the wall. It took seconds to find her slippers and slide her feet into them. *Part of me may as well be comfortable, even if I feel like I've been dropped from a plane without a parachute.* No matter how much she longed to hole up in her apartment, see no one, give vent to her feelings unobserved, and act like a child sent to her room for time-out, that luxury wasn't an option. Patti waited downstairs.

Martha, busy at the counter preparing a fresh pot of tea, turned and winked when she heard Kathleen reenter the kitchen. There sat Patti on the floor, with her nose less than a foot from Snowball, completely absorbed in watching the cat eat his dry kibbles. The child remained oblivious to anything else, totally unaware of the picture she made.

Kathleen grinned, and before she could squelch it, the thought came unbidden. *I wish Danny were here to see this. No doubt he'd take their picture.* A sigh escaped her lips as mentally she gave herself a shake. She had to stop thinking *Danny* with every other breath. Where had she stashed her independence? What kept her from taking pictures? So what if she wasn't a professional. She certainly knew how to aim a camera and take a picture.

While Martha got down fine porcelain cups, and moved to the table with the teapot, Kathleen dashed back upstairs and grabbed her digital camera. Before Snowball could finish his supper, she had returned and snapped three candid pictures.

Martha smiled, her eyes danced with merriment behind the glasses that slipped down her nose. She poured two cups of tea, the orange-spice fragrance wafting upward on the steam. "A good cup of tea can make almost any situation better, I've found." Her voice low as she stirred sugar into the hot liquid.

"Snowball hasn't had this much attention since my youngest grandchildren were here at Christmastime." She smiled and nodded toward the tableau on the floor. "He's lapping it up along with his supper. I wouldn't say he's exactly grinning like a Cheshire cat, but he certainly looks pleased with himself. If cats can be said to smile, then he's smiling—or maybe smirking."

Kathleen sipped her tea and kept her eyes downcast. She hoped Patti and Snowball were enough distraction to keep Martha from noticing if her eyes were a bit red. Sooner or later, she needed to tell this motherly friend about Danny going to Israel. But for now, she could count on her not to ask questions.

It had been so easy to tell Danny she'd never expect him to change his lifestyle, or give up the career he loved, in the passion of the moment with him sitting beside her. Faced with the reality of what that meant, she could only wonder if she'd been a bit hasty.

She massaged the back of her neck; she needed to clamp a lid on her heated emotions and shove all the frustration to the back burner of her mind. A smile tugged at the corners of her mouth as she watched Patti stand and stretch in a fair imitation of Snowball's satisfied air after the cat downed his supper.

Martha chuckled as the cat rubbed his furry head against the little girl's leg, then hoisted his tail like a flag being run up a pole and marched to the back door. "Patti, would you like to let Snowball out for me? He'll let us know when he wants back in."

"Yes, ma'am. I like your cat. He's pretty. And he's big, too."

Task completed, Patti came back and plopped in a chair beside the table. She kicked off her sneakers, then knelt on her knees in the chair's seat. It put her almost at eye-level with her teacher. "Miss O'Brien, you look just like my mommy when she's sad. Are you sad?"

Kathleen winced and ran her tongue over her bottom lip. *So much for pretenses.* She thought about fibbing, but just as quickly rejected the idea, and answered with all the truth of a person on trial. "I'm sorry if I seem unhappy, but yes, you're right; I am a bit sad. I expected my special friend to come and see me this weekend, but he can't make it."

Patti left her chair, and with eyes grown round and solemn, she slipped her arms around her teacher's neck and hugged as if she were clinging to a lifeline. Instead of letting go, the child buried her face in Kathleen's neck, and started to sob.

Acting on instinct, she pulled the little girl onto her lap and held her close. A ragged sigh assaulted the lump in her throat and burst free to join the child's wail. Kathleen wondered how much torture her hurting heart could take. Guilt hammered her emotions as well. She blinked back tears. How could she be so blinded by her own needs and not recognize a child on the edge of despair?

Martha placed a box of Kleenex on the table. "Well, aren't we a soppy bunch? I wonder what Snowball will think of all the waterworks?" Her face creased in a teary smile; she quietly distributed a handful of tissues.

At the mention of Snowball, Patti lifted her head and gently scooted from the teacher's lap...Kathleen dabbed at her eyes, sat up straighter, and tugged at her rumpled skirt. She welcomed the distraction, though she suspected the storm might not be over.

Her "teacher's hat" suddenly seemed too small. She wanted to comfort and reassure far beyond the role of mere teacher, but if she gave in to her feelings of the moment, she'd howl too. *Big help that would do! Who's the adult here, anyway?* Determined to aid the child who had a stranglehold on her heart, Kathleen smiled and nodded encouragement.

Patti blinked, sniffed, and blew her nose on the tissues handed her. "Is that ole cat ready to come in, do ya think?"

Martha smiled and nodded her head. "I think if you go to the backdoor and call, Snowball will come on a run."

• • •

The cat marched to the kitchen, like a VIP ready to inspect his lodgings, accepting attention as due him. He checked his dishes for any forgotten morsel, then purred his contentment as he rubbed against his new friend's legs.

Martha opened a drawer and took out a new catnip mouse. "I don't know about you two, but I'm ready to find my rocking chair. Shall we move to the other room? Patti, you may give this mouse to Snowball if you like. He'll bat it around and put on a show for us.

Kathleen glanced at her watch for the umpteenth time; still she jumped when the doorbell rang.

Patti looked up from where she played on the floor with the cat. "I bet that's my daddy."

Al looked as if he bore the weight of the world on his shoulders as he stood on the steps.

"Come in. Patti's been waiting for you."

"No. Better not. We gotta get movin'. I promised to drop her off at Amber's for a while this evening. Guess this is her final day here." Al looked at Kathleen over Patti's head and grimaced. "Ready, Patti cake?"

She watched as he scooped his daughter up in his arms and trudged down the driveway, his long legs eating the distance with each stride. He called, "Thanks," over his shoulder. "I'll be talkin' to ya."

He opened the door of the truck and deposited his daughter in the seat, turned to see Kathleen and Martha watching, and galloped back for another word with them. Al looked back at the truck then down at his feet as he ran a hand through his hair. "I don't suppose you ladies would let me take you to dinner this evening? Call me chicken, but I think it's gonna be rough after Patti sees her mother. I promised to take the kid out for a hamburger later and I could sure use some adult backup."

Martha frowned and slowly shook her head. "Alvin, I'd help if I could, but I've promised to go over some material with a friend from church. She said she'd drop by later. But maybe Kathleen could go."

Words of refusal sizzled on her tongue. She didn't want to be perceived, by anyone, to be dating Patti's father. Gossip spread faster than chalk dust from beaten erasers, in this small community, but her heart hurt for Patti, and she did want to help. Besides, she could use the distraction, whether she admitted it or not, she was more than a little miffed with Danny.

"How about it? Could we consider it an unscheduled parent-teacher conference? I could really use your help. I'm floundering here. Can I pick you up, say in an hour and a half?"

"Let's do this. I need to do some shopping anyway; why don't I just meet you in town at the restaurant? Tell me where and what time, and I'll be there.

• • •

Coffee in hand, Kathleen chose a table farthest from the entrance to the restaurant, but with a clear view of the door and the play area. She arrived early on purpose; but it didn't do much to alleviate her feeling of unease. The fast-food chain had recently opened a new place in Fir Valley, and kids flocked here like crows to a corn field. *Half the school children will probably show up here.* The thought no sooner crossed her mind than in the door walked John Adams with his family.

It took John less than a minute to see her. His eyes lit up and he took his baby sister by the hand and pulled her along. "Hi, Miss O'Brien. What are you doing here?"

"Well, hello, John. How nice to see you…and who is this young lady with you?"

"This is Sissy. She's my baby sister. She'll be in kindergarten next year." He tugged the little girl forward. Sissy stuck her thumb in her mouth and tried to hide behind her brother.

"Don't be scared. This's my teacher. She's nice."

The server waited patiently for the unaware children to move so she could place the lady's order on the table. Unfortunately the congestion only worsened as Patti rushed up, excited to see John, his little sister, and her teacher, all at the same time.

"Excuse me, children." Kathleen gently drew them aside. "I think this girl would like to set a tray down."

"Thank you," she voiced her relief.

Patti scooted onto the bench across from the teacher. "See the doll my mommy gave me?" She held the flaxen-haired doll, dressed in a blue, spangled cowgirl outfit, complete with rope, boots, and hat, out to Sissy. "You can hold her if you want." The little girl took her thumb from her mouth and held out her arms.

"Sissy, can you say, thank you?" Mrs. Adams watched and smiled as her little daughter hugged the doll. She winked at Kathleen; then prompted her daughter. "Give the dolly back now, honey, and come eat your French fries."

Conversation became stilted or nonexistent, as Al wolfed down four hamburgers and an enormous pile of fries. Patti worried one small burger while she wriggled, slurped chocolate milkshake, and consumed several French fries (one at a time) after first drowning them in catsup.

Kathleen pretended a great interest in her salad, and somehow managed not to fidget as she pushed it around with a plastic fork before shoving an occasional bite in her mouth. Mentally, she squirmed, as Al candidly watched her. *What? He's never seen a teacher eat salad before?* Her mind spun.

I feel like I'm back in Mr. Short's high school biology class, being studied like a bug under a microscope. Why is he staring at me?

Patti tapped his arm. "Daddy, can I go play in the tunnels and slides with John and Sissy?"

"Huh?... Yeah, I suppose so." He looked through the window at the play area, and moved aside to let her out. "Sure, go ahead, just come when I call you."

His face creased in a lopsided grin as he pointed to her Styrofoam cup. "Get you a refill?"

"Yes. Thank you."

Al shoved his cup aside and rested his forearms on the table. He offered a sheepish smile. "Well, you know the saying 'Be careful what you wish for; you just might get it.' As you know, I wanted Patti in the worst way. Now I've got her. But I'm not sure I can even be a good father to her, let alone both father and mother... Amber and I were stupid kids. And we just compounded the problem when we got married."

"Why *did* you get married?"

"Oh, you know. The age-old thing. Amber got pregnant. Her mom was no help to her. Edna's the town drunk and worse. My grandparents insisted I marry Amber."

Kathleen nodded. "Tell me something; can she sing? Well enough to become famous, I mean?

Al pushed a saltshaker around and took his time before answering. "I never thought she had a chance to become famous—but I suppose I could be wrong if she met the right people. I teased her a lot, made fun of her, but yeah, she can sing the birds right outa the trees. Kinda like Loretta Lynn, I guess."

"I hope you won't make fun of her to Patti."

He gave her a sharp look. "Yeah. I'm tryin' to play it cool. I know runnin' her mother down ain't gonna win me any Brownie points. Clara's already been on my case about that."

"So, in regard to Patti, what do you consider your biggest problem right now?"

"You mean other than distracting her from Amber leaving?" He took a deep breath. "Well, I need to find a decent place for us to live. I'm having my trailer moved tomorrow, but it's too small for any length of time. And I can't park forever in Clara and Henry's yard, even if they are willing to put us up. And it ain't fair for Grandma to have to watch my daughter. She's got enough to do with Granddad. I need to find a reliable baby sitter."

Kathleen frowned. "What if I kept Patti after school and Saturdays until you can make other arrangements? Would that help you?"

"You'd do that?" He turned his head for a moment and watched his daughter at play. "That'd be *great* for me—and Patti thinks you have a direct line to God. But what about that banker guy?...Looks to me like you got a rock on your finger now. What's he gonna say about your time taken up with a kid?"

"Oh. I'm not engaged to the banker, and somehow I don't think Daniel Lee Davis is going to object."

Chapter 30

Al studied the backs of his hands for what seemed an inordinate amount of time. When he did lift his head, what blasted from his mouth totally surprised her. "Davis, huh? Wow! You do get around, don't you? And where is this guy now? How come he's not with you on a Friday night?"

Spring was said to be on the way, but a cold front settled over Kathleen. *And what business is it of yours, Mr. Williams?* Her teeth on edge, she spat the words. "Daniel is required to travel in his business. Tonight, he happens to be on his way to Israel."

"Whoa!—Kathleen…I'm sorry—I hit a nerve—didn't I?"

She glared at him. "I thought we came here to help Patti, not discuss *me*."

He held up his hands in mock surrender. "Yeah, you're right. And your boyfriend ain't none my business—But I'll tell you this, Miss school-teacher-ma'am, if I were engaged to a classy babe like you—I wouldn't be flyin' off to some godforsaken spot on the map. I'd stick to you closer than bark on a hemlock."

Upset as Al made her, Kathleen felt her anger dissipate almost as fast as her temper flared. He might be rough around the edges, and he did tend to act first and think later; but he could make her smile in spite of herself. He had Patti's best interest at heart. Of that, she was convinced.

Al waved to his daughter before she again climbed a ladder in the play area. He sobered as he turned back, his eyes two big questions marks. "I could sure use your help tomorrow, if you aren't totally ticked off with me. But I don't know; you may not want to get up as early as I would need to drop Patti off."

" How early are we talking about?"

"Six, at the latest. Before if possible. I'll have a full day trying to get my trailer moved and set up. I hate to say the kid would be in the way; but I won't have time for her."

Kathleen studied the man seated across from her, and a disturbing thought crossed her mind. She couldn't deny he oozed masculinity from every pore; no doubt, his rugged good looks turned more than one woman's head. How long would it be before he married again? Or found someone to live with? How would Patti handle it when he did?

"What if I kept Patti overnight? You wouldn't have to worry about dropping her off; and neither of us would need to get up early."

Al balled up papers, straws, and napkins, and shoved them aside. His touch on the back of her hand startled her. "I appreciate your help; I really do. Patti's been pretty good, but I get this feelin'somethin's gonna blow. Do you know what I'm talkin' about? You got any advice for an old hound like me?"

"I don't know. I'm a teacher, not a parent. I suppose, reassure her she's loved, and you'll take care of her. She probably feels the animosity between you and Amber. I don't know if you can do anything about that—but she may need to understand she has nothing to do with her mother leaving her behind."

• • •

John waved as he left the restaurant with his parents. Patti came back to the table looking glum, and minus her shoes.

Al smiled and tousled her curls. "Patti, go back and get your shoes before you sit down."

Sneakers on but untied, she squeezed her way past Al, retrieved her doll, and sat beside her father, leaning against his side. He put an arm around her, and drew her even closer. "How would you like to stay with your teacher tonight and tomorrow?"

Patti's lower lip protruded; she stared at something under the table, and shook her head. "I want to stay with you," she muttered.

Al's eyebrows shot up; his eyes mirrored puzzlement. "If you stay with me, you'll have to get up really early. I'm going to be very busy all day tomorrow getting the trailer moved and set up. It wouldn't be fun for you, Patti Cake. You'd be sitting in the car by yourself for a long time. Miss O'Brien has offered to keep you over-night, and I think that's best. We'll spend Sunday together; I promise."

Patti doesn't want to stay with me? What's going on? Is she afraid her father will leave her, even as Amber has? Or had she done something wrong? But what? Patti seemed okay when she left Mrs. Fisher's, and happy when she and her father got here. Kathleen's mind whirled faster than a merry-go-round, but it failed to spin out any answers. "Patti?"

A tear slid down the little girl's cheek; her eyes remained downcast, refusing to look at her teacher even when spoken to.

"Patti?" He hooked a finger under her chin. "This isn't like you—so what's gottcha all puckered up? You might as well spit it out. I thought you'd *jump* at the chance to stay with your teacher—so what's wrong?"

More tears pooled in her eyes and spilled over. Her chin quivered as she spluttered her supposed betrayal, and disenchantment of the teacher she idolized. "John said I'm teacher's *pet*. All the kids at school think I'm the teacher's pet."

Kathleen nearly choked. She couldn't believe her ears. She stiffened. Her back rigid, as if an ice cube had suddenly been thrust down the back of her neck. *How can that be? I treat the children the same. Don't I?* Cold coffee remained the only thing before her, but it felt as if she'd swallowed a glob of peanut butter, and it rested atop her windpipe.

Astonished to see merriment dancing in Al's eyes, Kathleen remained quiet.

"So, you're teacher's pet? Tell me, little darlin', is that a bad thing? Or is it something like being your daddy's princess?" He gave her a little squeeze. "What is a teacher's pet anyway?"

Patti stared mutely at her father before turning a reproachful look on her teacher. Kathleen started to speak, but Al held up a hand to silence her.

"You know, Patti, Miss O'Brien is more than a teacher—she's your friend. And, I think, my friend, too. She helped you through the rough time in Chicago. But I doubt you'll ever be her *pet*."

"I'd never intentionally do anything to hurt you," Kathleen quickly added.

Eyes serious now, Al continued to talk in low tones. "Patti, I know being called 'teacher's pet' makes you feel bad, but it's just another way for kids to tease. If you let it bother you, they'll tease more. Sometimes you just have to suck it up and pretend like you don't care. If they can't get a rise out of you, they'll soon quit."

Al winked at Kathleen. "And if you tell anyone what I'm about to tell you, I'll tie your shoelaces together. When I was your age, the kids called me 'slats' and that was just when they were bein' nice. The rest of the time it was 'hey, skinny.'"

"Really? What did you do?"

"Oh...I sucked it up. And waited for the day I'd get big enough to knock their block off." He grinned. "And you know what?"

"What?"

"I did get big enough. But I found out ignoring them worked better than fighting. Ignore them, Patti."

• • •

Kathleen slowly drove home, the day's events playing over and over in her mind. She felt as if her well-intentioned efforts to help had somehow backfired. The accusing look in Patti's eyes haunted her. Had she unwittingly given cause for the class to think she favored Patti?

By the time she reached home, her brain felt like it had been washed, rinsed, and spun dry. She wanted to creep up the stairs and hibernate until spring. But Martha heard her come in and called. "Kathleen, join me by the fire and tell me how it went with Patti. Is she upset over her mother leaving?"

"Maybe, but she seemed even more upset over a remark one of her classmates made to her while they were together in the play area at the restaurant." Kathleen related the incident to Martha and went ahead to tell her she had planned to keep Patti overnight, but because of the upset, she'd decided to wait and pick her up tomorrow.

"Well, Kathleen, I guess I'm not too surprised Patti's been labeled 'teacher's pet.' If you recall, I tried to warn you about being more than a teacher to that little girl. Why *are* you so involved anyway? Why do you feel you need to baby sit? I think Alvin would find someone, if you weren't so readily available. Keep her *here* overnight? Saturday, too?" Martha pushed the glasses back on her nose and scowled. "What do you propose to do with her here all those hours?"

Kathleen felt her face grow hot. She was speechless. Her landlady, however, had more to say.

"Sure, it was commendable to be involved when you found

Patti in Chicago. But she's home now. She has family here. I think you need to let Alvin do his job— he can find a baby-sitter if he wants one. I'm sure my granddaughter, Charlene, would be happy to take care of Patti."

"Martha." Kathleen swallowed hard. "Charlene isn't out of school yet when Patti would ordinarily be getting home. I'm sure Mr. Williams understands my help is temporary. I've only agreed to help until he can get moved and settled."

"Well, I just think you're setting a dangerous precedent. What if other parents think they can leave their children for you to baby-sit? And as for Patti, I think Clara is capable of keeping her great granddaughter an hour or two, until Charlene or someone else arrived to take over. I might help—if I were asked."

Kathleen stood to her feet. She bit her tongue, a retort stopped just short of being released. With Herculean effort, she managed to keep her voice from quivering. "Well, I've promised to keep Patti tomorrow while Al gets moved, and I don't plan to renege on my offer, however—" She broke off before she said too much, and fled for her apartment.

Behind the closed bedroom door, she let tears course down her hot cheeks. How could a day started with such anticipation and high hopes turn into something that felt so miserable. *If Danny had come, like he was supposed to.* But that kind of thinking only left her more miserable. *What had set Martha off?* It felt like an attack.

Crying made Kathleen's nose run and left her feeling more wretched than ever. She grabbed a tissue, and tried to repair the immediate damage. "Sucking it up" might be good advice for her as well as Patti, but what she craved was a sympathetic ear and a shoulder to cry on.

She tried to pray, but God didn't seem to be listening. She doubted her prayer went any higher than the ceiling.

And what am I to do with Patti for an entire day? After Martha's outburst, I don't want to bring her here. Kathleen's thoughts were as gloomy as the fog and dreary skies of the Willamette valley. For the first time since meeting Martha, she wished she'd opted for more independence and privacy. What she'd thought of as "homey," now felt like interference in her life and disapproval.

• • •

Saturday morning Kathleen dressed for comfort and neat-appearance in penny-loafers, gray slacks, and lightweight pink sweater. She donned her hooded raincoat, and grabbed an umbrella before tiptoeing down the stairs and letting herself out the backdoor into the rain.

She drove without error to the house and arrived five minutes early. Mrs. Williams greeted her at the door. "You must be Patti's teacher. Come in. Come in. Patti hasn't quite finished her breakfast. We'll have a moment to talk. I'm so happy to finally meet you. I've never properly thanked you for rescuing Patti and helping my Alvin, too. Stupid thing to do, snatching Patti like that. But I understand his motive."

Because they were friends, and near the same age, Kathleen had expected Clara to be like Martha. But they were very different, at least in appearance. Clara's cropped dark hair waved softly around her slender face. High cheekbones, with just a touch of color, drew attention to warm brown eyes framed by dark lashes.

This great grandmother exuded youth and energy of a woman far younger than her years. Tall and willowy as a sapling, she had to measure at least five foot six. Dressed in a green flannel shirt, tucked into casual blue jeans, silver and turquoise earrings dangled from her ears. She might be in her seventies, but she was still a pretty woman.

Clara smiled and extended a hand as though to draw Kathleen aside. In almost a whisper she said, "I just gave Henry his morning shot for arthritis and he's sleeping now. I'd like to keep Patti here—but Henry has mild dementia. He's easily confused and sometimes he's not very nice. He can yell like a banshee and swear like a stevedore if something sets him off. Other times, he's a lamb. I've tried to explain—but this upsets and scares Patti...Truth be told—it sometimes scares me."

Kathleen nodded and answered in a low tone. "I'm sure it must be difficult. I'm glad to help out until Patti's father can make other arrangements. Patti is a very bright little girl; I enjoy teaching her."

• • •

"Are we going to Miz Martha's today and play with that ole cat?"

"No. I think not today. Mrs. Kestler has invited us to her house. I thought you might like to go there and hang out with her kids. I think they have three or four cats you can probably play with. If it wasn't raining, I can think of a number of things we might do, but..."

"Cool. I know who Mrs. Kestler is. She teaches those big kids. She's nice. She gave us first-graders candy once. I think it was Halloween."

Kathleen smiled. "You have a good memory, Patti. Yes, Rosie Kestler is pretty thoughtful." *And let's hope* she *doesn't think I'm making you teacher's pet.*

Chapter 31

Rosie persisted the day before and wore down all excuses until Kathleen had agreed to have breakfast with her, Bill, and their children, then attend Sunday morning worship services. Guilty as accused, she had avoided church, as well as the bank, where she might have run into Edward. It should be safe now. According to his own avowed timetable, and the latest scuttlebutt (*he left alone?*) Edward had to be long gone from Fir Valley.

The house remained quiet as she left; she assumed her landlady chose to sleep in. Perhaps she felt no more eager to face Kathleen than she to confront her. Their relationship had been so comfortable; it troubled her to feel judged. Martha's criticism seemed harsh. *Am I really that misguided in what I'm doing for Patti and her father? Or is something else going on?*

• • •

"Eat!... Eat!" Rosie urged. "*What*? You don't like my cooking?"

"It's delicious, and I'm *stuffed*." Kathleen felt as if she wouldn't need food again for a week. She doubted she could hold another bite. Little link sausages, bacon, orange juice, coffee, eggs done to perfection, and pancakes light enough to float out the door on their own. All served up with a smile to make the sun (if only it would shine) envious.

The children saw nothing unusual in their Sunday morning fare. They ate and bickered good-naturedly as to whose turn it was to load the dishwasher.

"I did it last time."

"No you didn't, I did."

Kathleen smiled. "What if I load the dishwasher? Then you'll really be messed up."

Five-year-old Nathan giggled. "It's really Becky's turn, but she can take my place and feed the cats." He puffed out his little chest. "I'll help you load the dishes."

"Oh no, you won't, you little weasel. It's *my* turn on the dishes an I'm not feeding those cats that stinky food. They're *your* cats. You feed 'em. Momma said."

Rosie moved with ease and efficiency among her brood, directing, admonishing, and encouraging. "We leave for church in twenty minutes. Get a move on, girls. Good job, Nathan, now go wash your hands and face."

Once again Kathleen marveled at this family she considered a prime example of what home life should be. No wonder Patti had exclaimed she liked it here and wanted to come back and play with the Kestler children. Kathleen suspected

Patti couldn't put a name to it, but she envied children with brothers and sisters.

"You just as well leave your car here. Go with us, then come back and spend the day relaxing. We'll banish the kids to the rumpus room and threaten them with early bedtime if they bother us. Give us a chance to really catch up on the latest.

"It's tempting, Rosie—though your motives are suspect. I think you're trying to make me fat."

She snorted. "Fat chance of *that*! You eat like a bird."

Bill chuckled. "Yeah, my wife thinks food is the answer to life's problems. And if you don't eat like a logger, you must be sick. Why do you think I sport this paunch?"

Kathleen laughed. "I thank you for your generosity, but I've imposed long enough. Here yesterday, today. I think I'll drive to the mall after church and do some careful shopping. Or maybe not so careful. Maybe I'll throw caution to the wind and buy something I don't really need...like another pair of shoes."

• • •

Pews were nearly filled as Kathleen entered and sat toward the back. Nearby, familiar faces turned and smiled at her. Surprised at how comfortable and welcoming it felt after her considerable absence, she relaxed and tuned in to the service. The choir sang while a limited orchestra played favorite hymns.

Pastor Jim preached on choices, taking his text from the book of Luke, and how some decisions we make can affect our lives for good or evil and how we may have to live with the results of wrong choices for a long time. All too soon, the service ended, and members gathered round proclaiming they'd missed her and were happy to see her again.

No one mentioned Edward. Further evidence news in this small town traveled faster than a bad smell. Caught by surprise, Kathleen hesitated, and smiled, when a young woman she recognized approached her. She didn't recall ever seeing her in this church before.

"You're Kathleen, aren't you? I remember seeing you in the bank, and I did hear you sing one time. You have a lovely voice."

"Thank you…and you're Jeannie, from the bank? Where, if I may ask, did you hear me sing?"

Jeannie smiled. "Here. I visited once some time ago, before I…shall we say became embroiled. Pastor's sermon today kinda seemed aimed at me."

"Oh?—I don't think Jim singles anyone out. I'm sure we can all profit from his message."

"I suppose. But I don't think I'll hang around here much longer. I've put in for a transfer. This small town with all its gossip and everyone knowing everyone else's business is not for me."

"Well, I know it can seem that way." Kathleen mimicked the words she'd heard Martha use. "By and large they are good people and don't mean you harm. To where will you transfer?"

"You mean am I going to follow Edward to California?" Kathleen felt the blood rush to her face. Jeannie uttered a low mirthless laugh. "It's okay, everyone wants to know. Some ask, some don't. But, no—I learned my lesson in that regard. I think he just used me to try to make you jealous."

"Oh, Jeannie. I'm sorry."

"Don't be. I coulda made a worse fool of myself. At least I said 'no' before he did. I guess I can thank the gossips for that. Edward finally admitted the truth. Sorry, if I sound bitter, but I don't much like small towns and small town gossip. I like users and liars even less. When I leave here, maybe people'll find someone else to talk about."

Unfortunately, Kathleen thought, *that's probably true.*

• • •

Kathleen walked from one end of the mall to the other and back again. She browsed in shops she'd never been in before. She sauntered throughout department stores and sashayed into small boutiques. She perused book stores and became enthralled with choices newly on the market. So many good books to choose from, it was difficult to narrow it down to two novels and four children's stories.

Other purchases included a white cardigan sweater on sale, a pink camisole, also on sale, and another pair of dark blue slacks, perfect for school. Last, but not least, she bought shoes to match the trousers. Tired of traipsing the mall, and not yet ready to give up and go home, Kathleen treated herself to a coffee mocha.

She sat beside the small round table provided for customers, nursed her drink, and watched people in the mall without really seeing them. Her mind dredged up problems real and imagined, and she wondered about the choices she needed to make. Could one ever know for certain if some decisions were right or wrong until after they were made?

Two people entered her line of vision and moved closer before it registered who they were. *Oh no, I don't want to talk to them again today. Have they seen me? Maybe if I don't look at them, they'll not notice me and go on by.*

"Well, Patti, look who's here. Your teacher." Al pulled out a chair and sat down across from Kathleen. "Hope you don't mind if we join you. I'm here to tell you, this kid has about walked my legs off…Patti, you want a hot chocolate?"

"Hi, Miss O'Brien. Me and Daddy went to a movie."

"Daddy and I."

"Huh?"

"The proper way to say it is, 'Daddy and I went to a movie'."

"Oh, yeah. Daddy and me went to a movie." Kathleen smiled and let the slip pass.

Al returned with drinks and launched into an account of getting his trailer set up. "Well, Patti and I…we're now trailer trash." He grinned. "But we won't always be. I'll get us into a suitable house before too long. Had to go buy some more towels and bedding now the kid's with me. Suppose to get a phone put in tomorrow. I'll give ya the number soon as I know."

Kathleen wished she'd left half an hour ago, but she listened politely and made courteous comments when appropriate. *This seems to be the day for seeing people I know.* Walking purposefully, Mr. Fisher saw her the same time she recognized him. He scowled, nodded curtly, and kept on walking. His demeanor seemed somehow threatening, like dark clouds gathering for a storm.

Al broke off mid-sentence. "Kathleen, what's wrong? You look like you saw a ghost, or the devil tramped on your grave."

"What?...Oh—The president of the school board just walked past."

"You mean Frank? I don't like that—" He looked toward Patti. "I can't say now what he is—but I don't like that self-important stuffed shirt. He's one of the biggest gossips I know—worse than some old woman. And he needs to watch his own henhouse first."

"Well, I'm not going to ask what you mean by that." Kathleen excused herself, clutched her packages, and rose to leave. She had the uncomfortable feeling Mr. Fisher didn't approve of her. *I've done nothing wrong, but I feel as if I've been caught in some clandestine meeting with a secret lover. Does Frank think I'm dating Al?*

• • •

The last glimmer of daylight dropped behind the trees as Kathleen reached home. She used her key to unlock the backdoor. No lights shone anywhere on the premises. No fire burned in the hearth. No welcome 'hello' sounded from any room. It felt like it had when she came home from grammar school expecting cookies and milk only to find her mother not home. Martha had every right to be gone if she wished, but she rarely stayed away after dark. If she were planning to be away, she generally left at least one light on.

A cup of hot tea and a soak in a tub of warm aromatic water was what Kathleen needed to lift her spirits. First, she checked her e-mail. An offer to reduce her mortgage. One to sell her Viagra at a bargain price. Another guaranteed to match her up with her soul mate. Delete. Delete. Delete. The message she hoped for didn't appear. Nothing from Danny. Too soon. He'd be embroiled in assignments.

The phone jangled before she could make the tea or run water for a bath. She heaved a sigh and set her cup down. *That will be my mother. She'll want to know if we've set a date. Picked a place. She's not going to be pleased, but I may as well answer, or she'll just call again.*

"Hello."

"Kathleen?"

"*Danny*! I just checked my e-mail. I didn't expect you to *call*."

"Honey—I needed to hear your voice. I'm missing you like you wouldn't believe."

Kathleen caressed the phone and curled herself into a corner of the couch. She closed her eyes, hugged a pillow, and tried to pretend he was there beside her. "Oh, Danny. I miss *you*, too!"

"Things haven't gone too well. It's been the pits. We sat on the runway for a good forty-five minutes in Chicago before takeoff. Short hop to LaGuardia, more hurry up and wait before takeoff. Rough weather all the way to England. Then forever getting through Heathrow airport. Guess they had a bomb threat."

"Oh, Dan. I'm sorry. That doesn't sound like much fun."

"It wasn't, but that's not what bothers me most. We nearly lost two of my colleagues in Iraq. Roadside bomb. Kathleen, we all know how dangerous it is, but you somehow just don't expect it to happen to you, or someone you're close to. I know both these guys pretty well—News anchor and cameraman. Soon as I get over whatever this plague is I've got—I'm flying to Germany to see them..."

"Danny?—You're *sick*?" Her heart hammered in her chest. "What's wrong?"

"Oh, it's not that bad, honey. Cold maybe. I'm just feelin' sorry for myself, but it sure would be nice if you were here to soothe my fevered brow. Feed me chicken soup...So, how're things going for you?"

"Me?...I'm all right—missing you—You sure you're going to be okay? Are you in a hotel room?—Can you get a doctor if you need one?"

"Yeah, don't worry. I'm here in Tel Aviv at the Frank Intercontinental. Just pray for me. I'll be fine. And remember, if you should need to get hold of me—and can't reach me—contact my boss in Seattle. You've got his number. Don't forget—I love you. And I promise—we'll make up for time lost when I get back"

"I love you, too, Danny. And I miss you *so much*."

"Sweetheart, I hate to hang up. But I gotta go. Listen—Kathleen. If you don't hear from me for a few days, don't worry. It'll be because they've got me on the jump. Not because I won't be thinking of you. And I'll be back home before you know it."

Happiness ever-after seemed attainable when she talked to Danny. His voice reassured her their separations could be handled. She could cope with his job and long absences. Couldn't she? *Of course I can,* she thought. But then that niggling little worm of doubt would wriggle its way in to chew away at her self-assurance.

She longed to ask Danny's advice about Patti, Mr. Williams, the school situation, and at least a dozen other potential problems. But with the miles separating them, her needs paled in comparison to what she now believed Danny's to be. A clearer picture began to emerge. She didn't want to discuss her problems long-distance. Kathleen knew danger often played a role in the assignments he undertook. What she hadn't focused on was the tedium, loneliness, strange food upsetting to the tummy, and running on adrenaline that could suddenly vacate and leave you vulnerable.

Bolstered by the call from Danny, Kathleen felt a keen urge to tackle the inevitable. An impish smile played about her lips as she picked up the phone and punched in the auto dial for her mother's number.

"Hello?"

"Hi, Mom...I just talked to your future son-in-law. Would you like to guess where he is?"

Chapter 32

Monday morning, as Kathleen drove onto the school grounds, she passed Mr. Fisher leaving in his new red Toyota. She lifted her hand in a little wave, but the chairman of the school board didn't return the gesture though he looked right at her. The scowl on his face, combined with his early morning visit to the school, triggered alarm bells in her brain. *The Fishers are certainly acting odd, have I done something wrong?*

She didn't know Mr. Fisher well, although she'd seen him on those occasions when Martha called him for some need, or he dropped by to check on his mother and of course, at school board meetings. He had been cordial, until recently. An ordinary looking man in his late forties or early fifties, he garnered no special notice. His description could easily fit a dozen or more men: average height, stocky build, a developing paunch, bald on top, salt and pepper hair in back. Usually, he wore one of those caps with a bill; he was the kind of man, Kathleen thought, you see and promptly forget. She had no idea about the color of his eyes.

Mr. Steele pushed the door open and entered her room just as she finished locking her purse in the bottom drawer of the desk. "I hate to lay this on you first thing Monday morning." The principal shoved his hands in his pockets, stared at the floor for what seemed like an eternity, then faced his first grade teacher. "I suppose you saw Mr. Fisher stormin' out of here. For a minute or two I thought he might take it on himself to talk to you."

"I did see him. I assume his early morning visit has something to do with me."

"He claims he's gotten complaints about the Williams girl staying with you after school. Seems they think you're showing favoritism. And he wants it stopped for insurance reasons if nothing else."

The principal cleared his throat. "I tried explaining to him Patti is here after school on a temporary basis until Mr. Williams can find a satisfactory sitter—he cut me off. Said that's his problem, not ours."

"Oh, dear!"

"Yeah. I can't figure why he's so heated. The situation doesn't seem to warrant it. But there it is. We'll have to contact Mr. Williams and tell him Patti can no longer stay after school, starting tomorrow...I don't think we have a number for Mr. Williams either. I'll have to call the grandparents, I guess. I hate to do that, but I don't think I have a choice."

Kathleen started to reply, then stopped herself. Something told her the less she contributed about Mr. Williams the better.

"Try not to let this upset you, Kathleen. You're doing a fine job."

She swallowed. Her mouth felt dry and her words came out sounding rehearsed. "Thank you…I am…however…concerned about the 'teacher's pet' label—For Patti. Perhaps I can convince the class they're all my pets?"

Dick chuckled. "I don't doubt you can." With that, he turned and left the room; the door clicked sharply behind him.

Like a kite caught in the wind, Kathleen's well-developed lesson plans flew from her mind. She slumped into the nearest chair and bent her head to her knees, tried to slow her heart rate with controlled deep breaths. Only moments remained before the children arrived. *What did I plan for today, anyway?*

Like every other Monday morning, first-graders trooped into the classroom jabbering to each other; calling a cheery "Hello, guess what?" to their teacher, clamoring for her attention—except Patti. Patti flounced past without a word and went straight to her desk, the doll her mother gave her clutched in her arms.

Kathleen thought it best to ignore the coolness and pretend she noticed nothing unusual. Sticking to routine seemed the best overall plan. After she took attendance and they recited the Pledge of Allegiance, the usual fifteen or twenty minutes allotted for Show and Tell seemed a positive way to start the week.

The children were eager to tell about their weekend and nearly a dozen hands were raised when the teacher asked who wanted to share. "Molly, you may be first." Molly Ferndale, a rather shy little girl seldom spoke up, and she came hesitantly to the front of the room now.

Recently Kathleen had observed Molly and Patti playing together more than usual. Like Patti, Molly lived alone with her father; her mother had been deployed to Iraq. In the teacher's opinion, both girls could benefit by being friends. Molly did her lessons quietly and accurately, excelling in nearly every subject. The child, half American Indian, had beautiful brown-toned skin and liquid dark eyes that seemed to hold secrets.

The little girl opened her hand and slowly held out some seashells.

"Oh, I'll bet you've been to the beach. What do you have, Molly? Lay them here on the corner of my desk and hold them up one at a time so we can see them. Class, do you know what Molly is holding in her fingers?

Several children waved their hands. "Bobby?"

"I know. That's a sand dollar."

"Yes, that's right. A perfect one, too...What else do you have, Molly?"

"An agate?"

"Yes, and some very pretty ones. Will you have them polished, do you think?"

The child shrugged, gathered her treasures into her hands, and prepared to take her seat behind Patti.

"Thank you Molly, for sharing those. Would you like to call on someone to be next?"

She hesitated, looked at the teacher; then her eyes went to her friend before she said, "Patti."

Patti hugged her doll to herself and paraded to the front of the classroom. "My momma gave me this before she left." She held the doll up and turned it around so all could admire the doll's clothes. "My mommy has an outfit just like it. She's gonna sing on the *Grand Ole Opry*. She…"

"Ah, lookit da baby wid her dolly…Idn't dat cute? Does her want a boddow?" Bobby spoke in low mocking tones, barely above a whisper, nevertheless, heads turned to stare at him. A few snickers could be heard. Before Kathleen could react, Patti flew down the aisle like a hornet aiming for a target, and grabbed a handful of Bobby's hair. She yanked—hard.

Unshed tears glistened in Bobby's eyes. With both hands, he snatched the doll from her and gave it a sling, not caring where he threw it. Patti screeched her fury, tugged harder on his hair and kicked him on the leg as hard as she could. "You're mean. I *hate* you."

"*Patti—Stop it!—Now.*" Kathleen grabbed Patti by the arm with one hand and pried her fingers from Bobby's hair with the other. Bobby turned in his seat and kicked out at Patti. His foot connected with the teacher's shin.

"Both of you. *Stop it!*" She gave Patti a little shake.

"I'm not a baby," Patti shrieked. "And I'm not the teacher's *pet,* neither." She twisted around and aimed a well-placed kick to Kathleen's leg, catching her above the ankle.

The kicks hurt, but she didn't release her hold on Patti's

arm. Instead she tightened her grip, and forced herself to speak in a calm controlled manner while she maneuvered the out-of-control child to her seat. "Patti, you will be staying in at recess—Bobby, you also. I'll talk with you both later."

Kathleen turned and faced the front of the room. She felt the heat flush her face. There stood the principal holding Patti's doll and watching the goings on in her classroom. In all the upset, she hadn't heard him come in. *How long has he been standing there? How much did he see and hear? What will he now think of my ability to maintain order in my classroom?*

"I'm sorry, Mr. Steele." She tried to smile and her voice trembled a little as she said, "I'm afraid I didn't hear you come in. Excuse me for one more moment, please."

The first grade teacher squared her shoulders, stood up straight, and took a deep breath, letting it out slowly, before she spoke. "Class, I think we need a time out. Please close your eyes, lay your head on your desk, and rest for a few minutes. No looking around. If you can hear the pencil when it drops; I'll know we are ready to begin our day."

Dick frowned and handed the doll to Kathleen. The hat had been knocked cockeyed, but otherwise it didn't appear to be damaged. He motioned her to step out the door with him. "I came to tell you, I talked on the phone to Mrs. Williams, the grandmother. She wants Patti to ride the bus to her place when class is over for the day."

"Oh—Did she understand they don't have to do anything today?"

"Yes, I made that quite clear, but she was adamant that I send the child home to her, today."

"Thank you, Mr. Steele, for letting me know. I will tell Patti."

"That's fine then. Perhaps it's for the best." The principal slowly shook his head, as though he couldn't quite believe what he had witnessed, but his eyes twinkled, and he smiled at Kathleen before he turned to go. "I'd tell you to have a nice day, except it sounds so trite, but things will get better. You'll see," he droned before the door closed behind him.

Kathleen sighed and checked the time as she observed her students. All had complied, and heads were down on desks. Patti made little gulping noises; her shoulders rose and fell, as she quietly sobbed. But she kept her eyes shut and her head buried in her arms. No one looked around. Slowly and silently the teacher walked the aisles. Bobby didn't appear to be crying, but his fists were clenched on the desktop, and his red face alerted the teacher of his distress. Three more minutes before she dropped a pencil and ended the time out.

Have a nice day, indeed, she thought. *Things can't get much worse, can they?* By the law of averages the day had to improve.

Kathleen wished she could comfort Patti, assume the roll of mother for five minutes and soothe away her hurts. But she must retain the status of teacher, and that meant she had to discipline this hurting little girl. The reprimand she meted out needed to be severe enough to make a lasting impression, and get her over the label of "teacher's pet." And more important, cause her to think, before she exploded.

Bobby. What to do about Bobby? She would have to discipline him of course, discover, if possible, what had brought on his snide remark? Most of the time, he shone as a lovable, if mischievous, little boy. Never deliberately mean. Days like today, Kathleen could almost wish she hadn't become a teacher. Almost.

Rain fell in a steady fine drizzle from a low-hung sky, the color of No. 2 pencil lead. The air carried that scrubbed clean smell, an essence you wanted to breathe in and hold in your lungs. A fragrance better than anything chemists had on the market, though some came close.

Kathleen stood by the open door and watched her children file out to the gym for first recess. Most were solemn, due to the upset in the classroom this morning. She breathed deeply of the fresh air and turned her attention back to the two unhappy wary-looking students still sitting at their desk.

"Bobby, you may go to the restroom now, and then come back and take your seat. We need to talk. Patti, you too. You may go to the restroom. Wash your face and hands, then come right back and take your seat."

When she returned from grabbing a quick cup of coffee, both children were back in their places. Kathleen swallowed a fast gulp of warm, too strong, dark liquid, and set the cup on her desk. *Might as well get this over with.*

She left the coffee (it hadn't been worth going after) walked to the back of the room, grabbed two small chairs and set them facing each other. As instructed, Bobby sat in the "hot seat" and faced the teacher, their knees almost touching.

She tipped her head forward, kept her voice low, and spoke for his ears alone. "Well, Bobby, how do you feel?"

The child looked at his toes and remained mute.

"You got a little more than you bargained for didn't you? I'm sorry Patti pulled your hair and kicked you. That wasn't nice and I know it hurts. She was wrong to do that."

A look of surprise on his face, he stared wide-eyed at her.

She gave it a moment to sink in then asked, "What did you think would happen when you made fun of Patti and her doll?" He shrugged, and again became very interested in his shoes.

"Well, let me tell you something, Mr. Robert Daniels—" Kathleen lightly tapped him on the chest with one manicured pink-painted fingernail while emphasizing each word. "If you ever make fun of *anyone* during 'Show and Tell' in my class-room again, you will be going to talk to Mr. Steele."

"I'm sorry," Bobby mumbled.

"Okay. Here's what I want you to do. Go back to your seat and get out your tablet. Number the lines from one to ten. I want you to write ten sentences to Patti; tell her you're sorry you made fun of her and her doll. And this is not to be done during school time. If you don't finish before recess is over you will have to come back noon recess and work on it. "

"What if I don't know how to spell a word?"

"Do the best you can. If you're really stuck, I'll help you. Don't rush through it; do a neat job. When you're finished, I want to see your work."

Kathleen walked to her desk and took another sip of now cold coffee. "Patti, you may come on back now."

Still sniffling, and much subdued, the small blonde moppet sat in the chair facing her teacher. When Kathleen looked at her with solemn eyes and didn't immediately say anything; Patti began to squirm. "Miss O'Brien, are you mad at me?"

Kathleen bit back an easy reply, continued to look stern and kept her voice low. "Patti, it isn't a matter of being mad at you, or not. But no, I'm not mad at you...but you must understand, certain bad behavior results in consequences. What you did is totally unacceptable. It's *never* okay to pull hair, hit, or kick. No matter how upset you are."

"I'm sorry, Miss O'Brien." Tears spilled over and ran down her cheeks.

Two minutes remained before the bell would ring ending recess. "Patti, if this ever happens again, in the classroom or on the playground, I will send you to Mr. Steele. Now, you may take your seat; but you are to come back to your desk after you eat lunch. I will tell you then what I want you to do."

Kathleen smiled. "I have your doll; her hat is only slightly askew and can be fixed. I'll give her back to you after school."

Tears continued to run down Patti's face as she stood and wrapped her arms around the teacher's neck. "I'm sorry I kicked you, Miss O'Brien." Her voice barely audible she whispered, "I love you."

The rest of the morning went well and the children settled down to routine. The surprise came when Kathleen returned to her classroom after lunch recess. There on her desk were one dozen red roses delivered by the Fir Valley florist.

The children seemed as surprised as she. "Look," more than one exclaimed as they trooped in. "Flowers for the teacher."

She detached the card and read the message: All my love, Danny

Chapter 33

Ten minutes before class dismissal for the day, a knock on the door interrupted the schoolroom-quiet. Kathleen laid her pencil aside and rose to answer.

"Al, what are you doing here? How did you find out so fast?" His log truck parked along the road, close to the entrance of the school grounds, diesel engine grumbling in the background.

"Find out what? What are you talkin' about?" Al removed his cap and scratched his head. "I'm probably a little early, but I'm making runs fairly close to here now, and I thought I'd swing on by and pick up the kid. Take her with me to the landing. She's always buggin' me to ride in the truck."

He gave her a lopsided grin. "I'd take you too, if you could shake loose from this blackboard jungle. You ever been to a landing in the woods? You really should see one if you're gonna teach in good ole Oregon. Oregon is all about timber, ya know. At least here in the valley."

Kathleen scanned the room; the children were quiet and

busy. She stepped outside and pulled the door almost closed behing her. "Al, I can't take time to explain everything now, but Patti hasn't had a good day. Be gentle with her. Also, could you please tell the office before you take Patti?"

"Oh, I've already done that. I'm careful these days." Al grinned, then sobered as he watched her. "If you don't mind my saying so, you don't look like you've had a good day either—The principal told me I can't leave Patti here with you after school anymore. I hope that's not what's bothering you. It's not your fault, you know. You've been great. And something'll work out."

Kathleen felt a stinging behind her eyes. "I'll get Patti ready to go with you." She hesitated a second before opening the door, and lowered her voice even further. "Call me this evening if you want my version of the day."

• • •

The rain stopped and clouds broke apart to let sunrays stream through in small areas. It made Kathleen think of pictures of Christ kneeling beside a large boulder, hands folded in prayer as he looks heavenward. She drove slowly, in no hurry to reach home, a prayer for guidance on her lips. If she were truthful, she'd have to admit it felt good to be by herself. And Patti had looked happy to be going with her father, her doll hugged tightly under one arm, art work clutched in her hand.

She let her mind drift from one thought to another until she noticed a profusion of yellow daffodils blooming among the grass in a neglected orchard. *Why is it flowers untended often seem prettier than those given special care?* she mused. *Is it because they have to struggle to survive?*

Kathleen reached home and parked her car in the garage. Snowball came on a run from somewhere in the yard as she approached the back door. She shifted the materials in her arms and bent to stroke his glossy head as he wrapped his furry body around her legs, alternately purring and meowing a welcome. Maybe he just wanted back in the house, and counted on her to open the door; but his ministrations were a warm fuzzy and brought a smile to her lips.

No light burned in the kitchen and no enticing aroma of good things cooking wafted into the hallway. The house seemed too quiet; Martha's voice didn't ring out with a welcome as it usually did. Reasonably sure she was home—Kathleen stowed her things on the bottom stair step and peaked into the living room. There sat her landlady huddled in a blanket, chair pulled about as close to the dwindling fire burning on the hearth as she dared.

"*Martha*, what's wrong? Are you ill?"

"Oh, Kathleen," she rasped. "I don't know; I can't seem to get warm. Maybe you'd better not come closer, and don't let Patti near me. I can't imagine I'm getting the flu; I've had my shot, but I feel about as strong as a wet noodle."

Kathleen slipped off her coat and laid it across the arm of a chair before sitting down. "Patti isn't with me. Her father picked her up today. Martha, do you need to see the doctor? I'd be happy to take you. I think there's still time to get you there—an emergency—he'd see you."

"Oh no, dear. This'll pass…if you could maybe just build

up the fire a little. I hate to be such a bother." She reached for a tissue and covered her nose and mouth before coughing. "I'd call my son, or my granddaughter, but they're totally put out with me." Tears began to run down her wrinkled cheeks.

"Of course I'll build up the fire for you. I'm going to make you some hot tea, too. Just give me two seconds to change out of these clothes. I promise, we'll get you warm."

Snowball raced up the stairs behind her, meowing plaintively. "I hear you, pretty boy. I know...you want your supper. First things first. We have to take care of Martha."

In record time, Kathleen brought more wood from the basement and built up the fire. While water heated, she fed the cat. She carried a tray laden with teapot, cups and saucers, and soda crackers in to Martha and placed it carefully on a small table beside her chair.

The two ladies sipped their tea in companionable silence and gazed at the fire as if it held answers to life's most troublesome secrets.

"Thank you," Martha murmured. "This tea helps; I *am* beginning to feel warmer."

"Good. And I'll fix you some chicken soup. I know you have some in the freezer." Kathleen set her cup down, wondering if she should broach the question uppermost in her mind or wait for her companion to explain. When the silence began to hang heavier than a blanket left in the rain, Kathleen said, "Martha, do you want to tell me why your family is upset with you?"

Tears started afresh, but she nodded her head, gulped the last of her tea and began. "Charlene is grounded from now until who knows how long. If my son has his way, she won't get out of the house, except to go to school, until she's thirty...Or the Lord comes. I guess they won't even let her ride the school bus. They'll take her and go get her." Martha wiped her eyes. "I know my granddaughter, and I'm afraid she'll rebel big time."

"Oh dear. What happened to bring about those restrictions? Why are they mad at you?"

"Well, it's rather complicated, but maybe I can boil it down. Charlene thinks I told her dad too much and got her in trouble—and Frank thinks I knew things and didn't tell him. Truth is, I didn't know Charlene was lying to her parents—though I did try to tell them I thought she spent too much time with this boy. That he's too old for her. Frank and Estelle blew it off, like I'm an old woman and what do I know. Until they had to face the fact she lied about spending the night with a girlfriend. Instead she spent the night with this boy and probably not for the first time. Guess they planned to run off together. I don't know, maybe get married. Or maybe just live together. Somehow, Frank found out and confronted them at the mall."

Martha blew her nose, gave a tremulous sigh, and continued. "I guess she met this fellow on several occasions when her folks thought she was here with me. She'd maybe spend five to fifteen minutes here and her parents thought she'd been here with me an hour or two. Maybe longer. Doing chores."

After a short break in which Kathleen thawed soup and heated it in the microwave; she hurried back to take her seat beside the fire. Eager to resume their conversation, she opened the dialogue. "I met your son early this morning on the school grounds. He pulled out just as I entered the parking lot. He didn't seem very happy—I waved, but he only scowled in return. Maybe he's just upset over Charlene."

"Frank was at school?...What did he want?

"He told our principal Patti can no longer stay with me after school—to be effective immediately. He said he's had complaints from parents—and he mentioned something about insurance, too. I'm not sure what..."

"My heavens!" Martha interjected. "I wonder who complained. I haven't heard anything." The blanket slipped from her shoulders as she leaned forward in her chair. "I'm sorry, Kathleen, this must make you feel unappreciated. What's going to happen to Patti, who will care for her if you don't? I think Clara has her hands full with Henry."

Kathleen didn't think Frank concerned himself with what happened to Patti, but she bit back the sharp retort begging to slide off her tongue. She needn't be sarcastic with Martha. That would accomplish nothing. Instead she got up and added a couple more logs to the fire and went to check on the soup. It gave her time to puzzle over Martha's seeming switch in opinion. *Didn't she just tell me, rather harshly as a matter of fact, that I'm too involved with Patti?*

She got out T.V. trays and set one up for Martha and another for herself. They could eat their chicken noodle soup by the fire. Perspiration began to bead on Kathleen's forehead, but Martha pulled the blanket back up around her shoulders.

"Here I sit, feeling sorry for myself and letting you wait on me. Sometimes I think I've outlived my usefulness. Maybe

I should just turn this place entirely over to Frank, as he'd like, and go live in one of those retirement villages. Old people need to learn their place and have sense enough to keep their mouth shut and let the young people manage things.

"You have a good heart, Kathleen, and I should never have criticized you for being involved with Patti." Martha laid her soup spoon aside, reached for another tissue and wiped her eyes and her nose. "I thought if Charlene could baby-sit Patti—well, she's blown that hasn't she? I suppose I forgot; it's really up to Alvin, isn't it?"

"Martha there's no way you've outlived your usefulness. You're a vibrant woman, and I value your opinion. To say nothing of the wonderful meals you prepare. You know this community much better than I do—maybe better than anyone. And I believe you have an ear and a feel for what's going on."

Kathleen took a deep breath; before she could lose her nerve, she asked the question uppermost in her mind. "I have the feeling your son is upset with *me*; and it doesn't seem Patti could be the sole cause of his disapproval. Do you know what's bothering him?"

The lady she thought of as her mentor stared at her. She looked as startled as a child caught reaching for the cookie jar. The silence stretched, and Kathleen feared she'd get no answer to her question. She watched as color suffused Martha's face, a red that couldn't be blamed on the fire or even on a possible fever.

"I'm not sure how to answer you…I shouldn't presume to speak for Frank." She hesitated, cleared her throat, seemed to be thinking it over, then just spit it all out. "I *have* heard some rumblings—and I do know my son tends to jump to conclusions—especially if he's observed something with his own eyes."

"What?..."

Martha held up a hand to silence her. "I know when you hear this you're going to think it's no one's business. Standards and requirements are much different today than when I was a young teacher. What the public used to think totally unacceptable behavior is no longer frowned upon but quite commonplace. Still—" She hesitated and looked down at her lap. "Still, this community can be pretty conservative."

Kathleen held perfectly still and watched as the older woman finished the last of her soup and wiped her mouth with a paper napkin thoughts sped through her mind faster than a soccer ball kicked first one way and then the other. She gripped the arms of the chair until her knuckles turned white. *I don't know what Martha's going to say, but I don't think I'm going to like it.*

"This community takes great pride in its school—pride in our teachers. We've fought down consolidation time and again; often with shouting matches that almost led to fisticuffs at board meetings. Our teachers are observed and their actions are fair topics of conversation for almost any gathering. Interest in teachers is second only to the lives and actions of our doctors. If either one does something out of the norm, be it good or bad, it gets hashed and rehashed."

Kathleen brought Martha a glass of water and waited until she could quit coughing and continue her narrative.

"Thank you." She sipped from the glass. "This cough is awful. Now, where was I?...Oh, yes. Frank has seen you with Alvin on several occasions—as have others. Of course Patti was there, too."

Shifted to the edge of her chair, Kathleen pressed. "What are you trying to say?"

"Now don't get upset; hear me out. You wanted to know what people are saying and why Frank seems cool toward you. Well, he may be narrow, and he may be mistaken, but he isn't alone in thinking it's rather peculiar; everyone thought you were going to marry the banker, of whom most approved. Next thing we know, in less time than it takes to tell it, you're sporting a ring from a man no one here has ever heard of. Folks are asking me. And what can I really tell them? Danny seems very nice. I told them so. However, he isn't around much. In the meantime, they see you out with Alvin. They wonder about what happened in Chicago."

Martha gulped water, and again held up a hand, her eyes pleaded for understanding as she looked at Kathleen "I also tell them you're a very nice young woman, as well as a competent teacher. I know you wouldn't do anything immoral—I tell them."

Hot words sizzled on Kathleen's tongue. With enormous effort she bit them back. Her thoughts and emotions were harder to contain. She stood abruptly and gathered up the soup bowls and utensils, making them clatter. "It seems Jeannie was right."

"Jeannie? Who's Jeannie?"

"Jeannie is, or was, a bank teller in Fir Valley. She said

people would find someone else to talk about when she left—
I never dreamed it'd be me."

Chapter 34

Awake before the alarm clock rang, Kathleen reached for her Bible and turned to one of the Psalms. It comforted her to read about David's trials and tribulations and how he cried out to the Lord, but it didn't keep her from missing Danny. It seemed to have the opposite effect, and only made her miss him more. Faithful to daily check her e-mail, she didn't receive the message she so desired. *If only Danny were here, and I could talk to him. I know he'd have words of wisdom for me.*

She crept down the stairs and stood listening for a moment or two. Only the usual creaks and groans of an older house greeted her ears. Should she wake Martha and check on her, or should she let her sleep? She could call her later from school. But how could she go off to her job without knowing; what if the woman couldn't get out of bed? Or what if she'd lost her voice and couldn't talk?

Before Kathleen could fully decide, a light shone from beneath the bedroom door out into the hallway. In answer to a soft knock on her door, in a raspy voice Martha called, "Come in."

Martha sat on the edge of the bed, hands folded sedately in her lap. She wore an old-fashioned white nightgown, long sleeves down to her wrists, and a generous skirt hid her toes. A piece of red flannel hugged her throat and the smell of Vicks permeated the room.

"How are you feeling this morning?...are you ready for some breakfast?"

"Breakfast? Oh, I don't know—I feel like I've been dragged through the proverbial knothole backwards. My throat's sore." Martha grabbed for a tissue, covered her mouth and coughed, a wracking sound that made Kathleen wince.

"Maybe a cup of hot tea, but I can wait on myself, dear. Don't you have to get to school?"

"All in good time. I have almost an hour before I need to be there.

Kathleen hurried to the kitchen and put water on for tea. She took down oatmeal and raisins, determined to also make a hot breakfast for Martha. Snowball strode up to his dish, tail flicking, full of himself, cat wise, expecting to be fed. When he found his bowl empty, the plaintive scolding he emitted and the look of disdain on his face elicited a laugh from the young teacher. "So what are you going to do, my furry friend, have me evicted?"

In slippers and warm quilted robe, Martha shuffled her way to the kitchen. Chin nearly on her chest, as though her head might be too heavy to lift, she plopped down beside the table in the closest chair. Kathleen set a cup of hot tea in front of her.

"Oh, my! I'm not used to being waited on, but you surely are an angel."

Kathleen smiled, and poured dry kibbles into Snowball's dish before returning to the stove to stir the steaming gruel. A few more minutes and she spooned hot oatmeal into pretty blue daisy-flowered dishes. Next a bowl of brown sugar and a matching pitcher of cream were placed in readiness.

"Oh, my, I didn't think I wanted a thing to eat, but this looks good...you'll join me won't you?"

"Yes, thank you, I will. I took the liberty of making enough oatmeal for two. I'm afraid I don't often take time for a hot breakfast; though I know I should." She looked at her friend. "Martha? You'll be okay? You're sure you don't need to see the doctor? I could arrange to take you."

"Oh no, dear. I'll be all right. Or if I do need to see the doctor, I can drive myself...and leave these dishes. I'll tidy the kitchen. I have all day. Don't make yourself late to school."

Kathleen checked her watch. "Ten minutes. I'll pour you another cup of tea."

Martha sipped the hot liquid. "Thank you. Your tea with honey and lemon soothes my throat...I confess, I didn't sleep well last night. The windmills of my mind droned incessantly; that and having to cough.

"I'm worried about Charlene, and I don't know what I can do, if anything, to help the situation." Martha coughed again. "I think her folks expect too much of her. She can't measure up. Not to her quote 'perfect cousin.' Oh dear, I'm rambling again, aren't I? and you need to get to work. I have thought of someone, though, Alvin could get to baby-sit Patti. That's if he's interested."

"You have? May I ask,who might that be?"

"Me. There's no reason Patti couldn't come here after school. It makes perfect sense. I don't know why I didn't think of it before. Oh, I wouldn't want to keep her too many hours at a time, but you'd be here shortly after four. I'll phone Clara, and I'll talk to Alvin—Patti could come here as soon as I get over this cold."

Martha spooned up more oatmeal and squinted at Kathleen as she finished her breakfast. "But tell me, dear, Danny.... He hasn't been around much lately—and you haven't mentioned him in awhile; did you two have a fight?"

"I haven't *seen* the man long enough to fight with him—Danny's on assignment in Israel. Apparently everyone thinks, while the cat's away, and all that cliché, I'm running around having a blast, but I might as well be Rapunzel locked away in her tower and shorn of her tresses. Or perhaps I should just join the convent." *And give the wagging tongues a rest.* Kathleen smiled benignly and kept her more stringent thoughts to herself, thankful her friend couldn't read her mind.

Martha coughed until tears ran down her face. Kathleen cringed as she hurriedly stacked bowls in the sink. "Leave them," Martha gasped. "I've all day to tidy the kitchen.

As Kathleen drove to school, she pondered the events of the morning. Martha now seemed more in sympathy with Patti and her needs, and more understanding of the situation. Maybe it had something to do with Charlene and the upset there. *I have the feeling there's more to that story. What is she not saying?*

The sun had yet to clear the treetops, but it promised to be a nice day. A smile of amusement tugged at Kathleen's lips as she stood beside her open classroom door and watched children stream off the bus. Like ants at a school picnic, they scurried in all directions.

Two little girls erupted from the bus; Patti and Molly clasped hands and raced toward their teacher. "Miss O'Brien, Miss O'Brien. Guess what?" Patti shouted from halfway across the school yard.

Kathleen smiled, and held out a hand as the children raced up, almost bumping into her. "Whoa...slow down. Catch your breath, and tell me."

"I getta stay all night with Molly. Daddy said. And guess what else? My mommy called. And my daddy even talked to her. She's maybe gonna have me come see her this summer. I talked to Uncle Spike, too."

While Patti stopped to gulp for air, the teacher adroitly maneuvered the girls inside the classroom.

"Uncle Spike says my mommy sings real good. They're gonna travel on a great big ole bus if they get real famous. My mommy says she ain't...*isn't* gettin' on no plane for nobody. Uncle Spike can just get her a bus, or else figure how to keep a jet on the ground."

Molly poked Patti. "You have a note to give Miss O'Brien."

"Oh, yeah...I forgot. My daddy wrote you a note. I think it says I can stay all night with Molly."

Kathleen smiled and accepted the sealed envelope Patti handed her. She placed it on her desk; later, when lessons were underway, and curious children weren't gathered around like chattering birds, she'd open it.

Morning passed quicker than one busy teacher could believe possible. The classroom hummed with contented children forging ahead in workbooks after instruction in reading and arithmetic. Children finished their lunch and busied themselves on the playground before Kathleen remembered the letter.

Seated at her desk, classroom door locked, she slid the note from the envelope and read:

Kathleen,

Not sure if Patti needs note to get off bus with Molly, but there's one in her jeans pocket. Met Joe Ferndale. Nice guy. Doing better job of parenting than me. Talked to Patti, think I got the whole story. Sorry she kicked you. She cried. She won't do it again. She really likes you, you know. Also, I called every member on the school board. No one knew a thing about complaints of Patti staying after school. And that schemer, Frank Fisher, couldn't, or wouldn't, give me one instance of a complaint. I'll be at the next board meeting. You can bet on that. Board members can be replaced. And I think the bastard is lying. I still don't know how I'm gonna manage spring break. Granddad's worse. I may have to take some time off work. For sure Patti can't ride all day in truck with me. And I can't stick Grandma with her all week. I didn't know single parenting could be so difficult.

Al

Kathleen laid the letter aside. *Well, Al, I know how you can solve your dilema with Patti. I'll keep her over spring break. After all, I haven't anything better to do, have I? God alone knows when Danny will be back.* Kathleen allowed herself a weary sigh before going to the office. It probably wasn't necessary, but she'd cover the bases and tell Hazel Patti would be getting off the bus with Molly Ferndale.

• • •

Ready or not, the Friday before spring break arrived. Children chattered happily about their plans for vacation. Many were going somewhere with their parents. Others planned to visit the week with grandparents—Molly Ferndale among them.

Kathleen noticed Patti hadn't much to say. Probably spending the week with the teacher didn't rate high on the scale of exciting things to do. Well, Kathleen would cut out her tongue before admitting she wasn't exactly overjoyed with the prospect herself. She loved Patti, but frankly she needed a break from children's endless chatter. Uninterrupted quiet time, and hours spent conversing with adults—or one adult in particular—fit her idea of the perfect spring break.

Children called "Goodbye" as they stormed out the door and onto the bus to begin their week of freedom. Slowly and methodically the weary teacher went about picking up papers, dropped pencils, and straightening desks. Dick said they could leave a little early, but she had no compelling urge to rush home and listen to Mrs. Fisher's barking cough. Thankfully, the dear lady continued to improve, but coughing remained part of the daily regimen and made decent conversation nearly impossible.

Kathleen eyed the rocking chair, and as if drawn by some invisible cord, gravitated to it and sank down. *This chair really is comfortable. And it's so quiet with the children gone. Blessedly quiet. Maybe I'll just sit here and close my* eyes *for a minute or two.*

She would have been surprised to know she'd been asleep for almost an hour when she dreamed someone called her name. A pleasant voice. One that sounded familiar. Nice dream. She smiled. The dream voice said her name again. So soft. "*Kathleen? Sweetheart*?" Gentle fingers stroked her cheek. Dreamlike she moved her face to caress the hand. "Kathleen?...Carrot Top?...Honey, wake up."

Her eyes flew open and she bolted upright. "*Danny*!" she screeched. "Is it really *you*? I'm not dreaming? It's really you? You're *here?*"

Suddenly, she felt light as a spider's web blowing in the wind. She sprang from the chair and wrapped her arms around his neck. Danny lifted her off the floor and swung her around, nearly crushing her ribs in a bear hug, before releasing her and lowering his head to claim her lips in a gentle kiss. She wanted to sing. She wanted to dance. She wanted to shout and laugh. Instead she burst into tears.

"Ah, darlin'. Don't cry." Seated in the rocking chair with her snuggled on his lap, he rocked her as gently as one might rock a baby. She buried her face in his neck and let the tears soak his shirt. Several minutes passed before Danny lifted her chin and lightly kissed away the tears.

"I'm here—sweetheart—and it's just you and me for the weekend. We have some serious catching up to do. And if I'm not mistaken, this is the start of your spring break. I'd like to take you over east of the mountains to see the folks. They think they deserve to see their errant son, and I think I deserve to spend the week with the woman I love.

Kathleen managed a watery smile. For the first time she noticed his attire, cowboy boots, western shirt, tight-fitting Levis, and she didn't doubt a hat figured in there somewhere. She pulled back and giggled.

"What? Miss schoolteacher, ma'am ? You don't like my duds? I left my cayuse out thar in the schoolyard."

"Danny, you're crazy."

"I know. But you love me anyway. Seriously, I thought we might do a little riding next week over at the ranch. Mom's got the sweetest little mare you can ride. Get you out in that central Oregon sunshine. Put some hair on your chest."

Kathleen belted him before she burst out laughing. Danny laughed along with her, but looked puzzled when she jumped off his lap and began to wail. "I can't go, Danny. I promised to take care of Patti all week. Her dad's kinda in a bind. I had no *idea* you'd be back"

"Whadya mean, you can't go with me? We'll take Patti with us. The kid'll love it."

"Danneeee! Be serious. I can't just barge in on your folks with a six-year-old child for a week."

"And why not? My mom will love her. Dad, too. Why do you think they keep a pony over there? My mom loves kids. She's doggin' on me all the time to get married and supply her with a passel of grandkids." He winked at her. Kathleen blushed. "Mom'll be put out if you don't come and bring Patti. And believe me, after what I've been through, I have no desire to face her wrath. One little girl is no trouble at all."

" I don't know what her dad will say. Maybe he won't want her to go that far away."

"His choice, sweetheart. The man can't have everything. But I'm thinkin' he'll let her go. I'll meet him, talk to him. Let him know I don't have two heads."

Kathleen reached up and kissed him. "Danny, I think I love you."

Chapter 35

"Kathleen, honey, you're awfully quiet. You're not having second thoughts are you? Have I come back and interrupted your plans for the weekend? I'm pretty flexible; we can do whatever you'd like. I can ditch the cowboy garb, get dressed up, take you somewhere fancy, just tell old Dan what's on your mind. What's your pleasure?"

"Truth?"

"Yeah, Carrot Top, truth."

She stifled a yawn, and withdrew her head a fraction from his shoulder as she twinkled up at him. "You're not interrupting a thing. Except maybe sleep. I'm sorry I'm not better company, Dan. I'll confess to being tired—but I've waited a long time to sit here beside you—feel your arm around me—and know I'm not dreaming. I'm quite content you know, but if you want conversation..." She giggled. "I'm going to have to make us coffee."

Danny gave her a quick hug and withdrew his arm. "Why

don't I make the coffee? You relax. Just tell me where to find the fixings?"

"I'm afraid all I have up here is instant. I seldom make coffee for myself. Martha has the good stuff downstairs; she generally plies me with coffee or tea the minute she hears me come in. It's not often I can sneak past her, but she isn't feeling well. She'll be surprised when she learns you're here. And probably a little putout she missed your arrival."

"Instant's fine." He winked. "We'll catch up with Martha later."

Pleased to know he preferred to drink instant coffee with her, to perhaps better coffee shared with others, Kathleen rose to stand beside him in her miniscule kitchenette. Like teenaged conspirators, they bumped hips, and erupted into subdued giggles as she reached overhead and withdrew two blue mugs. Kathleen felt as if she were getting away with something forbidden, even while her brain told her not to be ridiculous. Just because she'd never entertained Edward, or any other man, in her apartment before, didn't mean she shouldn't invite Danny here now.

Seated across from each other, their fingers touched and entwined as their hands rested in the center of the tiny kitchen table. The questions Kathleen wanted so badly to ask Danny while he was away, no longer seemed important. She didn't want to talk about school, and she didn't want to discuss Mr. Fisher.

"Kathleen, I hated to leave you suddenly, the way I did, and I thought about you constantly. But I can't promise it won't happen again; it probably will. I can't even tell you

I won't be in danger. Unfortunately, danger—war, is what makes the news."

She withdrew her hands, reached for her mug and took a sip of coffee. "I know, Dan, and I won't pretend it's easy when you're gone. My emotions were all over the board. To have you go…when I thought I needed you, and God alone knew how much peril you'd face. I've had a lot of time to think…and I guess I'd rather have you part time than not at all."

He smiled and reached for her hands again. His grip on her fingers tightened, and his expression sobered as he looked into her eyes. "I hoped you'd feel that way, but I guess I wouldn't have blamed you too much if you'd decided to chuck it. My lifestyle won't be the easiest to live with. I do promise I'll take care of you, and life won't be boring."

He released her hands and reached for his cup. "Honey, if you're sure you'll have me, I really don't want to wait too long before we marry. But I'll try to give you time to plan the wedding you want."

"The wedding *we* want, Danny. *Our* wedding. My mother will have her ideas, *like inviting half of Portland*, but it's *our* wedding. Maybe we can make some plans this week. I need something concrete to tell Mom before she starts with the myriad suggestions she will have hatched since we last talked."

Danny chuckled. "We can always fall back on Plan B."

"Plan B? What's plan B?"

"You run away with me."

She laughed. "A lot less trouble than planning a wedding,

I'm sure, but it doesn't fill picture albums for us to reminisce over when we're old and gray…"

A plaintive cry from the top of the stairs halted conversation mid-sentence and alerted the couple to more current needs. "That will be Snowball," Kathleen said. "It sounds as if he wants his dinner. I'd better check. It's not like Martha to forget to feed her cat.

The feline rubbed his furry head against available legs. That accomplished, he switched his tail, looked up, and voiced his complaint with loud meows. Now that he had their attention, Snowball raced ahead down the stairs, making more racket than school kids on lunch break. The couple laughed and followed.

Kathleen, shadowed by Danny, took two steps into the living room and halted. Icy fingers of fear crawled her backbone like spiders up a drainpipe, for a moment she forgot to breathe. Martha sat slumped in her chair—her head listed at an awkward angle—chin obscured on her chest; glasses dangled precariously from one ear. Her face appeared waxen.

"Is she…?" Kathleen's voice came out in a ragged whisper as she clapped a hand to her mouth.

Danny squeezed her shoulder and pushed his way past. With an economy of strides, he crossed the room and checked Martha for a pulse. "She's breathing," he confirmed.

His fast response released Kathleen to action. She quickly scooped Snowball up, gave him a rapid stroke on his furry back and deposited him away from where he'd been traipsing back and forth, rubbing his head on Martha's feet. Kathleen lightly touched Martha, and repeated her name. Her frail attempt to respond set off alarm bells.

"*Danny?!*"

"She's in trouble. We need to get her to the hospital."

• • •

They sat holding hands in the waiting area outside the emergency room. "It may not be as bad as it seems. Don't hit the panic button yet. Let's wait until we know something for sure."

Danny's calm manner and soothing voice were all that kept her from losing it. It had been Danny who acted fast and got Martha to the hospital in record time. Danny who had handed her his cell phone and instructed her to call ahead. Danny who helped her find the number and call Mr. Fisher.

After an eternity to them, twenty minutes by the clock, Frank stormed through the door, and rushed up to the lady behind the counter. In a voice that carried, he demanded to know the condition of his mother. The receptionist calmly told him it might be awhile before the doctor could talk to him. She handed him a clipboard with attached papers to be filled out and directed him to be seated.

Clipboard tucked under his arm, he frowned when he turned and saw Kathleen, and Danny holding her hand. Ignoring the man beside her, Frank directed his questions to her. "What happened? What's wrong with my mother? Can you tell me? You just said an *emergency*. Get to the hospital."

"We're not sure what's wrong, Mr. Fisher." Kathleen leaned forward in her chair. "Martha seemed really confused when we tried to rouse her. Jumbled. You know? She wasn't making much sense. Her face seemed distorted and when she tried to respond, she nearly toppled from her chair. Dan caught her, and carried her to the car. We brought her here as quickly as possible.

"*You* brought my mother here? Why didn't you call an ambulance? Call the medics?"

Danny kept his voice low and controlled, but no one could mistake the steel underneath his words. "Mr. Fisher, you can blame me for not calling for an ambulance. Given the distance and the time factor, I thought it imperative to get your mother here as quickly as possible. We did call ahead, and a team of skilled personnel were awaiting our arrival."

"And *you* would be…?"

"Oh, I'm sorry," Kathleen interjected. "This is my fiancé, Daniel Davis." Danny stood, and the two men shook hands. Some of the starch wilted from the chairman of the school board as he slumped in a chair adjacent to the teacher. No one spoke as he bent forward, elbows on knees, head in his hands. Some moments passed before he straightened and began to fill out the forms he'd been given.

Danny squeezed and released Kathleen's hand. He rose, crossed the room, and disappeared around the corner. When he returned, he balanced three cups of coffee in his hands. Kathleen gratefully accepted the Styrofoam he held out to her. Frank nodded his thanks and reached for the hot brew offered him.

The door to the emergency room opened and a nurse called, "Mr. Fisher? You may come in now."

They watched him rise and quickly make his way to the room beyond. The door shut, and still their eyes remained glued to the entrance like nails drawn to a magnet. With an effort Kathleen forced herself to look away; she wanted to know Martha's diagnosis but feared what she might hear.

A look at Danny's face reassured her; she didn't need to be told he silently prayed. Kathleen said her own prayer of thanks for this man beside her. She needed his strength. Her palms were sweaty and cold, and her stomach felt like a stopover for migrating butterflies. Martha might not be family, but they'd grown close and in ways she seemed like a second mother. Kathleen studied the green squiggles on the white tile floor and tried to not visualize the worst on the blackboard of her mind.

A cool breeze entered through the open door as Charlene blasted into the waiting room, three jumps ahead of her mother. Quick to spot Kathleen, the teenager flew to her side and perched on the edge of a chair.

"Grandma? She's in *there*?—Dad? Where's Dad?—Oh, no!—This is just awful!"

Kathleen laid a hand on Charlene's denim-clad knee and tried hard to smile. Danny quickly stood and offered his chair to Mrs. Fisher. Not wasting time, Kathleen murmured a short introduction, then gently told mother and daughter as much as she knew of the situation concerning the elderly Mrs. Fisher.

"Frank is with her then?" Estelle muttered, not really asking a question. Her eyes shifted from Kathleen to her daughter, and quickly moved on to stare at the entrance to the emergency room.

Danny picked up a magazine and thumbed through it. Kathleen wiped her palms on a tissue. She tried hard not to fidget as she remained seated between Charlene and Estelle. Charlene squirmed in her chair, watched for her father, and sporadically reached to clutch the teacher's hand.

The door leading to the emergency room swung open and Mr. Fisher pushed through. He took a few steps into the waiting room and abruptly stopped. Kathleen sucked in her breath. Frank, his face chalk-white, looked bewildered. Estelle rushed over and put her arm around him; she gently led him to the chair Kathleen quickly vacated.

They waited in silence for Frank to regain his composure as he slumped in the chair between his wife and daughter.

"Daddy?" Charlene's eyes filled with tears as she watched her father. "Is Grandma—"

He shook his head, but remained mute. His face regained a little color as he turned to Danny and Kathleen. "I'm sorry I doubted you. The doctor said you acted wisely in getting my mother here as quickly as possible."

Estelle reached for her husband's hand.

"My mother's—had a stroke. How bad—they don't know—yet." Frank pulled his hand away from Estelle and raked fingers through sparse hair. "Lungs are congested. Bad. They're admitting her—to ICU. No visitors. For now. Except immediate family." He wiped moisture from his eyes and reclaimed his wife's hand.

"I'm so sorry," Kathleen whispered around the lump in

her throat. She crossed the short distance and shook hands with Frank and Estelle. "If there's anything—anything I can do." Kathleen felt Danny's hand on her back as he, too, shook hands and expressed his sympathy. Wanting to escape before she broke down and mingled her tears with Charlene's, Kathleen bent down and quickly hugged the teenager who now openly sobbed.

• • •

Settled in the car, Danny wrapped his arms around her and pulled her close. He let her cry for a few minutes while he gently stroked her back. When she pulled away and blew her nose on a tissue, he started the engine.

"I feel so—*guilty*! I should have *insisted* she see the doctor. But. If only—she might..."

"Huh *uh*! Honey! Don't go there!" He halted her disjointed flow of words with a squeeze to the shoulder. "You *can't* take the blame. She's a grown woman, and from what you tell me—a stubborn one."

Only after pulling into the parking lot of a fast-food restaurant did she remember they hadn't eaten. "Oh, Danny, I don't know. I feel like I'm going to be sick."

"It's nerves, sweetheart. And the shock. You'll feel better when you eat something. A milkshake, maybe. That always goes down good when your tummy's a bit upset."

A look at her face, and he whispered. "Things'll look better in the morning."

Chapter 36

Awake before six, Kathleen fixed herself a cup of instant coffee. To her amazement, she'd slept, if not well, more hours than expected. But with morning came a fresh dose of angst. So many questions raced through her mind; questions for which she had no answers. *Will Martha be okay? If she's not, will I need to move? Could a stroke happen to my mom or my dad? They're younger but...*

Kathleen lifted the phone from its cradle and speed dialed her mom in Florida.

"Hello?"

"Hi Mom—It's me."

"Kathleen! I'm glad you called. I was just thinking about you."

"Not too early is it? You an' Dad having your usual late Saturday breakfast?"

"Yes. Yes, we did. Dad just now left for his walk on the beach."

"I'm glad he's exercising." Kathleen wrapped the phone

cord around her finger. "But you need to exercise too, Mom. You should go with him."

"Honey?" She paused, each word emphasized as she continued. "Is something wrong? Your voice sounds funny. You're not crying are you?"

"No, I'm not crying." Kathleen swallowed hard. "But I feel like it—Mom—I've got bad news. Martha's had a stroke. Danny and I took her to the hospital yesterday evening."

"Oh dear! No wonder you sound funny. That's too bad! I know how much you think of Martha. I'm sorry, honey. This *is* bad news. I hope this isn't the start of more. Trouble comes in threes you know." Margaret O'Brien cleared her throat. "But Danny? You did say Danny, didn't you? Danny's there with you?—Sounds like he got there just in time."

"Yeah, Mom, I guess you could say that."

"Kathleen, now you've got me worried. Are you going to be okay? Danny won't leave again real soon will he?...I wouldn't like to think of you being alone now. And what if Mrs. Fisher doesn't recover? Right away, I mean? Who's in charge? Will you have to..."

"Mom! Stop with the questions, already. I don't know. I don't even know how bad Martha is."

"Well, maybe it's not as bad as it seems right now. People do recover from strokes. With therapy. But tell me about Danny. You weren't expecting him, were you? Will he be there for your entire vacation?"

"Yes, he'll be here a week or more. He wants me to go with him to visit his folks in Central Oregon."

"Well, that sounds like fun. Didn't you tell me they have

horses? And while you're together—for goodness sakes—make some plans—for your wedding! Set a date!"

Kathleen settled on the edge of her bed. "Yeah, Mom."

"Don't 'Yeah, Mom' me, young lady. It takes *time* to plan a wedding. We'll need to secure the church."

She heaved a sigh she hoped her mother could hear. "*Mom.* Relax. We'll handle it."

"Well, I suppose so but I don't think you realize…"

"I promise we'll come up with a date soon. But I'm not sure I'll go with Danny to visit his folks."

"What? Why ever not?"

"I promised Mr. Williams I'd look after his daughter this week. He's rather in a bind. The grandmother has her hands full caring for the grandfather. And—"

"Well, my goodness, you made the promise before Danny got back. Mr. Williams should understand and get someone else."

Snowball strutted across the bed and eased into Kathleen's lap. "Danny wants to take Patti with us."

"Well, that's generous. Some men wouldn't want to share you. So what's the problem?"

"What if Mr. Williams doesn't want to let her go? It's a long way from here. And Patti can't go home to her daddy at night."

"Well, if he doesn't want to let the child go, then it's up to him to find a sitter. Kathleen, you owe it to Danny, and to yourself, to spend the time with him. If you're going to marry this man, there'll be plenty of times your plans will have to change."

They talked a few more minutes and she hung up, refusing to respond to her mother's assertion. But her mother's statement bothered her. She wanted nothing more than to spend every possible minute with Danny; but did that mean she should cancel her own plans, and break promises, all on a moment's notice. *Danny doesn't expect it. Does he?*

Other remarks her mother made niggled at her mind, though she'd tried to shut them out. Kathleen couldn't deny being head-over-heels in love with Danny, nor could she deny a willingness to marry soon. So how could she be so in love and yet clueless about what he might expect of her? With all her heart she desired to be a good wife. But what did "Good Wife" mean to Danny?

Kathleen stroked Snowball's silky head. She cringed when her mom reminded her she'd once considered marrying Edward, and urged her to be sure she knew Danny. She *did* know Danny. Of course she did. And how dare her mother speak his name in the same sentence with Edward. Didn't she know they weren't to be compared?

She and Danny practically grew up together. They shared the same values, attended the same church—listened to the same sermons. All pluses but that didn't always mean agreement about how to apply faith to life.

She loved the way Danny didn't waver in his belief. The way his strong faith supported him. She felt sure his faith ran much deeper than her own, a good thing. An encouragement to her, unless it defined narrowly how she should behave.

They needed to talk, she and Danny. He'd said he'd never expect her to give up teaching—a definite plus. Because of his uncertain schedule, she could even continue to teach at Pleasant Grove for awhile if that's what she wanted, he'd said. Though he hoped she'd want to move to Seattle. Generous, but what if Danny changed his mind after they married?

The way he accepted Patti warmed her heart. The fact he wanted to take her with them to his parents, well, it was just stupendous. But what if Patti couldn't go? And what if she didn't want to go without Patti? Would he be angry? All these doubts were making her a little crazy. She was even beginning to question how to broach the subject of his expectations of their life together. What if her uncertainties angered him? Maybe she could start by asking how many children he wanted.

• • •

They sat in the back booth of the recently opened restaurant on the edge of Fir Valley. Danny asked her preference, and then ordered bacon and eggs with whole wheat toast and coffee for both of them. "I'm glad you called, another ten minutes and I'd have risked waking you."

"I don't know—the house feels really strange without Martha there. Snowball feels it too; he slept on my bed last night." Kathleen sipped hot coffee. "I fed him this morning, but I brought his dishes upstairs to my apartment. I have this weird feeling; I'm trespassing when I enter Martha's kitchen."

Kathleen stared out the window before turning her attention back to her companion. "Guess what? It's raining—right on schedule for spring break."

He chuckled. "That's right, it always rains in the Willamette Valley during Spring Break, doesn't it? Well, it's nice to know you can count on some things."

"I'm sorry, Danny. This hasn't been much of a welcome home for you."

"So, who's complaining? You're here. I'm here. We're together. That's what counts. We'll get through this thing with Martha. The sun'll shine again."

With her foot, Kathleen sought his leg under the table and lightly tapped him on the ankle. "Oh stop being so disgustingly cheerful! I want to stay in the dumps for awhile."

Danny pulled a long hound-dog face and shoved his coffee cup across the table. "Okay. Move over, and I'll share your soggy blanket of doom and gloom."

Trust Danny to make her giggle. She made a cross-eyed face at him worthy of a first grader. There was no denying she felt better.

"Sweetheart, since it's raining, and there's not much we can do here, what would you say if we collected Patti and took off for the folks' a day early?"

"Oh shucks—I forgot. I haven't asked her father if he'll let Patti go with us." Kathleen checked her watch. "It's too early to call. Saturday morning. They may be sleeping in."

"It's okay, honey. No rush. Finish your breakfast, and then maybe we can drive out there. I'd like to meet Mr. Williams and talk with him. Maybe meet the grandmother as well."

She took a few bites and kept her eyes on her plate. "What if Mr. Williams says no? If he does, and I feel I should stay *here* and keep Patti, will you be terribly upset with me?"

Kathleen laid her fork aside and resolutely faced him across the table. "I did promise."

Danny kept on forking in bacon and eggs, pausing to sip coffee, with no more reaction than if she'd asked him if he thought it might stop raining. "I don't think Mr. Williams will say no. But if he should, we'll simply go now, today, to see Mom and Dad. And we'll be back in time to baby sit Patti Monday morning."

She stared at him. "You're serious? You'd give up your week with your parents to help me care for one little girl?"

"Well, sure darlin,'" he drawled, a glint of mischief in his eye. "Someone has to keep you focused."

• • •

Kathleen turned her head to check on Patti seated in the backseat of the rented Toyota Camry. In her lap, she held the doll her mother gave her. Snuggled beside her sat the teddy bear her father had bought her in Chicago. Unaware of being watched, Patti continued combing her doll's hair and softly singing to her two inanimate companions.

The words were barely audible to the couple in the front seat, but what they heard made them choke back laughter. A mishmash of choruses learned in Sunday school and perhaps some of her dad's country western were being rehearsed. "You picked a fine time to leave me Lucille," blended with "Jesus Wants Me for a Sunbeam."

Beginning to relax, Kathleen gently massaged Danny's shoulders while he drove. "My mind has been so on overload I haven't even asked about you or your trip to Israel.

I'm sorry. I do want to hear all about it. What's it like over there? How did things go for you?" She rested her hands in her lap. "Did you get to Germany to see your colleague, the one injured in Iraq?"

"Is that three or four questions? Guess I'll take that last question first," he teased. "I did see Rocky in Germany. His spirits were amazingly good." Danny hesitated, flicked the windshield wipers up a notch, and reached for her hand. He smiled, but it didn't quite reach his eyes before he sobered. "I doubt he'll ever return to broadcasting—at least not the news as he's known it. His face is still heavily bandaged—for sure he's lost the sight in one eye, and my guess is he'll be pretty badly scarred when he does finally heal. But of course there's always plastic..."

"Oh no! We didn't hear any of that on the news. Just that he's recovering in a hospital in Germany." Kathleen took a deep breath, and tried not to shudder. "But we'd have to know the damage is great, wouldn't we, when a roadside bomb explodes in your face. Oh *Dan,* war is so *awful*! I hate it!"

"Yeah—but Rock's one of the lucky ones. He's coming home. They'll bring him back to the States. And they'll do a good job of patching him up. He'll be with his family."

Kathleen didn't answer. No doubt he was right. But she wondered how *right* it could possibly feel if Danny came home disabled, unable to do the job he loved. She shied away from the thought, closing her mind to the awful possibility.

Raindrops glistened like jewels on branches of fir trees, and on weed-infiltrated grass alongside the two-lane highway over the Santiam. They passed the small community of

Mill City and later on Gates. Occasionally a well-kept home peeked from a clearing in the forest. Pretty. The steady hum of tires on wet pavement soothed Kathleen with an almost hypnotic affect. Another glance in the backseat told her Patti slept.

Detroit Lake appeared in a somber mood as Danny skillfully negotiated the curves along the edge. Rain peppered the water making little expanding rings on the gray surface, like minnows gulping for bugs.

Danny broke the companionable silence. "Carrot Top, I think I can about tell what's running though your mind. And probably you don't want to talk about this, but I think we should. Maybe I can reassure you a bit. Of course there are no guarantees in this life, but I can tell you we take all the precautions possible when in a war zone, and for the most part reporters and photographers are respected and reasonably safe." He touched her hand. "I have no desire to get myself killed.; I'm certainly not suicidal, and if it's blatantly foolish to cover an area, I'll refuse. But the world deserves to know the truth of what's happening over there." He lightly squeezed and released her knee. "Besides, I'm not always taking pictures of things blowing up; sometimes I photograph very pretty ladies in very skimpy bathing suits."

"Uh huh, and that's suppose to make me feel better?"

He grinned. That impish gleam shone in his eyes. "Sweetheart, I'll take your picture in a bathing suit anytime, and put it up against any of them any day."

• • •

The rain changed to large feathery snowflakes before they reached the summit of the pass. Kathleen debated waking Patti to see nature's beauty, hesitated a little too long, and the fickle snow stopped. The sun broke free. Sodden dirty piles beside the highway were certainly nothing to inspire Patti to write a "My Vacation" story, or for the teacher to chance dealing with a grumpy child awakened too soon.

Before they reached the touristy town of Sisters, Patti woke, stretched, and morphed into something of a chatterbox. "Where are we? Are we there yet?"

"Not yet, but it's not too far," Danny said.

"What are those trees? They look funny. Why is the bark all cracked like that?"

"Those are pine trees, Patti. Ponderosa pine," Kathleen said. "Aren't they pretty?"

"Yeah, I guess. Boy, this road is sure straight. I can see a long ways. What's at the other end? I have to go potty."

Danny shot a look at Kathleen. Kathleen stared back. "How far are we from Sisters?"

"About twenty minutes, maybe ten if I push it."

"Patti, do you think you can wait, say as long as a recess time?"

"I dunno. I gotta go kinda bad."

Dan spotted a more-or-less level place to pull off the road and made a quick stop. Kathleen untangled her squirming charge from the straps in the backseat and helped her from the car. "I don't know, Patti, there's no restroom here. Can you manage to go behind a tree? I'll stand guard. No one will see you. Just go behind that big tree there."

Patti ran back. "Miss O'Brien, this is kinda fun. I'll stand guard if you wanta go."

Chapter 37

Danny guided the car down the long fenced lane, pulled up and parked in front of the three-bay garage. The occupants barely had time to clamber from the car and treat themselves to a lazy stretch before the front door of the ranch-style house jerked open, and a miniature whirlwind with flying blonde hair raced across the lawn. "You're here!"

Her companion followed only slightly slower, his long legs eating the distance.

"Mom—Dad. You know Kathleen. And this little cowgirl is Patti."

"Kathleen, I'm so glad you came and brought Patti." Carolyn Davis gave her a quick hug and turned to her youngest guest. "Hello, Patti. Welcome. I love your boots and your hat."

Patti hung back and looked up at her teacher. Kathleen smiled and gently urged her forward with a hand on her shoulder.

"Thank you, Mr. Danny buyed me my hat."

Carolyn beamed at the child, and winked at Kathleen, but she couldn't wait a second longer to launch herself at her son. Danny bent, wrapped his arms around his mom, gave her a bear-hug, and a noisy kiss on the cheek, before he released her.

Jim Davis looked on, blue eyes twinkling. He retained an athletic build, and except for Danny's blonde hair, his son resembled him. Jim was starting to gray a bit around the temples, other than that his hair remained dark. He wore a super-sized grin that left no doubt of his pleasure in seeing them.

"Kathleen, good to see you again. It's been far too long." Jim opened his arms and gave her a hug. "I can't tell you how happy I am this son of ours has had the good sense to ask you to marry him. I just don't know what took him so long."

"Patti. Forgive us." Mr. Davis, recovered first, smiled. "We get a little carried away when we haven't seen our son in awhile…I hope you like kittens. There's some in the barn."

Eyes wide, she stared up at him, but didn't answer.

Danny draped an arm around Kathleen's shoulders and took Patti by the hand as his mother urged them to the house and ultimately the large country kitchen. "I'll come back and get our things later," Danny said. "If I know Mom, she'll have something ready for us to eat." He spoke for Kathleen's ears, but Jim, lagging behind, heard.

"I'll help you bring luggage in later, Son. I have an idea our future rodeo queen here is hungry. How about it, Patti? Do you like pizza?"

Patti grinned. "*Yeah!…*I mean, yes sir."

Mr. Davis chuckled. "Yeah, I like pizza, too."

"Jim makes the best pizza ever, and he's turned out three different kinds; they're ready to go in the oven. We can eat before our tummies have too much time to complain," Carolyn announced as she surveyed her kitchen. "You girls can help set the table if you like," she said as she began to take things from cupboards and drawers.

"Sure. We can do that, can't we Patti? Maybe we should wash our hands first."

"There's a bathroom down the hall second door on the right, but you can wash here at the sink, too, if you like."

A long, highly polished trestle table, that looked as if it might have come from an abbey, graced one side of the light airy kitchen. It could easily accommodate a dozen or more people. Danny watched a minute or two then quite efficiently went about removing the extra ladder-back chairs from the table and placing them in the pantry. He purposely bumped against Kathleen and whispered in her ear, "I think Mom and Dad expect us to fill these chairs with grandkids."

Kathleen's face turned a shade to match her hair. Danny wanted to tease her further, but he knew he'd probably goaded her enough for now. She'd need time to get reacquainted with his parents.

If Carolyn Davis noticed her future daughter-in-law's red face she chose to ignore it. "I like my long table, but shouting down the length doesn't appeal to me." Carolyn laughed, pushed hair back from her face, then rinsed her hands again. "I like to be close and cozy. Those films, you know, where the master sits at one end of the table and the mistress sits at the other end? And this austere butler always looks down his nose while he shuffles sedately from one to the other."

Carolyn reached in a drawer and took out more napkins. "I always have this urge to laugh, even if the movie is serious. Jim and I once sat at opposite ends of our long table when we were feeling provoked. We ended up throwing biscuits at each other and laughing our fool heads off."

Kathleen smiled, repressed a giggle, and candidly directed her attention back to helping Patti with placement of pink mats on the table. The child needed no coaching to place matching paper napkins on the left side of the plates her teacher adroitly set out.

"Good job, Patti," Carolyn said as she bustled over. "But I think we may need more napkins with pizza. I'll just set these extra on the table."

"I like your plates, Mrs. Davis. They're real pretty."

"Well, thank you, I've had them since Danny was a little shaver not much older than you. Some pieces have a few nicks and chips, but I like them, too. They're Franciscan ware, desert rose pattern."

Danny strode back into the kitchen looking innocent as a cat with cream on his nose and feathers stuck to his whiskers. He aimed a smirk at Kathleen and lightly ruffled Patti's hair. "Well, ladies, your luggage is now deposited in your room. I took the liberty of unpacking for you and putting your things in the drawers."

Kathleen arched an eyebrow, the look on her face made Danny want to hoot. He struggled to keep his face straight and his eyes innocent looking when she said, "You didn't?"

He knew he treaded dangerous ground, but he couldn't resist the chance to tease.

"What? I wasn't supposed to?"

When Kathleen shot him a look guaranteed to peel paint, Danny erupted into laughter. Before she could think of ways to kill him, he grabbed her from behind, lifted her off the floor and swung her around.

Jim, finished with barn chores, shucked his boots and entered the kitchen in time to witness his son's shenanigans. A large grin wreathed his face. On wool-stockinged feet he crept up behind Carolyn, gave her a playful swat on the bottom, and nuzzled her neck.

"Well, old woman, is the pizza ready?"

She turned and smiled up at him. "Couple minutes. Just time for you to wash up."

They held hands at the table while Jim bowed his head and returned thanks. "Dig in," he said as soon as heads lifted. "What kind would you like, Patti?"

"That one." She pointed to the pepperoni and he slid a slice onto her plate.

They stuffed themselves with pizza, and went through a pile of napkins while wiping greasy fingers. The adults carried on a happy banter; the talk consisting mostly of, "Do you remember?" Patti stuffed herself on pizza, listened, and remained quiet except for an occasional giggle when an adult recalled a story she thought funny.

"Jim, this is the best pizza I've ever eaten," Kathleen said. "I hope you'll teach Danny how to make it."

• • •

After visiting awhile, Dan's parents excused themselves and retired. At last, Danny had Kathleen all to himself. Cuddled on the couch before the open fire in the family room, he did what he'd been longing to do all evening. He pulled her to him and kissed her until they were both breathless. A glow suffused their faces, heat that had nothing to do with the fire on the hearth. Gently but firmly, Kathleen pushed him away.

"I thought Patti might be afraid, and want her daddy or her grandmother when it came time to go to bed, but she didn't hesitate at all." With some inches now between them, Kathleen laid a hand on Danny's knee. "I let her choose the twin bed she wanted to sleep in and she hopped right in and settled down without a murmur. Of course I read to her until her eyes were so heavy she couldn't hold them open any longer."

"Honey, I don't mind telling you, my heart melted when she came out here in those fuzzy pink bunny pajamas and hugged my neck. I wasn't expecting that. She smelled so clean and nice after her bath. You must have shampooed her hair, too?" He caressed the hand resting on his knee. "I hope someday, in the not-so-distant future, we have a little girl just like her."

Kathleen scooted to the corner of the couch, tucked her feet under her, and faced the man that turned her knees to jelly. "Dan, I know you want a family. And I know you grew up by yourself. So—how many children would you like to have?"

"A dozen," Dan blurted and then sobered. "Honey, come on back over here. I promise to behave and to talk sense."

Kathleen stayed where she was, but she did plant her feet on his leg. "Dan, I'm serious—how many?"

"Well, I don't want to raise one alone if we can help it. So, I'm thinking at least two. Three or maybe four strikes *me* as even better. But I'm fully aware you're the one that will be doing the work of bearing them. Dan watched her face as he slowly massaged her feet. "It seems only fair to leave the decision of how many up to you. I plan to be the best dad possible, but you have to know—I won't be there all the time."

Dan continued to absently rub her feet as he studied Kathleen. "Sweetheart, I hope you know if you change your mind and don't want to work when we're married that's cool. You can stay home. Take up hobbies." Dan shifted her feet, and crossed his legs. "I've already told you, I don't have a problem with you working if that's your desire. And you've said you want to teach, at least for now. But even when we have kids you can work if you want. We'll put them in daycare or hire a nanny. Sometime, I'd like to take you with me on assignment."

No way could all the questions be answered in one evening—especially since they didn't even know all the questions. The future only revealed its self one day at a time.

"Kathleen, with me you'll be pretty much free to do whatever you like. I hope we'll be teammates. I certainly don't view myself as lord and master, or my word as necessarily the final word." He stretched, stifled a yawn and reached to draw her back beside him. "Just let me know if you decide to sell the house while I'm gone, so I can find you when I come home."

His arm around her, she surprised the daylights out of him when she said, "Dan, do you think we could pull all the details together and be ready to get married by say the middle of July?"

"*Wow!* You mean it? Babe, just tell me what you want me to do." He stood and pulled Kathleen to her feet. "Come on, let's have that bowl of ice cream Mom offered us earlier and take a look at the calendar. Maybe we can nail down a date and go from there."

They sat at the table, shoulders touching, and spooned in French vanilla ice cream. Dan produced a small calendar and a yellow scratch pad, but forgot a pencil. He rose, rummaged around in a kitchen drawer and came back with two. For about ten minutes they worked on lists.

"I'm sorry, Danny. I can't concentrate; I'm about to fall asleep right here. And if my guess is right, Patti will wake early, eager for adventure."

"You're right, and I'm being a thoughtless jerk." He gently tipped her face toward him and kissed her lips with a caress as promising as sunrise. "I didn't realize it's after midnight. Go to bed Carrot Top; I'll clean up here."

• • •

"Good morning merry sunshine," Dan said. "You ready for a pancake or two?"

"I can't believe I slept so long." She stifled a yawn. "Patti, how'd you sneak out without me hearing you?"

"I was really quiet, huh?" She crowed while shoving another bite in her mouth. "Mr. Danny said I should let you sleep. Me and him made blueberry pancakes. I stirred in the blueberries."

• • •

By one o'clock the sun warmed enough to venture outdoors. Dan brushed and then saddled Trigger, the buff-colored Shetland pony with the flaxen mane and tail. Patti's eyes were round as silver dollars as Danny lifted her into the saddle and shortened the stirrups to fit her legs.

"Okay, kiddo. Hang onto the saddle horn right there. Here we go." Kathleen watched as Dan gently led the pony around the corral. Once, twice, seven times before he stopped, looped the reins over the pony's head and handed the reins to Patti. "All right, cowgirl, you're ready to ride on your own." He gave her instructions how to guide Trigger. Dan walked beside them as the little horse carried Patti slowly around the ring.

By the middle of the week Dan had taken enough pictures of Patti, Kathleen, and horses to fill a small gallery. It took a bit of coaxing to get Kathleen on Carolyn's black mare the first time, but after that she seemed eager to ride. She rode as though she'd been born to it.

Patti and Danny bonded. Only once did she seem to have a touch of homesickness, and chattering to her dad on the phone took care of that. The child lost her shyness around Dan's parents and delighted them with her happy chatter.

Kathleen tried several times, unsuccessfully, to call family members and learn the state of Martha's health. Finally, she let it go. Wrapped in a rosy glow, the week sped by too quickly for Dan and Kathleen. That is until very early Thursday morning.

Out of long habit Dan kept his cell phone on. Around four in the morning, his boss called and apprised him of a train wreck near the Oregon/Idaho border. He hated to ask—but since Dan's parents resided only minutes away from the scene if he traveled by private aircraft—would he grab his cameras and go?

Dan had two minutes to decide if he should wake Kathleen, or dash off a note and let her sleep. A note seemed the coward's way out. Hoping she also slept with her cell phone on, he dialed her number, trusting not to wake Patti.

A bleary-eyed Kathleen, rubbing sleep from her eyes, appeared at his side just as he pulled a cup of instant coffee from the microwave.

"What's up? You said it's urgent."

"Yeah. Want a cupa coffee?"

She shook her head, and he quickly outlined the problem.

"*Dan!* I don't believe this. You're on vacation—you just got *back* from an assignment. Can't they leave you alone for *one-lousy-week*? Do you really have to rush off?"

"Honey, I won't be gone more than a day—maybe half a day. I'd take you with me, but there's Patti. We can't drag her around. And I don't suppose you'd want to leave her here with my folks?"

Dan left with a heavy heart. Kathleen hadn't bothered to

dignify his last remark. She'd simply slumped into a chair and stared at him. She'd kissed him goodbye with no more warmth than a robot. Probably, in her eyes, leaving seemed like a dirty trick. He hated to think so, but maybe this was the acid test, the test to determine if they could make it as husband and wife.

Daniel Lee Davis prayed harder than he'd ever prayed in his life.

Chapter 38

Elbows plopped on the table, Kathleen yanked on a lock of hair and twisted it around her finger until it reached her scalp. *No point in going back to bed; I'll never sleep now.* Why did life have to be so unfair? Why couldn't she have fallen in love with a garbage collector, a plumber, or a goat farmer, anyone that didn't go racing off when the phone rang? But Danny? Danny seemed eager to go. *Eager!*

The instant coffee she overheated in the microwave burned her tongue. It just made her angrier, as if that were Danny's fault too. *In a way it is,* she reasoned. *He's the one got me out of bed at this ungodly hour. And for what? To tell me he's leaving. Leaving! That's what!*

She tugged harder on her hair; the physical distraction did little to lessen the mental anguish, but it did remind her not to cry. Her thoughts mocked her as her emotions rose and plummeted faster than kids on a teeter-totter. She'd been so sure she could handle absences required of Danny as he followed his chosen profession. Hadn't she spouted something about news anchors and their wives? Walter Cronkite and his wife Betsy for an example? If they could handle separations, she could. A brave assumption. Also an untested one.

Illogical as it might be, Danny's overseas assignments seemed easier to deal with than his leaving her now. For one thing she needed to wear a happy face in front of his parents. If she were home she could do as she wanted. Keep herself busy. Lose herself in work. Or simply grouse with no one to observe.

She liked Jim and Carolyn Davis well enough. Though she felt they were just now getting acquainted. Ten years had passed since they'd seen one another, and this was entirely different than breezing in and out of their house as a teenager. Kathleen felt like Danny had dumped her, left her on display like some prize filly to be evaluated and observed for defects while he galloped off in search of greener grass.

Then there was the remark about Patti. He'd take her with him if not for Patti. So did that mean he really hadn't wanted to bring Patti here after all? *But that's ridiculous. Isn't it?*

Maybe it was the coffee, or maybe it was just having time to fully wake and think; but an uneasy feeling began to stir in the region of her solar plexus, swell and lodge in her throat. She coughed. Maybe she'd assumed too much. She *had* insisted she take care of Patti. Danny had been pretty accommodating, but perhaps she hadn't given him much choice.

Stop already! Kathleen clamped hands over her ears as if she could shut out the turmoil reverberating in her brain. One thought popped to the surface and refused to be stilled.

If I marry Dan, this is the way it will be isn't it? He'll forever be leaving at inopportune times.

If only it wasn't dark; she could go for a walk. She needed exercise; time to compose herself before she faced Patti. Maybe she should go to the barn and shovel horse biscuits. That's what Danny called them. Right now, she could think of other names for the stuff on the barn floor. Names that more nearly matched her anger.

A slight noise caught her attention and she glanced up startled to see Carolyn enter the kitchen, her slippers scuff-scuffing against the vinyl floor, eyes blinking at the unaccustomed light. If this teacher intended to compose herself, she'd better do it in ten seconds or less.

"I'm sorry," Kathleen said. "Did the light wake you?"

"*What?*" A hand flew to her chest. "*Oh*—you frightened me—I didn't see you sitting there." Carolyn shuffled her way to the table and dropped into a chair beside Kathleen. "Huh uh. No. The light didn't wake me. Just couldn't sleep. Thought I'd come out here. Get a glass of milk. You couldn't sleep either?"

"Actually, I slept quite well until I was awakened—" In an economy of words, with a voice she struggled to keep well modulated, Kathleen related the news of the call that sent Danny into action.

Eyes wide, Carolyn Davis dropped her jaw and stared at her young guest. "*What?* Well—that takes the frosting off the cake." She heaved a sigh. "How awful for you. I don't suppose he could turn the offending cell phone off. Men are such aggravating animals. And most of the time they haven't a clue."

It was Kathleen's turn to stare. She hadn't expected Mrs. Davis to sound put out with her son.

"Well—this calls for a pot of my special Irish crème coffee." She rose from the table, cinched the belt to her robe with a jerk, and reached for Kathleen's cup. "That stuff you're drinking has to be terrible." She made a face. "Let's dump it."

In moments steaming cups of coffee, with the most heavenly aroma wafting upward, rested on the table in front of the two women. A plate of warmed sticky buns, melted butter swimming on top, tempted them to nibble. A supply of napkins waited near by.

Carolyn tore off a chunk of pastry, licked her fingers, and reached for a napkin. "Jim's business, thank God, never required him to travel. I could depend on him to be home each night. But what he did do when we were first married was go hunting. And I'm not talking a weekend or even a couple weeks. Oh, sometimes it was no longer." She sipped coffee and peered at Kathleen over the rim of her cup. "But on this one annual hunt, he disappeared for more than a month."

"A *month*? What was he hunting?"

"Oh, bear, elk, moose, birds. You name it. He hunted it—often in the wilds of Canada. I never knew for sure where he was; only that he was off in the wilderness miles from a phone." Carolyn sighed and twisted her napkin. "He coulda died out there somewhere for all I knew. He'd show up on our doorstep weeks later looking like a mountain man I barely recognized."

Kathleen reached for another cinnamon roll. "How did you cope with that? Surely he wasn't out there alone all that time."

"Oh, he had a partner. But that was small insurance. I still had to wait—and I'm afraid I didn't handle it very well." There was an unmistakable glimmer in her eye as she faced the woman seated adjacent to her. "I went home to mother."

Kathleen smiled and nodded.

"I thought I'd give Jim time to miss me. You know? Like I missed him. But it didn't work well when he only got home a day ahead of me. I walked in to find him in our bed snoring his head off. A huge pile of dirty clothes in the middle of the floor." Carolyn Davis kept her voice low as she sniggered at the memory of the joke on her.

"After that I simply gave him the best send-off I possibly could. He left with no doubts of being well loved. I tucked little heart-shaped R-rated notes in his gear for him to find when he was out there freezing his whiskers, so he'd be reminded what waited for him back home."

Carolyn grinned as she took time to drink coffee. "But I did keep him a bit off balance. It got so he didn't know what to expect when he came home. One time when he left for his hunting expedition, I painted the whole house—each room a different color—and all of them gaudy. He came home to a royal blue bedroom. Another time it was pink flamingoes all over the yard. One for each day, he was gone.

Kathleen laughed politely. The intended message didn't

escape her, but she also knew she had to work the situation with Danny out in her own mind. No one could do it for her. As tastefully decorated as the Davis home now appeared, she found it hard to visualize Carolyn ever being anything but appropriate. Orange walls, however, did conjure up a certain obstinate appeal—that and throwing biscuits. Kathleen decided she really liked this woman.

• • •

The day inched forward; her thoughts never far from Danny. She found she could carry on a conversation, chop vegetables for the hearty soup Carolyn wanted to make, and later read to Patti; all with only part of her mind on the task at hand. After nearly thirty years Jim and Carolyn Davis seemed so much in love. Could it possibly be that way for her and Danny? Certainly Dan seemed blessed with the same sense of humor his mother exhibited, and underneath she sensed a strength akin to his father's quiet confidence.

Their heads together over the checkerboard; Jim had infinite patience instructing Patti. She fast became a worthy opponent and didn't want to quit playing. Up at an early hour, Carolyn gave in and napped in her room. Glad to have some time to herself, Kathleen put on a warm jacket and headed for the barn.

The sun shone, but a cold wind straight off snowcapped mountains whipped around the corners of the buildings. Coaly nickered to her, and Jim's big horse, Ace, leaned his head over the door to his box stall. "Hello, big guy." Kathleen rubbed the blaze on his face. "Quit pushing," she laughed. "You'll get your treat."

Baby carrots were dispensed to each of the horses in turn in the exact manner she'd seen Danny do it. Coaly and Ace each got four. Little blanketed Trigger got two, but only after he nosed the pocket they were hidden in. Kathleen laughed to herself and petted the small animal for some minutes before she picked up a brush and stepped into the large box stall to brush Coaly.

The mare turned her head and watched with what Kathleen hoped was approval before she switched her tail and went back to munching hay. The brush slid over the horse's coat effortlessly and Kathleen thought she wouldn't mind doing this on a daily basis. Surprised at how much heat one horse could generate, she soon became too warm, slipped off her coat, and laid it across the stall door. Brush-stroke, brush-stroke, brush-stroke. Her thoughts unraveled with the brush strokes. It was almost like having a friend in whom to confide her doubts and frustrations. When Coaly looked at her with those large liquid brown eyes; Kathleen imagined the horse understood her feelings.

"You going to clean her hooves too?"

Kathleen whirled around. "*Dan*—you're back!" She dropped the brush and rushed to throw her arms around his neck.

He opened the stall door and stepped inside. They remained locked in a tight embrace until Coaly nudged him for the third time looking for the expected treat.

"Ummm darlin', you feel so good. You smell a little horsey though. And you've got dirt on your nose."

Kathleen swatted him on the shoulder, and just as quickly sobered. "Was the wreck bad? People hurt? Did you get all the pictures you wanted?"

"It was a freight train, honey. Twenty cars off the tracks, most on their side. Some down over an embankment. One brakeman slightly injured." He paused to wipe the dirt off her nose with the red bandana he carried in his jeans pocket. "The worst part—they were hauling toxic chemicals and they caught fire. My pictures will be on the evening news."

"Dan, that sounds so dangerous—were you…?"

He silenced her with his mouth on hers. Kathleen clung to him, her knees felt weak and she forgot her question.

"Honey, what say we gather up Patti and head for the valley? I expect you've had about enough of Mom and Dad by now. And I have the greatest longing to have you all to myself."

Coaly stamped her foot and shoved her nose rather hard against Dan's chest. He chuckled, petted her neck, fished a sugar cube from his pocket and fed it to her.

Kathleen laughed. "Dan, you have two women in love with you. Should I be jealous?

Chapter 39

An animated Patti giggled and bounced in the backseat before leaning forward to tap Danny on the shoulder. "Knock knock."

"Who's there?"

"Kent."

"Kent who?"

"Kent you tell by my voice?"

Danny laughed and said, "Okay, here's one for you. Knock knock."

"Who's there?"

"Isabel."

"Isabel who?"

"Isabel working? I had to knock."

Kathleen relaxed and listened to the happy banter. She needn't worry that Danny invited Patti to his parents just to please her. He truly enjoyed the child. This level of hilarity couldn't be faked. The man continued to amaze her with his abilities. How did he know so many jokes? Was there no limit to his repertoire? Or his patience with a child's silliness? She taught school, and she didn't know *any* Knock knock jokes.

Danny reached over and squeezed her hand.

"Okay, Patti. One more. And this one is for Miss O'Brien. Lets see if she can guess the answer....Knock knock."

"Who's there?"

"Ab-e!"

"Ab-e who?"

"Ab-e C D E F G H...!"

She laughed, more to hear Patti's delighted giggle than from the joke itself. "Oh, good one for the teacher, huh?"

Danny smiled and winked, but remained quiet as he gave his attention to the highway ahead. They rode in companionable silence for a few miles. Kathleen let her mind skitter from one subject to another even as her fingers lightly massaged the back of Danny's neck. Part of her brain planned their wedding; she no longer feared the long separations she knew would punctuate their life together. She didn't have to like it—but she could cope, and she'd have an ally in Carolyn Davis. Only death could truly separate her from Danny; she knew that now, he'd return, and their time together would be that much sweeter. In his absence, she'd know to lean heavily on the Lord.

During the past week, Martha had never been far from Kathleen's thoughts. Now, while headed home, those concerns pushed their way to the forefront of her mind and lodged there, like a log caught on a snag in the river. Each day she'd prayed for Martha, and chafed when she couldn't make contact by phone with family to find out how she fared.

As if Danny read her mind, he brushed his knuckles against her cheek and said, "Honey, you thinking about Mrs. Fisher?"

"I am. How did you know?" She sighed and forced a smile. "I hope we can see her tomorrow."

Patti slept soundly in the backseat. Windshield wipers made a rhythmic whish-click, whish-click, across the glass. Had it rained in the Willamette valley the entire week of spring break?

Danny squeezed her hand. "Hey, Carrot Top, wanna make a bet? The sun'll shine next week when the kids go back to school."

She laughed. "It's almost a given, isn't it?"

• • •

The porch light beckoned through the gloom. Clara Williams, alerted by a phone call, stood in the open doorway waiting to welcome them. Danny carefully lifted a tired little girl from the backseat and gently carried her into the house. Kathleen thought Patti might well sleep through until morning, though her regular bedtime remained hours away. A fun-filled week packed with surprises and challenges could be exhausting for a six-year-old.

Clara led the way to a small bedroom, drew back the bedcovers, and motioned Danny to lay the sleeping child down. Gently the grandmother slipped off shoes and covered her. Responding to Mrs. Williams' signal, the trio silently withdrew to the kitchen.

Kathleen noted the dark circles around Mrs. Williams'

eyes as the lady poured them coffee and set a plate of Snickerdoodles on the table. She forced a smile as she eased into a chair.

"I can't thank you two enough for caring for Patti this week. Things have been chaotic around here. Alvin finally convinced me to act: we moved Henry to a care center in Fir Valley. I just couldn't cope with all his needs anymore." Clara heaved a shaky sigh, then brightened and reached for her coffee. "I'll be able to care for Patti now—you won't need to worry about her after school hours."

Danny and Kathleen started to speak simultaneously. "You first," Dan said.

"I enjoy Patti, and keeping her after school isn't a problem for me, but as you know, the school board chairman has objected."

"Yes, I'm aware. My Alvin and Frank have locked horns over that. Those two don't like one another. Not sure why, Alvin won't say, and I don't pry." Clara sighed. "Martha wanted to help. You know, smooth things over. She volunteered to keep Patti after school. Such a generous soul." Clara wiped away a tear.

"Have you heard how Martha is doing? I've tried all week, unsuccessfully, to contact the family."

Clara paled and set her coffee cup down. "Oh, dear! I'm sorry. Then you don't know. Martha passed away yesterday morning about five o'clock. I tried to see her after we took Henry to Valley Care Center, but the hospital didn't allow visitors—only family."

• • •

Back in the car, Kathleen released the tears and let them flow unhindered down her face. Danny wrapped his arms around her and gathered her close enough she could feel his heart beat. They sat in silence. Kathleen liked that about Danny; he didn't rush in and try to fill the frame with meaningless words.

A few moments passed and Dan withdrew a handkerchief and gently wiped her face. She managed a teary-eyed smile, as he lowered his head and kissed her tenderly on the lips—A kiss that said more than words, a kiss as compelling as flame to a moth, a kiss undeniable as love to bind her heart to his.

He started the engine and drove slowly back to Mrs. Fisher's house, a protective arm around Kathleen.

They sat in the driveway and stared. Every light in the house appeared to be ablaze. "Dan, this is weird. I don't see a car, but someone's here. All the lights are on—even my lights upstairs. What in the world is going on? Why would someone be in my apartment?"

"Well, if it's burglars they're not being very subtle. My guess is family members are here, but I wouldn't think they'd invade your apartment. Come on, honey, let's go see what's happening."

Kathleen didn't need her key; the backdoor stood ajar. The first thing she noticed on entering the house was the odor. Apparently, Snowball had been confined all week and no one had bothered to clean the litter box. Somewhere in the house a radio echoed.

Stopping to listen, neither sensed danger. Still she moved

cautiously down the hallway, Danny beside her; his hand reassuring against her back. Footsteps sounded on the stairs. Kathleen waited and came face to face with a surprised Mr. Fisher as he reached the bottom of the stairway.

"Kathleen! I didn't expect you back today. I thought you weren't coming back 'till tomorrow or Sunday."

"Obviously—what were you doing in my apartment?"

Face a mottled red, he glared at her. "What was I doing upstairs? What was I *doing*? You think I don't have a *right* to go up there? For your information, *Miss* O'Brien, I *own* this house. Mother's gone—I'm in control now."

Dan stepped forward. "Mr. Fisher, you still haven't explained what you were doing in Miss O'Brien's apartment. As long as she's paying rent, it's her private domain. You enter by invitation—unless you want to get a search warrant."

Fire blazed in Frank's eyes. He looked as if he wanted to take a swing at Dan. He had to think better of it before he blurted, "I was looking for that blasted cat. He's hiding from me—somewhere—but I'll find him. And when I do—that wretched hairball goes. This house *stinks*! Or hadn't you noticed?"

"Mr. Fisher, I don't know where Snowball is hiding, but I'm pretty sure he isn't upstairs. I believe I closed my doors before I left."

"Well," he huffed. "I might as well tell you now; I'm moving my family in here as soon as I can. I'd like you to vacate the apartment; though I *suppose* I could allow you to stay until school is out, if necessary, but you certainly won't have the run of the house the way you did when Mother was here."

"Mr. Fisher, I'll be only too happy to move." Kathleen didn't wait for a reply as she skirted around him and made her way up the stairs.

Dan followed, but couldn't resist a jibe as he passed the puffed up toad. "Don't forget to turn out the lights when you leave. I understand cats see very well in the dark."

Kathleen stood in the center of the room that had served as her kitchenette, dining area, and where she and Danny had so recently cuddled on the couch. Too angry to cry; her eyes felt as if they could start an inferno. She clenched and unclenched her fists.

"I don't think I can stay here another night. That man doesn't like me, and the feeling's mutual. I don't trust him—and I don't want to be in the same house with him."

Danny went to the tiny sink and filled a mug with water. He handed it to Kathleen and she drank it down. Her temper cooled; she took a deep breath and directed her anger into action. With Dan's help, they soon had the apartment vacated.

Three hours later they were on the freeway headed for Seattle. Even now, Kathleen couldn't determine if she wanted to laugh or cry. She was even less sure how they had accomplished everything in so short a time. Her meager furnishings were temporarily stored in Rosie and Bill Kestler's guest room, along with most of her clothes. Rosie had in her possession a set of keys to Kathleen's car, now parked beside the Kestler's garage.

A call to Dick Steele alerted her principal she would be taking some personal leave time as well as sick days. Dick had totally understood—told her to get some rest, and not to worry about school. An entire week of lesson plans, hurriedly, but precisely written out, lay on Kathleen's desk, ready for a substitute teacher.

Dan took the freeway exit for Olympia. "I need to buy gas, and let's see if we can find a decent restaurant still open. Italian maybe? Seems like I remember one here, stays open. Get some spaghetti?" He grinned at her. "You look as if you've been dragged through the proverbial knothole backwards. Not that I blame you. I probably don't look so hot myself. My eyes are beginning to feel like over-exposed film."

Kathleen bowed her head while Danny softly prayed. With plates of spaghetti and glasses of iced tea in front of them, she raised her eyes and watched as he patiently wound long ropes of pasta around his fork.

"How do you do that?...Never mind; I'm resigned to making a mess of it. I probably should ask for a bib."

"Never mind, darlin', just enjoy. You know don't you? Everything's gonna be all right. We'll find you an apartment in Fir Valley. Probably there's even someone in the community you could stay with for a couple months until school's out."

"I know. I'm not really worried about that. Rosie said I could stay with her; but I'd rather have my own place. My biggest regret is Snowball. Dan, Martha loved that cat. I wish I could take him, or at least find him a good home."

A waitress came by and replenished their iced tea, and refilled their water glasses.

"I saw you with your camera, taking pictures of Snowball.

Didn't take him long to come out of hiding, once the menace left, rub against my legs, and let me pet him…But why were you taking snapshots of my apartment?

He laughed. "Habit, I suppose. Insurance maybe. Hard to tell what may be useful in the future. You can always stick them in your scrapbook for posterity."

Kathleen smiled and checked her watch, thankful she'd called ahead and reserved a motel room. It'd be after midnight by the time they reached Seattle. Tomorrow they could retire at a more reasonable hour and she could bunk with an old college chum.

• • •

Saturday and Sunday, Dan and Kathleen roamed around Seattle and outlying areas playing tourists. They rode ferries and held hands the entire time—their fingers intertwining and sending delicious messages of being loved throughout her whole body. Monday they made an offer on an older two-story house overlooking the sound. A house with an amazing wraparound porch. A house with a large country-style kitchen. A wonderful house for their future.

Afterward

Three Years Later:

Kathleen sat on the porch swing, a pillow behind her back, legs stretched full length, feet and swollen ankles propped on a footstool. Maggie reclined on a lounge across from her daughter and thumbed through the wedding album for the third time in as many days.

"These pictures turned out well, didn't they! I have to admit having your wedding in Oregon Garden rates as a stroke of genius. The roses are gorgeous, and the manicured lawns look perfect." Maggie sighed and brushed away a tear. "And coming down those stairs on your father's arm, well, I still choke up when I think about it."

Kathleen looked up and smiled as Danny approached bearing a tray with glasses and a large pitcher of lemonade. Only four days ago, he'd been in Iraq.

"How you doin' babe? The boys giving you a hard time?"

"Actually, they're pretty quiet today. I think they may be resting for their big push into the world." She sighed and took the frosty glass he handed her. "I hope so—Lord knows I'm tired of feeling like a beached whale. It's been months since I've seen my toes."

Danny sat beside her and lifted Snowball onto his lap. Kathleen absently stroked the cat's silky head, thankful he'd become part of their family. She hadn't gotten him without delay; Rosie had kept him for her after Charlene spirited him away from Mrs. Fisher's house.

A letter from Rosie and one from Patti lay on Kathleen's desk in the room she called her office. Life in the community where she'd taught school before marrying Danny progressed well according to all reports.

Patti said she loved school. Her pride in her father was obvious, when she told of his appointment as school board chairman. Al Williams hadn't remarried, in the years after his divorce from Patt's mother. It surprised Kathleen; he was, after all, a virile man. Of course, he could still marry, if he found the right woman.

Rosie and Bill Kestler were about the same. Rosie was Rosie, a dear friend. She promised to visit as soon as the twins were born, and Kathleen felt like having company.

God had really blessed their marriage, Kathleen thought. With His help, they'd learned to deal with the separations connected to Danny's work. Kathleen had continued teaching in a school near Seattle. Now, three years into their marriage, God chose to bless their union with twin boys.

A twinge started low in Kathleen's back and persisted

until it reached her abdomen and increased in intensity. She sucked in her breath and reached for Danny's hand. "I think it might be time to phone the doctor."